BANANA PIER

ALEX CHISHOLM

Matador
9 Priory Business Park
Wistow Road
Kibworth Beauchamp
Leicester LE8 0RX, UK
Tel: 0116 279 2299
Email: books@troubador.co.uk
Web: www.troubador.co.uk/matador

This book is a work of fiction and, except in the case of historical fact,
any resemblance to actual persons, living or dead, is purely coincidental.

ISBN 978-1780880-143

British Library Cataloguing in Publication Data.
A catalogue record for this book is available from the British Library.

Cover photograph courtesy of Aberdeen City Libraries, Local Studies.

Typeset in 11pt Aldine by Troubador Publishing Ltd, Leicester, UK
Printed and bound in the UK by TJ International, Padstow, Cornwall

Matador is an imprint of Troubador Publishing Ltd

The world is a dangerous place,
not because of those who do evil,
but because of those who look on and do nothing.

Albert Einstein

1. AFFECTING THE DORIC

Aberdeen, Scotland: Saturday 27 July 1991

'When Colin told me he wouldn't be aroon for a bit, I never gave it much thought. Colin could be a funny guy - up one minute doon the next. Wi him nae being aroon usually meant the man was headin' for a bucketful, a metaphorical drownin' o' whatever sorrows happened to be plaguing him at the time. For ages you wouldna see him then one day there he'd be, sneakin' into some bar or other. Nae the bars he kent I usually went to. Like he needed that part o' his life separate. Nae that it bothered me, like. I've never lived in the man's pooch. But, ken? He could really piss you off. This time though I seen him. Real bad shape, ken. Tried to talk te him. Was he carin'? Was he fuck? Seen mair gratitude from the paper mannie on Union Street than Riddle that night. Mind his eyes. Real cold an' grey like wee granite curlin' stanes. Nae a flicker o' gratitude. Nae that I was expectin' it y'understan', but he might have said somethin'. As cauld as Aberdeen granite. And I mind the voice. That kind o' nasal whine like it's full o' snot. Whinin' bastard, bleatherin' on an' on. As long as he'd money, he'd be on the piss. When the money ran oot he sobered up. Sometimes he'd disappear a the'gether. Just vanish, like. Colin Riddle that's the man. Riddle as in piddle nae Rid-del. Nae a Frenchman. Disappear. Whoosh! Christ kens far. I'll be seein' you, pal. That's what he'd say. I'll be seein' you pal, then I'd never see him for a week, sometimes a month or mair. Then oot o' the blue there he'd be. The cocky wee Gordon. I'd drop in by Ma's and he'd be there, pint in hand. First couple o' times it happened I says t'him, "Where've you been, man?" Made on he never heard me. Suppose he might've been embarrassed so I never mentions it te him again.

The thing aboot Colin is - well there's two things really. One, he was aye daft wi money. Ever since I first kent him. And number two,

1

his weakness for the old juice. When he'd money, he'd spend it on the booze. When he didn't, me an' him was best o' pals. That last time I seen him in toon, he was goin on an' on aboot bein short o' the auld readies. Comes oot wi this story aboot havin' been to see the bank manager. I tried nae to indulge him, like. Kent it would go straight into the barman's till. Anyway, he was moanin' on aboot this bank manager that says te him, "Better dead than red," as he turfed him oot o' his office. Meanin' there was nae gonna be a handout for him. Kent he'd never see it again. Colin wasn't too bothered. Smilin', like, and then comes oot wi his wee appeal for some buckshee from yours truly. "That John's attitude was way oot o line," says he. He called guys John. You an' me, Ian, we'd say Jim – the Aberdeen wye. Nae their name, y'understand? Hypocrite, probably up to his ears in debt, himself. Des res in the west end, flash car, kids in private schools, the lot and nane of it paid for. Helpin' himself to my money! In the name of God … so I says, "Give it a rest. How could it be your money? You're aye broke, man." Colin looks at me, all plaintive, like, the long nose twitchin' – smellin' out chances. That's how he was, a bit o' a chancer. Mind? Worked sometimes. Mostly made do on the social. Had a bitty pension. Nae much. Never worried him. Me? I hated nae bein' in work but it was, like, Colin found it hard te settle to anything lately.

Chalk and cheese, me an' him, as ye might say. The start o' it in the Odeon picture hoose. After that, him an' me, well we wis just like one. Nae bein funny, ken? Can't mind the film just this bloke standin there wi the titles goin' up. Takin' a' the time in the world, unwindin' scarves, mair than one, peeled off gloves an' pulled folded newspapers oot from inside his leather jacket. What a carry on! And what a racket! The rest o' the folk tuttin' and mutterin' but did he care? Did he fuck. Carried on packin' the papers into a plastic carrier bag that he kicked under the seat before settlin' in, just as everyone's patience was wearin' oot. Then later he pops up in the Short Mile. Goin' through the same rigmarole but in reverse. After, drunk and incapable on his Triumph Bonneville 650, wi me onboard. An' that, as they say, was the start o' a beautiful friendship or somethin' o' the kind.

Tugged my sleeve, and says to me, "Tom, mate, I'm got this idea to get some real cash, nae the pishin' bit o charity they give you on the

Broo." Been drinkin'. Slid right doon the glassy granite wall. Way over the top. Straight street theatre. That's Colin when he's in that mood. Loves playin' a part. The arm comes around my shoulders, "I only need a bit, Tommy, pal. Just a bit to get me by." I says nothin'. He was playin' up. Colin on the slide. Playin' to the gallery o' one. Me. Hammin' it up but nae sayin' too much for maximum impact. He looks doon all coy, like, his straggly blond hair flappin' over his eyes, an' the great neb keekin' oot. I sees him watchin' me as he tosses back his greasy mane, like the flick o' a knife. "What's the matter now?" I says. Colin pulls himsel all the way up to his full five foot six. He kent he'd got me. I kent he'd got me. I even kent he kent he'd got me, but I didn't want him to think me an easy touch.

Maist folk would pass him on the street. Never notice him. Nae just because he was small but there was nothin' special aboot him. That could be a good thing. Nae to stand oot in a crowd. I'm nae sure Colin always seen it that way. He could be full o' himself when it pleased him. Well, he stands there, starin' doon at his shoes, manky hair tumblin' doon in front o' the sulky face. The tops o' his shoes that looked like battered haddocks, cracked, lumpy, turnin' up at the toes. Naebody'd guess to look at him that this scruffy guy'd spent most o' his life in Her Majesty's forces. What could I do? He clapped me on shoulder an' looked me straight in the keekers. Kent he'd won but at least he kent better than to smile. I'd a bit o' cash wi me. Wasn't much. If you'd seen his face, all doleful, like. Thought to myself then, aye Colin, man you could have won a BAFTA for sincerity, but nae for best newcomer. He'd this habit o' pursin' his lips so his cheeks were sucked in when he was embarrassed, or grateful, ken? Looked good. Suppose it was his tribute to method actin', all humble an' thoughtful, like. Looked you straight in the eye. Seen it all before. Mair and mair since the drink was taking its hold on the man. You've to hand it to him, he kent when to spread it on thick. I had to laugh. He says, "Thanks pal. I'll pay you back soon." Aye, play the other tune. But him an' me, we're a team. Good mates. Saw a lot o' each other. Times in the pub. Times maybe a trip to the hills, Braemar and Ballater, thunderin' along the Deeside road on the Triumph but mostly at the pictures laughin' at the baddies on the screen. Saw everythin' but best if it involved a bit o' sex and a lot o' violence. Nae necessarily the kind a film you'd spend hours talkin' aboot. You'd go into see it. You'd see it. You'd come oot into the cold. What's there to talk aboot? If it was intellectual conversation we was after it was a case of nippin' into the pub. "I've a job lined up," says he. "In a day or two. Need to get some stuff? Smarten up, eh? I'll send you what I owe. See you, Tom." So I says, "Send me? Where you off to?" Colin turns around, taps a finger on the side o' that hooter. "Can't say, Tom. Top secret, eh!" He laughs. Near laughed his head off his shoulders. Then he buggers off. Swallowed up into a mob o' loud, half-naked kids hangin' aboot Union Bridge.

I tried to sniff him out but gave up. Missed him, like. Thing was, Christ knows when he'd turn up – like the proverbial – so I nipped doon to the library, ken, at the Viaduct. It's where I go when he's nae about. I'm nae ashamed or anything, it's just when Riddle's around, well we do other things. When I'm myself I find oot stuff. The library has this thick carpet. You can creep around pickin oot books, nae botherin' anyone. Ellen says I should have went to the university but I'm nae sure. I've aye liked books but I find it hard to sit doon just to read sometimes. It's nae the ideas. I'm nae stupid but I've never found concentratin' that easy. I was just pullin' oot a book here an' a book there, lookin' for somethin' to grab my eye. Ellen, my sister, mind? Anyway, there was me couldn't settle to anythin'. I mean, if Colin had been about, well we'd have gone off to the hills or somethin'. It's like an itchy feelin'. Ken how sometimes you feel you've to get oot away from things? If I'm workin' I dinna feel it. Nae matter.

So there was I in the library lookin' at books on art and architecture. In another life I might've been an architect or an artist. Whatever. I'm nae. But anyway, this book's cover, all textured it was. I pulled it off the shelf – one o' them things jagged my mind. Somethin' on the radio aboot a Scotsman who'd gone to Russia. An ordinary jobbin' mason just grabbed his chance. Ended up the darlin' o' the Russian Tsars. Nae bad, eh? I minded this mannie because o' his name. I'd never heard o't before. Menelaws. That's what he was called. Adam Menelaws. I turned to the index at the back. Checked oot the Ms. Nae Menelaws. Just oot o' interest, I looked up Aberdeen. There it was. I turned to the pages. Nae Menelaws. No, I didn't think he was from

4

Aberdeen but there was a lot on another mannie called Charles Cameron. He was from here. He was a bigger fish than Menelaws. Major architect in Ruskie land. Probably him that was responsible for Menelaws goin' oot there in the first place. Aye, there it was. Cameron, architect to the aristocracy, like, in Imperial Russia. So I'm wonderin', where Menelaws fitted into all this? Stopped one o' the librarians, didn't look a day over twenty, hair pulled back in a ponytail and wi a fondness for big earrings, you might say, mentioned his name, but Menelaws never meant anythin' to her. She'd got me to spell it oot. Well her guess was as good as mine, I'd only heard it on the radio but there's nae too many ways you can spell Menelaws I'd've thought. Showed the peasants how to build souterrains, I think they ca' them earth hoosies, ken? That was before getting into the big stuff; a' them palaces an things for the Tsars.

I noticed she had this raspy breath, like ye get when ye carry mair fat than's good for a body. Anyway, she squints over her glasses that was pressin' deep into the podgy face. "Have you tried the university library?" And glances at her watch. I could see she was nae that interested. Ken fit I mean? All the time she was fidgetin' wi a copy o' the *Blue Guide to Prague*. "Or the School of Art? Gray's are bound … and Scott Sutherland – the School of Architecture." She turned on this wee nippy smile. Och, that's nae a nice thing t'say. It was quite a nice wee smile like one o' them fat kids that used to be on bairns' birthday cards standin' back wi their hands on their hips, rollin' their eyes and laughin'. That's what she reminded me o'. Wee chubby cheeks, though in her case they were nae so wee but it was a case o' the smile on one minute melting faster than a grilled icicle the next. Quick as a flash she was back lookin' at pictures o' the Charles Bridge and Wenceslas Square. I noticed on the library clock it was half-past twelve. The librarian shoved the Prague book back on the shelf wi the porky dimpled hands. Didn't seem much point hanging around there and losin' good drinkin' time into the bargain. As I was leavin' I whispered to her, "Maybe I'll try the art school. Did you ken Scott Sutherland came from Torry?" But she never took me on so I went off quiet-as-a-moose on the plush carpet so as nae to disturb the other readers hunched over desks and up to the gate at the issue desk. There was this

5

bourach o' staff doin' their best to ignore a smelly asthmatic dosser who was hangin' about just where you ging oot. The librarians were nae interested, awful important jobs to do evidently. It was the man himself in his shiny stinkin cast-offs that grasped the situation and stands to one side ushering me through the exit wi a flourish o' his hand. Quite the gentleman. Drops in by Ma Cameron's. Oot the door with folk but as for Colin Riddle, nae sign so I nips doon here to the Prince. Can't beat the pungent essence o' stovies and beetroot when you come in from that dark lanie. Nae sign o' the bastard here either. Anyway, thought I'd have a bitty dinner. Broccoli quiche wi beans an' chips. Nae the same withoot chips, eh? And a pint o' Flowers. That's when I hears your voice, Ian! How're you doin'?'

The other man shakes his head. 'No bad, man. Is that just the brew, Tom, or have you been stoking up on something a bit more potent?'

'What can I say, pal? Sorry, like. I'm on these pills. And wi the beer … well I get a bit carried away. Sorry, man. Just tell me to shut the fuck up.'

Ian Ross gives Tommy MacHardy's arm a friendly squeeze. 'Well, it's good to see you and hear your news. Been a while, Tommy.'

'So, what takes you back up?'

'Oh, things, y'know.'

'Aye.'

But Tommy MacHardy doesn't know. It's been nearly a year since he saw Ian, though he has come across a couple of his articles in the press.

Ian Ross is a newspaper man. One of a diminishing breed of well-informed, articulate journalists who put integrity ahead of sensation. Strictly broadsheet material, which is why MacHardy rarely happened on his writing. The two born within a few months and a few doors of each other in Aberdeen's Torry district, they knew each other well as young children and that early link was never quite severed despite long periods apart.

Tommy MacHardy's mother had taken him to live in Ireland when he was six but virtually every school holiday until he was in his teens was spent in Aberdeen, staying with his aunt in Victoria Road. This same aunt looked after Tommy's sister, Ellen, when he and his mother left, as she had just begun working as a clerkess at Grandholm's textile mill and refused to go with them. Caused a major row – Ellen never spoke to her mother again and didn't attend her funeral. Cut herself off completely from that side of the family and her relationship with MacHardy suffered for years; only re-establishing itself once MacHardy returned to Aberdeen in 1989.

Similarly, MacHardy's friendship with Ian was also a fractured affair and, in time, the boys took very different paths in life. Ian Ross graduated from Aberdeen University in 1968 with a 2:1 in English and walked straight into a job as rookie reporter with D C Thomson in Dundee. In a few short years his by-line featured in several nationals including *The Times*, the *Guardian* and the *Observer*, making Ross' reputation as an investigative journalist. But MacHardy was never going to be university material. He left school at fifteen and sat in his bedroom for ten months until his mother lost patience. Told him to get out from under her feet. With his self-confidence at rock bottom, he borrowed money from his uncle, checked he had a supply of Imipramine in his back pocket, boarded the ferry to Stranraer and hitchhiked up to Aberdeen.

To begin with it was as if MacHardy had never been away; when he and Ian got back together, they mucked about, as if they were children again. But soon Ian started to go all serious, stayed in to study, went to university, got into politics. Tommy MacHardy did none of these things.

On Saturday 31st July 1965, nineteen year-old MacHardy had just come out of Woolworths with a copy of The Byrds' *Mr Tambourine Man* when he was confronted by a stream of young demonstrators marching noisily down Union Street. Banners flying high: Aberdeen YCND, Aberdeen Anarchists, Syndicalists, Aberdeen Young Communist League – around a hundred young people singing and chanting anti-war slogans. Standing beside MacHardy on the pavement was a middle-aged man with ginger hair sprouting from his ears, screaming, 'Get back to China.' A diminutive girl of around fifteen with long dark hair and a placard with *No hegemony over Vietnam* scrawled across it turned to him, laughing disdainfully, and shouted back, 'Moron.'

'Hey, Tom! Come and join us.' Ian Ross had spotted Tommy and

to him. MacHardy hung back. He didn't belong with these
.ı was chanting, 'Hey, hey LBJ, how many kids did you kill
.ey, hey, LBJ, how many kids did you kill today? Hey, hey, LBJ,
hυ. any kids did you kill today?' And their cries were heard 2000
miles away in Washington DC, where Lyndon Baines Johnson and his
thinning-haired inner-circle declared, with more than a whiff of
sulphur, that it was the USA's duty to kill babies to preserve freedom
and democracy. With the sound of the marchers ringing in his ears,
Tommy MacHardy made off up the road, crossed into Belmont Street,
noticed that anarchists had been deploying catapults again against the
armed wing of the state, glanced thoughtfully at the cracked army
recruitment office window then stepped inside.

Tommy MacHardy eyes Ian Ross over his pint: slim, wiry frame, dark
neatly styled hair, fingers yellowed from the tabbies he is forever sticking
between his teeth, casually dressed but expensive casual, no scruff.

'Don't suppose you've seen anythin' o' Colin since you've arrived?'
MacHardy enquires, pushing aside his empty dinner plate with his free
hand.

Ross shakes his head. 'Colin?'

'Yeah, my mate … the guy I've been tellin' you aboot.'

'Aw, no. You goin' te tell me about him?' Ian Ross lights another
cigarette and offers the packet to MacHardy.

'Nothin' te tell. Man, your mind's on the slide.' Tommy
MacHardy shakes his head to decline a smoke. 'The three o' us went
oot on the pish. Last time I seen you. Maybe that's why you can't mind
it.'

'Could be.' Ian Ross lays the packet and lighter on the table
between them.

MacHardy sits back and drums his fingers on the table.

Ian Ross watches him. 'So, fit else is happenin' round here?' he
asks brightly.

Fit else is happenin'? It is plain to MacHardy that Ian Ross is playing
the local card. Affecting the Doric. He never, for a moment, believed
Ross spoke like this in those Knightsbridge bars or wherever he hung
out, but it was nae big deal. He could speak any way he wanted. He was

as Aberdeen as anyone and, MacHardy admitted, a bright kiddie who had never sunk to churning out mindless tabloid pap. But still MacHardy keeps mute.

'So he's left ye in the lurch, this bloke?' Twin shafts of slate-blue smoke blow like rocket vapour from the newspaper man's nostrils.

'Aye, something like that.'

'Far you workin' noo then, Tom? Is it TAGOil?' The Doric is coming thick and fast now. Ian is all smiles.

'Oh, just casual, like. Better though.'

'No been well?'

'Aw, nothin'.'

'Are you sick, man?'

'Och, nae really. A bit doon, like. Nae bad, though. Takin Phenelzine.'

'Phenelzine? What's that do?'

'Oh, y'know.'

'You have to watch yourself, Tom. Seein' a doctor?'

'Shrink?'

'No, I meant … '

'I am – seein' a shrink,' Tommy MacHardy chips in.

'I'm sorry, man.'

'Nae a problem.'

'Is this Phenelzine for that?'

That is never specified but Tommy MacHardy's shrug of apparent indifference more or less confirms that Phenelzine is his current preferred anti-psychotic medication. He's aware of Ian Ross watching him intently … or maybe it's the psychosis.

Ross savours a mouthful of beer. 'Great to taste a decent pint for a change.' He looks around the bar; once his old stomping ground in the sixties and early seventies. 'Well, it's my shout. What'll you have?'

They sit and talk for around an hour about nothing in particular, certainly nothing that has much to do with their own personal lives. MacHardy gets the feeling Ross is tip-toeing around him, like he has something he wants to speak about but is scared he might trigger a reaction that he won't be able to handle. But whatever else has happened to them, the early bond formed as children remains intact. It is an odd phenomenon that we often know very little about the lives of those who are closest to us. Much of what we think we know is assumption. We assume so we don't ask. Ross, for example, has seen so little of MacHardy since their teens that he presumed Tommy had stayed on in Aberdeen, apart from some time in the army, and Tommy had never shown any inclination to talk about that. There are other things to speak about – friends in common, music, films, what is happening in Aberdeen, always bad.

Ian Ross drains his glass and turns down Tommy's offer to buy him another beer. 'Well, I've a few things to do. Working break, y'know? Catch up later. Here's my number at the B & B.'

Tommy inclines his head. 'Somethin' up, Ian?'

Ian Ross raises an eyebrow and bites on his lip. 'Awe, things not too great at home, Tom.'

Tommy MacHardy nods like he understands.

Ian Ross hovers awkwardly. 'Got a couple of kids. Yeah … ' He sidles out from behind the table. He says 'Catch you soon, Tommy,' and, as an afterthought, gives his pal the thumbs up.

Tommy MacHardy returns the gesture.

2. BETSY AND BROTHERS

Aberdeen: Two days earlier – Thursday 25 July 1991

Thick splinters of glass lie around the bus shelter. It reeks of pish despite the prevailing easterly wind howling through it like a coyote on the prairie. It is Northfield; wildlife is to be expected. Perched on an orange plastic bench is an old man dressed in that uniform of old men: pressed pewter-grey trousers; short, brown lace-up boots; knee-length coat on a spectrum from grey to black and a flat cap of no discernible colour whatsoever. An urban guerrilla camouflaged for a stake-out in a bus shelter. A grey man in a grey bus shelter in a grey city on a grey day. Tommy looks at the old man and reckons it is the orange seat that gives him away. The radical element. Take it away and you'd never see Joe Public at all.

Tommy MacHardy's sister, Ellen, gives him one of her looks that can mean anything depending on the circumstances. She closes the kitchen door against the racket of bickering teenagers and a blaring TV before asking her brother what's wrong. She knows what's wrong in the larger sense but wonders what has sparked this particular episode. Incessant talking. Anxious, taut expression. Mouth set hard by fast clenched teeth. Every muscle and sinew in a rigor mortis grip. It makes her nervous. Not of him but her own confused emotions. One moment Ellen sees a carefree wee boy running along Torry's streets to the plotties at Nigg and down to the Banana Pier to wave off their Dad or flying his kite on the Gramps or reading adventure stories on the beach at the Bay until his belly tells him it's time to go home for something to eat. The next moment she's being confronted by a stranger who says things she doesn't want to hear and suppresses what she does. A fragile relationship crippled by circumstance.

When Ellen first heard Tommy had been back in hospital, she went

11

to see him. Tried to coax from him whatever it was that troubled him with such devastating effect. Never succeeding. There were things in her brother's head he could never talk about.

Ellen pours two cups of coffee and splits the cellophane from a pack of Kit Kats. Tommy cups his hands around the steaming Gold Blend, mesmerised by the play of kitchen lights on the dark liquid.

'Tommy, fit's goin' on? Are ye in bother, Tommy? Have ye been taking anythin'? Are you still on yer medicine?'

'I'm fine.'

'Aye, that's obvious. Just tell me.'

'I'm fine.'

Ellen notices tears in her brother's brooding eyes.

He was six years old, spending the night with his Granny MacHardy, as he often did on a Friday night. The neighbour who banged on their door was incoherent with shock as she led Ellen and her mother along the road to old Mrs MacHardy's flat. The young policeman panting from exhilaration and running uphill in his eagerness to attend a real crime at last. He touched the small boy's head as Tommy backed away from the scene; his little face twisted and tormented, fat tears streaming down the pale cheeks. Later they found him a mile away, cowering by the Banana Pier.

Trained nurse as she is, Ellen feels helpless when confronted by her brother's distress. The table between them measures in years. Ellen sees the man but not the person opposite. Tommy had internalised his mental illness, for he knows that whatever people say, none can comprehend what he's experiencing. His shrink told him he concentrated too much on himself, should remember there were other people in his life who mattered, but Tommy finds it difficult to connect with other people. He mutters something about Riddle then clams up. He checks himself when he mentions Riddle in front of Ellen. About him being there and then not. Ellen reckons Riddle is the crux of her brother's problem.

What Tommy knows is that his sister has no idea what is going on in his head. He can see that other folk would find Riddle a right calculating bastard, like the time they'd been out on the pish in the Dutch Mill. Riddle went to the bog and next thing he was speaking animatedly on the phone. Sounding different. Stepped out of dialect into anglo-army speak. Low voice register, something about getting in touch with a guy in Kettering. Soon after that, Riddle was away again on one of his jobs.

Ellen's kids are doing their best to raise the roof with their screaming and yelling. Tommy gets up to leave.

'Look, wait and I'll get ye somethin' te eat.' She takes a frosted plastic bag of haddocks from the freezer, drops it into the sink and lets cold water run over the flesh. 'I dinna suppose yer lookin' after yersel.' Ellen touches her brother's hand but he shrugs her off. 'Fit's wrong?' She looks bewildered.

'Can't you turn it off?'

'Fit, the water? What's got inte you?'

'It's just me. Forget it. I'll be goin'.'

'Look, if it's botherin' ye.' She crosses to the kitchen sink and screws down the tap. 'Talk te me, Tommy. Let me try to help ye. I only want te help if I can. What's happenin' is nae your fault.'

Tommy shakes his head. 'I'm better on my own. I'll see you.' He calls out over the din. 'Bye, kids.'

Like a green and yellow caterpillar, the corporation bus crawls up to the terminus, obviously ahead of time. The driver swings it across the road and brakes just short of the shelter. Stiffly, the old man rises to his feet, fumbles through his pockets. A grim-faced young woman hurries up, pushing a buggy with one hand and dragging a whimpering bairn behind her with the other. MacHardy offers to help with the pram. Without a word, she unbuckles the child, picks it up and carries both kids onto the bus, leaving Tommy to work out how to fold the buggy. Glancing self-consciously towards the driver, who's apparently taking forty winks between passengers, Tommy is ready to give up. Brandishing his bus pass, the octogenarian revolutionary presses forward onto the platform as the pram collapses and an embarrassed Tommy MacHardy follows him aboard. He dumps the buggy in the luggage area, watched by the woman, who turns to the window. MacHardy sits beside the urban guerrilla who is wrestling with a newspaper. Its headline is on the political crisis in the USSR.

'In for a few changes there,' remarks Tommy.

'It's them bloody cooncillors fa doesna care fit they're doin' as long as they get their jamborees aroon the world. Shoppin' centres! Fit do wi need wi mair shoppin centres? Far's a the money comin' from, eh?'

Tommy MacHardy doesn't have any answers. His companion is obviously no international terrorist.

King Edward was aye outside the men's lavvies on Union Terrace at Union Street. On his pink granite plinth the stony-eyed monarch has long since turned his back on Aberdeen's dropouts, red-faced alkies, moon-skinned women, carousing and tussling with one another by the crescent of benches. Down-at-heel brown suede shoes, the badge of male solidarity, and women who know their place. Most Aberdonians avoid Edward's diminutive empire but many a tourist, weighed down by cheap bargains from the shabby shopping malls, claim its asylum from the city's grim hospitality. Across the road at the Monkey House, Tommy MacHardy watches a refugee in his cotton zipper jacket, blue open-neck shirt and cream slacks help his wife onto a bench. She is a big woman swathed in pink and white tricel. The pair stare at passers-by and suck sweets. A trickle of youths followed by a small pack of mutts wander up, sprawling over seats on either side of the couple, who gawp at the blue-black hair and ankle-length coats giving way to Mickey Mouse boots. Records and tapes out of plastic bags are shown around as Alsatian dogs, with jaws as big as whales and tails tucked between their legs, sniff at the oldies who put away their bags of sweets. Edward takes no interest, insensitive and indifferent, unconcerned that the hilt of his sword might be an offence to public decency. The frock and cream slacks abandon their place in the sun and head off for a cup of tea somewhere less public. MacHardy buys a newspaper from the vendor at the corner on his way to the Star and Garter. He glances at the headline, *Russia in Crisis*, and turns to the back page.

★ ★ ★

Detective Inspector Bonnie Young and her sergeant, Dave Millar, are about to grab a bite of lunch while checking out the latest crime stories in the local press when DI Young's phone rings.

'Dave, you take it,' Young says as she pulls the top off a carton of salad.

DS Millar, lowering the sandwich halfway into his mouth and muttering something about wishing he'd gone to the canteen, leans over his boss' desk and picks up the telephone. 'Chief Superintendent for you.'

DI Young pushes her salad box aside, forms a comb with her fingers and drags it through her blond wavy hair before taking the receiver. 'We've got a job on. You right?'

Dave Millar grabs what's left of his bacon softy with one hand and his car keys with the other.

'Hang on.' Bonnie tugs at her raincoat hanging on the coat-stand by the window.

'It's sunny out there. We're driving, no walking.'

'You never know.'

Millar reaches into his desk for his notebook. Not the police one, his own. Since around the age of eight he's kept diaries; something not unconnected to his battle with reading and writing at primary school. His mother had got him into the habit of practising at home, writing down what he'd been doing through the day. Usual diary stuff. It stuck with him.

★ ★ ★

The phone box reeked of pish. 'That's great. Thanks very much.' The woman at the Maritime Museum had said it was likely they did have information about the *Betsy and Brothers* but Tommy would have to find it himself.

Tommy picks out the Lloyd's register for 1782. The list has it as *Betsy* not *Betsey*, and written in the old manner as *Betſy*. The page is divided into columns. Tommy checks information against the given keys. Gradually it begins to make sense. *Betsy* was a popular name for boats.

As well as the *Betsy and Brothers* there is a plain *Betsy* and *Betsy and Ludwell, Nelia, Polly* and *Sally*. Tommy uses a finger to track Menelaws' vessel. The museum keeper explains that if it was a ship it would have had a bowsprit – a spar jutting out from the bow and three square-rigged masts including lower mast and topmast and a topgallant.

'The *Betsy and Brothers* was double-masted therefore a brig or brigantine, square sails on her foremast and fore-and-aft sails on her main mast.' The keeper draws Tommy's attention to an illustration of ships in a reference book.

Tommy MacHardy has a Ladybird book version of this in his head – fully rigged pirate brigs and schooners riding foamy breakers on heavy saltire-blue seas. That's his *Betsy*, newly launched at Scarborough in 1764 and watched by her owner, a man called Forrester who had her contracted to run between Britain and the Russian port of Ark' angel. The museum keeper leans on the table.

'Here it tells us she was modified as a ship in 1784; look, double decks cut down to one. E1 hull, that's good but not excellent, not A1.' He drags the nail on his index finger down the page. 'See here, the master's name was Johnson and she sailed between St. Petersburg and Leith. What year were you interested in, again?'

Tommy MacHardy grins broadly. '1784, the very year. Brilliant. Cheers, man.'

★ ★ ★

From the road it is clear this is a substantial house; some might say grand, others, pretentious. Detective Inspector Bonnie Young and Detective Sergeant Dave Millar approach the Rubislaw Den mansion at the very moment its door opens and a woman wearing a navy and white uniform emerges. She gives a start and grins self-consciously. The detectives assume her to be Mrs Bell until she calls back into the house.

'Thanks, Brigadier, I'll pop in again tomorrow.'

'No problem, Ellen, stop worrying.' A hollow-faced man, late fifties or a little older, follows her out and stands framed by sombre dressed granite.

16

'There are people … ' the woman begins.

'Brigadier Roderick Bell? I think you were expecting us, sir. I'm Detective Inspector Young and this is Detective Sergeant Millar.'

The man's attention doesn't move off the woman getting into her car until she has reversed out of the drive. Only then does he acknowledge the two detectives.

'Good of you to call. Come in.'

Brigadier Roderick Bell, known as Roddy to his friends and family and Dinger to his men and comrades from the Gordon Highlanders. Not so much used nowadays but Dinger he has been since the early seventies at Glencorse army training barracks. It stuck to him in West Germany and while senior instructor in covert operations with the Special Intelligence Wing in Ashford and throughout operations in Northern Ireland and Cyprus.

Brigadier Bell has the appearance of being taller than he actually is for he holds himself upright, shoulders back. There is, however, an unhealthy leanness about him and his skin is faintly yellowed and opaque. He has what might be described as a well-lived-in face: dark toothbrush moustache, keen green eyes and dark hair streaked grey, like iron filings, and swept to the left. Bell leads the detectives into a large square room furnished in oak and mahogany with layers of colourful, intricately patterned rugs arranged on the floor. The air is stifling, heavy with the smell of lavender polish and densely shaded from the summer sun by lowered slatted blinds. Barely discernible in the shadows is a second man. DS Millar catches the eye of his DI. Both recognise the weel kent face of one of the senior managers at North-Sea company, TAGOil.

'Thought it best to see you here. Office a bit public.' Roderick Bell has a soft, reassuring timbre to his voice. He introduces Donald MacMillan who leans into the half-light for an exchange of handshakes. Brigadier Bell clears his throat. 'Pity you've been troubled over this. I'm sure it'll turn out to be something and nothing. Wasn't our decision. Mrs Bell's I'm afraid. Friend of the Chief Superintendent, y'know. Happens to people like us. Silly really. Please, take a seat.' An emaciated, pugilist paw motions vaguely in the DI's direction. Bell sits down at the opposite end of a long couch occupied

17

by MacMillan. He has not shifted his attention from DI Young. Like he fancies her or something. 'Would you like some tea, perhaps?'

Bonnie Young declines. 'No, we've just had lunch, sir. Nice house,' she adds, unnecessarily but consistent with Bell's cordial manner.

Roderick Bell doesn't pick up on the compliment. 'This will probably turn out to be a waste of everyone's time.' Then, as if just noticing that the two detectives have remained standing, flaps his hand towards two armchairs and adds, 'Please,' and waits for Young and Millar to sit down. 'MacMillan here has also … also been targeted.' Bell produces a sheet of paper from his jacket pocket and smoothes it flat on a side table.

Bonnie Young pulls on a glove then reaches over and takes it onto her knees. 'That's a lot of money! It says they've information that would embarrass TAGOil. What do you think they mean?'

Brigadier Bell looks blank as he shakes his head. 'Nothing whatsoever comes to mind, just someone chancing his arm I imagine.'

DI Young glances at Donald MacMillan, who has taken off his spectacles and is staring resolutely into the middle distance. 'They don't say what – assuming you know?'

It's Brigadier Bell who again does the answering. 'Like I say, TAGOil has no skeletons, eh, Donald?' Bell's manner is urbane, affable. A thin smile flits across Donald MacMillan's lips.

'As for the money, well, it's ridiculous,' Bell adds.

Bonnie Young nods in agreement. 'Can we go back a little, sir? This arrived when?'

'17th June,' Bell replies straight away.

'Mmm and you both got them? At the same time?' She looks from Bell to MacMillan and back again.

Brigadier Bell continues with his own train of thought. 'He, or they, whoever they are, warned against bringing in anyone, police, uh, but my secretary, Miss Cromarty, and Margaret, thought, well, you can't give in to blackmail, can you? I mean, what kind of society would it be? Bad enough nowadays, derelicts, scroungers, stirrers, all up to no good … doing down the old country. Don't know what a day's work is most of them but expect everyone else to provide … uh, Miss

Cromarty, Sue, came into my office brandishing the thing. She appeared rather flustered and insisted I go to the police.'

'But you didn't.'

'Needed time to think about it. Something like this is a shock to the system. Remember, we were warned off going to the police.'

Detective Sergeant Dave Millar resists a smirk. He doesn't see the Brigadier as the type of guy who'd buckle under easily and certainly not from what appears to be a none too sophisticated attempt at extortion; a vague threat of an embarrassing exposure unless cash is handed over.

'You're not from here, Brigadier?' DS Millar's question comes across as boorish.

'Eh! What's that got to do with anything? You only deal with those born within the sound of St. Nicholas? That it? Suggesting I should get in touch with Interpol?'

'No, sir, I'm just trying ...' Millar avoids looking in his DI's direction.

'Actually I am from here. Been away. Lost the accent. Not always a bad thing.'

'I don't think my sergeant ...' Bonnie Young begins.

'No, no, forget it. No point in getting off on the wrong foot. Actually wasn't born here but spent much of my childhood ... then career took me away. You lose it, you know. Most people do. Moved back around two years ago, after Hugh died ... brother ... needed to keep an eye on the business, TAGOil, y'know. Margaret couldn't be left to struggle on by herself.'

'And Margaret is?'

'Hugh's widow, sister-in-law.' He inclines his head towards a piano where a beautiful, youngish, raven-haired woman, her arms locked around the neck of a chocolate Labrador, smiles circumspectly out at them from a photograph framed in intricate silverwork.

'What was your career, Mr Bell?' DS Millar asks.

'Serving my country, dear boy, professional patriot, that's me. Can't question my credentials. Solid as they come. You don't become a Brigadier by sitting on your arse on street corners.' Bell scrutinises the young Detective Sergeant from his slightly scuffed, cheap shoes to the over-groomed hair that he recognises comes from a certain class.

DI Young examines her feet. 'And now you've moved into the oil business, Mr Bell.'

'Brigadier,' snorts Bell pointedly. 'My brother's business. Oil and gas: equipment hire, expertise, that sort of thing, dealing mainly with offshore companies. Well established and successful. Good team. A lot to thank Donald for.' The quick eyes are on the man in the shadows. 'Didn't want to risk losing the family connection.'

'So you stepped in.'

'Not that I was a great deal of use for a start. No, Donald has been the one directing things, so to speak.'

Donald MacMillan shares an awkward semi-quaver of a smile with Bell and Young.

'TAGOil is very successful, I believe.' Young has a way of making statements which are intended as questions.

'Nothing much to do with me, I'm afraid. Others to thank for that.'

'Your brother.'

'That's right … and others, Donald, of course. But Hugh certainly had a good business head on his shoulders.'

'Great tragedy … his … his sudden death.'

Intelligent green eyes search the DI's face. Bonnie Young meets the look and steers the conversation back to the enquiry.

'How did you find out you'd both been targeted, Mr MacMillan?'

'I phoned through to Roddy.' MacMillan's voice is hoarse as if unaccustomed to speaking. 'After …'

He is interrupted by Bell. 'Donald got onto me. That surprised me … that he'd also been a target.'

Bonnie Young looked at MacMillan. 'After?'

'After it arrived.' His voice almost a whisper.

'Felt I had to say something. Relieved to find out it wasn't anything personal … to do with TAGOil.' Bell clears his throat.

'You thought it might have been personal?'

'Not really. Well, I didn't know.' Bell stiffens, draws a finger down his moustache. 'We compared them. Identical. Been Xeroxed.'

Suddenly, MacMillan comes to life, firing on all cylinders. 'It arrived shortly before our weekly seminar. Senior management meets up on Monday afternoons. I was finishing off a report for the meeting, or trying to, kept being distracted by that,' he points to the blackmail note.

'Tell me,' asks Young of both men, 'has anyone else at TAGOil received one?

Bell shakes his head.

Young probes deeper. 'And no disgruntled clients or staff who you might suspect? Her question is directed at the Brigadier but he appears to regard it as rhetorical.

'Have you got yours with you, Mr MacMillan?'

'Eh … no I didn't know you'd be here … thought we might play a round … they're at home …' the small voice evaporates into the highly polished atmosphere.

'They?'

'Donald's not here to answer questions, he's my guest. In fact, this isn't a great time,' breaks in Bell.

DI Young studies him, considers saying something, then changes her mind. 'That's fine, sir. Tomorrow will be fine. So, who might have handled the demand?' She asks, almost as an afterthought.

'What do you mean?' MacMillan has a tendency to look past people he's talking to as if their right ears are more interesting than their faces.

'Anyone at home, sir?' The DI's tone is just a tad impatient.

'No, no-one.'

'Your wife, perhaps?'

MacMillan clams up. Young is wondering how someone with such a high business profile can be so diffident. MacMillan stares straight ahead, semi-detached from the conversation. She tries a different tack. 'This Sue Cromarty, did she hand you the note, Mr MacMillan?'

'Not handed … but delivered with the rest of my mail … in the mail tray.'

'So she didn't alert you as she had Mr Bell?'

'I suppose she didn't notice it. It was still folded. Sue doesn't actually read our mail, sorts it generally and passes it on.' Donald MacMillan smiles unexpectedly and DI Young notices how handsome he is behind the troubled expression.

'But she would've given it a cursory once over, surely? She'd seen the Brigadier's.' Young isn't taken in by a pretty face.

MacMillan examines the plaster work on the ceiling. 'Well, she didn't.'

Without prompting, Bell picks up the narrative. 'When Donald phoned me we talked things over and decided to say nothing. See what developed. Then Margaret discovered … in the desk here.'

The three others in the room follow his eyes to an antique bureau. 'She insisted we call Queen Street. And there you have it.'

'Well, I agree with your sister-in-law, Mr Bell,' DI Young leans forward, obviously uncomfortable in the chair, 'this sort of thing should never be ignored. We could be dealing with anyone.'

'As you say, Miss,' Brigadier Bell evidently deciding that disrespect for titles runs both ways, 'a line has to be drawn under this.'

'We'll have to get fingerprint samples from everyone who's handled them – your secretary, Mrs Bell and yourself,' declares DI Young.

The Brigadier is on his feet and plants himself in front of a smouldering fire. Young thinks this peculiar on such a beautiful summer's day when all that is required is to open the window blinds.

'Is this really necessary? I mean, it's not as if any blackmailer who'd go to the trouble of cutting out words from a book or paper or whatever would then leave prints over the document.' Bell rubs his hands up and down over his backside as he speaks and Young's nose wrinkles at the unpleasant reek of singed wool.

'You'd be surprised, sir, what we can pick up. It's only routine; for elimination.'

Again, neither man reacts to Young so DS Dave Millar pitches in.

'What happened to the envelopes, sir? I assume they came in envelopes?

'I'm not sure.' Bell is staring at Young's lap.

'They must have,' Millar glances at the documents, 'there's nothing to indicate who they're for so presumably they came in addressed envelopes. Or were handed in. Pushed through the letterbox at TAGOil but addressed.'

'I should have thought to ask Sue,' retorts Bell.

'Does she handle all the incoming mail, Brigadier?' asks DI Young.

'Generally, yes. There are two of them. Sue and … uh, Greg. Not sure of his other name.'

'A postmark would be the obvious place to start a search.' Bonnie Young sweeps aside a wayward strand of hair.

Bell sucks on his moustache as he strides imperiously back to the sofa. To DS Millar, Bell is a strange exotic caricature of a type he was never presented with during his stint with the Strathclyde police force. A man who demands respect. Uncomfortable with people such as himself asking damn fool questions.

Bonnie Young taps a cheap biro salvaged from a charity Christmas appeal against her notepad. 'Has anything of this kind happened before at TAGOil?

'Whatever do you mean?' Bell leans back and catches the DI's eye.

'Blackmail. When your brother was in charge, perhaps?' And then filling the ensuing silence, Young elaborates, 'It can happen that if blackmail has been successful and not reported that the blackmailer will try again.'

The Brigadier lets her question dissolve into the shadows.

'No mention of a handover,' Millar throws into the conversation.

'They must be intending to get back with instructions.'

'I imagine so,' Brigadier Bell says curtly, 'if they're serious, which I still doubt.'

'Well, you're certainly taking this very well, Brigadier.' Detective Inspector Young has a quizzical expression on her face, as if she is trying to read her man. 'Don't think I would be so relaxed if someone was squeezing me for 3 million. Not that that's likely given police salaries.' She smiles at her own remark and as no-one else appears amused, continues, 'This sort of thing would unnerve most people.'

'I'm not most people, Miss. I've been in the thick of conflict. Believe me, this is the work of some degenerate trying it on.'

No, Young can't read him at all.

'Can either of you think of anyone, anyone at all who might be responsible … ?

'I, I …,' a husky voice cuts in. 'No, it's all a great mystery … who might … ' MacMillan's words crumble and roll from his tongue.

'Oh, for the days of the old typewriters,' pipes up Millar, 'when it was dead easy to match print patterns. But these computers and printers, they're making life pretty hard.'

Bell turns on DS Millar.

'The words are cut-outs.' The green eyes lighting up at DS Millar's evident discomfort.

Millar looks back at them but will later make a note that he reckons Bell was trying to intimidate him.

Young catches Brigadier Bell checking his wristwatch.

'We're grateful for your time, gentlemen. We'll have to talk with Miss Cromarty and … and … Greg was it? Try to track down where they were sent from. But, one last thing, are these the only communications you've had from the blackmailer? Been in touch in any other way? Phone calls, that kind of thing?'

Bell shakes his head. MacMillan is not finished with examining the ceiling.

'Well, thank you, gentlemen. We'll take this. If he gets back in touch, come to us right away. In the meantime, we'll get started.' DI Young picks up the blackmail demand from the table. 'Mr MacMillan, do you want us to call?'

MacMillan is on his feet. 'Um, no, that won't be necessary, I'll drop in by the station tomorrow.'

Young moves to the drawing room door. 'That'll be fine. We'll see you again, gentlemen. Thanks for your time.'

Aberdeen: that evening

Bell pours his guest another nip. Donald MacMillan, some fifteen years younger than Brigadier Bell, has become a frequent visitor to his Rubislaw Den mansion. Those who knew him before Bell arrived have noticed a change in MacMillan following the death of his wife. Once prominent in Scotland's company circles, he retired more and more into himself, leaving much of the social side of business to TAGOil's Finance Director, Stanley Shaw.

Roderick Bell feels it only right to offer Macmillan whatever support he can as a colleague and he enjoys his company after all. 'Are you ready for a top-up?'

'Yes thanks, Roddy.' Donald MacMillan half rises out of his chair to meet the hand with the Laphroaig. 'Just a wee splash of lemonade.'

'You know, I've never been able to understand adding a child's fizzy drink to one of the world's most sophisticated spirits.'

'Whoa, there! Not too much. It'll kill the flavour!' MacMillan is a different man from the one confronted by the Grampian Police's brightest as he tilts the tumbler.

Bell tops up his own dram with water and the two relax into their chairs. Late sun sneaks between the blind slats creating marbling on the carpet. MacMillan sighs. 'Do you think the police will turn up anything?'

Brigadier Bell bumps his glass against the side table. 'Doubt it. Didn't seem awfully bright. What did you think? I mean their whole attitude ... the force here's riddled with lefties and perverts whose idea of carrying out policing is driving around in a heated car harassing motorists. Present them with any real crime and they're completely at sea. Education system lost its way, you see. The wrong types are being recruited. And women! Why on earth would a woman want to be mixing with the filth and corruption of policing? Not natural. Very attractive young woman, wouldn't you say?'

Donald MacMillan neither agrees nor disagrees.

His host continues, 'With a bit of luck this will all go away. We don't want every Tom, Dick and Harry trampling through TAG, pushing their noses into what doesn't concern them.'

MacMillan looks deep into his glass. 'I can't help thinking it's someone at TAG. It crossed my mind Sue Cromarty might have something to do with it?'

The Brigadier's head leans against the back of his chair so his eyes fall on the chandelier. 'Can't see it myself,' he says after a moment's consideration.

'Whoever's behind it could bring down the whole company with their, their ...'

'Blackmail, Donald. Call a spade a spade,' Bell bellows. 'Blackmail. Look, I don't believe this will go anywhere. And don't you lose any sleep over it.'

25

'Well, I do, Roddy. I don't understand why you're taking it all so lightly.' Another sigh brimmed full of anxiety.

The Brigadier's eyes are closed. 'We had far bigger worries in Northern Ireland. Far greater problems, Donald. Count yourself fortunate you didn't have them to deal with. Too much of this.' He waves his whisky glass in the air. 'It's as if they were genetically predisposed to drinking to excess. Not an admirable quality in a population.'

'Is that what makes them do it? Go out and kill each other, I mean.' MacMillan ventures.

'Nothing wrong with a spot of expeditious annulment when required, but, with some of them, yes, it's the consequence of drink, misplaced religion and unadulterated ignorance. There's precious little you can do against any one of those, but when they come together, as they do in Ulster, well, you're asking for trouble. That's what our British boys are up against: animals roaming the streets ready to blast anyone whose face doesn't fit. And the women. The women! Screeching banshees, the lot. Half a dozen brats trailing at their skirts. God help them! Makes you despair for civilisation. One of the worst days of my life when Mountbatten was blown to pieces. Bastards! We gave them a hot time after that, I can tell you.'

Donald MacMillan squints at Bell and the two fall into silence broken only by an occasional hiss from scarlet soldiers sparking to life at the back of the fire. One of the things that happened to Bell after being diagnosed with cancer was an unusual sensitivity to cold. His doctor put it down to a psychological need for comfort, such as whisky.

The two men sit quietly dozing, mesmerised by the fire's glowing embers. Brigadier Bell is just about to crack open a fresh bottle of Laphroaig when the drawing room door opens and in walks Hugh Bell's widow.

'Margaret. Ah, Margaret. Come in. Come in. How was your evening?' He helps her off with her jacket. 'You're damp, old girl. Is it raining? Here, dry out.' He ushers her over to the fireplace.

'It was only a summer shower. I'm not wet. Don't fuss.'

Margaret was Hugh Bell's second wife. She had been acquired during a visit to the Philippines, where it was said they fell in love instantly. Hugh Bell's return with a beautiful young bride provided his neighbours with ample opportunity for gossip. There was further speculation when she showed no sign of moving away from Aberdeen after her husband's death and even greater conjecture when the Brigadier moved into the house. The fact is that Margaret Bell is rarely at home in the city. She loves travelling, mostly overseas. Hugh Bell had bought houses in several sun-spots which Roderick Bell assumed she visited, although he never took much notice of her escapes to the sun. It was none of his business, what she did with her personal life.

'Are you for a drink?' Bell still holds the unopened bottle.

Margaret takes herself back to the doorway before answering. 'Thank you, no. I'm a little tired so I think I'll go straight up. How are you, Donald?' she asks.

'Very well, Margaret. Just having a nightcap with Roddy. We had a visit from the police earlier.' MacMillan still feels discomfited at being such a frequent visitor in what is really Margaret's house without her invitation.

'Police? They were here this evening?' Margaret Bell's hand freezes on the door handle.

'No, earlier today. We haven't been drinking all this time, if that's what you're thinking.' The Brigadier retrieves a piece of coal that has fallen onto the hearth. 'Went out for a meal, that place in Chapel Street. What's it called …? But, yes, a couple of detectives turned up asking questions about those idiotic blackmail demands.'

The slight figure in the doorway stiffens but the smile on Margaret's face is dazzling. 'I'm glad. In fact, I was talking to Chief Superintendent Ritchie this evening, we happened to be in the same part of the dress-circle … '

'Yes, how was the ballet?'

'Quite delightful, thank you, Roddy. As I was saying, Chief Superintendent Ritchie is most determined to find those responsible. He said you should have gone straight to him about it. I told him I advised you … '

'You did indeed, Margaret, but as I explained to the detectives, it's more than likely this whole affair is some elaborate hoax. Nothing in the world to be concerned about, is there, Donald?'

Donald MacMillan shakes his head dolefully.

'No sense in you worrying, Margaret.' Roddy Bell pauses. 'They will, I expect, come back to talk to you but if you don't want to speak to them I can put them off.'

'I'm happy to talk to them but there's not much I can say, only that I found it in that desk.' She points to a finely carved secretaire at the back of the room.

'They might ask why you were looking in my desk in the first place,' the Brigadier remarks coolly.

'I'll …,' his sister-in-law's face flushes, 'I'll tell them the truth; that I was looking for my car tax documents. You know what a scatterbrain I've become, Roddy. Thought you might have picked them up with your papers. You going into hospital like that, well, it is very easily done.' She catches Donald MacMillan's eye and looks like she wants to explain herself to him. 'I thought perhaps my papers had got mixed up with Roddy's. So I opened the desk … to look. My car tax was due.'

'I'm always losing things.' Donald MacMillan blinks a smile.

'Of course the desk wasn't open, was it, Margaret?' Roderick Bell crosses so he is standing between Margaret Bell and MacMillan.

'You had only just been admitted to hospital, Roddy, I couldn't have asked you. So I forced the lock. It was only a little lock, it didn't take much force.' She makes herself take on the Brigadier. 'I'll have it replaced.'

'Don't want the police imagining we have a criminal in our midst,' Bell quips dryly. 'Didn't look much like a car tax document, though?'

'It was late, I was frantic. I opened anything.'

'Check out the same things again and again,' MacMillan chuckles, 'hoping they'll turn up. Blind panic. All been there.'

'Well, if that's all.' Margaret takes a deep breath and pretends to stifle a yawn.

Donald MacMillan stands and straightens up, a good head above Brigadier Bell. 'And did you find the car documents?'

'Oh, yes, I did, thanks. In the bottom of my handbag.'

'What did I say? Always look again, the thing you're looking for usually turns up. Goodnight, Margaret.'

'Goodnight, Donald.' And, not quite meeting her brother-in-law's eye, 'Goodnight, Roddy.'

Roderick Bell reaches out and holds open the door for her. 'Sleep well.'

'Well I suppose I should go. I've taken up far too much of your time today. Feel guilty, taking a day off work like this. Skiving, eh?' Donald MacMillan flaps an arm towards the mantle clock.

'No, stay and keep me company for a bit yet.' The Brigadier is making for the silver salver with MacMillan's glass. He pours out a light, peaty dram and passes it back to his colleague. MacMillan is leafing through a magazine.

'Help yourself, if you'd like to take it away,' begins the Brigadier.

'Whatever else I am, I don't subscribe to the green-welly-four-by-four-if-it-moves-shoot-the-bugger-in-the-interests-of-freedom-brigade.'

'Donald, Donald! What are we going to do with you?' Roderick Bell considers the drawn features opposite him. He has grown to like his TAG colleague but knows their differences mean they will never become close friends. It infuriates Bell that the Donald MacMillans of this world see themselves as occupying some moral high-ground, questioning his integrity, after the years of service he had given to the country. His being at TAGOil is further proof, if that were needed, that he recognises where his duty lies. It had never been Roderick Bell's intention to go into business, but then Hugh died and Bell had been summoned to London where some friends from British intelligence's Tart section explained that, unfortunately, he would have to forsake his pencilled in appointment to become Britain's High Commissioner in Hong Kong for the time being, to take over the helm at TAGOil. As he left the Tart building, Bell recalled his father's dying words, 'Duty, duty is what we're here for. Always take the right course. It's up to you now, my boys.' Then, as the cancer finally claimed the laurel wreath of battle, 'You're driving too fast, slow down', leading to speculation among his family around his bedside that God might be operating a taxi service when it came to the final journey.

Since his return to Aberdeen in 1987, Roderick Bell had made few friends. There was Robin, of course. Never his name. The young, swaggering squaddie got hold of the wrong end of the stick, 'I'm no goin te be anyone's batman.' His captain had laughed, 'Who's asking you to be a batman? But you can be a wee robin, if you like.' Reliant

Robin he had called him until they found something better.

At the beginning, Reliant Robin had little idea of what he was getting into. Still, he listened. And he had been listening ever since. He became a reliable Robin. Bell was quietly proud that he had spotted the potential in the scrawny recruit at the start of the seventies. He had picked him out from the others. Or perhaps it had been Robin who had stood out. Not the sharpest, although he could be quick, a survivor. Not the cleverest, although he had a certain way of retaining information. Not the soundest bell in the belfry but certainly a canny Joe. Find one who needs you. Make him need you even more. Like a drug. Vulnerability in a man is no obstacle to the service. In fact, it can be an advantage. A certain recklessness and penchant for risk-taking.

A year or two back he would have trusted Robin with his life. That was the whole point of the exercise. Not now. Now he had real doubts about him. Bit late, but it was as if he had misread the signs. Back then in West Germany it had all looked so different. Then they were both younger, playing off one another. He felt he had really got to know his man. That was his job, after all. Funny how things work out. Both ended up in this backwater. He snorted; where better in the circumstances? Except, of course, Aberdeen is not really a backwater but Europe's main centre for oil and gas, which led him to be there in the first place. As for Robin – it was obvious which way that wind was blowing. Tart had been against using him again, loose cannon, but Bell had argued for his man. His fragility was a worry. Some days Reliant Robin looked ready to sell his soul to the booze, or was it drugs? Bell could never be sure. There was the time Robin offered to take him up to Loch Muick after Hugh's body had been recovered. He hadn't relished the idea of being there alone with Robin. Ridiculous. Turned out Reliable went along that day anyhow, with some friend of his, he said.

3. TOMMY AND GOD

Aberdeen: Ten months earlier – Wednesday 3 October 1990

'Sit down, Mr MacHardy. Now, according to your file you've been un-employed for three months. What've you been doing to find employment?'

'The usual things: paper, job centre,' Tommy recites to the wall but there is anxiety in his voice. It's like speaking to my sister, he's thinking. She's forever going on about how he has to sort himself out, settle down with a job. What does she know about anything?

On the other side of the Perspex divide the civil servant is shuffling her sheaf of papers.

'Have you tried applying to companies direct?' She could be reading from a script. 'Cold calling can have positive results where other methods don't.'

Tommy lifts his head and realises she's little more than a child. Probably hates asking this stuff as much as he hates having to be here. Why blame the messenger when it is the system that stinks?

The girl must have sensed a break in hostilities for she catches Tommy's eye. 'I'm sorry, Mr MacHardy, but we have to ask these questions. I know it's no' your fault you haven't a job.' She opens her mouth as if she wants to say more.

'I'll give it a go.' Tommy gets up.

'Eh, Mr MacHardy, I hadn't actually finished … '

'Look, quine, I ken the routine. I've been lookin,' and he walks away before she can carry on with the mantra about losing his benefits if he fails to supply details of his efforts to find work.

Aberdeen: Friday 5 October 1990

Tommy pays the assistant in John Menzies for a *Press and Journal* and a bag of Liquorice Allsorts, then walks a few yards to the kirk steps, where he parks himself and opens the paper. It's Friday and Friday means jobs. He takes a look. Everyone wants people with specialised knowledge or previous experience. Tommy sinks his teeth into a cerise coconut ring stuffed with liquorice and squints up at the poster above his head blasting out in thick heavy capitals GOD KNOWS. MacHardy rummages around in the bag of sweets, attempting telepathy with God. 'Which one, Lord, the blue beady one or the black and white sandwich?' The judgement, joint or otherwise, comes down in favour of the sandwich. Tommy stuffs the bag into his pocket. On the bus home he reads a business feature on TAGOil. Could be a sign, he ponders. God knows – his thought for the day. Then he notices his horoscope: *Every so often circumstances start to push you in the right direction, today is one of those days so let go of any arrangements which represent the past.*

Scrunching up the newspaper, Tommy MacHardy places it into the bottom of the fire grate, arranging kindlings on top, and takes a match to it. Once they've caught, he adds coal, rubs his hands together and goes into the kitchen to make some tea. When he returns, the sticks and paper are charred and the fire quite dead. Tommy rips off another couple of pages of newspaper and is rolling them up when he spots a boxed advertisement for a Man or Woman Friday at TAGOil. More hassle. More disappointments. Perhaps he shouldn't go to TAG? He phones Ellen. Does she think he should try for it?

'At TAG?' she repeats. 'Yeah, nothing to lose.'

Easy for her to say. Tommy wishes he had never mentioned it.

Aberdeen: Friday 19 October 1990

Ellen has warned Tommy to keep off the booze, and he mostly has. He locates his only white shirt from the black rubbish sack that serves as both dirty washing bag and wardrobe. It doesn't look too bad so he irons out the worst of the creases to the point that under a jacket it looks passably presentable.

TAGOil's headquarters at the Bridge of Don has nothing to hide behind its great wall of reinforced glass. At reception the glass theme is combined with leather and lots of stripped wood. Little expense spared, except on staff salaries. The Man or Woman Friday TAG seeks apparently expected to settle for the feel-good factor of becoming a TAGOil employee rather than a decent wage.

'Christ! Ross, what the hell're you doin' here?'

A startled Ross spins on his heels. 'Tom! Ask you the same,' Ross splutters.

'Got an interview. Broo on ma back, ken?'

'Aye, like to see the old employment bureau doing its job. Keep riff-raff like you off our streets. Good luck, pal.'

'So what's brought you here? Nae work I take it?' MacHardy slips his friend a knowing grin.

'Lookin' for a job … here? No likely. Just like to keep up with what's happening in the city. Anyway, must get off. Good luck, pal.'

'You in town? Want to meet?' Tommy asks.

'Flying visit, I'm afraid, Tom.' Ross raises his hands in apology. 'See you next time I'm up.'

And with that, Ross starts off, nearly colliding with a sharp-suited, bap-faced man with spectacles and his nose glued to the front page of the local newspaper. The businessman enters the lift ahead of MacHardy. As the doors close together, MacHardy absent-mindedly runs a hand over his shirt in an ironing motion and catches a whiff of armpit juice. If it's mine, there's nothing I can do about it now, he tells himself.

What follows is less of an interview than confirmation he is Tommy MacHardy and ready for work. TAGOil are keen to take on former military personnel struggling to make it in civvy street, he is informed. Regards them as reliable. Not into trade unions, that kind of thing. On his way out, MacHardy passes by a pair of dour individuals with identical brown briefcases who announce themselves to reception as auditors.

This being Tommy's last afternoon of liberation for the foreseeable future, he heads to the fourth floor of the university library, where the architectural books are housed. To his relief, the room at the back is deserted. Searching shelf after shelf, he happens on a section arranged by nationality and tracks down the Rs. The Russian volumes in Cyrillic and English occupy no more than two feet of space. He finds what he's looking for: Scottish Presbyterianism personified in the architecture of Cameron and Menelaws, which supplanted the extravagances of rococo and baroque with the purity of neoclassicism. Various plates illustrate Menelaws' most famous creations, including his Egyptian bas reliefs for the gates at Peterhof for Nicholas I. MacHardy finds some of the academic art terms difficult but perseveres: *The Scottish mason Adam Menelaws followed the European fashion for the aesthetic principles of edle Einfalt und stille Größe (noble simplicity and quiet grandeur) established by German philosopher Johann Winckelmann.*

Tommy quickly sketches a none too accurate thumbnail of a detail from Menelaws' oriental-style apartments for the royal elephants but when two students come into the room he quickly covers it up and copies down some accompanying text … *this work from an architect whose eclectic style and mastery of deceit cleverly tricked the eye into believing in illusions craftily created.*

Ian Ross springs into his head when he reads about Menelaws' work for his neo-Gothic arsenal. Ian the armchair pacifist definitely would not approve. Ross blasted bad laws, corrupt politicians, cosy trysts between governments and arms manufacturers, usually referred to in political-speak as defence contractors, weapons consortiums and the like, holding them culpable for the growth in slaughter of innocents in wars. He could rattle off statistics: ninety percent of deaths in conflict are civilian and eighty percent of these are women and children. Tommy would let him get on with it. Knew Riddle would answer back if he'd been around. Something along the lines of, *Well, it's good for you, huh? Got you your fancy lifestyle, no problem. Fair slice of cash. D'you never think, pal, that you're making a good living out of other peoples' misery?*

Tommy phones his sister Ellen to let her know about the job. She sounds relieved.

'That's great. They're good employers.'

'Only part-time, a few hours. Wasn't sure I'd get it though,' her brother confides.

'Of course they were goin' te gie ye it, ye dafty,' she laughs.

Aberdeen: Monday 22 October 1990

Tommy MacHardy is being shown around TAGOil headquarters by Greg when a very tall and distinguished-looking man strides through reception. 'Good afternoon, Mr MacMillan.'

Evidently he's not heard Greg, preoccupied as he is trying to attract the attention of the bap-faced man MacHardy encountered the previous Friday. As the two walk by, the bap leaves a question in his wake: 'Donald, what's all this about?'

'Trouble?' Tommy asks Greg.

'I don't suppose anything much. Always something going on here. Could be something to do with the unions. TAGOil doesn't believe in unions.'

'How can you nae believe in unions? They exist. It's nae the same as fairies or the Loch Ness Monster. They exist. They're here.'

'Well, you know, they're not here. Union, no job. Job, no union. Keeps life simple for them. But some of the men keep trying.'

'So you reckon that's what this is about?'

'Don't know. There's those two, the accountants ... Mr Double Entry and Mr Reckoning,' adds Greg. 'Is it a coincidence that they arrive and MacMillan turns up before 2 o'clock?'

'You don't like him?'

'No, I like him. He's okay, away a lot. They're all away a lot, gallivanting. Not so much Bell but, then, he's sick. MacMillan, he's off to Russia again soon.'

'Russia? That's great.'

'Is it, why?'

'Well, y'know.'

Aberdeen: Thursday 8 Nov 1990

The phone on Detective Sergeant Millar's desk is red hot. 'J-e-e-esus!'

Bonnie Young looks up.

Dave Millar replaces the receiver and pulls a face. 'It's our lucky break, DI Young – our names are going up in lights.'

'So, we're heading for page fifteen of the *Evening Express*, Sergeant, classified section? Lost property?'

Dave shakes his head. 'The word in the tenement lobby is TAGOil's been dealing off the bottom of the pack.'

'As in?' Bonnie fishes.

'As in keeping dodgy accounts, imaginative bookkeeping, slipping a bung or two, who knows?'

'What's the source?'

'A boy has to have his secrets, Gov.'

'Team work, laddie. C'mon, TAG's pretty big time, must be raking it in. Why finger dodgy practice?'

'Who knows; who cares?'

'I'm not buying into this until you tell me what's going on. Despite what the Brigadier wants us to think, they've a sizeable chunk of offshore business, haven't they? How many people work for them?'

'Doesn't mean they're supporting them all from the North Sea,' chips in Detective Sergeant Millar.

'This is getting silly. Let me have it.' Bonnie Young is frowning.

'Word is they've been fiddling.'

'Whose word, Sergeant?'

'I can't divulge … '

'You can to me, teamwork let me remind you – and I'm pulling rank.'

'Okay, the husband of a friend's been involved in checking TAG's books. Word is they're not adding up.'

'A friend? You been discussing cases with a friend?'

'Only small talk.'

'Mmm, so we can expect a few headlines from TAGOil sometime?'

4. BANANA PIER

Aberdeen: Six months later – Thursday 16 May 1991

Beyond the Banana Pier, an ageing, rusted trawler, dwarfed by oil supply vessels, slices through the swell heading into the eastern dock. Further out, a small pilot boat escorts a red and white cargo ship seaward. An ordinary day at Aberdeen harbour. MacHardy follows the to-ing and fro-ing from the pier. If she knew where he was, Ellen would say it was about time he stopped running there and faced up to his problems. MacHardy doesn't care. He likes to watch the screeching seagulls glide on air currents like acrobats without a safety net. Gingerly, he feels the lump on the side of his head. 'Unlucky,' the police had said. 'What've you bin doin, Tommy?' his sister had asked. Staff at the hospital had not been overly concerned by his condition either.

The day he heard he'd got the job with TAGOil, Tommy MacHardy stopped taking his happy pills, with the result that he had accumulated several "spares". He ripped a few from the foil strip and looked at them for a long time. Couldn't cope with the tedium at TAG. Didn't like the people and they didn't get along with him. But mostly he couldn't get Colin Riddle out of his head. Here today, gone tomorrow Riddle. Here today, gone tomorrow, back again Riddle. Just a matter of when. Always one to show up when least expected – usually with a stuffed back pocket, which was nice. Tommy had had that feeling the previous day when he'd left TAG as usual at five-thirty to walk the three or so miles back into town.

MacHardy walks across the grass by the Don estuary then turns down onto the beach. Stampeding white sea horses are dashed into feathers and froth by steely waves; flying foam crashes and tumbles along the damp sand around his feet. Autumn is blowing in from the north yet it's not yet summer. Tommy turns up his collar and stuffs his hands deep into his jeans' pockets. Sand has wedged itself into the stitching of his shoes. A plastic bottle bobs in and out with the tide. He approaches a curious contraption sticking out of a sandbank. Impaled on a brush handle is a huge turnip with a Margaret Thatcher mask fastened to it. This hideous apparition peers out imperiously over the vast watery expanse of the North Sea. A solitary man ambles along the sands. Tommy has been looking back up the coast towards Balmedie and when he turns and spots him and assumes he is a down-and-out in his short camel-coloured car coat and shabby flared trousers. He's up close now; his neck tanned like leather, cracked like crazy paving. It cheers Tommy that an alkie shares his love for this tranquil spot.

The golden glow of the late afternoon darkens to lead and ochre. Tommy climbs the concrete stairs to the esplanade and, from the tail of his eye, catches a streak of camel in the high grass. Up top, a heavily-bearded driver in a parked Ford Orion is taking a catnap. Directly in front of the Orion is another car with its windscreen to the sea, boot into the flow of traffic. A crouched figure with a car jack is changing a wheel. Rain is starting to fall; large, pendulous droplets. Tommy quickens his pace. Passing the Orion, he sees something yellow in the wing mirror as a muffled voice says, 'Give me a hand, here.' But he cannot. He is trying to do something, is clumsy and uncoordinated. Thinks he can hear the drone of a fuel pump. It's hot, stifling. He's gasping for air. Shaking. Someone is shaking him. Nothing is making sense. Rain is falling straight onto his face. Something is being said in Russian. Why is someone going through his pockets? The Russian is now speaking English.

'It's not him. This is some different guy. We've got wrong one here.'

'No, this is right one.'

'You are mistaken. This is not him.'

'You think I do not know my job. It is him. I have a picture. We follow him from TAGOil. Believe me, he is right one. He will do.'

'Don't be stupid. What happens when the real one turns up? Believe me, this is not him.'

MacHardy pulls himself upright and tries to shake the kapok out of his head. His body hurts.

'Just get a taxi. I'll pay for it.' Ellen sounds exasperated. 'Good grief, Tommy, fit hiv ye bin up till, now? Why was ye walkin' anyway? Where's yer bike?'

'Off the road.'

Ellen's two kids sit wide-eyed taking in every bruise and cut on Tommy's face and head.

'Awa an' watch TV, you lot.'

Their protests are rejected. Long ago, Tommy realised his sister tried to keep him and her kids apart as much as possible, as if his depression would rub off on them. It is clear from her reaction that she does not buy his story. 'You need t'see friends, Tom.'

'Riddle's gone,' he utters unhelpfully.

'Aye, that's the usual story. Is that fit's the matter wi ye? Tommy, ye've a job now. Ye need te keep well. Are ye still takin' yer pills? When did ye last see yer doctor?'

'He's busy.'

'Hiv ye tried?'

'You got me it, didn't ye? The job.'

'Has someone bin sayin' things?'

Two kids are scampering down the steep bank, running helter-skelter for the pier. Their father's voice is raised, shouting to them to be careful, to keep away from the edge. One pretends to trip up as he runs past Tommy MacHardy. The father sees the lager can and yells at his kids to come back. Thinks I'm a wino, snorts Tommy. Hold onto the piery kids. It'll aye be there, nae like your Da. Neither child is taking any notice of their father, who's reluctantly scrambling down the dirt. He reaches out and claims the hands of the youngsters, walking them to the end of the Banana Pier. Tommy is already up the steep bank, looking down from Girdleness Road at a father swinging a giggling child into the air.

The barman in the Star and Garter raises an eyebrow when Tommy starts on a tale about being abducted in the boot of a car and dumped at Westhill. He's just served him his third vodka. Humouring

MacHardy, he wipes down the beer taps. 'And they talk about fishermen's tales. Taken it to the law?'

'Waste of time,' comes the reply.

'Have you had enough, pal?'

'I'm nae drunk.'

No, they never are, thinks the barman as he wrings out the cloth.

'I need t'get oot o' this toon.'

'Going on holiday are ye?'

'I'm workin'.'

'Oh, aye. That's good.'

'TAGOil. Ken? Bridge o Don.'

The barman nods. 'So where're you going?'

'Goin'?' MacHardy presses out a tablet from a foil strip and washes it down with a mouthful of spirit.

'On holiday? When you get the money together?'

The barman recognises the type: on a downer, been lax about taking the happy pills, topping up the mood with several drinks too many. Still, all cash in the till. He looks at the only other customer in the bar: a woman sitting on her own at a table next to the window.

'Something else?'

She takes no notice of him as she delves into her handbag.

MacHardy is still stalling. 'Russia … probably never happen.'

'Now that is different.' The barman whistles to demonstrate how different he thinks it is and sees the woman looking. She collects an overnight bag from under the table together with her handbag and walks out without a word. The barman drops the cloth he's been using to spread sticky beer spill across the bar's surface and collects her glass from the newly vacated table, his nostrils twitching at the whiff of perfume left hanging in the air.

5. ASHEN-FACED DAISIES WITH JAUNDICED EYES

Aberdeen: Saturday 27 July 1991

Donald MacMillan is vaguely aware of the crunching granite chips beneath his Jaguar's tyres as he draws up in front of the Rubislaw Den mansion. He turns off the ignition, withdraws the key and lets his head rest against the steering wheel. Several minutes go by then he turns at the sound of tapping against the window and stares into the face of Roderick Bell. Searching the gaunt and pallid features, MacMillan fixes on familiar, keen, emerald eyes. He feels guilty about his ingratitude. Bell has helped him over the last two years when he was floundering in the aftermath of his wife's death. Now Bell is fighting his own battle, against pancreatic cancer, and if the prognosis is correct, it's a losing one.

Swooning, ashen-faced daisies with jaundiced eyes fail to thwart the two men's progress. Bell leads the way between mixed herbaceous beds and the lawn to the sunny end of the long garden. He's taken to sitting outside when not at his desk at TAGOil and he fetches a couple of ironwork chairs from inside the greenhouse.

'Can I get you some tea, Donald? Or something stronger perhaps? You don't mind sitting out, do you? It's a little windy but too nice to be indoors.'

Brigadier Bell is quite adept at caring for people; that's the way he's lived his life – responsibility for the welfare of the men and women in his unit – protecting them, as much as humanly possible, operating in dangerous circumstances.

Bell recognises MacMillan's importance to TAGOil: it is in the interests of the organisation to get him back to full health. And he had succeeded until recently when MacMillan's manner grew more distant, even antagonistic, towards him. The Brigadier puts his colleague's behaviour down to weakness of character. Roderick Bell's world is strictly monochrome. He has never pandered to people's sensitivities, although he would argue he is not without compassion. In the end, he believes someone either has it in them or they don't.

'There's too much going on, Roddy. I don't think I can cope anymore.' Donald MacMillan's voice is barely audible.

No, Bell could never imagine Donald MacMillan surviving freezing cold bashas, having to live off his wits for weeks at a time while being stalked by an enemy. It is Donald MacMillan's good fortune in life that there are others willing to risk their lives for him and those millions like him.

'It's a difficult time, Donald, but I'm sure you've dealt with worse.'

Donald is nervously pacing up and down. 'Once I might have, but now it's as if everything is spiralling out of my control. My whole life is tied up in TAGOil … '

'Sit down Donald,' Bell says kindly.

Donald MacMillan raises his spectacles with his hand, squeezes his eyes and drops down back into the chair.

Roderick Bell adjusts his cotton hat so the brim deflects the sun from his face. 'You're worried what the auditors will find? Is that what this is all about? What can they find?'

MacMillan appeals to the Brigadier, 'What if they find something? I mean, is what we're doing strictly legal?'

Bell casts a disparaging look at the slumped figure – a conference room bunny if ever there was one: slick business speak, vacuous pronouncements, jargon junky, could turn out a report in the blink of an eye, every line of which would have hidden meaning behind it. He is a procedures man, bureaucrat to his fingertips, ivory tower dweller with a tendency towards pomposity. Brigadier Roderick Bell regards himself as the complete opposite of the system's type, insensitive to his dependency on countless unacknowledged underlings. He never was. Always there for his men and women, usually men. A team bonded by shared convictions, driven by him. He could not operate without relying on them to do their jobs and they in turn trusted him for planning and support.

'Look, man, TAGOil has clients across the world. Our service is second to none,' Roderick Bell says dryly. 'We have personnel taking their technical expertise and equipment to the four corners of the earth the minute it's needed. Oil and gas production are the foundation of this century's global economy and you know as well as me that TAG has to grasp every opportunity, whatever that might be.'

Reflection is a trait linked to terminal illness and, just now, Brigadier Bell is resentful at the selfishness he sees afflicting British society when he and his men have made constant sacrifices for the country. Bell considers himself as protector of the realm. Sixteen years ago he was involved in secret talks to negotiate peace in Northern Ireland along with some very ordinary individuals. Often in such circumstances, ordinary is precisely what is called for so as not to alert the excluded, nor raise unrealistic expectations. As it was, one little man carried an immense burden on his shoulders while talks took place. On his back was the government, keen to find a solution of sorts for Ulster's predicament, demanding the laying down of weapon caches. On the government's back were loyalists demanding this and that and promising resistance if the little man's endeavours were successful. So that was the end of that. The IRA accused the government of deliberately setting up talks to destroy them. It was a point of view. There were many points of view. So nothing changed. The killings continued. There was 'H' Block and Sands. The Brigadier has no patience with the concept of martyrdom. He can fully understand why someone would fight to defend his country but not the desire to martyr himself for an ideology. Martyrs are always criminals in Bell's black and white world.

'I just feel we might be out of our depth, Roddy.' Donald MacMillan fidgets with his lead crystal tumbler, vigorously spinning the whisky around and around.

The little man had worn a red carnation and carried *The Times*. A cliché from fiction. Deliberately so. Ordinary with a twist. Often, least attention is paid to something glaringly apparent. So, red carnation and newspaper it was. If there had to be an Irish nation then so be it, it was said, but look out for the loyalists' response. The spooks played their part, too. Such events can't happen without input from them. It's a long running drama.

'Donald, you have never been out of your depth. You are the one who kept TAG afloat between Hugh's ... demise ... and my arrival. The family will be forever grateful. Without your commercial background, TAGOil would never have become the trading success it is today.' Brigadier Bell places a reassuring hand on his colleague's back.

As far as Roderick Bell knows, Donald MacMillan has only the vaguest of ideas about TAG's international involvement. The skilled boardroom negotiator, the respectable face of TAG responsible for the company's international profile, is not the best informed about the extent of TAGOil's interests. There are matters its Chief Executive will not share with the Marketing Director. He has no involvement with Tart. It is Bell who has been ordered in to TAGOil by the Tart wing of British intelligence to maintain links with the USSR. Hugh Bell had come to the job from an industrial background but he was a Bell, nevertheless, so was trusted implicitly by Tart whereas Roderick's route was directly via intelligence, which explains his dependency on TAG's senior managers. Donald MacMillan had taken over from the deceased Hugh Bell as TAG's negotiator in matters relating to Oktneft's, or aspects of them.

'We've all been under a lot of pressure lately, Donald. My advice is that you book yourself a break from it all. Do you the power of good. What d'you think?'

'I can't possibly leave just at the moment ... not with all this hanging over us.' MacMillan takes a couple of sips from his glass.

'The very time to take a bit of leave if you ask me. Come back to us refreshed, ready to tackle whatever lies ahead.' The Brigadier moves his seat in line with the shifting sun.

1970s and boom time in the North Sea. Multinationals and those new to the offshore energy game were setting up in Scotland, around Aberdeen, creating a highly skilled, itinerant workforce and specialist tool entrepreneurs. Tart was quick to recognise the potential for infiltrating the Soviet's energy giant, Oktneft. And for those dinosaurs in suits, whose whole raison-d'être was to continue the good fight of the Cold War, the advent of Scottish-Soviet détente over abrasion-resistant cutters and drilling fluids satisfied their humble needs most neatly.

'TAG relies on you, Donald. As senior advisor to the Board, it's

because of you that we've made inroads into the Middle East, Australia, West Africa and the USSR. You're behind our international portfolio.' MacMillan raises a hand to quell Bell's generous praise. 'Not the Soviet Union, that was Hugh.' The reedy little voice, brimming with emotion. 'And only the initial advances. Hugh was responsible after ... '
'Yes, but you started the ball rolling. Really, Donald, it couldn't have been done without you ... all this,' he pauses and thumbs towards the imposing house which has so long aroused MacMillan's curiosity as to just how Hugh Bell could afford it: the several overseas homes, charter jets for business and pleasure, expensive cars, expensive clothes for Margaret Bell, extravagant dinner parties.

'Get through this latest visit to Oktneft and then take off for a spot of R and R. Wish I could come with you.' Roddy Bell is still talking.

MacMillan is scheduled to fly out to the USSR to meet with the chairman of Oktneft. Mikhail Gorbachev's perestroika is continuing to encourage Soviet managers to take greater responsibility for their industries, equipping them with fresh attitudes – ambition to build up their businesses, incentivising them with target-related bonuses for increasing output. It is all in the cause of greater achievements, higher successes, reinvestment. Still very much a covert co-operation. Very early days. But TAGOil is far from alone in attempting to break through the layers of opaque bureaucracy surrounding the Russian trade sector. Where others have fallen by the wayside, co-operation between TAG and Oktneft is going well. Except this afternoon, with the current envoy silent and hunched in his seat. Brigadier Bell contents himself dead-heading his fading Wee Jock floribundas with his Swiss army penknife.

6. THE MADNESS LIES NOT IN THE MIND BUT IN THE SYSTEM

Aberdeen: Sunday 28 July 1991

When Tommy MacHardy phoned Ian Ross at his B & B to see if he fancied going out, almost the first thing Ross asked was if Riddle had shown up. It struck Tommy that for someone who had no recollection of the man only twenty-four hours earlier, Ian had developed a singular interest in his pal.

Outside Duthie Park's Winter Gardens, undeterred by the threat of rain, joggers, cyclists, and dog-and-children walkers take no notice of Ian Ross puffing hard on a cigarette as he listens to his friend.

'I decided I'd unearth the bugger. Went round to his hoose. It wouldn't have been the first time he'd decided to have a lock-in wi Bells. Always turns up eventually, sober, flush but wi nothing very much to say for himself. Anyway, he might have been on the booze or maybe sick. Nae able to get oot. I nips along to his place. Came on his neighbour oot cleanin' her windows. Standin' havin' a chat, like, when Colin's door opens and this woman appears. Kind o' did a double take that took in the neighbour as well. Maybe in her forties, a bitty older than Colin, nae bad lookin, wee lines aroon her eyes. Thing that stood oot was her bright orange lipstick. Aboot five seven, same as Colin and carryin' a bit o' weight. Or maybe that was just the skirt and jumper clingin' on for dear life. Ken, what I mean? She says, "I'm looking for Colin Riddle." "Oh, aye, I says." Saw the neighbour look at me, then at her, like, then she went off inside. Woman was one ice cool dame. Made me edgy. I was splutterin' something aboot him tellin' me he was goin' away for a bit.

"When he gets back I'll tell him to call you. Who'll I say it was?" She flashed her white teeth between them blindin' orange lips.

"And you are?"

'I'm only the rent man," I tells her and waited till she took off in a Rainbow taxi that was waitin.'

'Might have been in bed with flu or a little lady.' Ian Ross' eyes narrow behind his own smokescreen.

'No, had a good look round. No Colin.' Tommy stretches out his legs.

Ian stubs out the last half inch of his tabby, draws a packet from his pocket, tips out another fag and lights it with a stylish black and silver lighter. Tommy has noticed Ian's initials engraved on the silver. Ian takes a deep draw. Ashen clouds drift in from the west but there's heat in the sun.

'Well, fit's life like, eh man? You still bidin' in the same place?'

'Oh, aye.' Tommy MacHardy balances the heel of one shoe over the toe of another.

'Your friend's run out on you and some woman turns up at his house – so what do you think is happening, Tom?' Ian speaks through coils of smoke.

You've dropped the Doric for starters, Ian Ross, thinks MacHardy.

The reporter is holding up his cigarette, sketching figures of eight with the smoke. Tommy turns to him.

'Maybe,' he hesitates, 'maybe Colin's been seized by aliens from a distant planet and wifies wi big orange lips are takin' over the earth, startin in Garthdee. When you see a wifie wi tangerine kissers you'll ken she's one o' them alien folk. That'll be their Achilles heel, in a manner o' speakin', because we'll lure them into the council chamber an' leave them to the mercy o' the philistines.'

'And how does that help us get Colin Riddle back?' Ross exhales away from MacHardy's face.

'Well, if he was daft enough to take up wi a woman wi bright orange lips then he deserves whatever's comin' to him, is my thinkin'.'

Ian Ross isn't playing. He sucks on his fag and scratches his chin. 'But really?'

'Really, Ian? I've no idea,' replies MacHardy. 'Probably he's just offshore or flown to somewhere else: Africa, Australia, who knows? That what he's like. One minute he's there, next … '

'D'you know who he works for?'

'Look, it doesn't matter, mate.'

'Okay, take it easy, Tom. D'you think we could get in out of this cold?'

The dappled-grey sky is eclipsing the fast-thinning sunlight and a stiff westerly breeze is working itself up into frenzy.

'You've gone soft since movin' doon south.'

'If you say so.'

In the evening, Ian Ross is back on the phone to his friend checking up on how he is.

'Fine.'

Has he found his pal, yet?

'No.'

Is he doing anything tonight night?

'No really.'

Does he fancy a beer?

Why not, thinks MacHardy as he searches through the black plastic bin bag of washing for a shirt.

A handful of loose change clanks over the flags in the Blue Lampie. Tommy chases them as far as a thicket of denim-clad legs. One of the posse of students, a pock-faced colossus in an Aran sweater, bends down and flicks a fifty pence piece his way. 'Here, take this, little man,' brays the sweatered youth sardonically.

'Prat. Fuck off.' Tommy MacHardy kicks his coin back.

The others snigger. Tommy shrugs off a consoling hand on his shoulder. It's Ian Ross.

'What's going on here, then, Tommy, mate? Take it easy, man.'

'Aye, aw, it's nothin'. C'mon, let's sit doon over there.'

Ross buys two rounds to Tommy MacHardy's one. Tommy is telling Ian about his latest interest, Adam Menelaws, a mason who left Scotland for Russia in the late eighteenth century.

'Catherine the Great was after skilled workmen, – reliable ken? – clerks, masons, labourin' brickies. Gave them proper contracts and bits o' land if they wanted. Menelaws, he was time-served, proper skilled, ken? Thirty-six – dangerous age, eh, Ian? What were you getting up to then?'

'Much the same as I'm doing now, actually.' Ian Ross creases his brow. 'And you?'

But Tommy is ploughing the same furrow.

'He spotted a notice in the *Edinburgh Courant*. Same time that lots o' Scots men and women and their families was movin' to Poland and all round the Baltic. Plenty work for traders, ken? Merchants and mercenaries – aye jobs for someone that can fire a gun, eh? The promise o' adventure if no a fortune. Then again, always the chance o' a fortune. Worth givin' it a go. Menelaws himself signed up for three year on good money and since he was a journeyman he'd oversee the younger ones. They sailed from Leith on the 3rd of May 1784. Menelaws and another seventy-odd Scotties headin' east.'

'1784, taking the Scottish Enlightenment to the Ruskies, eh, Tom?' Ross raises an eyebrow. 'And I suppose they all made their fortunes?'

'Some did, like Menelaws, aye. Did okay. Became a big famous mason. Building them posh palaces in Russia.'

Ian Ross peers thoughtfully over his beer glass at Tommy MacHardy.

Although it had been him, Ross, who had gone to university, Tommy had been a smart kid who absorbed everything he heard and read. Could pick up facts in a flash and recall them when he had to. Pity how things turned out for him. Ross sometimes wondered if Tommy ever begrudged him the success he had found in life. He roots around in his jeans pocket and produces a tenner.

'Same again? Another pint?' He's trying to catch the barman's eye as he calls over to Tommy. 'Your pal, Riddle, what is it he does?'

'Into different stuff. Bitty this, bitty that, mostly wi TAG.'

'Private contracts?'

'What d'you mean, private contracts? Casual work's always on contract. You make him sound like some big shot businessman, jeez! That's like sayin' Scotland's got a world class fitba team. Hardly appropriate, ken what I mean?'

The barman hands Ian two straight pint glasses, froth running down their sides.

'You're awful interested in my pal, are you no?' MacHardy sucks the head off his beer.

Ian notices how Tommy's left leg shakes nervously when he's talking.

'Just making conversation, Tom. Just that you seem real worried about him. Bit of a mystery, eh? I like a mystery. They're there to be exposed. Drink up.'

Ian shrugs like he really doesn't care so Tommy MacHardy lets it go.

Ross is ranting on about the outrage of Third World debt. British companies raking in obscene fortunes from impoverished, debt-ridden countries. Setting up useless schemes which line the pockets of UK directors but do little for poor countries other than push them deeper into debt.

'They're left to struggle to pay off the worthless schemes by diverting monies from health care and education budgets.'

Typical Ian Ross, thinks MacHardy. Thinks he was born with a mission in life to expose all the world's injustices.

'Fit' have ye te dae to get served here?' Tommy taps on the bar with the bottom of his glass. Miracle. The barman spots him. 'Another one?'

Ian shakes his head.

'Naw. Feel like some fresh air. Fancy a bit of a walk?'

Tommy turns his back on the barman, giving him a taste of his own medicine. They're going out the door when Tommy cosies up to Ian, a bit drunk and in fine fettle.

'One day, Ian, I'll give you a story to make you sit up.'

'I'm sure you could tell a few, Tom. I'm listening.' Ian Ross is standing on the pavement watching a pallid moon turtle-roll through a convoy of pearly clouds.

'One day. One day. I'm too young. There's mair to do.'

'Keeping me on tenterhooks, Tom.' Ian's brain is running in neutral.

'Patience, man. I'm keepin' it under ma hat.' Tommy takes his pal by the elbow and steers him between two cars to the other side of the street.

'Very inscrutable, MacHardy. Ever thought about becoming a milliner?'

'Aye.'

A cold current of salty air hangs over the length of the Gallowgate. Both men dip their heads between their shoulders and turn up their jacket collars. It takes them nearly half an hour to walk down Market Street, along through Torry and out to the allotments at Nigg Bay. Ian Ross is a step or two ahead of Tommy, tripping and sliding down the grassy slope. They are two wee boys again.

'Last one to the pier's a hairy kipper.' Ian leaps onto the iron capstan on the jetty, raises his arms over his head and bellows at the pale moon, 'There's no morals in politics, only expedience.' Tommy pulls him down but Ian scrambles up again, screaming at the scudding clouds, 'The scoundrel's useful because he is a scoundrel.' Tommy MacHardy catches hold of Ross' leg but Ross kicks him off and bawls out to the sky, the sea, the land, couples in steamed up cars at the Torry Battery, 'Remember those words of Vladimir Ilyich Lenin: my fellow citizens, my comrade Tommy.'

Tommy MacHardy runs out to the end of the Banana Pier, raises a fist and hollers seaward, 'I've had a perfectly wonderful evening, but this wasn't it.- Groucho Marx.'

Ian Ross jumps down and joins Tommy on the pier and they jostle with each other on the narrow ledge like they did as children. Dashes of light trace a line from the harbour mouth up to Torry Dock. The faint hum of an engine synchronises with the north wind, sweeping away ghosts of their Aberdeen childhood. Ian Ross reaches into his coat pocket and takes out a pack of cigarettes. He nudges Tommy with it. MacHardy glances down then looks away. Ian lights up and pockets the lighter then Tommy extends a hand. He'll take one after all. Ross passes across the packet and lighter and a pen that has got stuck between them. Fag ends glow like two bloodshot eyes in the vermillion darkness of the bay. They smoke in silence. MacHardy doodles on the packet in his hand. Not looking at it but staring ahead. Four feet dangling from the pier, men grown apart, strangers really but still that easy familiarity between them, born of another time.

MacHardy breaks the stalemate. He plans to visit Russia, to see Menelaws' buildings for himself. Wants to do something with his life. Get rich maybe. He might have said, "get well," but he doesn't, not in front of Ross. He doesn't admit to that in front of anyone. Saying it

51

would mean he wasn't well in the first place. Tommy throws the spent cigarette into the water.

'Leningrad.' Ian Ross leans his head back so he's staring up at the sky. 'All those neo-classical palaces. Man, you'd love it. What's that palace called, the one where now they hang pictures instead of people?'

'The Hermitage?' MacHardy bends his head towards Ian and winks, then he's up on his feet looking down into the black, oily water lapping rhythmically against the pier wall; the same vermillion as the night but dappled with electric blue from ships' lights.

Back on Guild Street, Ian's eyes pick out a woman paying off a taxi at the railway station. Tommy follows his gaze. 'I wouldn't bother with her, that's Colin's woman. The one I told you aboot, mind?'

'Are you certain that's her? This Riddle's bird?' Ian Ross asks. A memory is trying to surface in his beer sodden-brain. They're outside the Criterion Bar when it comes to him. London. A drinks party at the Home Office. Just another government department jolly organised ostensibly to meet real people but, in reality, packed with weel kent faces. Ross had been one of a handful of journalists there that evening. Remembered being cornered by an Under Secretary at the Northern Ireland Office, memorable only for his halitosis and dyspepsia. He had castigated Ross over a piece on RUC collusion with loyalists. The woman who had just walked into the Joint Station had spent the entire evening in a huddle with Cabinet ministers. Same satsuma mouth. The blast of a car horn. Ross hops onto the pavement as a line of traffic speeds past. On the amber, Ross sprints across to the station, reaching the concourse in time to see the London sleeper creep stealthily into the night.

Ian Ross wakes and stretches out on the bed, hands behind his head, considering his next move. A few moments later, he's up and slipping on his jacket. Falling drizzle etches his face on the short walk along Crown Street to the red phone booths outside the post office.

'C'mon, c'mon,' he hisses impatiently into the receiver.

A click on the other end and a sleepy voice croaks, 'Hello, who is that? Do you know what time it is?'

An afternoon in the sun with the Brigadier has not done Donald

MacMillan very much good and the phone call late in the evening heralds an even worse finish to his day.

'Hello. Mr Donald MacMillan?' Ian Ross explains he's researching an article about alleged links between political groups in Northern Ireland and Eastern Europe when the line goes dead. Ross stares into the receiver for a moment and re-dials. 'Mr MacMillan, don't hang up. You'll find out I can be a persistent bastard. Still there? Okay. Now, what about a meeting?'

Recent pressures on Donald MacMillan were such that he had started attending church most Sundays. A neighbour had recommended it to him as emotional sticking plaster and, not wishing to offend her, MacMillan had allowed himself to be drawn in, that is, until one Saturday evening around six months later. That was the day his emotional journey of joyful intensity and saccharine kindness struck a reef. What began as a perfectly normal social gathering with casual chit-chit turned into his reality check. Part way through the evening it struck Donald MacMillan that the people around him held particularly strong and rigid views on life that were alien to his own so he stopped attending church, turned down invitations for coffee and went back to spending long, depressing Sundays alone and increasingly brooding about TAGOil and Roderick Bell.

Ross is back in his hotel room in less than 10 minutes. He picks up his cigarette pack from the bedside cabinet. Empty. Squeezes it and aims for the wastepaper bin, sees Tommy's doodle, goes over and retrieves it. A simple line drawing of a man's face and a good resemblance at that, muses Ross, idly laying it down on the bedside cabinet.

Moonlight filters through the cluster of chestnut and beech trees where Ian Ross is waiting. He sees a car advance slowly towards the park gates, rising and dropping over each sleeping policeman like a ship in a heavy swell. Ever closer. He notices the driver has come alone. Slightly older than middle-aged, clean-shaven and wearing dark-rimmed spectacles, the man peers about apprehensively as he reverse parks his Jaguar to face the car park exit. He lets the engine run but switches the headlamps to dip. Ian Ross slips out from his cover, checking the vehicle's rear seats before approaching from the rear, pulling on the passenger door and leaning in.

'Turn it off, and the lights.' Ross sounds angry or nervous, MacMillan can't tell.

'What the hell does this mean? What do you want from me? Why meet out here?'

'Turn off the lights, please,' Ross instructs the driver again.

This time MacMillan obeys.

'And the engine.'

MacMillan turns the key. Ross is more at ease now it is dark and quiet. Each man sizing up the other. 'Ian Ross,' he stretches out his hand. MacMillan returns the handshake but without enthusiasm.

'Now explain to me, what all this cloak and dagger stuff is in aid of.'

'I think you know, Mr MacMillan.' Ian Ross' head gives an involuntary twitch.

'I assure you I don't. I take it you're the blackmailer … well, let me tell you … '

'Me, blackmailer? Are you being blackmailed then, Mr MacMillan?' Ross laughs. 'That's interesting, I haven't heard anything about this.'

'So it's not you? Well, I don't believe it.'

'I'm a reporter, MacMillan, I don't go around blackmailing people. I expose that kind of thing. So tell me, why, if you're being blackmailed by someone, did you agree to meet a stranger late at night in a deserted park?'

'I suppose because I want to find out what's happening to me. To be honest, I really don't care much anymore. I've nothing to lose.'

'Well, spare me the sob stories,' Ian Ross grunts. 'You're a top executive. You've got the lifestyle. Nice car. Do you want to walk?' He prefers the dark to someone else's car.

'Why do I get the feeling you're more nervous of me than I am of you?' MacMillan is finding his voice as his confidence rises. Ian Ross doesn't reply but notices that MacMillan doesn't lock the car. 'So tell me what is it you want?' The older man falls in with Ross as he leads towards the park entrance.

'Just some information. I want information about arms shipments destined for Northern Ireland from the Soviet Union.'

'Good God!' MacMillan blusters and stands rigid mid-pace. 'I know nothing about that sort of thing. Look, you've got the wrong end of the stick ... '

Ross turns on him, 'I've been sniffing around. Not only here but down south and across in Belfast. Your name's come up on more than one occasion. So what I want from you, Mr MacMillan, is your side of the story.'

'My name?' MacMillan removes his spectacles and wipes them on his handkerchief. 'This is absurd. I work in the offshore industry. I don't deal in arms. I've never heard ... ' He pauses to adjust his glasses, letting Ross press on with his attack.

'You're in the oil and gas business. Frequent visits to Russia, getting fresh with Oktneft and cutting deals on arms shipments.'

Donald MacMillan stares at Ross. 'You're raving mad!'

'I'm an investigative journalist. I work for a national newspaper. We've been onto this for months. Just how much do you know about your chairman, Brigadier Bell?' He waits for a reaction. MacMillan is looking at the ground, thinking, so Ross pushes on. 'You're the envoy sent out to shake hands. You're nobody's fool. You have to know what you're doing.'

Donald MacMillan clears his throat before he answers. 'Now, before you start accusing innocent people of ... '

'I thought you might welcome the chance to clear your conscience.' Ross talks quickly, impatiently. 'You know, the decent bloke drawn into this racket? Here's the chance to get it off your chest.' Then he checks himself; no point antagonising him and shutting him up. 'And you're being blackmailed? Well, that's interesting. Just you? TAGOil? To whom it may concern? What're they asking for?'

'Money,' is MacMillan's singular response.

'Police involved?'

'Yes.'

'Okay. Can I use it?'

'Use it?'

'Yeah, in the paper. My piece on TAG.'

'Christ, no. We don't want any publicity.' Again, MacMillan's voice sounds like it's on the verge of collapse.

'We?'

'Bell.'

'He knows about it, does he?' Ross presses on.

'Of course he does, it's not just me.' MacMillan slows down.

'So who else?'

'No-one that I know of.'

'What's the threat, exactly?'

'That has nothing to do with you.'

Ross wheels around in front of MacMillan. 'Been a bit naughty?'

'Absolutely not …' MacMillan recoils. 'They claim to have something that could bring down TAGOil if we don't pay up, which is total nonsense.'

'What kind of something?'

'I have no idea. There isn't anything.' MacMillan's voice quivers.

'What're they asking for?'

'3 million.'

'And are you paying?'

'Of course not.'

'What do you think they are going to expose?'

'I said they have nothing. There is nothing to reveal.'

'Such innocence. Can you run a big enterprise and remain virtuous? Don't think it happens, do you?'

'Look, you drag me out here and make ridiculous assertions without a scrap of evidence. I really should go.'

'Really? You aren't curious about what I know?'

MacMillan makes to turn back to the car park and scrutinises Ian Ross over the top of his spectacles.

'I know your game. Someone's told you some absurd lie and now you're frantically trying to make it work for you. You've taken on the role of agent provocateur in an attempt to worm out a story. Bell warned me about the likes of you.'

'Did he now? Well I bet that was an interesting conversation. And did you ask Brigadier Bell just how it is that he knows so much about the likes of me?'

'Well you'll get nothing out of me,' Donald MacMillan rubs his hands together, 'because I have had nothing to do with anything like this. I work for a legitimate oil company. We deal with Russia … all above board. Have you got that?'

MacMillan turns and walks back to the car park. His breathing is laboured.

'Before you go …' Ross catches up with him. 'What is it you do, exactly, on these visits to the USSR?'

'That's none of your damn business. The only thing that is going on is happening in your head. I'm sorry to disappoint you, Mr Ross, but someone's fed you misleading information and it's not going to take you anywhere.'

'I understand Brigadier Bell never visits the Ruskies, is that right? You're the one who does. Why you? Speak Russian?'

'I do speak a little Russian, business talk, and I have an interpreter.'

'Provided by Oktneft?'

'No, actually, usually someone from here.'

'Oh? Has that someone a name?'

'It's really … '

'I know, it's really none of my business, but if everything's out in the open, where's the problem?'

'We've had different interpreters since working with Oktneft. I'm not at liberty to say.'

'Do you know any of their names?'

'They've escaped me. Didn't mix with them. One I had a drink with … I believe he used to be in the army. Picked up a bit of Russian then, I think. He used to work with Hugh, as I recall, and the Brigadier kept him on. I've seen him more recently at Tag. Don't know what he's been doing. Nothing for me, that's for sure.'

Ross holds onto the Jaguar door to stop MacMillan closing it. 'You must know more than that about him.'

'I'm afraid not.'

'Mentioned family? Where he's from?'

'No, we seldom spoke, if you must know. In Russia he went his own way when he wasn't working.'

'How old did you say he is?'

'I didn't. Hard to say … around forty. I'm not good with people's ages.'

'How does he get on with the Brigadier?'

'I don't think I've ever seen them together.' MacMillan looks straight at Ross and asks him, 'What exactly are you accusing us of?'

'I'm sorry, Mr MacMillan, your innocent line doesn't wash with me. No-one who's so much involved in TAG's business could possibly be ignorant of what's happening. Where's your morality, man? Doesn't it disgust you? Tell me, when you look at yourself in the mirror in the morning, what is it you see staring back out at you? Where does your allegiance lie?'

MacMillan turns the ignition. Ross reaches into his jacket pocket and produces a large envelope.

'I can't imagine that you don't know what's been going on. My best bet is that greed has swept you along. Just remember that the money your company is bleeding out of Russia is being used to finance small-arms trafficking in the Third World. Does it never occur to you that the money that should be spent on schools or medical services or social support in these places gets diverted into war hardware? Don't you care about the torture and killings made possible by your involvement? Of course, for men like you the bottom line is always money. No, money doesn't get to it.'

MacMillan stares into a night sky the colour of bruised skin and, still, Ross' accusations continue to rain down on him.

'Have you ever thought how many women were raped at the point of one of your assault rifles? How many innocent protestors were rounded up and tortured as a consequence of your lust for riches?' Ian barks. 'Still playing the innocent? Who do you think is being set up to take the rap? Consider your position, Mr MacMillan, you don't have a lot of choice. Hugh Bell? Why do you think that happened to him? An accident? Suicide? Were you in on his sudden demise? And on the subject of Bells, how well do you know your partner in crime? Just read that, man.' Ross drops the envelope onto the passenger seat. 'Oh, and there's evidence of another transaction, closer to home. Still tracking down the evidence on that. Then I'll be back. Ask your Brigadier about where he gets his weapons from for his loyalist pals.

You've been providing a courier service for TAGOil and God knows who else … secret services? If any of this is news to you then, boy are you being used!'

Donald MacMillan gives a small shake of his head. Ross watches the man's trembling fingers press a swollen vein on his temple.

'Look, Ross, what am I supposed to think, to say?' The voice reduces to a rasped whisper. 'I must go.'

'I'll call you again.' Ross straightens, closing the car door. 'We'll speak again, Mr MacMillan. Just read it, man.'

MacMillan's sleek limousine turns away from the car park. Ross is angry with himself for failing to persuade MacMillan to talk. The innocent victim part had been played convincingly and Ross considers that he might be way off track with his theories about TAG. But it's only a small doubt. He'll get his scoop yet. He begins the walk back to Queen's Road to find a taxi. In front, the tail lamps on MacMillan's car, bump, bumping over the speed bumps.

7. HOME AND AWAY

Aberdeen: Monday 29 July 1991

Greg hands Tommy a cup of black coffee. Eyes like black olives on white saucers stare ahead.

'What is't?' enquires Tommy MacHardy.

The olives grow larger. 'He's deid. Him. He's deid.' Greg's mouth grimaces.

'He? Who's deid?' Tommy cups the warm mug in his hands.

'The mannie MacMillan. Deid.'

'Oh, I thought it was somethin' serious. Thought I was for the chop.' Tommy MacHardy sips the hot coffee.

'This is serious. Christ! He'd everythin'. Christ! It's no funny,' Greg rebukes Tommy.

'Really? You're no havin' me on? What happened?'

'They're sayin' the 11.45 from Dundee ploughed straight through his car.' The young office worker shakes with emotion. 'Doon the railway embankment near Stonehaven. On his way home, I suppose.'

'Well! That's a turn up for the books. An accident?'

'Fit else,' comes a sluggish reply. And then, as if something occurs to him, 'But he wis pretty depressed.'

'You think he might have topped himsel'?'

Greg stands up as though about to go somewhere then sits down again. 'Him and the mannie Bell.'

'But he's no deid is he? What d'you mean? He's deid an' all? Christ!'

Greg glares at Tommy then catches on. 'Och, no! No him. No Colonel Carry On. No such luck. No. His brother, y'ken. Him they found in the loch.' He looks for some awareness from Tommy. Finally it comes.

'Oh! That guy. Up at Loch Muick. Aye, I've heard aboot him.'

Just then, the door swings open and Sue Cromarty comes in.

'He's been telling you, then?'

'Aye, Greg's just been sayin'. Awful business. You okay?'

'Why shouldn't I be? He wasn't anything to me. A boss, that's all. There's plenty more where he crawled from. Maybe he'd something on his conscience he couldn't live with. If he had a conscience, that is. Now, am I the only one here who's got work to do? Perhaps you need a little more time to get over your loss? Tommy, the boss wants to see you.'

'Hard-faced bitch,' mutters Greg under his breath.

'What's she getting at, somethin' on his conscience?' MacHardy asks.

'Oh, just somethin' been happenin' here. Bit hush-hush, ken fit I mean?' Greg screws up his face. 'Sorry. Just her on her high horse. Poor guy.'

Tommy MacHardy finishes his drink and steps into the corridor. A man in his thirties with chestnut wavy hair and an older woman several inches shorter than him walk past. Their clothes scream out, "look at us, we're cops!"

Aberdeen: Thursday 1 August 1991

The queue for the airport bus receded and advanced. Convoys of vehicles splashed filthy rainwater from the gutter over the pavement. Tommy MacHardy shook his damp trouser legs and cursed each and every driver but there was no denying he was feeling good about himself again. Better than he'd felt in a long while.

8. GORBACHEVLAND

Moscow: Thursday 1 August 1991

It is the hunched shoulders that Tommy MacHardy first notices on his arrival at Sheremetyevo Airport. Looks a lot like Riddle does these days. Of course, it isn't him at all. Nothing like him, in fact, when he sees the guy's face. Only the stoop. He has Riddle on the brain. In front of him in queue for roubles is a very short and extremely pungent nuisance of an Orthodox priest with a rapid-fire mouth. The diminutive cleric gathers his bundle of toy-town currency, surveys the sea of weary-faced travellers and picks out MacHardy.

'Mrs Thatcher is leader we should have. Great leader. Great woman. Your country very lucky, very lucky, for such a woman! We have pygmies. I spit on them.' Then, abandoning theory for practice, he spits copiously onto the floor in lieu of Mikhail Gorbachev.

A Scottish voice behind MacHardy calls out, 'You're welcome to her. She's despised in Scotland.'

The cleric closes in on the queue, sniffing out the audacious one. The stench is intense. MacHardy thanks the currency clerk, pockets his money and begins to walk away, pursued by his prolix antagonist. So, when a dark-haired man steps up and dismisses the clergyman with a few choice phrases in Russian, Tommy MacHardy smiles gratefully and goes off in search of a lavatory. By the time he emerges from the airport to find a taxi, his rescuer is already waiting for him and introduces himself as Dmitri Fedotov. MacHardy shakes a tattooed hand: a tiger wearing a feathered hat grins out from a four-pointed star.

'I have cab.' Dmitri won't take no for an answer. He picks up MacHardy's only piece of luggage, a black leather holdall, and leads him around other waiting cabs to his own. 'Airport cabs are all run by local mafia. They will skin you to pay their boss so they can keep working this place. You have hotel? Because if you ask them, they will skin you more.'

'Yeah, I have somewhere booked.'

'Then that is good for you although I could offer you room that is very comfortable and cheap. Would you like to think about it?'

'You're okay. I have a place, already paid for.'

'That is pity. I could do you good deal.'

'I'm sure you could, Dmitri. Next time, maybe,' MacHardy laughs.

Dmitri drives fast into metropolitan Moscow. If Tommy MacHardy is on the look-out for examples of Adam Menelaws' style of architecture on the journey in he is out of luck. The run from the airport becomes a showcase for the grinding poverty that marks the lot of so many Russians. By the time they are filtering through traffic in downtown Moscow's fume-filled streets, MacHardy has learnt that Fedotov originally came from Ukraine and had moved to the capital early in the eighties. When not driving taxis he is employed in an engineering workshop. Tommy pays off his cab at the Intourist Hotel on Ulista Gorkogo, slipping Fedotov a British ten pound note as a tip.

Nadia, the tall, slim and exceptionally pretty receptionist chirps when Tommy MacHardy asks her name. Once the paperwork has been seen to and his passport confiscated for the duration of his stay, the beautiful Nadia is about to hand over the key to room 110 when a middle-aged man emerges, it seems, from under the reception desk. He whispers something into Nadia's exquisite ear and the slender hand shoots back and a different key is issued, for room 212. Satisfied, the man goes back to his lair.

MacHardy unpacks, tries the radio, decides it is dead beyond revival and satisfies himself that the shower and lavatory at least work. He looks out of the window so often he could draw the scene blindfolded.

Moscow: Friday 2 August 1991

The phone's ring makes him jump. Listening, he scribbles down an address then checks it against his map.

Robert Coulthard consults his wristwatch. It is ten to eight. He undresses, goes into the bathroom and turns on the shower. A cascade of boiling hot water stings his skin like wet acupuncture. Coulthard lingers in the heat and steam, relaxed by its primordial calming until he realises he is paddling in muddy water. Rubbing dry his hair, he uses a corner of the towel to clear a circle on the fogged up mirror and reassures himself that only a little of the dye has leached out; his hair is a shade lighter that's all. He finishes dressing and looks for his wristwatch: on the floor, under the bed, under the bed clothes, under the pillow, in the bathroom, in the bedside cabinet, in the drawer, on the chair, in his holdall but without success. So he goes through everything again. Everything. Everywhere. He remembers checking the time before showering. Or perhaps he imagined it? Coulthard tugs at the door. Locked. There, just visible, a corner of paper between the carpet and the bottom of the door. In a split second he is out into the corridor but there is no-one there except a service maid loading dirty linen into a laundry basket. The woman takes no notice of him as he dashes past her. He hears the lift doors slide shut. Too late – he slams a hand against the steel. For a split second he considers taking the stairs, only to think better of it. What would be the point? He wouldn't be able to identify anyone.

Coulthard returns to his room under the wary eye of the housekeeper. Could someone have sneaked in while he was in the shower and taken the watch? Coulthard finds his cash and bank cards are still folded inside a copy of *Izvestia*. Why the watch? Looking at the rest of his belongings, it is clear why. The thief probably overlooked the newspaper, or perhaps left hurriedly when the shower was turned off. It is not making sense to Coulthard. If someone had been in the room, they would have left the note inside instead of passing it under the door, unless he had had a thief with severe memory loss. He looks out along the corridor. The laundry basket has been abandoned. Coulthard turns it over and shakes the sheets and pillowcases, finding nothing beyond a few creases. It has got him thinking. Same old story? Same old paranoia? Not that he's too bothered. Paranoia can be a useful survival tool.

Coulthard finds Kalinina Prospect packed out with Muscovites and heads down on the regular march to work. Not yet eight in the morning but his sixth sense is triggered. The early bird catches the worm and Coulthard feels as vulnerable as a nematode on a bird table. He takes his time, checking reflections in each shop windows he passes. All looks normal but then what is normal in Union of Socialist Soviet Republics? Are the two middle-aged women with look-alike straight hair styles really housewives hitting the queues early? Or that man in the black cap? Wasn't he a couple of streets away without his cap and wearing a blue neckerchief? Coulthard dallies by a plate glass window in one of the larger stores, disappears into the shop, makes a quick circuit of its magnificent interior and comes out by another door. It is surely one of the burdens of the Westerner in the mean streets of Moscow: collect your paranoia as you check through passport control.

Store windows are clearly platforms for creativity but it is only Coulthard who appears fascinated by their tinned fish displays, arranged as pyramids, on shelves covered by jagged shark's teeth of black and blue crêpe paper. Full credit to someone's resolve and dexterity. Coulthard speculates on the levels of bureaucracy which lie behind the shop displays: remarkable standardisation; indistinguishable stock; presented identically; at the same government set price. This week Moscow's big loss leader is canned fish. Next week Moscow's big loss leader will be not dissimilar canned fish. Mountain ranges of stockpiled tin cans, some as old as the 1960s, preserved in food depots. Retro food no-one wants to eat. Not here – not even in Ethiopia, where Soviet attempts to off-load some of its more mature reserves as famine relief have been rejected. If people won't eat it, rebrand it is the maxim. Rebranded food. Artistically presented. Crêpe paper artists slice sharks teeth from one end of the Soviet Union to the other. The equivalent of painting the Forth Road Bridge. Snip snip. An activity perhaps regarded as a waste of time elsewhere, but in Soviet Russia that might be the point.

The early day sun blinks a sleepy eye on the city. Millions of choking dust particles gyrate and spiral on currents of air, stirred up by spinning car wheels and hundreds of pairs of scuttling feet. Hot-headed drivers tailgate anything in their way; crashing through gears whenever a yard of space frees up: foot down, gear change, brake, logjam. Robert Coulthard loves it all. Big city life. Lots of boltholes. Aberdeen's a little city. A one horse town. Not on the radar and so just the spot to slip into obscurity until fate declares war on obscurity and then it'll be a village with nowhere to hide. By the time he has crosses the Moskva River, Coulthard's feet are beginning to suffer. The leather of his new shoes is still stiff, not yet moulded to the shape of his feet. He can feel a blister each time he puts weight on his right foot but he knows he's almost there. It has taken him around twenty minutes steady walking from the hotel to the rivet-like ashlar tower blocks lining the broad avenue and a further few minutes to track down the actual address. Inside, he's accosted by the stench of putrescence. Possibly disinfectant. Secret ingredient X. The unique Soviet factor X. Unique because in any other place it would be banned as a public nuisance. The staircase is scrubbed spotless. Robert Coulthard passes a small window in the lobby. So small it is ineffective as a light source. It goes with the territory of suspicion: if you can see out, someone else can see in. Was there ever a nation whose people were as distrustful of one another? Neighbours. Family. Everyone. A legacy from the country's violent past. Good reason to be wary of the neighbours. It reminds Robert Coulthard of Ireland. Careful who you speak to and what you say. Never make yourself a target for others. If you need to know, you'll know. Ireland, the land devoid of sign posts. If you don't know where you're going, you probably shouldn't be going there at all. So it is in Russia. Anonymous families behind locked doors. Coulthard recognises this as the place. Couldn't really mistake it. Black leather pierced by metal studs. Pure Gothic. Aberdeen, now that's more your Scotch Baronial.

Knock, knock. Knock, knock. Coulthard can hear the jangle of keys and two locks being turned. There is a single bead of sweat on the back of his neck. A chain rattles. Medieval. The pasty face of a man appears in a crack of light. Coulthard introduces himself. The ghosty guy looks Coulthard up and down. Takes his time.

'From Cassidy, ' Coulthard says so that only the man behind the door can hear. He might have uttered the Russian equivalent of open Sesame. Clink, clink. The door swings open. The ghost is around his early fifties, just possibly late forties if his life has been tough. He is some four inches taller than Coulthard and in good physical shape apart from a nose which shoots off at an angle. Metal-framed John Lennon spectacles with strong lenses magnify his Bambi-like brown eyes. Thin, twiggy fingers rake his once fair, now beige, hair. The man is dressed in maroon tracksuit bottoms and a green woollen jumper which he tugs at constantly, revealing a shirt and garish tie, amounting, in Coulthard's view, to being a person of contradictions.

'Welcome, my friend, welcome, I am Alexei Grigoryev.' Bambi takes Coulthard's hand in his. He satisfies himself the corridor is empty then secures the apartment door. Alexei Grigoryev shows Robert Coulthard along the narrow hallway, both sides stacked with painted canvases. The room at the end is bright though smoke-filled and has been used as the artist's studio. A large window overlooks the front of the building. Sitting on a small couch with backs to the window are two men and, alongside them in an armchair, is a pretty woman in her mid-thirties with her feet tucked up under her skirt. Grigoryev introduces Coulthard.

'Ah,' says the taller of the two seated men with a sweep of a hand. 'Robert Coulthard from England. We hear much about you.'

'Eh, Scotland, actually, Aberdeen.' Robert Coulthard coughs. The delegation is a surprise. He was only expecting Grigoryev.

'Ah, Scotland, of course – Aberdeen – yes, they beat Real Madrid to win European Cup Winners' Cup, 1984.' The big man gives Coulthard the thumbs up.

'1983,' Coulthard corrects him again.

Grigoryev has been standing, his hands clasped in front of his chest as though about to break into a dance. He invites Robert Coulthard to sit down. Robert takes the remaining single chair, leaving Grigoryev to squeeze between the two giants on the settee. The trio, cigarettes pinched between their fingers like a line-up of drag artists, weigh up the Scotsman through corkscrews of blue smoke. If this had been an airport, the planes would have been fog bound. Grigoryev introduces the men as Sergei Dolgoruky and, the taller of the two, Yuri Zhdanov. Coulthard is struck by their size: tall and built like the proverbial brick shithouses. Zhdanov sits bolt upright but is relaxed with an angelic face, delicately featured with hazel-speckled green eyes veiled by heavy lids and long lashes which sweep his cheeks when he blinks. At least he blinks; the other shithouse, Sergei Dolgoruky, is more uptight than upright. Gauche. Dolgoruky is not someone you could forget easily: a flattened head suggestive of an encounter with an assailant wielding a sizzling hot frying pan; curly hair melted into a thick frizzle. He is every inch Frankenstein's monster with a droopy mouth; a scary dour clown with an electric perm. Coulthard takes an instant dislike to him. It is not only that he catches Dolgoruky watching him the whole time, but the cruel twist of his mouth exudes hostility.

The woman is Luda Semenova. She is in her late twenties, stylishly dressed in a skirt and fresh cotton blouse and nearly as tall as the men. She has a habit of winding her blue-black hair around her ear whenever she speaks in what turns out to be fluent English. She appears to be the girlfriend of Yuri Zhdanov but Coulthard wonders why she is there. He is left wondering why any of them are there apart from Alexei Grigoryev, whom he arranged to meet.

Grigoryev makes no reference to any of this other than that Zhdanov and Dolgoruky recently rolled in from Leningrad to be closer to the action in Moscow. Unlikely as it seems to Coulthard, Grigoryev describes them as enthusiastic campaigners against Mikhail Gorbachev who will add their not inconsiderable weight to the growing dissident movement in the city. It appears these entrepreneurs were introduced to Grigoryev by Zhdanov's cousin, and colleague of Alexei. Grigoryev had turned over his studio to them for their stay in Moscow and to show their gratitude they had invited Grigoryev into their latest scheme – selling imported Western goods for high mark-ups. Reading between the lines, Coulthard concludes that Grigoryev's hospitality has been hijacked by a couple of small-time hoods chased out of Leningrad by a bigger outfit and who are now desperately trying to establish themselves in Moscow. Whatever their reasons for being in the flat, Coulthard is unhappy at this turn of events. He listens as Zhdanov talks animatedly about how the Soviet state is nearing crisis point following the loss of its Eastern bloc – GDR, Poland, Romania, Czechoslovakia, Hungary, Bulgaria – with pressure mounting from inside the Soviet Union with people like himself eager to get off to a flying start on their comrades by testing out the free market.

'There are still problems, but every day we have hope this will not be for long. It is getting much easier, we have not same difficulties,' Zhdanov cannot contain his enthusiasm. 'We know TAGOil is doing business with Soviet oil and gas through Oktneft.'

Coulthard fixes his eyes on Alexei Grigoryev but the Russian doesn't appear to notice. It appears to Coulthard that a fair amount of information has been shared with these Leningrad guys.

Yuri Zhdanov squeezes the life out of his cigarette and drops it into a jam jar by his feet. 'We have good trade offer. We are all city men, you say?'

'Businessmen,' Grigoryev breaks in.

'Men of business.' Yuri Zhdanov rubs his right thumb against his fore and middle fingers. 'And as you are from West, sent out by big oil company, you are also open to do business with us, yes?'

Coulthard looks at him. Zhdanov is a first-class reader of character.

'I'll listen to what you have to say.' Robert Coulthard studies the company of would-be entrepreneurs with their plans to have a middleman with access to Western banking, someone who can open virtually untraceable multiple accounts, under a string of identities, into which he will deposit the takings of the Russians' various ventures. The seated giants each claim experience dealing in commodities back in Leningrad. It all sounds improbable but Coulthard is living through his own personal crisis. The way ahead for him is none too certain. So while narked at Grigoryev for landing him in this predicament, Coulthard is in no hurry to turn his back on these Leningrad shithouses, at least not until something better turns up.

It's still there though, the voice in his head – Dinger's, who else's? What was it? Something about no more chances. "Blow it this time and there's nothing I can do for you, Tart won't stand for it." More or less his exact words.

In many ways the timing is not ideal for Robert Coulthard yet, perversely, the timing might be perfect. He is going to need something when Dinger drops him and, to quote the great man again, "Chance is the providence of adventurers."

With the main business of the day postponed until he can get Grigoryev on his own, Coulthard finds himself agreeing to accompany

Grigoryev and the men from Leningrad to the city's main post office where an imported package is waiting for collection. Being important entry points for Western goods, airports and post offices are areas where it is essential for syndicates to have trusted people on the inside to ensure there is no unwelcome interference into their commercial activities. It takes cunning and perseverance to beat the Soviet regulations on foreign imports and exports but many try and most succeed. Zhdanov and Dolgoruky are going to test out their insider and, in a way, Coulthard.

'We try out you and we try out her.' Zhdanov means the woman in post office security who has taken his thirty pieces of silver. 'She knows us but will she try to trick you as foreigner and our courier? We will be there but not where she can see us. There is nothing dangerous in package. Nothing compromising. It is not so difficult now to move goods in and out but many don't reach right people.' Not sure how to read Coulthard's expression, Zhdanov says reassuringly, 'Do not worry, we are professional, my friend. We have not emerged from cabbage plant.' His manner is easy-going but Coulthard sensing Dolgoruky's eyes drilling into him, looks and sees they are doing just that. Coulthard has a growing dislike for Dolgoruky.

'A drink perhaps? To welcome you.' Zhdanov produces a litre of Stolichnaya from a bag next to the jam jar. Luda Semenova fetches small glasses from a china display cabinet; they toast business, the free market and the downfall of communism.

Alexei Grigoryev's pictures lean against surfaces and are strung up on every wall. He picks up a couple of examples and talks a little about them. Dolgoruky and Zhdanov don't appear too interested but Luda Semenova is more appreciative of his talent and reveals that Grigoryev's work decorates the office of at least one member of the Politburo.

Three generous nips of Stoly into the morning and Sergei Dolgoruky is on his feet announcing it is time to leave. 'Party is over my friend.'

Coulthard savours the taste of the vodka. He could do with just one more. He watches Dolgoruky. Russians loved political jokes. It might be the alcohol, but the man is making an effort. The mouth stretches as if trying to join in the fun then loses its battle with gravity. Dolgoruky, a dour comic.

Down the reeking stairway they go and out into the road, where they all pack into a black Zil. Zhdanov is at the wheel, veering fast around potholes and collapsed stretches of road. They hit a point where the traffic is backed up, forced into a lane going nowhere by a cortege of government limos. In the resulting gridlock a driver winds down his window and spits, 'Nachaltsvo!'

Moscow's foreign mail post office looks like it has been designed by a depressive with a grudge. Coulthard waits while a middle-aged woman with siren-red hair harangues a postal assistant. Her mail has been disappearing. The female assistant is impervious to the barrage of insults and accusations. She demonstrates an air of cool contempt which can only come from a lifetime's application. Abandoning the fiery-headed woman, the assistant summons Coulthard with an impatient hand movement, disappears with his document and re-emerges with the package. The redhead eyes Coulthard and his parcel suspiciously, mumbling incoherently as she wanders away to find an ear that will listen.

Dolgoruky holds the door open for Coulthard. 'Stupid old woman, should be home cooking for family.'

'I thought the revolution liberated Russian women from the kitchen sink?'

'Communist dogma, my friend,' Sergei Dolgoruky takes the box from Coulthard, 'you won't find many communists in Russia. They are all in your country.'

It unsettles Coulthard to see those drooping lips twist upwards in a grotesque parody of a smile.

Smuggled consignments of Bibles were one thing and, popular as they were on the black-market, they were never going to become a lucrative trade. There would be several more weeks of such imports until the post office handlers became accustomed to the regular consignments and only then would selected batches have their pages replaced with bags of narcotics. A quality product. Coulthard learns that a group of criminal Muslims has a racket going which produces and distributes cheap synthetic drugs, but the trend is for a healthier alternative.

71

Coke in, weapons out rings sweet with Coulthard. He has dabbled from time to time, bit of flake, but that was way back. Always ready to justify himself, who didn't in Berlin? Apart from Dinger. Knew which way his bread was buttered. Dinger was a traditionalist who had no truck with the drug markets. His own particular predilection was for single malt Scotch whisky.

It was in Ulster that Coulthard first realised the potential of drugs as currency. Paramilitary organisations had men dedicated to their sourcing and distribution while vigilant to keep such activities away from the older generation, who argued that drugged minds wrecked political awareness. For the majority on both sides of the religious divide, the obscene profits narcotics brought in far outweighed any other consideration. Happy dust was, after all, just another commodity. From blow to blow up in a few simple steps.

Drug culture might be huge and growing in Ulster, but in Gorbachevland, there are signs of it being on an altogether grander scale. Alexei Grigoryev had been the silent partner until now but here he is jangling a ring of keys and sounding upbeat.

'You must have seen signs of our drug addict on our streets. In Soviet Union we have over a million young junkies and on average each one spends around 200 roubles every day.'

'Yes,' grins Zhdanov, 'they need us and we need them. Everyone is happy. What we have here is big and will get much bigger. This is future!'

'Yes, sadly that is true.' Grigoryev suddenly looks glum. 'We have so many poor, struggling people in Russia that are hooked on ekoknar C. But this is … '

Sergei Dolgoruky shouts over Grigoryev, 'Koknar is just garbage. Bloody shit. We need to develop refinement in our young. Make them more … eh … discriminating.' The leering lips laugh.

Zhdanov looks back over his shoulder as he drives out into the line of traffic.

'Our hospitals are main source of cocaine here and we get some that way but this is not enough. No, market is bigger than we get from hospitals. Believe me, this will be big enterprise.' He stresses "big". 'But not always easy.' He is checking out Coulthard from the driver's mirror. 'Government supplies in this country are – what you say? uh, we need make certain that drug supply is strong. You know, keep eye on production. Know what is going on. Like this summer's crop in Odessa is one of best. Maybe good prices. This is just business sense. Everywhere are other dealers, competition, so we have to be stronger than them and keep on top. You get benefit too. Sound okay?'

★ ★ ★

The road sweeper has a quick eye. He has swept the man's wristwatch out of the gutter. It has weight. He turns it over. On the back, something is written in a foreign language. Not Soviet, he is sure. Fate is not usually so charitable.

9. SHAW'S OXTERS

Aberdeen: Friday 2 August 1991

'I take it you're Greg,' DI Young isn't really asking. She and DS Millar are in a small office behind reception at TAGOil HQ. Seated behind a long table lined with wire desk trays and a set of postal scales is Greg Anderson. Not long out of his teens, Greg has an elongated head that looks like the result of an awkward birth and the lean gaucheness of a man struggling to emerge from his stick-willow frame. He welcomes in the detectives with a friendly 'Hi,' but it is clear he is not at ease as he glances from one to the other. Millar is not exactly relaxed either. He notices Greg wears a gold stud in his left ear lobe.

'We hoped to find Sue Cromarty here.' Bonnie Young watches the interaction between the two men. It hasn't passed her by that Millar has come up from Glasgow with one or two prejudices.

'She's just popped out. Powder room,' says Greg, trembling under Millar's scornful gaze. He is saved when the door opens. 'Speak o' the devil.' Sue Cromarty locks eyes with Greg the moment she enters the room.

'It's the police,' announces Greg, 'they're here to speak to you.'

'To speak to both of you,' Bonnie Young corrects him.

Greg gives an involuntary shiver.

'How can I help?' Sue Cromarty is as confident a young woman as Greg is timid. She has what might be described as a pert little face; round with delicate features surrounded by a cascade of dark curls cut short.

'You are Sue Cromarty?' Young pulls up a chair and makes herself at home as the woman nods her head. 'You work in here? And deal with the mail?'

'Yes and yes. Some of the mail. Greg, or whoever's in, checks most of it. I handle stuff for our directors.'

'Yeah, we often have temps working here, or, if someone's not too busy and there's a lot of mail, we might need a hand from someone down the corridor,' says Greg, helpfully.

'Doesn't opening mail need people who know their way around the company so they can redirect it?'

'Yes, which is why it's usually me and Greg. One of us will be around to help if needed.'

'But you are mainly Mr Bell's assistant, aren't you?'

'Brigadier, Shaw and MacMillan ... until ....'

'A shock for everyone.' Young lowers her voice sympathetically.

'Mmm, we're all shattered. He's a nice man to work for. Was, I mean. Everything seemed to be going wrong for him. It's a real shame.'

'Going wrong?'

'His wife dying, y'know.'

'Of course.'

'Hit him hard.' Sue Cromarty grimaces.

'Anything else?'

There is a pause during which Sue Cromarty appears to be considering what to say next. She looks up for inspiration. 'The auditors were in. He did seem, well ... worried.'

'Auditors. Did he have reason to be?'

'What d'you mean?'

'Well, was he unduly worried would you say?' Young asks.

'No, I wouldn't. Everyone gets uptight when they're being inspected, don't they?'

The DI leans in towards Sue Cromarty. 'What can you tell us about blackmail notes sent to Brigadier Bell and Mr MacMillan.'

'Such as what?'

'Such as when?'

Sue turns thoughtful again. 'First one came on a Monday, I remember that ... must have been a month ago or a bit more ... maybe six weeks – I'd have to look it up.'

'Okay, but you're sure it was a Monday?'

'Yes, before the weekly meeting.'

'Seminar?' Millar interjects.

'You've been talking to the Brigadier.' Sue Cromarty giggles. 'He likes to describe them as seminars. The rest of us call them meetings.'

'And what was your reaction when you saw what it was?' Young coaxes.

'Well … I shouted to Greg when I found it … gave me a fright. Then I took it into him.'

'And how did he react?'

'Oh, didn't say much. Just looked at it then tossed it aside. He's a cool customer. Not much fazes our Brigadier Bell. Told me not to worry about it. That it was probably the work of a nutter and we should forget about it.'

'So what did you think about that?'

'It was his business,' Sue taps the table, 'not mine. If he wasn't bothered, why should I be? I run around enough after this lot, I'm not going to do their worrying for them as well.'

'What about you, Greg?' As Bonnie Young speaks to him, Greg Anderson's fragile body releases another shiver.

'Much the same as Sue, really. Fit's it got te do wi me. None o' my concern, like.'

Bonnie gives him one of her nice smiles, no teeth. 'Sue, did you pass Mr MacMillan his demand at the same time as the Brigadier's?'

'MacMillan? I didn't. I saw it though, lying on his desk. It didn't come through here.'

'Are you sure?'

'Yes, I'd have seen it if it had come in the post, unless someone else was in, handling it at the time, which is possible.'

Young and Millar look at each other.

'You said them, Sue. Did Mr MacMillan get a second demand?' Asks Young.

Now it is Sue and Greg who turn to each other.

'Well I saw one, but then I heard them speaking about two. Both got two,' answers Sue.

'When did the second arrive?' Young's face is a picture of surprise.

'I can tell you exactly. Just a minute.' Sue Cromarty takes an A4 sized volume from a shelf behind the mail table. 'Mail book. It'll be here. Yes, look, there it is.' Cromarty jabs at an entry for July 1st. 'See, it's highlighted.' There is also a hash sign with a 2 beside it. She turns the book around for the detectives to read. 'But that's not our writing. One of the temps.'

'And this is in addition to the one on the 17th of June?' Young asks.

Sue Cromarty flicks back the pages and points at a line under Monday 17th, where someone has noted #1. 'Actually, probably someone from the other office since it's numbered. Someone who knew there were two. Everyone here knows about it. Not a secret.'

'That's against Bell's name.' Millar leans in.

Sue Cromarty peers at the entries for the 17th and 1st. 'Oh, yes. Maybe Mr MacMillan's slipped through. Not sure.'

'If you didn't see the note or notes for MacMillan, how d'you know they were the same as Bell's?'

'I never said they were. But they were similar I'd say … from what I saw lying on his desk. Well only one of them. I didn't see another for Mr MacMillan, actually. I felt sorry for him. He's been, well, pretty emotional, y'know? I told him I'd seen one like it for Brigadier Bell. I think he was surprised but relieved, y'know. He phoned through to the Brigadier, who came by and I left them to it.'

'You know? What do you mean?'

'I'm sorry?' Sue Cromarty looks puzzled.

'You said, "you know",' DI Young talks slowly, 'as if to suggest MacMillan wasn't really upset or surprised by the note.'

Sue Cromarty's eyes dilate with anger. 'No, I didn't say anything like that. How do I know what he was feeling? He's been through a bad time. Yes, he was upset. I don't know if it was that blackmail thing or something else.'

'Okay.' DI Young brushes aside the remark. 'And you, Greg, did you see anything addressed to Mr MacMillan?' asks Young.

'Just Bell's.' Greg shakes his head.

'So how do you think MacMillan's arrived?' DS Millar's question is to both of them.

Sue Cromarty cocks her head to one side. 'I've no idea.'

Greg looks at the table and says nothing.

'Sue, when you saw the blackmail letter, didn't you think of reporting it to the police?' enquires Millar.

'Well, it wasn't up to me, it was up to him. Up to them.'

'Did you hear them mention the possibility of contacting us?'

'Um, I don't remember. Not to me.'

'Didn't you suggest they should?'

'As I said, it wasn't up to me.'

'No, but did you offer this as a suggestion?'

'Can't really remember. I think I might have … '

Millar stops her, 'When? When d'you think you said that?'

'Well … if I did, it would have been when the first arrived for the Brigadier. Yes, I think I said something then. It's hard remembering back. Think I might have.'

'You know that neither the Brigadier nor Mr MacMillan reported this until very recently.'

'I've no idea what they've done.'

'And how did the Brigadier react when the second came through?' asks Young.

'I didn't handle it but I did see them both on his desk. He was staring at them one morning. And breathing quite hard in that noisy way he does sometimes. I felt quite sorry for him. He's sick, y'know. And, it's a shame.' She looks around for someone to agree with her but none of the three others say anything.

'And what happened then?'

Sue Cromarty is herself breathing heavily. 'I think I suggested he get you in.'

'So you knew it hadn't been reported?' Millar sounds irritated.

'Well, I thought, maybe, he hadn't.'

'And what did he say to that?' Young's questions are less combative than her young sergeant's.

'He just stared, not at me, not at anything really. Just stared into space. Y'know. Thinking. He was thinking what to do I suppose. I asked him if I should phone the police and he said he'd take care of everything, so I left him to it.'

DI Young turns to Greg. 'And you never took in the next one?'

'I never saw it but Sue telt me aboot it. I was late in that mornin'. I'd gone te the dentist.'

'What do you feel about your employers being the subject of this sort of criminal activity … surprised?' continues DI Young.

'Aye. Of course. We tried to think fa might have done it.'

'And?'

'Didna have a clue.'

DI Bonnie Young places a hand against her forehead. She is curious as to why Bell and MacMillan tried to sit on the blackmail but she is tired, her head throbs and she has not eaten for too long. She guesses that if she asks for a cup of tea and a biscuit, she'll be pointed in the direction of a vending machine. She brings up the subject of the missing envelopes with Sue Cromarty.

'What do you remember about the envelopes the Brigadier's demands came in? Were they both the same or different. What were they like?'

'What? The one I gave the Brigadier?'

'Yes. Size, shape, colour, writing, printed or longhand or typed, postmark. What do you remember?'

'Um, just that it was a long, ordinary brown envelopes with the Brigadier's name and TAG's address, of course.'

'How was it addressed, to Brigadier or Mr Bell or what?'

'Just the name: Bell.'

'Okay, good, and the postmark?' DI Young encourages her.

'Well … it looked like London but it was smudged and something was written after the London. Maybe postal area. It's hard to say.'

'What do you do with envelopes, normally?'

'Throw them away.'

'And you did that with the Brigadier's blackmail note?'

'No, I passed the lot over to him.'

'You sure about that?'

'Yes I am.'

★ ★ ★

'So what you are saying, Mr … Shaw, is that Donald MacMillan was responsible for your Soviet dealings?'

DI Young and her colleague DS Millar have made their way, via TAGOil's carpeted lift, to the upper storey where the executive offices are situated and are now in the company of TAG's Finance Director,

Stanley Shaw, who is about to respond to a question from Bonnie Young.

'He was mainly responsible. He'd been out there a few times, after Mr Bell.' Shaw breaks off for a moment and opens a window. 'He interfaced far more with them than anyone else in the company recently.'

Shaw is short with a squashed, pock-marked face. His shiny black, wavy fringe flops carelessly when he speaks. Jacketless, he sweats liberally in the over-warm office; grey wet patches evident when he raises his arms off the executive desk.

'TAGOil started dealing with Russia during the late Mr Bell's time here. Is that right? Was there any particular reason for that?' Young rubs at a white mark on her skirt, which she suspects she picked up in the mail room.

'Only that he showed more enthusiasm for our involvement with the Soviet Union energy sector than the rest of us. We weren't against it, don't get me wrong, but he was first to spot the possibilities and … well … followed through. We all discussed our projects. He just made the running for us and then, after … ' Stanley Shaw's voice trails off.

'After?' Inspector Young raises her right eyebrow. Shaw's shrug irritates her. 'After?' repeats Young. The eyebrow arched perfectly.

'Bell used to handle most of that side … ' Again the voice drifts away as though the speaker has run out of steam. Shaw brandishes a hand dismissively.

'Brigadier Bell used to run the Russian operation?' DS Young asks.

'No!' Shaw laughs. 'His brother. The Brigadier's brother …' Shaw is either very bored or experiencing some difficulties.

The stain on DI Young's skirt is proving stubborn. She discreetly licks a finger and scrapes at it with her nail. 'And the circumstances of his death haven't been cleared up yet,' the thought slips from her mouth. 'Did he speak Russian? Mr MacMillan … speak Russian?'

Shaw lets his face settle into a scowl. 'A few words. Enough to be civil. That's all, I'm sure. Not a linguist. No, I don't think so. To be honest I don't know.'

'So why him?' Bonnie Young gives a half smile.

'To the USSR you mean?'

'Uhuh.'

'Well … we deal all over the world. We talk with similar companies. Sometimes we take them practical help. One of our services is to provide equipment that helps with extraction, you see … '

'Without the detail, Mr Shaw, if you don't mind,' DI Young cuts in. Shaw coughs. 'The oil world isn't really that big. We deal with each other.' He shrugs. 'It's often essential to send out a man with a piece of kit. Sometimes we send someone from the Board to speak to other executives about trends, keep up to scratch with what's happening. All part of the globalisation of the industry.'

'Why him?' The question is not going away.

'Well … he was Bell's man.'

'What d'you mean by that?' The DI is listening, waiting for Shaw to say something to justify her salary.

'Nothing really.' Shaw's hand conducts his reply. 'MacMillan worked closely with Bell. That's all.'

'So going to the Soviet Union was a perk?'

'In a way, yes.'

'And when Mr Bell disappeared and his brother took over the business, what was MacMillan's position then?'

'Well, no different,' answered Shaw. 'There weren't any major changes at all. The Brigadier isn't a businessman, you know. He just trusted those of us who knew the ropes to carry on as usual.' The greasy head wobbles on top of the shoulders as he speaks.

'And the Brigadier's brother? Did he speak Russian?' Bonnie Young returns to her earlier line of questioning.

'He may have.' The white-sleeved arms shoot forward onto the desk. 'A little. We hire translators to aid our communication. It's not essential for members of the Board.'

'So, who looks after the Russian side of the business now?'

Shaw clears his throat. 'I will be.'

'And do you speak Russian, Mr Shaw?'

'Not so you'd notice, Detective Inspector,' he replies lightly.

Young switches her attention to a photograph on the wall showing men in short jackets posing before a grounded helicopter. Her face scrunches up like she's trying to focus her eyes.

'You fly, Mr Shaw.'

'Pilot? Used to be. Then I moved into this business.'

'Like riding a bike, I suppose. Was it up here? North Sea assignments?'

'No. I used to work in the south … of England, mostly.'

'Oh, so you've been with TAG how long?'

'Let me see … around four years.'

'What brought you here?'

'Get away from the rat race. People have time for each other here. You know …' a hint of a smile registers on the current bun face, 'that sort of thing.'

'Less rats up here, eh?' DS Millar quips.

'Fewer, Millar,' his DI mutters. Shaw laughs. 'Mr MacMillan was being blackmailed. Did you know about this?'

'Yes, of course. We discussed it.'

'But you weren't,' Young means it as a question although her intonation is flat.

'No.'

'Can you think why Brigadier Bell and Mr MacMillan were selected for special attention?'

Shaw spends a second or two organising his thoughts. 'Both seen as heading up the company. I have really no idea. Isn't that your job?'

Bonnie Young bridles. 'What impact did the blackmail demands have on TAG as a company?'

'Not much. It's only recently become widely known. Got the impression the Brigadier wanted it kept hush-hush. MacMillan would do whatever he was told I suppose. Seemed alright when he spoke to me about it. Appeared to be coping well enough. Though now that I come to think of it, just lately he did seem a bit out of sorts. Not his usual self, you might say. Distracted I suppose. Signs were there but it's easy to be wise after the event. I don't think anyone realised how he was handling things.'

'Any reason you can think of why someone might want to blackmail Brigadier Bell and Mr MacMillan?' DS Millar pipes up.

Shaw shrugs again and shakes his head.

Millar tries a different angle. 'Any strangers hanging about the place?'

Shaw thinks for a moment. 'We're a busy company. Get all kinds of people coming in and out the whole time.' Clearly something has come into his head. 'There was someone, one morning being a bit of a nuisance. Nearly charged into me trying to get out. A reporter, I think. Yes, sure that was it.'

'And that was recently? When, exactly?' DS Millar is interested.

'Like I say, can't remember. But he didn't come across as anyone involved in this business.' Shaw gives an exaggerated shake of his head.

DI Young returns the focus back to Shaw. 'How d'you get on with your colleagues? Do you like them?' Her question sounds casual.

'Do you mean am I the blackmailer?' He gives a squashy laugh.

'Do you like them?' Young persists.

'We have a working relationship.' Shaw sits back. 'Don't have much to do with them outside of here. It's work, nothing more.'

'And Hugh Bell, did you like him any better?'

'Yeah, he was okay. Didn't know him too well,' a glint of a smile from Shaw, 'bit out of my league.'

'Meaning?' DS Millar asks.

'Just he was loaded. I'm not. Didn't mix in the same circles.'

'Do you think MacMillan was the type of person to take his own life?'

The Detective Inspector has at last succeeded in eliminating the stain from her navy skirt and is keen to similarly resolve other outstanding issues.

Shaw contemplates what she's said. 'Commit suicide? Terrible. Can't help you. No, sorry. As I said, I really didn't know him that well.' Leaning back into his chair, Shaw folds his hands behind his head. Two damp circles like bug eyes stare out from the underarms of his shirt but Bonnie Young doesn't need to see them to know they are there.

'Did you have the impression he might have had money difficulties?' Young puts to him.

DS Millar rolls his eyes. Money difficulties. She is asking if he is up shit creek and looking for £3 million to tide him over. Stanley Shaw studies Bonnie Young's face and decides that for a policewoman of a certain age she is pretty attractive.

'Think there was a bit of speculation, a while back, when Hugh

Bell … died, um, that MacMillan expected to take over, um, but then his brother came along … I know he'd just bought a new house … could have overdone it.' The bun brow wrinkles in a show of concern.

DI Young opens her mouth as if to respond then checks herself. 'Think we'll look round his office now. Thanks for your time Mr Shaw,' her outstretched arm forces the man to spring to his feet.

'Sorry I couldn't have been more helpful. Let me show you the way. I take it you do have a warrant?'

Young stops mid-stride. 'We're dealing with an unexplained death, Mr Shaw.'

The bun beams benignly and holds open the door. 'It's through here.' He leads them to the room next door to his.

'Just one last thing.' DS Millar points his index finger as if to caution Shaw. 'Did you know any of his friends or family?'

Shaw ignores the finger. 'I met his wife. Tragedy. Only the once. Donald kept the rest of his life private. We never mixed socially but I believe he did have friends, although I've no reason for saying that. It just seems likely he would have. Sometimes mentioned going out to the theatre, for meals, that sort of thing. Not really the kinds of activities people on their own do I suppose, although some might. Is that all?'

'That'll do for now,' replies Young while suppressing a yawn.

Dave Millar thanks him. 'Oh, before you go Mr Shaw, Do you still have your pilot's licence?'

'Er, yes, but …' is his hesitant reply. Shaw shrugs, his face quizzical.

Millar nods and returns the smile.

The detectives search every inch of MacMillan's office. Every paper clip in its place. Pens neatly arranged. No sweet papers stuck to the inside of drawers. No dirty magazines stuffed behind files. MacMillan kept a tidy outfit. His desk diary contains several names and numbers and pencilled-in appointments. Bonnie Young reads entries for the two days up to his death: a morning appointment with a person named Macleod of RND Products at Altens, which she recognises as suppliers of hardware to the oil industry, and the other is a memo to "phone PM".

DS Millar is a shade out of sorts: he resents being slapped down by

Young in front of punters and her mention of the Brigadier's brother is needling him as she hadn't discussed anything about this with him.

Hugh Bell died before Millar arrived in the north east, although he does recall the report on the BBC's *Reporting Scotland* programme so it must have been a fairly major event to have made it past the usual stories of "man dies from eating too many chips in Glasgow's east end". Millar files away his resentment for the time being.

'He might have killed himself out of despair.' Millar can sympathise. 'After all, with his wife dying. Couldn't live without her. Then some guy demanding money or else he'll expose ... whatever needed exposing. You can understand it. All that's bound to weigh on his shoulders, even for a hard-headed businessman and all that.'

'Something here stinks and not just Shaw's oxters.' Young wrinkles her nose. 'A bit glacial that man, don't you think? Way he looks at you. Can't put my finger on it.'

Moscow: Friday 2 August 1991

Coulthard is dropped off at his hotel, where he changes into jeans and trainers before hitting the bar for a couple of large vodkas. Having absorbed the aperitif, he goes looking for a bite to eat in the café he's spotted around the corner. It doesn't look up to much; distressed wood panel door opening into a dismal interior of some dozen aluminium tables and matching chairs and the aluminium serving bar completes the silvertone effect. A chef in high hat and full-length apron, neither of which appears to have seen a laundry in years, stirs each of four great steaming cauldrons in turn with the same ladle. It is late for lunch and only a few stragglers are still eating. Coulthard sticks to his preferred liquid diet and settles for soup. What it is he neither knows nor cares. It has a thin and sharp flavour; not unpleasant. Industrial soup from an industrial aluminium pot – a measure of tap water, glimpse of a carrot and a dash of Alzheimer's is Coulthard's guess. Die of Alzheimer's? I should be so lucky to live that long, he thinks as he takes a mouthful.

He is dunking his bread when a young woman he has spotted walking past the window comes in. He sees long tanned legs beneath a brown skirt and a striking blue and white check jacket over a white t-shirt. She looks around at the stragglers then at Coulthard, gives him a bright smile and walks straight over.

'Is the food any good?'

'Eh, yes, if you're hungry enough.' Coulthard studies her; definitely his type: woman.

'May I join you?' Her wide toothy smile and shake of long dark hair settles the matter.

'Please,' is his eager response.

The chef fills up her soup bowl and piles a plate with sliced white loaf. Robert Coulthard is sure she is German or Austrian. Northern Europe, certainly. He clears a space on the table.

'Here, let me.'

'Thank you, I can manage.' She sets down the soup bowl and bread plate and collects an aluminium spoon from the counter. 'Their cutlery is like their money: cheap and nasty.'

'Utilitarian,' Coulthard agrees. The young woman's beautiful smile has charmed him.

'My name is Mance Stresemann,' the smile's owner presents him with her hand.

'Pleased to meet you, Mance, I'm Robert Coulthard.'

Mance bends forward and sips the soup. 'Oh! It is hot!' She makes a face and stirs it to cool it down. 'Where are you from?' she asks.

'You don't think I'm from here?' Coulthard teases.

'Definitely not. I would say you were British. Am I close?'

'Pretty well spot on,' he replies. 'And you are … German?'

She tilts her head. 'Well done.'

'Which part?' he asks.

'I work in Cologne as a technical author with a financial services organisation. And what is it you do?'

'I'm what's known as between jobs at the moment. Do different things. Communications mostly.'

'Sounds interesting. In telecommunications?' she asks.

'That kind of area.' Coulthard doesn't elaborate.

The next few minutes are taken up with staccato exchanges and tourist chat. Coulthard's mind flitting back to brick shithouses and a time-warp 60s Beatle, but the girl is gradually winning him over. Turns out she is the tactile, continental type that makes life easy for someone as uptight as he is. She touches his sleeve when the cook lets some cutlery drop noisily onto the floor. Her eyes grow wide and she giggles. Coulthard laughs and shakes his head at the torrent of words being discharged from the counter. Even when Mance Stresemann's fingers have gone back to playing with her soup spoon, Coulthard can feel their impression on his arm; curving elegantly on top of his wrist, slender and tapered, nails scrubbed clean and no varnish.

'How do you think it stands up, especially in this heat?' Giggling, she points to her head and fans her face with a paper napkin.

Coulthard sneaks a glance at the cook with his white chimney hat. 'Russians have a big hat fetish. Probably someone writing a research paper on it right now.'

'Could be a Nobel prize winner.'

'We could drink to that,' says Coulthard.

'Do you want coffee? Except, I don't imagine they have coffee here.

Tea?' Those fingers brush Coulthard's wrist then linger just where they are.

'I'll give it a pass.'

'Okay ... well.' She hesitates.

'But I wouldn't mind a proper drink. Want to join me?' He thinks about placing his hand over hers but doesn't.

'Great. That would be great. Where will we go?'

'My hotel's just about next door. Got a bar. Soft seats.' He stretches his back and the flimsy aluminium chair flexes under his shifting weight.

The bar is quiet. Afternoons are mainly for visiting tourist sites or striking deals in smoky Soviet offices. Mance Stresemann tells Robert Coulthard, when he asks, that she is not staying in a hotel but in a private apartment. She orders a Polish Strick cocktail and they watch the barman pour a measure of Zubrowski bison grass vodka into a silver shaker followed by a half measure of apple schnapps, the same of lime and apple juice and a dash of vanilla syrup, at which point he raises his index finger and disappears towards the kitchen for a moment before returning with a handful of halved green grapes which he arranges on ice in a long glass, gives a few turns of the shaker and pours out the green liquid over the fruit on the rocks.

'Your pudding?' chuckles Coulthard as he throws back a double Stoly and follows it with another.

Mance asks him straight out if he is in town with anyone and seems to like his answer. He does not ask her. It makes no difference to him if there is another man. No guilt, no jealousy, no conscience.

Their drinks definitely enliven the conversation. He finds her fun. It makes him feel good that someone as stunning as Mance Stresemann is happy to spend time with him. She puts him at ease with her relaxed chit-chat. Mance declines a second cocktail, opting instead for a Coke. She reveals she was a student for a time in Scotland and so they discuss places they're both familiar with, although it is clear she is more familiar with them than Coulthard is. When she presses him, he tells her it is because he went into the army as a youth and spent much of his time away from home. It's more than an hour later when she leaves – with the hotel phone number and having kissed Coulthard on the cheek. He watches her go. Only then does he notice that the bar has filled up with some high-spirited tourists and clusters of formally-clad foreign businessmen quietly conversing with polo-shirted local entrepreneurs.

Coulthard nods his thanks to the barman and goes to fetch his room key from the reception desk. He is a bit boozy and already his cheerfulness is dissipating. He stares blankly at the TV screen in the lobby. News from Moscow like news from every major city – myopic by inclination. There is a report on an accident in the city involving a foreign tourist. Nadia is speaking.

'Excuse me, sir, but there is message for you. Urgent he said. The message is *Call again cowboy*.' Coulthard lets out an audible groan. He forgot to make the call. Ding-a-ling Bell at ten to ten; cowboy time. He guesses Scottish 1950s culture would be lost on young, pretty Nadia and hopefully the Gollum from under the reception desk. Still hours to go until the next one. He retraces his steps and collects a sugary black tea from the bar. Dinger might not be sober when he makes the call but he'll be expecting Coulthard to be.

Dinger had selected him for special duties while he was still a pawky wee trooper with Her Majesty's Forces; he had taken him on, sobered him up and helped him sort out a few personal issues so he could move on. If ever there had been an occasion when Coulthard looked like hitting the skids again, Dinger would turn up and talk him back up. He owed his life to Dinger. He would always owe him.

Coulthard lies down for a bit and thinks about what has happened since his arrival. Despite agreeing to co-operate with the four in the apartment, or rather three plus Luda Semenova, Robert Coulthard now regrets becoming so easily tied in with them. He had been caught up in the moment. What is done is done. There are other reasons for him being there. Bored, he wanders back down to the bar. It is under occupation from more boisterous tourists than earlier. Everyone, it seems, is having a great time except for him, Lenny the Lonely. The evening stretches before him like knicker elastic. He orders a lager and whisky chaser followed by two more and all he can think about is Mance Stresemann and not even all of her but those bottomless, dark eyes. He knows she is in love with him; he knows he is a good reader of women; the way she touched him as soon as they met. She wanted him as much as he wanted her. Along the bar, two extremely tall and very blond Russian girls make eye contact. Coulthard nods his approval and waves his beer glass. He is brightening up. It is a phenomenon of Russian women, he muses, that those over a certain age change from lemon meringue pie to clootie dumpling virtually overnight. The pair along the bar, still very much at the whipped cream stage, meet with his wholehearted approval. When the boldest sashays up to him and simpers, 'Are you looking for special friend?' and is followed by her tiptoeing companion asking if he would like to buy them a drink, Coulthard has to admit he is and he does.

It's late when Coulthard turns the girls out of his room. He watches them wobble away from the hotel, no doubt to catch up with homework for school the next day, as a taxi cab drops off a foreign man and a heavily made-up Russian woman forty years his junior. She passes muster with the KGB man at the door, who vets locals trying to gain entry, and gets his wink of approval. Coulthard hangs around the lobby phone kiosk until it is time for the call.

Clearly someone has been talking to Aberdeen. Dinger is in a filthy temper, accusing Coulthard of endangering the mission. Not that he says it as openly as that but Robert Coulthard has been primed to read what is not said as much as the sheer bloody obvious. Dinger stops short of ordering him home. Repeatedly asks if he is ill. Does he need to come back? Coulthard reassures him he is coping fine. Only one more thing to do then he will be home. Not to worry.

So who has been on to Dinger? Coulthard knows it will not have been the pair of brick shithouses, so that left Grigoryev and Luda. His bet is on Grigoryev. Dinger is a cunning bastard. Leaves nothing to chance.

He needs to walk off the booze. He's eaten very little all day and is hungry. The new McDonald's on Pushkin Square is shut. He is not the only one there – a steady influx of people drift up to peer through its windows. The night is still and warm. Coulthard sits on a bench a few yards from the restaurant. A skinny kid sidles up asking if he has Plan, which he knows is what the locals call hash. Coulthard tells him he doesn't have any but the youth clearly doesn't believe him.

'You take ten roubles,' he slurs his words, 'for Plan or koknar?' Getting no response he shifts his attention to Coulthard's feet. 'You sell trainer shoe?'

'No, pal. They keep my feet on the ground.'

The youth shuffles away. Coulthard admires the addict's grasp of English, doubting if any of Aberdeen's beggars could solicit cash in anything other than Doric. Coulthard wishes all Soviets were as easy to handle. It is confirmation Gorbachevland is open for business.

Early next morning, Coulthard tries to contact Grigoryev but is told he has been called into work unexpectedly. He'd left a message that the Monday meeting is still on. Coulthard spends a long time in the shower. Another night without sleep. He really isn't himself.

10. LOOT THE LOOTERS

Moscow: Saturday 3 August 1991

Dmitri Fedotov embraces Tommy MacHardy like a brother when they meet on the hotel steps late the following afternoon.

'I ask at reception for you. They would not help me. Then I describe you to a friend of mine who is service attendant and she say you were not out of room yet, so I wait.'

'How long have you been here?' Tommy asks coldly.

'It is nice day. Very nice so I don't care. I sit here and watch pretty women walk in, walk out, walk in again. I should work in hotel. I am honest man. There was tourist in there making fuss, say someone stole jewellery from her room. This happens all time – in hotels like this one, Russians see foreigners with everything when they have nothing so sometimes someone will take little things. That is way. We have term for it: expropriation of expropriators. Does not make big difference to your life but maybe so to Russian's. But I am honest man. Your friend. So, Tommy, I take you tour of my city and, if you would like, to meet my family.'

Which is how Tommy MacHardy comes to be sitting up front beside Dmitri Fedotov in his hire car holding tight to a kilo of tomatoes Dmitri picked up from a roadside stall. He waved aside Fedotov's invitation to sample the city's many museums while recognising the Soviets' near faultless dedication to heritage, coming as he does from a city where virtually nothing is remembered far less commemorated. No, the heritage most interesting to him when they set out is Moscow's buildings from the period of Adam Menelaws but it is Yuri Gagarin's soaring statue splintering the sun's rays which creates the greatest impression.

Dmitri ducks his head to get a better view through the windscreen. 'Gagarin is great hero from space, world's first cosmonaut. Such a man!' He presses the accelerator and the car roars out of Yuri Gagarin Square, leaving the lonely spaceman soaring forever into the clouds; a shining role model in titanium. Pure Dan Dare. Wondering what Menelaws would have made of it, Tommy concludes he would have been equally mesmerised by its power as a breathtaking symbol of Russian identity. They filter into the traffic on 60 Years of the Great October Revolution Prospekt on their way to the Ptichii Rynok.

At the entrance to Moscow's bird market, several malnourished old women proffer tiny, timid kittens and passive puppies; pitiable specimens mewing from hunger. The rest of the market is packed out with people and animals and birds, domestic and exotic. Dmitri steers Tommy to a stall set out with assorted pieces of machinery.

'I recognise this man,' he says under his breath into Tommy's ear, 'he is from engineering institute where I work. It happens all time. People steal and sell on.' He points to a collection of used machine parts in a cardboard box. 'See here – I go to work and one more machine out of order and one day I go in and all machine is gone.' The stall holder is hopping from foot to foot, glowering at Dmitri. 'People have two jobs, three, maybe. We do not get paid enough money to live. People have to do something. You agree?'

'Well … I dunno. Maybe it's the system that has to change? So you're not just a taxi driver, then?'

'I am taxi. I am engineer. And my house is hotel. They are dealers. Anyway, it all belongs to all of us. We are system,' he chuckles.

'If this happened in my country, the police would pull them in,' exclaims Tommy as they walk away, to the stall holder's obvious relief.

'Not here!' The driver shakes his head. 'Here it depends who you talk to in police. We have to be … what you say … ?'

'Sleekit?' suggests Tommy.

'Sleekit? I like this word.'

'It's Scottish.'

'I learn Scottish now. I start with sleekit. We Russians are sleekit. Yes! This is how we live. We steal to live. We have special name for this kind of stealing. Nesuny. You will not see person who work in meat plant standing in line for meat in shop. You take from factory for your family and sometimes for your friends. This is always what we do.

Everyone. Millions. It will never stop. You understand this? We take and we share in kooperativy so all have goods.'

'Kooperativy, yeah, well we ca' it the co-op.'

Dmitri is not listening to Tommy but calling to a couple of men carrying shoes boxes. 'My cousins,' he explains, 'they work in institute that make shoe. You know?'

'A factory for shoes,' Tommy helps him out.

'Shoes. Factory sell shoes over all country. In village and city. Price of shoes set by government, yes? In institute – factory, they set price for shoes, load them into truck and drive out of factory then drive back in with same shoes at different price, higher price. You see how it is? Look, in Russia we must invent to live. If our leaders cannot feed us then we take what we need. If people want new shoes, they must pay high price. This is why my cousins have nice house and nice car.' He thumbs in the direction of a sickly looking woman. 'Not everyone can do this. We think different from you Scottish men. We are open but also secretive. Let me tell you. In my institute we design and produce machine parts. Sometimes we cannot get material we need to make parts. Well this is bad so we must get them somehow. That is where comrade Amosoff comes in. Ssshhh!' He presses his index finger against his lips. Checking no-one is close enough to have overheard, he continues, 'He is our man to get what we need. We say tolkach. He will get favours by doing favours for others. You understand?' Tommy lets him talk. 'What we need, he will arrange that this product will be marked as reject. As many as we need. These rejects then find their way to us.'

'But they're not rejects,' says Tommy.

'No, there are no rejects. You understand?'

'They are sold on? The bosses turn a blind eye?'

'Our boss is Soviet government. In work place, boss is representative of government. They have many tricks up sleeve. They might employ ghosts. Many, many ghosts.' Dmitri's laughing eyes are circled by deep weathered lines.

'What do you mean, ghosts?'

'Officially institute say it employ 400 men and women, but only 200 ever turn up for work, you understand? Others get paid and you

93

have many happy workers. This is how we live. Like private enterprise in West. You want something, you must do someone favour or pay them money, but sometimes this is hard so you do comrade good turn. Same maybe if you are sick and need operation or medicine. This is only way we survive. In your country doctors are rich but here they are very poor so sell on black market. It is our way. It work. Sometime it work.' He throws his arms in the air.

'And the police know what's going on?' Tommy has to shout as a police car drives past, its siren screaming.

'Of course; police, party members, everyone. You want driver licence? You oil wheels. You must know who to speak to but there are ways we find out.'

'Sounds pretty complicated to me, Dmitri.' MacHardy splutters, his throat irritated by noxious exhaust fumes.

The driver shrugs. 'In Russia, everything has two sides.'

'Including you?' Tommy glances at his friend.

'For sure. Including me.'

Fedotov pours diluted black Russian tea into a porcelain mug decorated with red and gold bucking horses. The kitchen in his parents' apartment is pokey and the two men take up most of the postage stamp-sized table once they pull up their chairs. Since collecting MacHardy from the hotel, Dmitri has hardly stopped talking long enough to draw breath. Now he is denouncing Jimmy Carter's stance on the Soviet war in Afghanistan.

'Instead of backing us in war against spread of Muslimism that creep up from southern republics, Carter's CIA spend millions of dollars equipping Mujahidin to fight us. This is mad policy.'

Tommy asks the obvious question, 'Did you serve in that war?'

Dmitri neither confirms nor denies he did but speaks with the conviction of a man whose second cousin single-handedly led the assault on Kabul.

'We chase them. They run fast. Hide in cave. So boom, boom – rockets, you know?' His stubby fingers rap on his left shoulder.

'Shoulder-launched rockets,' MacHardy catches on.

'Yes, fuel-air, you know?'

'Vacuum bombs.' MacHardy continues to be helpful.

'Vacuum bomb? Maybe – boom, explode eye straight out of eye hole.'

'Sucks the life out of everything.' MacHardy pats his belly.

Dmitri roars with laughter. 'Great shock. Very shocking. They run faster. Too fast sometime. Nice place. Sunny. Smell nice. Wait, I show you.' He goes out of the room, returning with an iridescent blue gemstone cupped in his hand.

'Lapis lazuli, isn't it?' Tommy holds it up to the window. 'D'you know, artists used to crush this to make ultramarine. It's an amazing stone, man.'

'It come from Hindu Kush, in Afghanistan,' Dmitri adds for clarity. 'One time it is more valuable than gold.'

'Yeah, you got it when you were in the army?' Tommy enquires.

'I got it,' is Dmitri's enigmatic reply. 'You know, crew in Soviet helicopters they shoot dead our men if they are surrounded by Mujahedin. You think that good or bad?'

Tommy puts down his mug. 'Maybe they were tryin' to protect them from a fate worse than death.'

'There is fate worse than death?' Dmitri rubs his thumb around his chin and drops the gemstone onto the table at the moment a lipsticked, cheery-faced woman, who MacHardy takes to be Dmitri's mother, breezes into the kitchen.

Her darting eyes switch between her son and Tommy. 'Dmitri, Dmitri!' she reproaches her son, 'You keep your guest hungry and we have so much food in cupboard.' She pushes in behind Dmitri's seat to get to a row of white painted wall units bordered with garish red dahlias with blue centres and yellow Maltese crosses. For every door there is an A4 sheet of paper neatly taped to it. Her son takes a deep breath but has learnt from experience not to get involved in an unwinnable situation. Raiding her stock of canned fish, rice, buckwheat, oil from Turkey and jar upon jar of jams and pickles, the smiling mother watches that Tommy does not run off.

'We do not get to meet foreign people, this is privilege for us and my son starves his guest. What am I to do with him? Tell me?'

MacHardy's protestations that he is not hungry do nothing to dissuade the woman from arranging little side plates with pieces of smoked and brined fish, pickled cabbage and gherkins, chunks of heavily crusted white bread and fresh cucumber; from their dacha, she tells him.

'My mother tries to keep store of provisions so we do not go hungry. Our government call people like her hoarders,' grumbles Dmitri.

His mother rarely stops smiling but she cannot disguise the fatigue in her expression. She lays a hand on her son's back and addresses MacHardy.

'During great patriotic war, Soviet people had little to eat but we were kinder to each other then. If you had food, you share it with neighbours. Now we do not even speak to neighbours. We fight like dogs over scraps they sell in market and shops.'

'Your English is very good. Like Dmitri's.'

The smile grows a yard wide. 'I try very hard to learn.' She points to the pages of neat script along the front of the cupboards. 'I copy from books and study them when I work. I have same in bedroom. There is words and some poetry. Do you like poetry? I have book with British poems and try to remember some. Then I will copy other ones. This,' she peers at a stanza of verse, 'is by Voloshin. You know him?'

MacHardy shakes his head.

'Voloshin was in my family. He is famous. Poet. Painter. But his poetry I try to write out in English. This,' she reads off the cupboard door –

'I've had delusions, no doubt
temptations, weaknesses at times.
Despite all that, whenever I
faded in sorrow and delight,
my light has never gone out.'

Dmitri's mother beams at the two men and MacHardy can see where she has found the inspiration for her endurance.

Her son squirms, embarrassed by her behaviour. It is then that she spots the tomatoes and lets out a gasp.

'So red, Dmitri!' And, kissing her son, asks, 'What did the thieves take from you for them?' As she turns the plump fruits in her hand.

'Eight dollars.'

'Oh, Dmitri you have not eight dollars.' Then, looking at Tommy MacHardy, 'Do you buy this for us?'

Immediately Dmitri jumps in. 'No, Matya, I buy them. Now are you just going to talk about them or serve them to my friend?'

And so the tomatoes are rinsed off and given a saucer of garlanded rosebuds all of their own. Precious delicacies, each mouthful will be savoured at that Soviet table.

They are joined by Dmitri's father. He moves slowly – his weariness apparent in his body. But his eyes are intelligent and alert. He acknowledges Tommy with a polite nod as he takes his seat.

His wife calls out and a shy youth wearing a dark canvas cap, Dmitri's brother, and their young sister press themselves into the remaining gaps around the table. They eat in great intimacy, the woman swollen with pride.

'Today we feast. So much food. We eat like royalty!'

Only Dmitri, his mother and Tommy converse during the meal. The others eat, observe and listen but contribute nothing beyond nods and grunts. They all participate, however, in the frequent toasts made to all and sundry and much vodka is consumed along with the food. When a large proportion of the eight US dollars' worth of tomatoes, all the fish and most of the preserves have vanished from the dishes, Tommy MacHardy excuses himself.

Gingerly, he raises his head from the pillow and carelessly throws out an arm. Something drops to the floor. The blue lapis lazuli. MacHardy sits up and looks around. He is in a room as small as the kitchen and packed floor to ceiling with boxes. There are footsteps on the linoleum outside. The mother's kindly face peeps around the door. She wears full make-up; scarlet lips, dressed to go out. Tommy apologises. He must have passed out but she waves his apology aside and beckons him to follow her.

'Would you like tea or coffee?' The words carefully enunciated.

'Tea would be great, thanks.'

The clock on the kitchen wall says 6.40 and only then does MacHardy realise he has slept through the night. 'Look, I have to go,' he croaks. Dmitri's mother frowns. 'Not without eating something. Your breakfast is already prepared. Please.'

MacHardy tries to insist. His head is pounding and his eyes sore. He doesn't think he could swallow anything that is not liquid but she has already poured him a small bowl of sweetened porridge and is slipping an omelette onto a warmed plate. There is even one of the tomatoes, sliced and salted to enhance the eggs. Tommy obliges her, eating slowly and swallowing hard to make sure what goes down stays down. He drinks copious amounts of her tea poured from the pot and diluted with boiling water from the kettle.

Tea is usually Tommy's drink. Coffee smells. Smells give you away. Tommy watches the red lips prattle on about food shortages. She sidles up to him, her voice lowered into a solicitous whisper over the meal she has provided, describing the difficulties of procuring even the most basic of foods since her family lost its privileges. She means the two tier service run by Soviet stores. If you are one of the select, you get zakazi. Zakazi ensures the privileged never feel the real extent of the nation's shortages, but Dmitri's father has lost his entitlement to monthly supplies of sausage, jam, sugar, butter and every other essential. The woman says she hopes Tommy understands this is why they mostly have to eat vegetables grown at their dacha, a train journey away on the outskirts of the city.

Gastronom No. 1, known familiarly to Muscovites by its pre-revolutionary name of Yeliseyev's, supplies more than 70,000 zakazi every month. The majority of its stock is allocated to the USSR's crème de la crème; members of government, and selected translators, secretaries and drivers who enjoy its richest pickings. Other shops run similar systems for trade unionists, co-operatives and military personnel. Kick-backs working both ways. One well remunerated manager at Yeliseyev's finding it impossible to spend his vast accumulated wealth resorted to papering his apartment with hundred rouble notes. Well, wallpaper has long been a scarce commodity.

Dmitri's mother tells Tommy MacHardy how she has a friend in Finland who is forever urging her to settle there. 'I would like for that to happen. Very much it is my dream. But I need dollars. I have been saving for long time but this is slow and I want very much to go.'

Tommy encourages her. 'You'd like it there. Not so much queuing for food,' he teases.

The woman looks at him earnestly. 'I have been there, already, several times. Food in shops is a wonder. That is very much what I want. I would get job and live there with my friend.' She stares deep into his face and he understands her meaning.

'Would yer husband get a job there, then?'

'My husband, he does not want to go. He is retired. He was mine engineer. I have to think of my life. I am not so old. He would stay here where he is happy. He has dacha. He would be happy.'

'He would miss you and you him.' Tommy is at a loss for what else to say.

'In Russia families often get separated. This is fact of our lives. People do not belong to each other.'

There is an awkward few moments before the woman repeats her appeal. 'But I need dollars for this.'

'Eh, I'm no exactly well-off, y'know. Um, I haven't got much money.' Tommy wants to go. He knows she has been generous to him. Knows it is tough for her and the rest of them. Suffering from Western guilt, he digs out some of the dollars he has taken as back-up currency. Dmitri's Matya quickly conceals them in her hand as her son walks in.

Dmitri hugs Tommy but ignores his mother. Tommy thanks them both and insists he must leave when Dmitri slips an arm around his shoulder.

'You will need to get back into centre. I have no time – I have to go to institute today – but I will get you cab.' Tommy brushes aside the offer. He will find his own way back to the hotel. Dmitri accompanies him to the main door, where three stoned or drunk teenagers skulk on their haunches. Tommy recognises one as Dmitri's teenage brother, his canvas cap pulled down over his face. Dmitri pays them no attention.

'Maybe you like our house and would want to stay. Be our guest. Would be better than expensive hotel and real food. Not rubbish. It would be home. Like your home.'

Tommy smiles back at him but declines the offer. Dmitri leans his head to one side.

'You see us as we are. A good experience, huh? You stay.' He presses home the point on Tommy's shoulder and is reluctant to see him go. 'Listen, Tommy. Stalin, Khrushchev, Brezhnev and Gorbachev sit on train crossing Siberia. Train breaks down. Stalin shouts, "Shoot driver". Train does not move. Khrushchev shouts, "Rehabilitate driver". Train still not move. Brezhnev he leans forward, closes curtains and settles back, "Let us pretend train is moving" he says. Gorbachev, he runs down corridor, shouting, "Everybody out." When everybody is out he jumps over people onto the engine and calls out, "Everybody push and I will give you pay rise later." This is our Russia, Tommy.'

'But it's home.'

'Yes, it is home.'

'Your mother was talking about going to live in Finland.'

'She say that to you? Do not listen to her.'

'She seemed pretty determined.'

'She will go. One day she will go.'

'But not you?'

'I stay and look after my father. He is good man.'

Tommy MacHardy notices Dmitri picking at the image of the plumed tiger on the back of his hand.

Dmitri glances up to an upstairs window. 'My father worked in the mines? She despises my father. He was engineer. Responsible for men's lives. He tried to get managers make it safe for workers. But they do not care. My father make protest against poor safety and is arrested. They send him to Dnepropetrovsk Special Psychiatric Hospital and they inject him with Sulfazin. Every two days, into his eh … how you say?' Dmitri pats his hip. 'He is not able to walk, you know? Much pain. They give him Haloperidol. You know this drug? It makes you not sleep.' Dmitri jumps up and down to demonstrate. 'You are this way all time. Even now he needs vodka to get him sleep. Even so, his body does not let him sleep. He is no longer easy man to live, you know? Matya hate him now. They cannot get food in shops. She must queue all day sometimes. They do not speak. So she will go. We will stay. He is good man, my father.' Dmitri nudges Tommy. 'Why is individual at heart of communism? So he is easy to kick from all sides.' He laughs hard.

The canyon of apartment blocks recedes into a distant socialist ideal of housing for the masses. Britain might have ended up like this after the war if the Labour government had found the money and there hadn't been problems with crumbling concrete. Grey, most likely they would have been grey in Britain. Here they are painted blue and have small balconies like giant ashtrays running along their length. Streets colourful with an abundance of flowerbeds, grassy islands and a peppering of trees. Unambiguous urban planning and it works. Municipal symmetry, a mirror of the Soviet political structure: regimented, functional, utilitarian with just a suggestion of concession to the spiritual needs of its citizens. Magically, a cab appears.

'You change your mind, maybe?' Dmitri squeezes MacHardy's arm.

Tommy flags down the car. 'I've enjoyed myself. Apologise to your mother. Look, I need to go.'

11. PITILESS HYPOCRISY

Moscow: Sunday 4 August 1991- Evening

'You don't look happy, Robert.'

'Just thinking. Is this a German's idea of a good time?' Coulthard casts a jaundiced eye around the near-deserted restaurant.

'Oh! It's still early. Just be patient.' Mance Stresemann lifts Robert Coulthard's hand and runs her slender fingers along it, circling his index nail with her own.

'Fancy a drink? Or is it too early for that as well?' he asks.

'Thank you, Robert, I'll have a pertsivka and a Pepsi.'

Apart from the other four occupied tables, the rest have reservation cards propped up against their flower vases, including Coulthard's and Stresemann's. They sit at it all the same. The restaurant is a bleaker version of Aberdeen's Civil Service Club on Crown Street, and hardly bigger than a couple of tenement sitting rooms. What it lacks in ambience it makes up for in the bad taste of its decor. He was glad to get Mance's call asking him out but it is not the most exciting start to a date. Ten minutes later, it is obvious waiting on tables is an optional activity for the staff, none of whom have so far cared to take it up. Coulthard follows the racket from a TV and sticks his head into an adjoining room. A handful of people who might be waiters are watching Russia's answer to *Blind Date* on a black and white set. Coulthard coughs and makes no impression. They could be saving themselves for the rush when, and if, the Soviet mafia deign to turn up for a spot of dinner; always a nice little earner for staff able to double their state salary in a single night from tips alone. Then again it might just be that these ardent fans of *Blind Date* think they deserve half an hour of peace and quiet to enjoy the show. Robert Coulthard raps on the door and pushes it open. Someone behind catches it and peers up at him. 'Can we have some drinks out here? Piva. Pertsivka. Pepsi.' The man behind the door kicks the leg of a chair and a youth in white reluctantly rises and follows Coulthard into the restaurant while holding his attention on the screen until the door swings closed.

Mance Stresemann smoothes out the creases on the inside elbows of her blouse. 'When we met, you told me you had once been in the army. You didn't say when you left.'

'No?' Coulthard looks to see where their drinks have got to.

Mance tugs on her cuffs. 'In Britain it is not compulsory as it is in Germany? You chose to be in the army?'

'People like me don't choose to go into the army. You know, tearaways at school. Bored out of our skulls. Always falling behind. Told you're a useless so and so. Can't wait to leave. Then the army comes round, somebody needs us, promises an exciting future, good money, so there's no contest. It's like there's nothing else. Not for me when I was a kid anyway.'

'So you joined from school?'

Coulthard lets the question sink without trace.

Stresemann is making all the small-talk. 'And you found the excitement?'

'Yeah. Had its moments.' Coulthard winks. 'Filled the gap between bored youth and bored middle age.'

'And it taught you about life?'

'What's this? Twenty questions?'

'I am sorry?' Mance looks puzzled.

'No, it's okay. You're right. It's not that you come out of the army with a degree in philosophy or with an explanation for the meaning of life but it teaches you – well, it must have taught me something. Everything in life does.'

'Makes you proud of serving your country.' His companion leans in, engaging him with her brown, brown eyes.

'Yeah, that's part of it.'

'And did the army look after you?'

'The army does everything for you but wipe your arse. Protects you from the big bad world. Home sweet home. Food on the plate. Cheap drink. And you don't have to mix with outsiders. Yeah, it's a good life if you can hack it.'

Mance springs back in her seat and makes a face. 'Hack it? What is this?'

'Put up with it.'

'Obviously you could hack it.'

'Obviously.'

The drinks arrive. The waiter pockets the reservation card and re-positions the vase before setting down their drinks without a word. Four more people arrive followed by a party of three men. Within an hour, the atmosphere has livened up with loud conversation punctuated by laughter. The air is blue tobacco fog.

'Were you ever sent to Ireland?' Mance fingers the Pepsi bottle.

Coulthard tips his head from side to side, easing tension in his neck. 'Most of us were. That's where the job was.'

'That must have been difficult for you?'

'We were piggy-in-the-middle.'

Mance's forehead furrows beautifully in support of Coulthard. 'Stuck in the middle of people with strong ideas. Such a complicated situation, yes?'

Coulthard tries to read his companion. 'They gave us lectures about it so we knew what to expect. But when you're out on the streets being spat on by scrawny wee housewives who call you every rotten bastard name under the sun, it's something else. Except at the start there was only one lot we'd any respect for.'

Mance smiles beatifically. 'The protestants.'

'The proddies. Aye. Doesn't mean much to Germans, I suppose. The troubles – eh?'

'You might be surprised how many of us know about what is happening there.'

'I would.' Coulthard reads the beer residue on the inside of his beer glass.

'We can see some comparisons with our own country. So we sympathise with people who worry that their traditions are placed in peril. A nation must have deep roots so its people can grow strong.' Mance's hands grasp the air as though conjuring up the right words to express herself.

'And who's threatening your country?' he asks casually.

'No-one at present, but in the recent past our country has had to defend itself. We must remain vigilant.

'We?'

'Germans, like me.'

'And who is likely to attack Germany?' Robert Coulthard swirls the last inch of beer around his glass.

Mance shrugs. 'Both people within and outside of our state. This is what we have learned from history. But we too must attempt to help other nations preserve what belongs to them. Many people in Europe agree with us and we get stronger each day. It is very encouraging.'

Mance pulls in her chin so her chocolate brown eyes are almost all Coulthard sees. He is humming a few chords from the "Linden Tree". Then, without taking his eyes off Mance, he raises his glass. 'Same again?'

Later, Mance Stresemann contrives to bring the gentle meandering of their exchanges back to Northern Ireland.

'I read somewhere that British soldiers would go to loyalist meetings to show solidarity with their cause. Do you know about this?'

'That would be a pretty stupid thing to do. Inviting trouble. Sure there were Johns who felt a bit of sympathy for them. Orange boys. Most of the blokes, I suppose, but that's as far as it went, y'know? If the media ever got hold of anything, wow! Headlines! Enquiries! Are you media?' Robert Coulthard starts on a fresh beer.

Mance Stresemann suddenly laughs. 'Oh no, Robert, I am not from the media. We can change the subject, if you like. I am interested, that is all. It was right you were there to protect the British state from breaking apart. I thought you might have been won over by some of the arguments. Perhaps not!' She lulls him with reassurances.

'Yeah. As I said, most of us saw the prods as less of a threat and, remember, we were fighting for Queen and country, and so were they. Bound to be some affiliations there.'

'Some people in my country would also like to help the loyalists.'

'Fancy that. And you?'

'I know some of these people. What they want is to make a transnational movement of workers to preserve each state's cultural inheritance. Similar but separate, that is how we see it.'

Coulthard takes his time to consider Mance. He's frowning. 'These people, exactly who are we talking about? Not cultural attachés, I take it?'

Mance strokes the right side of her neck, leaving a streak of crimson. 'Oh, everyday Germans: we are students, business people, professionals – all types of citizens who would like to share ideas with similar people in Northern Ireland.'

'And why are you telling me this?'

'You have spent time in Ireland. You might know of people or groups we can make contact with.'

It is hard to make out Mance's silky voice over the din in the restaurant. It has also become very warm. Coulthard takes off his jacket and arranges it across the back of his seat.

'Do I look like a dating agency?' He extends his arms, hands turned up in supplication, like pictures of Jesus from kids' bibles.

'We are serious, Robert.'

'There you go again: the we. I'd like to know who you're speaking for.' Mance holds him in a gaze then in an instant her mouth opens in a toothpaste grin. 'Do they, you, have a name?' Coulthard is all curiosity now.

'Oh, that is not important. Not yet,' she sighs.

'Come on. Who exactly? You're making it sound like some big conspiracy. Why should I play along when you're being so secretive?'

'I understand.' She hesitates. 'There is a group of us, well, there are many organisations, as I say.' More hesitation while her chocolate button eyes search Coulthard's face. 'We work together to halt the slide into Zionist globalism.'

Coulthard looks at her intently. 'Is that all? I thought you were being serious for a minute.'

'Of course I am serious. What do you mean?'

'Are you some kind of Nazi? One of these right-wing skinhead bods? And you think you can start your revolution in Ireland? A touch unlikely, take my word for it. And you think I'd be interested in crap like that?'

'I know you are.'

'You know I am? Who are you? What're you doing here? What d'you want with me?'

'Robert, since I have spoken with you, I have got the sense that you might have sympathies for what we stand for.'

'Why? What have I said?'

'Okay, it is a gut feeling.'

'Gut feeling, my arse! Listen, just tell me who you are.'

'Just Mance Stresemann.'

'And who exactly is she when she's at home?'

'I don't know what you mean?'

'You know exactly what I mean. Look, I'm leaving.' Coulthard knows he hasn't drunk much by his standards, but he's wary about where this conversation is leading. As he stands up, he knocks over his chair. It's not deliberate but he can see from Mance's expression she thinks it is. He pulls out a handful of cash and drops it down on the table. Mance collects her jacket and hurries after him. He lets her take his hand and they walk on in silence. Later he will put his reaction to what she has said down to his paranoia.

Mance draws Coulthard into a doorway out of the drizzling rain. He brushes the worst of the wet off her hair and inhales the perfume of her shampoo. He places a finger under Mance's chin and draws up her head. There is intensity in the kiss, and they draw apart only when a group of youngsters barge past to get to the door behind them. As it opens, the pounding of live rock music rises from the gloom of the basement. Mance and Coulthard follow the sound down a stone staircase, worn on one side by decades of ascending and descending feet. A set of double doors opens into a noisy and sweaty dance hall where the music is loud and banal. Nobody seems to care that only the drummer can hold the beat. The rest of the band randomly strum their guitar strings. A trestle table serves as a makeshift bar where young men hang out while the girls dance. Coulthard and Mance buy a couple of Egyptian beers from a stern-faced teenager. A youth in a hot orange shirt and black leather waistcoat lunges in their direction, throwing up in front of Coulthard; hot yellow froth splashes onto his new shoes; strands of green-yellow mucous drip from the boy's mouth. He retch again, bringing up solids. The other dancers retreat, leaving him the centre of attention. Every gag and spew is cheered. He's doing better than the band. The kid starts laughing once he realises he's become the main attraction and wheels around in time to the music, spewing as he spins. For the second time that night, Coulthard and Mance escape onto the streets.

'Russians drink until they are stupid with it. Like you Scots.' Mance gulps in fresh air.

'You're such an expert on everything tonight. Such an expert.' Coulthard retorts.

On the way back to Red Square, Coulthard and Mance linger by the tomb of the unknown soldier in the Alexandrov Gardens. Despite the lateness of the hour, the area is still busy. From the five-pointed star, the eternal flame gutters in the light wind which ruffles the petals of the bouquet a bride has placed on the bronze draped cloth. Coulthard and Stresemann lean into each other, transfixed by the scene and sleepy from alcohol. Mance slips her arm under Coulthard's. He has set aside his earlier misgivings about Mance Stresemann. Her closeness is electrifying. He reaches a protective arm around her and presses in closer as they set off towards the Troitsky Bridge and Red Square with its knots of nocturnal musicians.

Brunei, Cyprus and Northern Ireland, the army postings Robert Coulthard mentions in passing as he and Mance Stresemann curl up in his bed. Not regular pillow talk but he's careful not to go into detail. He says nothing either about joining up at Bridge of Don Barracks in Aberdeen in 1970, Fort George in 1971, West Germany 1972, Northern Ireland special intelligence cell in 1976.

Mance tells Coulthard of her ambition to become a business translator after graduating from Cologne University, languages being her thing, and how she has been taken on by a financial company to act as a technical author. Lying there beside her, Robert Coulthard knows he is right – she is seriously infatuated by him. This confident, beautiful young woman with her deep, dark, intense eyes, she is hanging on his every word. He has fallen for her. Whether or not it is love or just falling in some other way, Coulthard neither knows nor cares. All that matters is she is with him, her long dark hair fanned out over the pillow, pale eyelids closed and he flatters himself that the long years of misery really are behind him.

They are both hungry. There hasn't been time for breakfast if they are to fit in the visit to Gorky Park Coulthard has promised Mance. And he has an appointment at 2pm. While Mance drops into one of the nearby shops to buy something to eat, Coulthard continues slowly towards the park entrance, where he waits for her. For how long he cannot be sure because he still hasn't replaced his watch but even by Soviet shop standards Mance is taking her time. He rolls and smokes a spliff before retracing his steps to the shops but there is no sign of her. Coulthard is at a loss. This type of happening is not unique in his experience – being summarily dumped by women. Picking them up is rarely an issue but holding onto them is a trick he has yet to master. Still, he is surprised. Gorky Park was entirely Mance's idea. She could just as easily have left him at the hotel. He wonders if, somehow, they had passed each other. Though not exactly busy, there are one or two tourist coaches parked on the road and groups of visitors milling around. Coulthard goes off to check if she is already inside the park: a sprinkling of people are watching teenage boys messing around on a stage, giggling kids chase each other around trees, happy riders disembark from the big wheel, but none is Mance Stresemann. Resigning himself to having been well and truly abandoned, Coulthard turns to his most faithful companion, vodka, his wet elastoplast until it is time to meet up with Grigoryev.

12. ELASTIC POLITICS

Moscow: Monday 5 August 1991 – afternoon

Robert Coulthard had been in the Soviet Union before, with Hugh Bell and MacMillan, but this was his first, and he supposed only one, as TAG's sole representative. Coulthard is not your usual envoy: no business executive; no expert when it comes to matters of energy extraction but he is a consummate actor whose specialism is long-standing parts. If he were in town only for the oil and gas convention, Coulthard might already be soaring above the Firth of Forth on his way back to Scotland, instead he is in his usual abode – the hotel bar. He is a man who can drink himself happy and drink himself sad. He can get that way without drink as well. It makes him feel good that he has successfully bluffed his way through three hours of technical jargon without compromising TAGOil's cosy relationship with Oktneft but he doesn't like not having Mance at his side to celebrate the achievement. His grip tightens on his glass. One more official duty to carry out then he's free to do whatever he likes. At least that is how he has read the arrangement with Dinger. Operational name like his own. He raises the glass to his lips, 'To you, Coulthard … and all the other bastards you've been.'

Just another anonymous three-story office block in downtown Moscow. Alexei Grigoryev is waiting for Coulthard and gives him a troubled look when he turns up ten minutes behind time.

'Something wrong, Robert?' he asks solicitously.

'No, should there be?'

'It just you look … well … not sleeping?'

For some inexplicable reason, and it has never happened before to Coulthard as far as he can recall, he suddenly clenches his fists; not to strike out but to force back tears. Grigoryev turns away, embarrassed. Coulthard's breathing is laboured.

'We'll take a few moments,' says the Russian quietly.

Coulthard makes no reply. He is scared by how he feels. Like there's a war going on in his head. He cannot find words and is struggling to speak.

'Woman trouble.' He has no idea as he opens his mouth what he's going to say. Coulthard lets words spill out. 'I thought I had something going but she's gone.'

Grigoryev's face relaxes. 'It happens. Holiday romances. People return home.'

'No, you don't understand, she really disappeared.'

'Well, Robert, this is a big city. People do.'

Robert Coulthard can see Grigoryev has no idea what he's talking about. He can't explain himself. Why did Mance go off like that? Can she have known how desperate it would make feel about himself? She was different to the others. And none of them went away without saying something. Never had one just vanish in broad daylight. He needs her. Might even love her. Whatever love is.

'Still need some time? They'll be waiting for us.'

'Let's do what we have to do. You know these guys?' Coulthard is furiously trying to bury all thoughts of Mance. He has to wait for Grigoryev's reply until they've negotiated the busy road.

'Only one of them. They're going to be a bit mob-handed. Do you mind? It's the way they wanted it. I don't think they trust each other.' He chuckles, 'It goes with the territory here.'

A thin-faced man in his mid-thirties takes Grigoryev and Coulthard into a room where five men are chatting amiably and chain smoking. Coulthard is surprised to see them in uniform, looking like they've just stepped out of their offices for a break. He finds it peculiar that they are so open but then he finds that most things in the Soviet Union are beyond his understanding. Coulthard and Grigoryev sit next to each other in the arc of chairs. There is a small square table where someone has left a uniform cap, a bookcase stuffed with periodicals and a chair by the door, where the thin-faced man sits, directly behind Coulthard. A small window halfway along a wall is half-hidden by a single, drawn curtain. The atmosphere is stifling and reeks of sour sweat.

Grigoryev's contact is an army colonel with black swept back hair. He handles the introductions which are kept to a minimum – military rank, no names – apart from Coulthard and Grigoryev – there's a second army colonel, bald this time, followed by three officers from the Voenno-vozdushnye sily Rossii, or VVS, the Soviet air service. Robert Coulthard indulges in a moment of insecurity: the occasion, the company, the reason for them being there. A year is a long time to be out of the game. A bout of shadow boxing kicks off negotiations. Familiar views. Gorbachev must stand down and allow the Soviet people to move forward into capitalism and wealth, contentment and blue birds on every windowsill. There's a rant against Gorbachev's handling of the war in Afghanistan. Expecting victory when he slashed the military by half a million men. Withdrew ten thousand tanks. Abandoned weapons rusting away in silo dumps.

'So what to do? Leave them there with our families starving or do we find market for them? You tell me.' The dark colonel is confident he is talking for them all. 'We do special price for tanks.' He draws a circle in the air with a finger like a car salesman orchestrating a deal. 'Tanks like new, not used,' Noticing one of the airmen shift uneasily in his seat, he raises his voice, 'What, comrade, you think me disloyal? Everyone know our tanks do not work. I am honest trader. Mr Coulthard, many of our tanks have defect, so you know. But they look scary.' He smirks. 'Enemy run away, so they work.'

Tanks are not on Coulthard's agenda but already he is thinking outside of Tart's official shopping list. As has been said, pretty much everything in the USSR is up for grabs, including his own future. He knows there will always be buyers for ground force tanks; it's just a case of knowing where to look and who to talk to. It's either that or some unlucky peasants scratching a living on the tundra will be obliged to take them in lieu of tractors.

Forced to retreat from Afghanistan by a combination of inept tactics, unremitting global derision and a Mujahidin fortified by US stinger missiles and British surface-to-air blowpipes, the present representatives of the state are determined to salvage something out of the debacle.

The bald colonel strokes his fleshy face and flexes Brezhnevesque eyebrows. Here's a reminder for Coulthard that not so long ago the two of them had been on opposite sides. Such are the ways of the man-made world. Allies or enemies. Never absolute. He asks Coulthard if he knows the American Jeff Bull. In a roundabout way he's letting him know he's in with them. Jeff Bull, popular with every weapon-hungry warlord in need of killing machines. Once, Coulthard would have bad mouthed the American and his trade. But times move on. Coulthard catches the eye of the bald colonel just for a fraction of a second. It strikes him that he has just read his mind.

As is the practice in such negotiations, the ground rules have been agreed in advance. Coulthard was not party to any of that behind the scenes stuff. He is simply there on behalf of his paymaster, Tart from British intelligence. It was Dinger who had briefed Coulthard. Little was expected of him short of being there in person but when a chair scrapes on the hard floor, Coulthard feels his heart racing under his shirt. Not a great sign. He knows he is not nervous. Not really. This is child's play compared to some of the situations Dinger has got him into. No, not nerves. It is just he isn't himself.

Alexei Grigoryev notices it too. 'Would you like a drink of water?' he whispers.

'I'm fine. Bit hot in here.' Coulthard runs a finger around the inside of his shirt collar.

One of the airmen, a captain, fiddles with the catch on the window but can't budge it. He offers Coulthard a cigarette and lights it for him. 'This will help.' Then takes one himself. The guy's right. It does. He inhales, breathing slow and deep. He can't afford to mess up. Can't let Dinger down considering the way he's gone out on a limb to put him here in the first place. Down to Dinger too that he's thinking about striking out on his own. All that talk about the sinking communist economy and its rats scrambling to the surface for air. "We supply the air. At a price. Always remember there's a cost to everything. Nothing for granted. Never assume what you think is happening is what's happening. I've lost good men because they forgot that. And never trust the word of anyone. Ultimately, the only person to rely on is oneself." Coulthard knows it. They all learnt that lesson fast. Dinger told them so often they couldn't ever forget it. There was always someone to give the orders, however, and Dinger was that someone.

Coulthard's client is never named during the meeting, but these guys are experienced enough to hazard some passable guesses if they don't know for sure. The idea that the British state should go to such lengths to procure weapons for a conflict it steadfastly refuses to acknowledge as a war probably rests quite easily in the Soviet mind. Governments are pretty much the same the world over – can't slip a postage stamp between their policies on home security is Coulthard's own view. The war which isn't a war in Northern Ireland is proving a difficult nut to crack for Westminster. Tough enough to need a shed-load of shadow strategies to deal with it. Part of the hidden agenda being provisioning the British secret service and military intelligence with unlimited powers, the freedom to act unconstrained by legal restrictions normally attached to official policy. Coulthard's role negotiating with the disenchanted of the USSR's once mighty military machine is a footnote to this overall strategy.

The Brezhnev clone peers out from hooded eyes partly obscured by shrubby brows. He reminds Coulthard that the West is indebted to them for holding so much scrapped military equipment. His words are greeted with a ripple of laughter. Scrap is the expedient term for any supplies which may be re-designated by any opportunist with an eye to a profit and shouldn't be confused with a reflection on quality necessarily.

Coulthard's heart is still battering against his ribs. High on adrenalin. That's good. "Adrenalin keeps you alert. Lose that and it's time you got out. Watch your back and cover your front – never easy." Dinger's quiet aside before he flew here. Something about not drinking himself courageous. Annoyed him then. He didn't need Dinger or anyone to tell him he was drinking too much. He knew it. The way they got him out of NI. His way of coping. Today is not the same. Today he is edgy and stone-cold sober. Well, not so sober. He could have downed a couple more. Who would blame him? Mance going like that. What if she didn't walk out on him? What if something has happened to her? He knows her. They'd spent the night together. He can read women like her. Something must have happened.

Alexei Grigoryev is leaning in towards him again. 'Sure you're okay?' Smoke from the airman next to him catches in Coulthard's throat. He coughs and draws the attention of the others. Grigoryev resumes his quiet pose and Coulthard tries to concentrate.

One of the VVS guys is speaking about virtual mountain ranges of decaying armaments and the Third World crying out for supplies. Another reason to hook up with Bull, Coulthard tells himself. He never let onto Dinger he had been contacted by Jeff Bull. It had come straight out of the blue, Bull calling him. Told him his name had come up in conversation. Funny how these things happen. Serendipity. Just the time his relationship with Dinger and Tart had flat-lined. Bad smell about the whole thing. Could not reconcile Dinger's attitude with everything that they had been through together in Mire.

Mire, their affectionate name for the Joint Force for Research Unit. It wasn't as though he was going to get a pension or anything. Not the likes of him. Not like Dinger. They had just bunged him some quiet money. That and what was paid into his bank account every month he was in NI. That was then. Coulthard can't see why he shouldn't get in tow with Bull. Strictly self-employed. Same as being a Tart field officer. Tart doesn't run to contracts for operatives like him – slip up and he's on his own. A year they'd left him out in the cold. Okay, he admits grudgingly, he'd needed some of that but a long twelve months. So much for putting his neck on the line for his country. He knows Tart was against Dinger using him again. Ever. Maintained he was compromised. Dinger told him that, probably to try to keep him sober, watchful. Dinger unlikely to last much longer. Then that would be it. Tart wouldn't touch him, not with his handler gone. It would be up to him and only him. Bull's call had come like manna from heaven. Tart: the fickle employer. Everyone knows the London toffs never give Johns like him a second thought, no matter what risks they run. Pick up, run and dump. At least he and Dinger have a relationship. Dinger is his man, or at least he's Dinger's. Dinger the boss. A top bloke. Always there for his men.

In his own modest way, Coulthard believes he has done the walk, step by cold calculating step, straddling the fuzzy line between good and bad, acceptable and unacceptable. Government sanctioned. He needs to put this negativism behind him, to bury the angst and ethical dilemmas. The world is full of *bampot* dictators and dodgy freedom movements propped up on the moral high-ground by sanctimonious and Machiavellian Western democracies. If he's to be honest with himself, he recognised that a long time back. He's not the one starting conflicts. He could sit at home watching the news on television, tut-tutting whenever another poor shot-up bastard turns bleeding eyes to the cameras, but what good would that do? Who's to say the shot-up Johns are the good Johns? We all do things. If people decide I'm a bastard that's up to them, he thinks. They don't understand how the world works.

A pack of cigarettes is passed round. Coulthard takes one and stretches forward for a light from the dark colonel. It's not exactly an EEC summit but it might have more impact on the world. Hanging out with the bad Johns, or are they the good Johns? Here, they're probably bad Johns, so did that make them good in the eyes of the West? He never once heard Dinger question the system. The British state, that is. Such a thing wouldn't occur to him. For everyone else it has of course. But Dinger is part of the establishment. He, on the other hand, is no-one. Eminently disappearable. Fade in, fade out. It's why Dinger has stuck with him. Lucky according to some. Coulthard believes in a bit of luck. Work through the possibilities. Then work on what you don't think is possible. Check and re-check. Every situation from every angle. Don't leave anything to chance. But, then, sometimes something happens. Call it luck. Or bad luck. Then bang. You're gone. Company like this. Past enemies. Just happy to know it's not the other way round. Brits selling off the last line of defence. That kind of thing. Here they're practically taking out ads. It's like it's a national disease. Selling off the family silver. Selling off your engineering tools. Auctioning the nation's meat supplies on the black market. The anti-capitalist state is a nation of entrepreneurs by default. As they say in these parts, the state thinks it's in control and the people let it believe it. So Coulthard negotiates. Basher would be proud of him. Not that he'd like to run into him again. The life he used to have. Call it life? The conundrum that is the province: paramilitaries, military and RUC – spy rings within spy rings trying to determine who's supplying what to whom; money, weapons, information, the low-down on the routes taken by those supplying the bars with blow. Predictably, the Soviets are pushing AK-47s. Something to do with overstretching on a deal with rebels in Mozambique. Cut to the chase; they can offer Coulthard a very favourable deal if he is interested. He isn't.

'Not Kalashnikovs. Not the way they advertise themselves.'

The black colonel raises a hand in disbelief. 'But who does not want AK? Child's play. Yes, maybe noisy. Is true. But is reliable. We sell with chrome bores. Make them very good. Last long time. Lifetime.'

Coulthard's not for persuading. 'Too heavy.' He draws deep on his cigarette and exhales a line of delicately curling smoke. The nerves have gone. 'We'd have a job offloading them. They haven't got the reliability we're looking for. It's got to be no.'

Coulthard knows you need to be sure of your weapon when the time comes. He used to like the Heckler & Koch G3. Got that from Dinger. The G3 assault rifle, compact, light to handle and, most important of all, dependable – clip in the magazine and watch it rip. Some of the Ulster boys liked a G3. Trouble was, as soon as the military got some nice kit, the provos would hunt down a source and the advantage was lost. The American M16 was standard issue when he first joined Dinger's team in Germany. Not one for the faint-hearted. Get a smack from that and you can wave goodbye. What he wants from these guys is something like the SVD rifle or the SVU OC-03-AS. Same calibre. Bit of refinement. He's getting some negative noises. 'They are only good for close combat.' 'Not so easy to get.' Then the rider. 'Not impossible.'

It's one of the airmen speaking. 'Will take time to source.' And, 'Yes, fine weapon. Little noise and there is not much flash so that helps conceal your man.'

'None of them are my men, let's get that straight,' snaps Coulthard sharply. Table talk. He realises he's sweating. Doesn't suit him being part of someone else's call. There's nothing for it but to carry on. He goes with the SVs and then it's rocket launchers. Agree on RPG-7s from reputable sources. They get onto personal hardware and when he broaches Tula pistols neo-Brezhnev chips in with the PSS.

'Is good for undercover. Very quiet. Silent. You know? You could fire it past head of sleeping baby and wouldn't wake. No flash, so is perfect for night job. Cartridges. All inclusive. No problem. Is very good small arm. You agree? And light. Only half kilo.'

'More,' someone else's opinion.

'Not much. Fraction. Beautiful weapon.'

There appears to be nothing Coulthard brings up that the Soviet military can't be persuaded to provide: arms, ammo, light armoured vehicles, artillery pieces. The enthusiasm of these men to bargain strengthens Coulthard's conviction that he's right to contemplate a move.

The Ireland-bound arms will take the normal route, first by road then they'll be shipped out. Off the Irish coast they'll be transferred by fish baskets to fishing boats off County Down, most likely overseen by UK intelligence aircraft and navy submarines maintaining the tradition of maritime free trade. These must be some of the most protected shipments around. Rarely intercepted. Expedience being the driving force in conflict. Allegiances as firm as shifting sands. For low level operators such as Coulthard it's all about carrying out instructions; former enemies become the new allies. Elastic politics.

Coulthard models himself on Scottish SAS adventurer Fitzroy Hew Royle MacLean. He can see himself stealing into the Kremlin and ordering Gorbachev out at gunpoint like MacLean did with Iran's Fazollah Zahedi. But he knows how that story ended: with Zahedi and the equally despised Shah being reinstated by Britain and the US. Never absolutes in his line of work. "British intelligence and our cousins in the CIA must always keep an open mind." Rammed home to them by Dinger in West Germany and again in Ulster, in case they'd forgotten. Even Coulthard could see through that one. Dig deep enough in dirty politics and you'll hit on oil. Not a Dinger sentiment, of course. That was Tommy MacHardy's newspaper pal, Ross. And not just oil, he'd written. Not always oil – could be ideology and, sometimes, both at once. Tommy had started listing them – Iran, Afghanistan, Argentina, Brazil, Cuba, Chile, the Congo, Ghana, Guatemala, Iraq, Nicaragua, Turkey then Coulthard switched off. The Soviet Union is a different ball game. It would take more than a few street marauding agents provocateurs, black propaganda and corrupt officials, mouths stuffed with traitor's gold, to penetrate the well established power lines stretching from Moscow to Vladivostok. Which is why it is a far more subtle game in progress.

The meeting's drawing to a close. He has come through it and feels great. It gets better when, having heard someone ask about US export licences for purchasing American arms, he's able to tell them they're currently around $15,000 for an end-user permit and no-one flinches. He is reassuring too on speculation that the UK government might be tightening up on arms trading. That the comrades are showing interest in purchasing deals with him personally comes as a pleasant surprise. He supposes, if they are in cahoots with Jeff Bull, they can only be looking to him for a discount deal. Same rules. West pays in dollars, Sovs buy with gold.

'Nice doing business with you, gentlemen,' Coulthard is shaking the hand of each man in turn and his speculative enquiry concerning MiGs and Sam-7s is met with unreserved assurances of availability for the right price.

As they leave, the lean individual who took no part in the talks but spent the whole time by the door extends his hand and pats the Scot's elbow. 'Nice work, son.' Coulthard cocks his head, is he American? He can't be sure; with so many Russians learning English from American radio, most of them sound like regular Yankees.

'Have we met before?' he asks, but a half nod is all he gets by way of response before the man is swallowed up by the spill-out from the meeting and he and Grigoryev are being shown out of the building by strapping door jambs packing pistols.

'What d'ye make of that? The guy there.' Coulthard looks back as they are hurried along.

Grigoryev shakes his head. 'Nothing, Robert. It does not matter who he is.'

'I thought you knew everyone who was here. How do we know we can trust them if we don't know who they are?'

'In Russia it does not matter. No-one is more friend than enemy.' Grigoryev sighs. 'You know it was your Lord Palmerston who said a nation has not eternal friends nor enemies only eternal interests.'

Coulthard does know. It was one of the things Dinger used to say when they were on manoeuvres. Funny to think Grigoryev and Dinger have the same line in Palmerston quotations. Then again, it could have been that Palmerston didn't have that much to say for himself.

Alexei Grigoryev buys Robert Coulthard a coffee. They both need a change of subject and conversation switches to Grigoryev's sideline of painting. He mentions he is going along to a meeting of the artists' group, Tovarischchestvo Russkikh Khudozhnikov later in the evening and extends an invitation to Coulthard to join him which is why Coulthard found himself in a once grand apartment, mingling with a very diverse bunch of painters and sculptors, from the neat and conservative to studied eccentrics in an elegant room, painted off-white to retain the light and with fine rococo-style plasterwork along its cornices.

Another of Dinger's influences. Used to encourage his young recruit to borrow copies of his Thames & Hudson art series when they were in West Germany. *All round education* was a Dinger maxim. Coulthard one of the few who responded enthusiastically and it didn't go unnoticed by Captain Bell.

Very little conversation concerned art as such. The majority of exchanges were good humoured, but there were disagreements over the current state of the country, with the old guard cautioning against being swept along on a wave of naivety – 'that the Party will reign supreme no matter what'.

Lying on his bed, head in hands, elbows extended, Robert Coulthard considers whether or not this is true. It isn't what Tart envisaged. Not why TAGOil is courting Oktneft.

Coulthard's eyes close. He sees Mance as she was when she came into the cafe. Her striking appearance. He thinks of them together in bed. That security of knowing she was there with him. With him. And he sees another girl. In NI. He opens his eyes; picks up a magazine. The strength of feeling at the TCRK surprised him. Their reaction to selling to the Western market. Especially the ones who believed they had to compromise their strict aesthetic principles to satisfy the voracious appetite of American consumerism. And there was Alexei Grigoryev defending the practice. 'Without these markets we will earn less whatever.' Coulthard reaches into the bedside drawer for a medicine bottle. 'They had become cash cows for parasitic art dealers,' it was said, 'who buy cheap in roubles and sell on dear.' And special indignation over Soviet émigrés to the US seen as the worst at exploiting the USSR's cultural legacy, having found their own Western Shangri-La. Coulthard swallows a pill, then another.

The old guy came up to him as everyone was on the point of leaving.

'I hope you will return home with understanding of what we think here. You must tell people in West that we desire change. We are impatient with our government. Everyone has become weary about promises to do this and do that. Talk. That is all.' Then, as an afterthought, 'These,' he flaps his arms flamboyantly, ' these people are my friends. We are future of Russia. All artists. All intellectuals. No change can come without discussion.'

Coulthard tries to read the magazine to stop the familiar creep of melancholy but his eyelids are heavy. His old mucker makes an appearance. Sometimes just thinking about MacHardy helps. Tommy MacHardy open as a page in a book. Tommy MacHardy straight up. Not like him. *Tonning it up* the Deeside road on the Bonneville; high-legging it in knee deep heather around the Cairngorms, dodging rabbit holes and lazing adders, trying to eat sandwiches with his shirt pulled over his head to keep from swallowing squadrons of hovering flies, air punching widows' veils of midgies in the sweltering heat at Sluigan howff, sitting by the cardboard ice cream cone that some crazy lugged up the hill and which MacHardy stood outside once as a joke, pishing himself laughing at the couple and their three bushed kids' request for *Five ices, please.*

13. TWENTIETH CENTURY WILD EAST

Moscow: Tuesday 6 August 1991

Grigoryev walks with Coulthard ahead of Dolgoruky and Zhdanov. His apartment in the Arbat district lies above an antique shop and is itself floor to ceiling with period clocks, Chinese vases and finely executed paintings. A seascape of a tall ship in full sail balancing on the arc of a wave takes Coulthard's eye as he is led into a room dominated by a vast circular table set with plates of fish, cuts of cold meats, mounds of vegetable fritters, salads, stuffed eggs and the piece-de-resistance, a crystal bowl piled high with caviar.

The door swings open and Zhdanov swaggers in like he owns the place. He calls Grigoryev out to the hall. Moments later, Zhdanov is back without Grigoryev. He makes straight for the table.

'You see tonight we eat peasant food,' he says, plunging a finger into the glass bowl. 'Beluga, finest caviar from Caspian sturgeon fish. You notice it is light colour. Light is best. That is what we say in Russia. Light is best.' He dips in his finger for a second helping.

The apartment belongs to Alexei Grigoryev, or rather his wife, Irina, but Yuri Zhdanov is making it his own this evening, playing the munificent host. He invites Coulthard to join him and is still picking away at the Beluga when an almighty commotion breaks out in the hall.

'One minute,' Zhdanov calls out.

Coulthard follows. Grigoryev and Sergei Dolgoruky are manhandling a struggling individual out of a lavatory. Zhdanov helps drag the man along the lobby and onto the landing. The other two have got hold of him now and Zhdanov ushers Coulthard back inside.

'What's going on?' he asks.

Zhdanov grabs some towels off the floor next to the lavatory and shrugs, 'Domestic problems.'

Coulthard can't do the food justice. Less to do with the incident at the lavatory than being left on his own with Zhdanov. He's chasing mushrooms around his plate when the doorbell rings.

Zhdanov's on his feet. 'Ah, Alexei is back.' But it's not Alexei. Luda Semenova steps into the living room. Coulthard catches something about a delivery of veal at the weekend. She looks over and says a quick hello to Coulthard then takes off her jacket.

'Want to join us?' asks Zhdanov.

'I'm not hungry,' she answers and brushes loose strands of hair from her forehead.

'Alexei is at football game with his boy,' explains Zhdanov, 'and Irina will not be back for while so we make ourselves at home. You must eat, Robert Coulthard.'

Zhdanov can't seem to get enough of the vibrant pink spongy meat and pickled gherkins. He smacks his lips together. 'Beautiful, huh? You want?' He holds out a bowl of halved boiled eggs laden with sour cream and yet more Beluga. As Coulthard shakes his head, a couple of eggs disappear into Zhdanov's mouth. He works his way around the table, sampling everything, scarcely pausing to savour any of it. His eyes flash down at Coulthard sitting patiently at the table as if waiting to be excused. Yuri Zhdanov wipes his mouth with the back of his hand. He looks as though he has a secret to reveal.

'Once there was old grandmother,' the voice low and conspiratorial, 'bent over from burdens in her long life. She work like slave to provide for family. She has many children, all as lazy as she is hard-worker. Every minute of day this woman do everything for her children and always they are more idle. One day old woman get ill and stay in bed. She ask oldest daughter to prepare herbal cure for her and explain which herbs and plants her daughter must use and where to find them in forest. But daughter is too lazy to walk to forest so she pick grass and roots from around house. When old mother drinks the brew, it tastes bitter and is bad. Woman spit out what is left but too late, poison is already in her and soon old woman dies. Her kids are happy. Now there is no old woman to call them lazy and no good but soon they discover it was scolding mother who keep them from starvation. Then oldest daughter is told by her brothers and sisters, "Now it is your duty to look after us" but, like them, she is ignorant and does not know what to do. So family become more poor and hungry. They divide up farm. Each take part of it to grow food but still they are lazy and stupid and nothing will grow. Soon they are beggars except for one son. This son has some of his old mother's wisdom but he is cold-hearted. He become bandit who steal from rich and poor. He make great fortune but waste it. When he died, his spirit became magpie. When you see this bird walk it is like peasant – yes? Roll from one leg to other leg.' Zhdanov demonstrates, rolling his shoulders from side to side. 'Magpie is proud of bright feathers. He think he is too grand for peasant country so flies to city where everyone admire his feathers and leave titbits for him on window ledge. When he eat, magpie look in through window and see shining jewels and thinks they will be nice to decorate his nest. So he hop in open window and steal trinkets. And people admire magpie for how he looks but he is sneaky scavenger. Always in life – eh?'

Robert Coulthard laughs. 'You Russians like your moral fairy stories,' he drops a spoonful of Beluga onto his plate, 'and stories about grannies!'

'Grannies?' quizzes Zhdanov.

'Yes. You know. Grandmothers.'

'Ah, yes. I know.'

'Grandmothers are very important in the Soviet Union, aren't they?'

'And not in your country?' yawns Zhdanov.

'Not what they used to be. Not in Britain. Families move and grow away from each other. In the UK, grannies are nearly invisible, but here, well, they're everywhere? Selling flowers and dispensing single sheets of lavvy paper. You don't see many grandas though.'

'Grandas?'

'Yeah. You know, grandfathers.'

'Of course. They are here also but you must know that many men from USSR were killed in Great Patriotic War so naturally there are not many old men surviving.'

'Wars, eh!' Coulthard quips as he savours the salty springiness on his tongue.

Luda Semenova returns with a tray of tea things and talk turns to the current situation in the Soviet Union. Once more, Mikhail Gorbachev comes in for a tongue-lashing. Luda Semenova grumbles about how life is harder now than it was with Gromyko as General Secretary of the Communist Party. It is Coulthard's impression that Luda was not born to suffer for the cause of ideology and is very much at home in the Grigoryev apartment with its expensive rugs and paintings, fine crystal and elegant furniture. What, he wonders, would she make of his dive in Aberdeen? He's often come up against the prevailing and mistaken idea held by so many in the Soviet Union that life is so much rosier in the great beyond which encourages political promiscuity in the scramble for entrepreneurial nirvana. Or is it expedience? He isn't really criticising them for it. They aren't alone. His own paymasters are doing everything possible to encourage these angry, disenchanted and disgruntled people to keep up the pressure to topple Soviet communism. Tart would be cheering on Grigoryev, Dolgoruky, Zhdanov and the rest of them as they wheel and deal their way to undermining the State. Forces doing whatever is required to keep the ball in play. Arguing black is white. Whatever it takes. They've been doing it forever. That's why Coulthard is confident that what he does for Dinger is excusable. Reasonable. Necessary. The spectacle of Soviet Russia in turmoil is being gleefully anticipated by scheming Western intelligence services and capitalists drooling over prospective pickings from the empire's stuttering industries. In response, Gorbachev is tinkering – empowering industrial managers with a measure of autonomy to liaise with foreign competitors while Soviet workers are systematically dismantling the whole, enormous edifice screw by screw, bolt by bolt and selling it off at weekend markets.

Zhdanov leans over his chair and picks up the vodka bottle which is all but empty. He holds it up to the light to get a better look then drains the dregs straight into his mouth. The effect is like a skoosh of WD40.

'Look around world. What do you see? Chaos! Where are strong leaders? Russian people have lost direction. And in your country there is division and death.'

Coulthard assumes he is referring to Ulster. He is correct.

'Ireland. I am talking of Ireland, where father is against son and brother against brother.'

'Not quite … ' Coulthard's words are submerged by Zhdanov's flow of consciousness.

'There is illness that affects whole world. Of spirit. Instead of open and loyal devotion to God and his laws, we have so many sects acting for Satan – against true path.'

'The Freemasons?'

'Indeed, yes. They have Satan's stamp, pentagram, same as symbol of Jewry.' At this Zhdanov made a sound like a spit. 'Freemason and Jew love money.'

Not averse to it yourself, thinks Coulthard.

Zhdanov continues, 'Jews create banking system when they deny sin of usury and lend money to make money. Why do people join secret societies like Freemasons? To benefit themselves at cost to all other citizens. They turn people from God. True way of Christianity and autocracy was blocked in 1917 in this country. Look around and what do you see? Here they sacrificed our leader and millions of good men slaughtered defending Tsar. Bloody-red rag of Bolsheviks is appropriate, yes? What we have to do, my friend, is destroy degenerate socialist system, then bring back heirs of our Tsar Nicholas to guide us to truth and meaning. Glasnost, perestroika – bah! Our people must return to traditional society of Russia.' Thus ends the lesson according to Zhdanov, who peers keenly at Coulthard for his reaction.

Coulthard lays down the tumbler. 'We sympathise with your position. Maybe there are alternatives which would attract more support to topple Gorbachev's crew?'

Zhdanov draws in his chin to his chest and looks across at Coulthard. 'You understand these things? Our country? You can travel from your country to my country. You have freedom to do this. You can carry messages between my country and your country. Documents. Whatever we have to do to spread ideas. You understand, Robert Coulthard?'

And he does. TAGOil might lose a couple of its personnel but it couldn't afford to lose its relationship with Oktneft. Robert Coulthard is the latest in a link, begun by Hugh Bell and passed to Donald

MacMillan, to some extent. TAGOil – Tart's baby. British intelligence worked to its own version of British foreign policy. A primary function of Tart is to meddle and to facilitate links with opposition groups that might bring about political change in the places Tart wishes to see this happening for all kinds of complex reasons. To oust communism in its heartland is a long-held dream nurtured by many men and women in MI6. So, wherever and whenever possible, Tart has its agents on the streets, in the government, in the apartments, in the institutes – eavesdropping, observing, encouraging and sometimes lying but always supportive of the likes of the artists' group, even Zhdanov and Dolgoruky, to put pressure on the system until it gives way. And someone within the drab utilitarian surroundings of Tart had decided several years back that the Union of Orthodox Fellowship might yet prove an irritation to the Soviet government.

Luda removes the empty Stolichnaya bottle from Zhdanov's feet and tucks it behind the leg of her own chair for she can see that Zhdanov is becoming agitated, his voice shrill, insistent that the time is right to push for change.

'Our faith must come before all else. Every day we face attack from system. Faith has to be the LAW.' His voice notches up several decibels at the word, "law". 'Lawful command. We must cut out influences of Talmudical Judaism from our nation. This evil gave us communism. Zionists crawled like vermin from synagogues, indoctrinating people with their trickery and lies. Buying people's silence and co-operation. They hold key positions. Money talks. Bible tells us how prophets warn Israel about financial dishonesty in Hosea 12: 1 to 8. How they work hand in glove, as you say, with builders of Solomon's third temple. Freemasons drive out spirit of our faith and let in atheism. It is time to come back to God. Return to doctrine of love and justice. Jews are crafty merchants.'

Zhdanov tilts his head back and drops his voice. 'This Jew says to his friend, "How is your sister who lives in Prague?" "Oh she is very well, and building socialism there," replies friend. "And how is your brother who lives in Budapest?" "Ah! He is very well and busy building communism." "Oh, and how is your other brother who lives in Israel. Is he busy building communism there, too?" "What, are you mad? Do you think he would do that in his own country?" Yuri Zhdanov looks directly into Coulthard's face for the smile, which comes. 'A Jew will complain about everything. Never at peace. Whine about fifth paragraph in passport, you know this? Next breath he will say, "We are different –we want to go to our own country." If they have country, they must be different nationality, yes? Always complain. We Orthodox Christians struggle every day for seventy years when this country abandoned moral authority. Without guidance of God.' He blows on the hot tea Luda has poured him.

Coulthard finds amusing the obvious contradictions between Yuri Zhdanov's polemic and his current activities but, if pressed, Zhdanov might justify himself by saying his actions are targeted at undermining a profane state.

Moscow: Tuesday 6 August 1991- Late Evening

Mance Stresemann is thinking about Robert Coulthard when Dolgoruky belches spirit fumes into her face. She runs her fingers through the hair that should have come with shock absorbers. As he heaves himself on top of her, the large Russian cannot help noticing Mance Stresemann's obvious lack of enthusiasm for his amorous foreplay, which takes the form of mumbled obscenities. He is clumsy, brutal, as if he needs to repossess her. Mance suppresses her repugnance and indulges him so that his anger ebbs away. Later, when she slips into the kitchen, Dolgoruky comes staggering in at her heels, demanding to know what she's looking for. He strikes her with his fist then drops down on his haunches, bawling loudly. Mance hunkers down beside him and they cry like kids who have been told the bogeyman is their father and afterwards they snort cocaine to the beat of heavy metal imports playing on Dolgoruky's state-of-the-art compact disc player.

★ ★ ★

Robert Coulthard slaps the hotel bar with the end of the business card the winking doorman had slipped him, dials the phone number printed on it and chooses to go to her.

★ ★ ★

It is half past eleven and in the Matveevskoe district its young men engage in their evening routine of cruising the streets in their beat up Ladas and leering out from wound-down windows at every pretty girl they pass. Two girls of around sixteen, both tall and skinny, become the boys' focus of interest. Typical Russian schoolgirls: long, shiny blond hair tumbling down their backs and long slender legs, unsteady on high heels. The girls giggle self-consciously, feeding on the attentions of the excited youths. One of the cars slows down and a boy pushes a door open, inviting the girls to get in. The pair cling to each other for dear life. Each protecting her friend. Tempted – it's obvious in their body language. Excitedly sniggering face to face. Swapping thoughts. Waiting for the right time. It's all too subtle for the boys, though. The car door closes and as it hurtles away another coasts up behind. Its young dark-haired driver whistles towards the girls. Laughing nervously, they tiptoe over to the vehicle. On the backseat the boys bunch up to make room for them. Everyone in high spirits. Keen to show off his prowess behind the wheel, the good-looking driver slips the clutch but stalls the engine as a hulking blue-cabbed lorry speeds around the corner of Nezinskaja ul, whipping up clouds of dust. No-one in the jam-packed car has any chance. In the moment of impact the car veers across the carriageway into oncoming traffic.

The deafening din of impact slams into a shroud of silence. Glass fragments, the dying and the injured litter the street. People turn out from nearby apartments. A green bedspread is drawn over one dead boy, a man's taupe jacket over a second, comforting words for a girl softly sobbing – a pale bone in her slim brown arm awkward like a chair leg in a vice. 'Larissa,' she gasps, a ghostly whisper barely audible. Larissa shows no sign of hearing. As it flew through the car's windscreen, Larissa's pretty young head was stripped of its sleek flaxen hair and in its place is a corona of jagged glass and metal shards. Someone has thoughtlessly propped her up against the upended Lada.

Thoughtless because Larissa is no longer a girl but a floppy rag doll: long pink legs splayed grotesquely, blank staring button eyes seeing nothing. When the police turn up, one of them sets up a diversion sign for the backed-up traffic while another checks out the lorry's load and makes a call from his patrol car.

The raucous ringing of the phone stirs them out of sound sleep. Dolgoruky returns the remaining coke to the kitchen drawer after taking the call.

'I have job to do. You stay here. Do not go.'

'Can't I come with you?' Mance Stresemann asks, sleepily.

'No. This is not possible. Why would you want to come?'

'Well, where are you going?'

'Okay. Calm down, Mance. I am needed by my friends. We have business, as I say. It is not your business. It has nothing to do with our organisation. Simply business.'

Within thirty minutes, Sergei Dolgoruky has pulled up alongside the wrecked blue-cabbed truck with a replacement lorry and a small posse of heavies, who transfer the consignment of meat into their wagon. The man from Leningrad is taking a risk moving in on the territory of local black marketeers and the Georgian gangs who dominate the capital's meat scams but he's been lucky tonight – the police attending belong to the Union of Orthodox Fellowship.

An angry voice speaks for many in the crowd, 'Grishin is behind this. What are you up to? Paying off your debt to him and his fat family for your Party card. There is no difference between Communist Party and mafia. We must clear out all this corruption that strangles our great country. Mosagroprom leaves warehouses full of rotting food while we starve.' A murmur of assent runs through the body of bystanders.

A second person picks up the baton. 'Train loads of food are sent back where they come from instead of being sold in the markets. Is this meat going back to the farms? Will Mosagroprom turn it back into cattle? No, it will be going into the mouths of the criminals who run our city.'

The police force their way into the throng of spectators, searching out the outspoken culprits. A section of the crowd moves towards the lorry and for a moment it looks as if there might be an attempt to snatch the supplies but the attention of Dolgoruky's bullies makes them think again. A man emerges, handcuffed between two policemen as the meat is switched into Dolgoruky's truck under protection of the law. A couple of ambulances have arrived. The animal carcasses are driven away in one direction and the human casualties ferried off in another. Theatre of the absurd.

★ ★ ★

Coulthard wakes to someone tapping softly on his door. 'Well, well, what have we here?'

Mance Stresemann looks upset and has a red mark on the side of her face. Coulthard raises a questioning eyebrow. 'Robert, I must explain.'

'Yeah, maybe that would be a good idea,' he agrees but makes no move to invite her inside.

'I did not mean to abandon you yesterday but Sergei came into the shop I'd ... '

'Sergei? Who's Sergei?'

'Sergei Dolgoruky.'

'Dolgoruky?' The name takes a moment to register with the weary Coulthard.

'He is a friend of mine,' Mance blurts out. 'He has mentioned you. He is jealous that I have seen you.'

'Look, I don't get this, come inside.' Coulthard takes her by the elbow and kicks the door shut.

'Who the hell are you and what is it you want with me?'

'I am Mance Stresemann and I have come to Russia to see friends.'

'Friends, right, go on.' Coulthard is standing very close to Mance, still holding her by the arm.

'My group, you know, I mentioned – I am here for meetings. It is not the first time I've been here and got to know Sergei Dolgoruky. When I was in the shop by the park, Sergei came in and asked what I was doing there. When I mentioned you he said he knew you also.'

'Go on.'

131

'Well, he was not happy that I should go with you to the park.'

'Go on.'

'That is all there is. Except Sergei is a jealous man. He must have been following me and when I was by myself in the shop, well he more or less forced me. Not forced me exactly but put pressure on me to go back with him. I am sorry, Robert.'

'I didn't have you down as the obedient little woman type.' Coulthard pulls on his ear lobe. 'But go on, where's Dolgoruky now?'

'At home.'

'At home? At your home?'

'No, at Grigoryev's studio – where he is staying. He has no place of his own here. His home is in Leningrad.'

'Spare me the geography lesson,' snaps Coulthard. 'Well that sounds all very cosy.'

'Robert.' Mance's brown eyes have taken on a muddied look.

Coulthard releases Mance's arm. 'I think you'd better go.'

'Please, Robert, I cannot – he has put me out.' She pleads with him but Robert Coulthard is not for moving.

'Not your lucky day then, is it? Look, I don't need complications. It's better you leave.'

'Of course. I am sorry, Robert. I know I must seem to have behaved badly but I do like you, very much.'

Coulthard is deaf to her pleading. He doesn't need to have his life any more complicated than it already is. Dinger always said, "walk away from trouble unless you're being paid to mix with it." No-one is paying up front this time.

14. A BAG OF AITKEN'S ROWIES

Aberdeen: Wednesday 7 August 1991

'What's the matter with you this morning?'

'Nothing.'

'Good.'

Sue Cromarty had been sighing audibly. Her colleague moves in closer and places a reassuring arm around her.

'I've brought in a bag o' Aitken's rowies. I'll even heat one up for you – an' you can have a daub o' jam if there's still some from our last raid o' the canteen. Aufa fine, y'ken you like them.'

'Can't you just shut up?' Sue slams shut the drawer of her desk and rummages through a batch of papers. Greg lifts his index finger to pursed lips. Neither speaks for several minutes going on hours until a bleeping phone demands to be answered.

'Ms Cromarty speaking. Yes, Mr Shaw. I'll be right along. Yes ... I will.' She glances at Greg.

'What's the big cheese want with you?' he asks.

'Wants me to go over Macmillan's transactions with Oktneft, he's arranged for us to meet up with that guy, you know, the supplier. See what's to be done in the short term. Terrified of losing contracts, I suppose, with all the carry on here. Anyway, he wants the files.'

'Does Bell know?'

'Search me. Someone's got to take the reins and he's not exactly fit, is he?'

'Have you noticed Shaw's been acting strange?'

'How can you tell?' Sue Cromarty croaks in mock astonishment.

'Can't see him staying, can you?'

'He might if he's the only one left here who knows what's happening. Bell's probably relying on him more than ever.'

'So why's no-one blackmailing him?'

'Don't know. I'm sure he's got plenty going on in his sleazy life that could earn a pound or two.' Sue Cromarty opens the drawer of a filing cabinet. 'I think TAG could go down. Get bought over, maybe. If anything happens to Bell, who'd be left to run it?'

'Hugh's missus might keep it on.'

'Somehow I don't think so,' Sue Cromarty laughs. 'She's never shown an interest.'

'Interested in the money, though, I'll bet.'

Greg gives Sue one of his looks as she adds, 'Don't see why she's hanging around here. If that was me, I'd be off like a shot to one of those places Hugh bought her.'

'With lover boy Shaw – I can just see it.'

'Ugh! She's got better taste than that.' Sue Cromarty crosses her eyes. 'But we'll have to keep our ears open, I'm sure he's up to something.'

'Lugs at the ready.' Greg flicks his ears back and fore. 'Um, haven't you a date with lover boy? Y'ken Sue, I think he's probably going through the male menopause. It's real, ken. Men like that can't stand gettin' old.'

'Can't stand growing up, you mean. You don't have him leering at you, feeling under your blouse, figuratively speaking,' she adds quickly, screwing up her face.

'Mmm. Sounds quite nice.' Greg moves his hands around his face coquettishly. 'Are you the office sex slave? Because if you are, tell me when you're a bit slack.' He reaches for his filofax.

'I don't think I'm quite your type, Greg.'

'Oh, well, people can change. So my father thinks.'

The phone rings. Sue wags a finger and moves to the door as Greg answers.

'Hello … yes, Mr Shaw, she's already left. Should be with you any minute.'

Sue circles her hand in an exaggerated wave as she opens the door, fortified by the thought that Greg would be keeping a rowie warm for her return.

'Ah, Sue. Fine. Okay. We're all here. Let's get started. Sorry for rushing you but I've to be at Dyce by one.'

15. EVERYONE IS A MOON, AND HAS A DARK SIDE WHICH HE NEVER SHOWS TO ANYBODY

MARK TWAIN

Moscow: Wednesday 7 August 1991 – Early Hours of the Morning

Robert Coulthard couldn't sleep after Mance's visit, so he took himself out into the night in search of someone, conceivably Mance, but perhaps just someone like her. He wasn't thinking that deeply.

The darkness of Moscow's mean streets weigh heavily on his shoulders: a lonely sort of feeling. Coulthard thinks about Fraulein Stresemann and tries not to think about her. A group of prostitutes huddle together in the shadows of a once bourgeois city house. Coulthard steps into an alley for a pee. He doesn't feel the blow which follows his sight of a boot advancing on his face.

The pain is quick in coming. One eye is fine. The other has seen better days, or nights. He looks around with his one good eye. Can't see much. Light is filtering through from the street at the end. Crouched, he feels along the line of throbbing ache, the rhythmic ebb and flow working through his head, along his torso and down his legs, Coulthard concludes he's been in worse order. Like a moth drawn to the light he's stumbling towards the exit when he pauses, listening for something he hears. There it is again. He feels for his Llama. It's gone. Coulthard backs up against a wall and shoots a glance in the direction of the rustling sound. A rat scurries away.

Rats he can deal with. How many? Over ninety that time they were holed up in Ulster. They were a man down so he had been shipped in for special duties. That was before he was put back in for the long haul. A lifetime ago. Joined the regular twelve-strong foot patrol in standard gear for a couple of days. Carried out a recce of the land. Used the regulars to set up a VCP, vehicle check point, bought time to make sure the area was properly inspected while the sappers were at work preparing the target building as a safe OP. Then early one morning, six of them slipped in, unseen by the locals. Staked-out for three days; short on mod cons, swapped bags of shit for sandwiches from the dead letterboxes under cover of darkness, slept with his M16, an M79 grenade launcher and usual light machine guns, oiled up ready for use. Boring as fuck once you were set up: decent spy hole for the John on HP watch, the Browning never off the shoulder, scope and camera trained on the surrounding area; always one on the radio, one kipping, no sound over a whisper. Struggling to stay vigilant when it was your turn on the SLR just in case a blast of tracers was needed as a marker in a quick getaway. Never knew when one of the bog boys would be alerted by a nosy farmer, all republicans to a man, eyes in the back of their flat heads. The last thing they needed was to be blown out of cover by some big-eared provo with a turnip trailer full of mortars. That was when you knew what being shit scared was all about. Just the time to call on one of the surface-to-air rescue beacons – good old Sarbes – in case things really hotted up, and the Wes from Bessbrook International had to be guided in. Blacked up and masked when the time came. Target due up from the south where he'd been hiding out. Expected to pay a little visit to the girlfriend. Three days holed up before he was spotted. An IRA staff officer. Bundled him into a field and radioed for the chopper but in the two or so hours it took it to get there the target had been shot trying to escape. As Coulthard later reported to Dinger, 'We were shitting ourselves the enemy would get there before the chopper but it turned out alright in the end. One less bastard at any rate.' All that hardware and not able to use any of it on the rats, obviously. Fine piece of advertising that would be. Little bastards, scurrying everywhere. Got you moving. Couldn't help it. Worst thing for undercover work. Poison worked best. Quiet. Trapped a few. Stamped them out of existence with the goonboots over soft shoes. Force but no prints. Professional soldiers.

★ ★ ★

A careful search of the lane fails to turn up his pistol. Coulthard curses his slackness and breathes deep and slow to dampen the pain pulsating along each vein and artery to the beat of his heart. Bruised and battered, he sinks to the stone kerb beneath a streetlamp. The Llama is missing but at least he is alive.

An approaching car alerts Coulthard and he sees them: two guys motioning to it. The driver gestures back. The guys are turning as he gets to his feet. He's running fast but they're faster. One makes a grab for his arm. Coulthard swings around and catches him across the face with a hefty left hook. The guy recoils and Coulthard wrestles the other one to the ground. But the first guy is back in the fray and pulling at him. Now the driver is out of his cab and between the three of them they have him restrained. His hands are bound with plastic and a bag is pulled over his head.

Coulthard is pinned behind the car's front seats by a pair of heavy size twelves and his arms are forced high up his back. He sweats inside the hood. Two men are talking fast, a little too fast to follow. Coulthard hears one of them sniffing as if he's having a problem with a nose bleed. Furious that he's allowed himself to be captured, Coulthard controls his anger by counting the journey time in seconds then minutes. If nothing else, it helps slow his breathing. The dusty bag sucks in against his nostrils as he strains for air; the extreme heat and the reek of cheap plastic from the car's interior make him nauseous. He slumps forward, light-headed and his limbs are tingling. A hand pulls the sack up over his mouth. He breathes deeply before the man next to him ties a rag around his mouth then removes the bag entirely. He's dragged up onto the seat next to the door and a pistol is pressed to his temple, forcing his head against the cold glass. Coulthard recognises it as his own Llama. The door lock is down. Very slowly he runs his mouth along the rim of the window to draw up the lock with his teeth, but the man beside him feels the movement through his gun hand. He strikes Coulthard a sharp blow against the side of his head with the pistol.

Coulthard can see people behaving unremarkably. No-one notices the backseat passenger's beseeching stare except a troubled reflection in the car window. They pull up at traffic lights. Surely now?

Coulthard chews on his gag and tries to lift his head, hoping to catch the attention of an adjacent driver. The man fumbles, lights a cigarette then turns in his direction. He looks, inhales and accelerates on green. A hand forces Coulthard's head towards his knees and he feels the cold certainty of metal against his head. He closes his eyes and sees Hugh Bell on the day he'd been taken on an unscheduled Land Rover ride to the helipad. Coulthard exorcises that demon, a learnt technique: clear the mind of difficult incriminating thoughts. Ridding them entirely from his conscience is a trick Coulthard has yet to accomplish.

This is not the first time Coulthard has found himself in such a dilemma, although, it is the first time as Robert Coulthard. It is a conundrum he is frequently trying to resolve: the question of who he is. From the time in West Germany when Dinger had taken him under his wing, Coulthard has become adept at picking up and dropping personae. Not too different from being back at school. One of the few positives from his alma mater was its drama department, in which he'd become a grounded star. Grounded for there was nothing he did which impressed his mother enough to attend any of his performances. Not once. His drama teacher had recognised the boy's ability but her encouragement was never going to satisfy the child with his difficult background. That experience did, however, teach him how to create his own safe haven behind a host of guises. As for the real him, the ordinary and invisible six year old had long disappeared from the world. Perversely, that had been a quality which attracted Dinger to him.

A familiar figure materialises on the misted glass. It looks like Tommy. Tommy MacHardy. An illusion. How could it be Tommy?

Christ! Tommy, man, over here. Coulthard wills his pal to heed his muted plea, I'm over here. Tommy!

Irately, the driver slams a hand on the horn and swerves, avoiding a car parked on the roadside with its bonnet raised. A wave of nausea sweeps over Coulthard and he retches.

'Hey, man, don't do that', Coulthard understands the angry protest from the guy next to him, but he can't help himself and retches again; sour mucus runs over his chin and down his jacket. Coulthard's companion draws away and threatens to plaster the Scotsman's mouth.

Coulthard sinks back into the seat. His head is light and heavy at the same time. He is dopey.

Loch Muick crimped blue and silver in the under-draught of the helicopter. Hover flying. Manhandling. Sweating like stuck pigs. A final thrashing of limbs and a splash drowned out by the engine's roar. Calm after that. A moment's misgiving. He was human after all. The Glen Muick track hard-packed from recent frosts. Silvered margins cracked under the heavy tread of a boot. January. Bleaching sun set pale in the cobalt blue sky. Air icy cold, catching the back of the throat. Deserted bothy. Backs on door. Beef sausages squashed flat in a softy. MacHardy's remembered the Aero bar. Flattens the beer can under his heel. Drops it back into the rucksack – quicker than digging a hole. Never leave traces. Time to look around. That stretch of glen picture perfect. Red Deer grazing. From beyond a bank of aubergine trees, flapping vees of silver-shot geese, collective cackling trailing into the twilight. 'I think I smell sna.' Tommy points his nose to a patch of leaden sky over to the west.

'Deer I can understand but snow?' The wind snatches the words off Coulthard's tongue, pitching them into the loch's dark snarling waters.

Coulthard estimates the journey has taken around twenty-five minutes from Gorky. His captors have taken the precaution of strapping his feet together. His kneecaps have been replaced by marshmallow; incredible what the Sovs can do. He lets himself be half carried, half dragged into a building where he's pushed to the floor. Coulthard's tongue lies immobilised in his mouth but he still has one functioning eye. The building, he guesses, might be a store of some sort although in the dark it's impossible to distinguish much. He takes a good look at the goons; the one he recognises, the one he'd slugged outside the alley, is the same gowk he'd seen being manhandled out of Grigoryev's lavatory. He's playing with his nose.

Coulthard strains against the gag. The gowk looks like he's going to relieve him of it then changes his mind. They leave him there. The bindings are cutting into his wrists. He makes his body relax. His mind is another matter. Always alert. The building never stops moving, banging, flapping, creaking. He feels like he's incarcerated in a wheezing prefabricated monster. Sleep comes in snatches. Too cold.

Can't build up heat. Trussed up like a chicken for the pot. He's up and hopping an ersatz Highland jig. Bending and swaying to get the blood circulating. Nothing's helping his head. Nothing dampens the pain of the pistol whipping. He's down again. Curled into a ball. He's come through before. Wills away the pain.

★ ★ ★

'Here, have this, Dooley,' whispers the fellow beside him.

He answered to Dooley as a kid growing up in Ulster. The outsider, keeping himself to himself, head down avoiding eye contact back in 1958 and twelve years old. Other kids stalking him – chanting Lonnie Donegan's hit, *Hang Down Your Head Tom Dooley: Hang down your head and cry, hang down your head Tom Dooley, hey, boy you're going to die.* The name stuck. From then on he was Tom Dooley in the neighbourhood. Only a name. Mire wanted him as Colin Riddle again. Operating under cover in the Ulster Unionist Faction.

Riddle stretches the navy wool tammy over his ears. They don't speak, him and his mate. Just the two of them. A Sunday. Like any other Sunday, you might say. Except, of course, it isn't. Riddle's been told this is to be his day. Not that he's had much say in it. Something of a rite of passage. Prove his commitment to the group. Riddle isn't especially worried. A bit fidgety, maybe. Just keen to get on with things. Always been a doer. Not one to sit around on his arse for too long and do sweet fuck all. Up and doing. Suits him to a tee. But, as he'll remind anyone who cares to listen, he's no golfer.

A normal enough Sunday. Much like the one last week and the one before that. Catholics had been out attending mass, protestant families in church. Of course, Riddle isn't much concerned about what the proddies do with their Sundays, apart from the big bastard eighteen inches away from him. A tap on his shoulder.

'Time to move out,' hisses the big bastard, the merest trace of a smile reveals mottled, uneven teeth.

Riddle's primed. Ready! Christ! Years preparing for just this sort of moment. Hears Bell's words, "You have great potential, son. Can't fault your attitude. Leave your emotions at home. No point in getting into any of this stuff if you're on the sensitive side. Your mindset is an inspiration to others."

140

Riddle never had any major issues with Mire's brand of ethics. Where others might have struggled with their conscience, Riddle found conviction. He became a confident and trusted operator within the unit, accepting implicitly every task given to him. Totally. It helped knowing there were people around as ordinary as him prepared to do whatever it took to underpin the security of the country. That was why the Joint Force for Research and Tart recruited his kind. "When you lay your cards on the table, it's men like you and me who understand true loyalty. Loyalty to Britain," Dinger never tired of reciting to his team.

Back then, Riddle virtually worshipped Dinger Bell and everything he stood for: order, stability, faith in him. Transformed the awkward green squaddie into a slick operator. An exhilarating time. Ulster was his wild west. Corralling catholics into their homes between eight at night and six in the morning to stop them and the prods kicking seven bells of hell out of each other. No-one could move around without the agreement of the regiment and only then if they wrote down their names and addresses and reasons why they might want to go shopping or visit Aunt Madge or attend hospital. Anyone who tried to argue just didn't get chosen. The boys had to have distractions to relieve the monotony. No harm in playing games with the Boggies, as they called them.

'Okay, you're a bit of alright, off you go – but not her. Turn the milk sour she would. Back to your coven.'

'Time to go.'

'Basher really is a big bastard' is how Riddle described him to Dinger. 'Classic paddy, backswept orange hair and freckly and, best of all, a lisp which gets real bad when he's angry. To look at him you'd never believe what he's done. A real nutter.'

Riddle was frequently within hearing distance of the lisp. Too close sometimes. Close enough to witness mounting shock and horror on the faces of his victims. Then the lisp adds to their distress. It's like Basher doesn't notice it. He's totally collected. In total control.

Riddle turns to say something and sees himself, his own look of anticipation coming back in Basher's dead fish stare. There aren't many who've looked into those eyes without flinching. Riddle doesn't flinch. He knows about being a tough bastard, being one himself, or so he likes to believe. Total self-belief. That's what he tells himself. But he likes to draw a distinction between himself and Basher.

He'd seen several like Basher in his time and all with the same expression before a job: cold, dulled, dead. Not too rare over there in NI. The UUF only took men who passed the eye test. Johns who got their highs through savagery. Violence, their habit. Basher was just one of many. Billy was his Sunday name, which, given their circumstances that day, was bordering on the ironic. For Basher and his pals, Ulster was a paradise packed with opportunities to indulge their sick levels of sadism. Sometimes that thought spooked Riddle. Not all violent activity was senseless, sometimes political exigency called for it. What else is war? Even the paramilitaries had their own codes of conduct. Comes down to who writes the rule book, of course. Straight gangsters and street fighters probably have their own codes of conduct. Having spent time in the Shankhill, Riddle had the right background to convince Tart and Dinger he could go back there as their man. Sit pretty. Wait for the invitations to roll in. Or the one that mattered – from the UUF. Which was exactly how it happened.

'Took their time about it. Fuck me, are they suspicious?' Riddle bleated over a mug of tea when he met up with Dinger for a couple of days debriefing one September in England, though not at the funeral he said he was going to. Nobody they knew and they both knew plenty of dead. It was Riddle's uncle who persuaded the UUF to have him. The first months were the most difficult. His first real test had been witnessing some kids being breeze blocked for thieving from their neighbours; gave one a split skull but his mates got off lighter with handfuls of broken fingers. It was disturbing for Riddle to have to watch, but he convinced himself they were obnoxious young shites who terrorised and stole from old people so, on balance, he thought they probably deserved everything meted out to them.

Once or twice he did seriously question the direction fate had taken him. Such as the time the UUF stretched his understanding of DIY by ordering him to cripple young villains with electric drills. But being in the UUF meant he had to suppress whatever humanity was in him so he would convince himself that the kids had known the score and gone on committing crimes within their areas just the same. Taken on the big boys and lost. And once a beneficiary of the UUF's community management procedures, it was a rare young man who persisted in his anti-social activities.

His family in Ulster was loyalist to the core so it had been inevitable that some of this would rub off on him. He grew up knowing that there was collusion between the RUC and protestant paramilitaries. Laughing at the local press' willingness to attribute the use of British Army issue weapons and uniforms in sectarian crimes to the result of raids on Territorial Army bases when everyone knew they'd been handed over to the loyalist paramilitaries with assurances that none would ever find their way into any government forensic lab.

Basher and his pals had access to the Bingo Book, as and when deemed necessary. Not everything, just names of nationalist suspects held by the military in Ulster. There were some operations it was simpler to get the loyalists to carry out rather than risk having the British public asking awkward questions. While the RUC co-operated fairly closely with British intelligence and the Joint Force for Research, even it didn't know the extent of covert activities.

"It's war over there and you can't load a rifle and not expect casualties," Dinger had dinned into Riddle before sending him back in. "I make a distinction between my own boys and the loyalists you'll have to work with. We're disciplined and professional. With them, well, you can't be sure what they'll be up to next. Still, love them or loathe them, if they didn't exist, we'd have had to have invented them."

Colin Riddle passed through the Killing House with a group of SAS lads. Christ, didn't one of them dither when going for cover! Got his brains blown out. Shook everyone until it was pointed out the incident was, in its own way, a test because if you couldn't cope with losing comrades, you were in the wrong line of work. Later, of course, the others got to thinking how lucky they'd been that some other poor bastard had bought it and not them. "Lesson, lads, survival depends on alertness."

After KH, Riddle took to carrying a Browning High Power: tidy and unpretentious and ideal for undercover activities. Dinger wore an Ingram 10 SMG. Liked having the security of knowing there was more firepower beyond the first burst.

'Not long to go now.' Basher's timekeeping is sound. They're outside Mick

McCloggin's house. Riddle's seen the name for himself on a list of IRA men passed by intelligence to the UUF. Desperate times require desperate measures. As much as the unit would have loved to, they couldn't have run the risk of eliminating him themselves. But, with the British government's policy of hands across the divide, the factional divide that is, it wasn't necessary. That was what groups like the UUF were good for. Minimal input from Dinger's Mire team. Collusion it was but it was up to the UUF to decide what to do with the dossiers passed onto them. If they used the information to extend their own death lists then so be it. There was always the possibility they would decide to do nothing and in that respect they were unreliable. That and their uncanny knack of bungling operations. Riddle had to resist the temptation to do a Dinger on the UUF and get them better organised.

First time back in Ulster was a three day and night job, strictly undercover. In and out without anyone knowing he was even there. Dinger had blooded him. Riddle knew he'd been discussed at the very top of government. Dinger hinted as much. Saw him as perfect for the role. Used to live there so had a toe in the door. Back to his roots, you might say. To live like a pig in a trough like all the other swine in a couple of pokey rooms. His drama teacher would have been proud. Got back into the local shuffle. Spread the thick brogue, too. It was a great game and he was up for it. A game with an edge, sure. That was the buzz for him. He was careful. Become sloppy and you'd make the headlines. Riddle was good. Dinger appreciated that. That was why he was willing to use him again.

Riddle knew someone else was embedded with the other side but he never found out his name. For all he knew the John was still in place and reporting back to the unit. This was where intelligence on McCloggin had come from. Basher's crew acted on this information. Basher with his habitual grin which never quite reached as far as his eyes.

'I'm not a v-vindictive man, D-Dooley, as you know,' he'd drill Riddle's shoulder with his forefinger, 'but I d-don't give a s-stuff about the scum round here except them that c-comes onto our turf and k-kills our loved ones. What man would turn a b-blind eye to that? I o-owe it to my f-family and them others that these b-bastards are trying to d-destroy. We won't let them, though. So we'll get it d-done.'

Riddle is buzzing. It's freezing cold. Freezing. The kind of night a man's breath catches the back of his throat. He's been up for this since it was confirmed the road block had been removed. This was the signal that the RUC would keep out of things until they got the wink the job had been concluded. This was the go-ahead. The all-clear. Colin Riddle realises he's panting like a dog. Apprehensive. Sure, he is. Wouldn't anyone be? Maybe not Basher. Basher's gabbing on. Quiet like, but unremitting. He doesn't look the least bit nervous. Riddle wipes cool beads of sweat from his brow. It's what sometimes happens to him in certain situations. Dinger's noticed it. He'd tell him to toughen up, that he had way too much humanity for this game; but it didn't alter his faith in him.

Ulster was the second theatre he and Dinger had worked as a team. Riddle did as his handler asked and worked on his toughness. 'If tough is what he wants tough is what he'll get,' he repeated to himself in front of a mirror. Though in a land of hard men, it was tough to be the toughest. Riddle knew he would never achieve that. This was not a place to ever let your guard down. Dinger asked him one time if he was okay. He asked him more than one time but one particular afternoon he'd seen something new. Asked Riddle if he needed professional help. As if Riddle would. Assured Dinger he was great. Always found it easier to convince himself than others.

The Plough. Orion's Belt. One stretch of his arm and he might touch them. Each blade of grass was fringed with frost. Breath as thick as chimney smoke. The Plough and Orion's Belt. Learned at primary school and never forgotten. Tommy perched on a boulder outside Derry Lodge, staring up at the black-blue sky shot with glittering diamonds, hands warming around enamel mugs of hot tea. Tracing starry patterns with his eyes. Riddle reckons Basher's not a man in touch with galaxies. Those grubby, stubby fingers stroking the corners of his mouth, sticky with slivers of saliva. The hard man flicks off the spit, nodding to let Riddle know it's time.

The middle-class neighbourhood has row upon row of neat, freshly-painted houses and trim little gardens out front; a community where people are happy to stay indoors rather than hang out on the streets nosing into everyone else's business. There's no-one on the street to see two men approaching. No witnesses unless they are behind curtains. And this is the sort of neighbourhood where people are embarrassed to be caught staring out of their own windows so the men stride confidently along. But noiselessly for all that. Well rehearsed. Just the one car parked by the hedge that runs the length of the bowling green opposite the houses. Some semis, mostly detached. There's a sign indicating opening times on the Bowling Green's gate. Basher and Riddle are in front of the notice. Just ahead is the car. A blue Orion left there earlier in the day. Their getaway. Not long now. The job won't take long. Riddle swings round. Basher's fiddling in his trouser pocket, jangling the car key. The car is on their left. Basher bends down and turns the key in the lock on the driver's door. It releases with a clunk. Then he unlocks the passenger door and catches up with Riddle. Ready at last. Like a couple of boy scouts. Always prepared.

It is dusk. The falling darkness has driven the birds from the trees which screen the smart houses from the well-maintained road. It's so quiet that Colin imagines he can hear the electrical activity in his brain. He drops behind Basher as they approach the house. Over pink gravel, each step precise and firm so as not to disturb the stones and signal their approach. The element of surprise gives an advantage. Blue light leaches through gaps in the drawn curtains of a ground-floor room. A television is on, turned up loud. A woman's laughter: high spirited and musical in tone. The ring of metal reverberating on a wooden floor – a man angry, yelling, 'You silly bugger. Watch what yer doin, won't you?'

The noise is a relief. Colin turns the polished brass knob and tries the door but there's no give. Basher draws his Star pistol and shoots off the lock. They are face to face with a young girl of around eight; she stares at them in wide-eyed amazement. She is crying. In her hand is a fork. Riddle and Basher brush past her. A man sees them and tries to get up from his seat at the table. Caught in the eye by a slug from Riddle's Browning, he straightens then jerks backwards. A woman freezes halfway between the table and the door; her mouth open in a gasp – a pause – a scream. A shriek from a startled baby. The man tips forward and flops, folding in half; his flailing hands feeling for the table but catching a plate of sausage and chips which he takes down with him. Fork, knife and plate clatter on beautifully waxed, stripped pine floorboards. Riddle aims and discharges three more shots. The diner on the floor convulses in a mess of blood, tomato sauce, morsels of burst sausage and shattered golden chips. The little girl, rushing in screeching, hysterical, drops down by her dying father, urging him to say something to her. Terrified dark eyes puncture his waxen face like constellations in *reverse. Eternally silent. No crumbs of comfort for the child who will remember her father's last words to her: 'You silly bugger.'*

The woman has stopped screaming and cowers in a corner shielding the baby and reaching out to the girl but her gaze is locked onto her dead husband. Basher gives her one of his grins.

'You'll no be h-havin' any m- more of them b-bastards in a h-hurry, ye p-papist whore. We'll leave ye them what you h-have as a gesture of g-goodwill.'

They meet a wee lad of around ten in the hallway, brandishing a toy rifle.

'Oh, oh, the c-cavalry's arrived,' crows Basher. He raises his hands. The trembling child is transfixed. 'The action w-was in there. You've m-missed it, s-son. I'm sure there'll be another o-occasion. M-maybe when you're a b-bit older.'

Riddle pulls him away before the neighbours start taking an interest. From the dining room he hears the wife whimper, 'Alan, Alan.' That's the point Riddle realises they'd got the wrong John.

After, when Dinger debriefed Riddle he reassured him, "Incidences of mistaken identity happen. Killing isn't an exact science and anyway this one will go down as a spat within the IRA. Go home, have a drink and forget about it." Riddle did as he was told but still the incident preyed on his mind, so he drank a bit more and the more he drank the more his predicament began to trouble him. In the end, Dinger had to get him out to get him sorted.

The only light is an intermittent gleam of moonlight through a single pane on the roof. The wind has got up and all around him is clanging and clanking. Coulthard realises he's been asleep. Now, with his good eye, he makes out bits of engines and wrecked vehicles, and what looks like someone striding purposefully out of the gloom. No, several figures. A corps de ballet emerge from the wings. All armed. Four men, one more than put him in there. The front man catches Coulthard clean on the jaw with his foot, propelling him backwards. Different feet jab into the small of his back. The remaining two join in, working him over. Too big for ballet dancers, he concludes once they've sated their anger and given him time to think. More akin to the cast of a Norse saga. The gowk is frowning yet oozing confidence. Who wouldn't be? Three tough guys up and his adversary down and secured.

'You got our message, Englishman? We warn you stop interfering in our country.'

Coulthard lets it go. The gowk nods to the fourth man, the biggest in the corps, who cuts Coulthard's gag.

'Look, I've no idea who you think I am.' Coulthard's bloodied words drip from his swollen lips. Odin half lifts Coulthard and pushes him into a chair which overbalances. He pulls it back up and steadies the still tethered Coulthard.

'Can't you take off the rest? You've got me outnumbered. I'm going nowhere.' Coulthard talks fast.

Odin pulls him off the chair as the gowk growls, demanding to know what Coulthard is doing in Russia.

Coulthard plays the tourist card.

'And this is what you call hotel?' The gowk is having none of it. 'Let me tell you, Mr Holiday Man, I am not interested in shit. Big man from West come to show ignorant Russians how to do business. Well you are not at home so you leave us alone.'

Coulthard stretches his neck, trying to relieve a niggling pain in his right shoulder. The gowk's still sounding off and brandishing Coulthard's Llama around.

'Democrats, reformers. Those Uncle Toms who mix with Western devils are on way out.'

Coulthard reckons the analogy misconceived. In his experience, racism and xenophobia went hand-in-hand in Russia.

'Gorbachev's hangers-on are finished – washed up men, finished, out on arse,' continues the gowk.

Is he going to kill me with my own gun? The thought runs through Coulthard's mind.

'Your friends talk of new revolution in our country – democratic revolution – this is future for Soviet Union they say: international trade, freedom and God – Godly freedom!' The gowk pauses and aims a kick at Coulthard's groin but this time Coulthard is ready for him and lifts his knees to deflect the blow. 'Here, I show you something.'

Coulthard is wary as the gowk squats down beside him. He spreads out some half dozen photographs onto the floor by Coulthard's bound feet. His attention is drawn to the faces of miserable looking men, women and children – Russians, he presumes, in primitive and filthy surroundings.

The gowk doesn't lift his eyes from the images as he continues to berate Coulthard. 'This is not centuries in past. These are Gorbachev's people. No money, no food, they live like wretches and what does Gorbachev do? He say to rich Westerners, "Here is our wealth, come help yourselves." This is bad, Mr Holiday Man. You are bad because you keep these people poor.'

Coulthard tries to stop the diatribe. 'Maybe Western countries will get help to your people.'

The gowk is not for listening. 'We do not want your opinion. Your opinion is worth shit. We will help our own people Soviet way.'

Robert Coulthard's interest in the finer details of ideology is wafer thin at the best of times and this is not even one of those times.

'You are afraid, Mr Holiday Man? A little fear makes man hear better. We want you understand your scheme it is finished – from now.'

Coulthard wonders which scheme he's talking about. What's the point of picking me up? he thinks. The Norse gods look on apathetically. The gowk leans in on Coulthard.

'Mr Markowski, he worries. He send us come for you. You come with us now.'

'Markowski?' Robert Coulthard lets the realisation sink in that the gowk is Markowski's gofer.

'Did we mention this is offer you cannot refuse, Mr Coulthard?'

At this point Coulthard's dormant stomach ulcer reminds him he's not alone. As green as he feels, Coulthard is determined not to show it. "Never expose your weakness to the enemy, son." Dinger's brief on Markowski was thorough.

Markowski only has his own ethnically pure brothers in his organisation and they're all signed up to the Vorovskoy Zakon, the Thieves Code, but employing outsiders is something he does from time to time, out of necessity. The gowk's boss was going to unusual lengths to speak to him. Coulthard would have preferred the telephone. It's a consolation to him though that had Markowski wanted him off the streets, he'd be dead by now.

Marat Markowski is a Soviet Jew from Odessa whose heart lies in Israel; a place he intends to take his billion dollar fortune once the permits make it through Soviet bureaucracy. Family connections got him his first job as a regional district government administrator dispatching small-time crooks to the gulag but it didn't take up all his time and he was able to set up a sideline embezzling from state coffers by creating pripiski, or false accounts, for agricultural subsidies. Markowski's family roots are steeped in criminality, going back beyond the Great Patriotic War. Active in the Thief's World, they had been vigorously anti-Bolshevik. The Thief's World armed with its own laws and courts, outlawed collaboration with the state. Volunteering for war service was a contravention of its codes and it was Marat Markowski's own father who gained notoriety after the Second World War for his ruthless conduct in the internal Suka Wars: Thief's World traitors who'd accepted Stalin's pardon in exchange for joining the Red Army and survived to return to their old habits and eventually back to the camps where they were summarily eliminated. Outside the camps it did his reputation no harm and he went on to build a powerful crime syndicate despite lacking the backing other criminal gangs had from within the Kremlin. The day his mistress failed to show up at Odessa railway station he took five gunshots to the brain and his multi-million fortune and business empire passed to the son. Markowski junior deals in zinc, copper, nickel, illegal arms, diamonds, gold, aluminium – anything with a lot of value – by air or road to Baltic ports. He is even more successful than his father, it is said. One night, the Estonian police raided his hotel room in Tallinn. Found US $150,000 in cash, a million dollars worth of diamonds and an attaché case packed with documents, which were scattered to the wind over trees and rooftops during the excitement of the search. Police arrested the pilot of an Antonov-24 transport plane the same night. None of the evidence stuck. The police inspector responsible for the raid was later reunited with a couple of Markowski's thugs, recognisable by the suppleness of their leather jackets and the thickness of their furs. It was the last meeting he would ever have.

Markowski knows the world of foreign and offshore bank accounts, foreign real estate, foreign stock holdings; he has capital investments spread between a hundred institutions and a further hundred transitory companies – warrens of impenetrable blind alleys. But Marat Markowski, aka The Angel, aka the Odessa Godfather, has one weakness in his organisation, which explains his interest in Hugh Bell and TAGOil. The oil and gas industries are magnets for speculators and criminals jostling for position of top dog in the event that communism's demise lies just over the horizon. And with Soviet eyes focussing more and more beyond the borderlands, one more valuable asset for criminal gangs becomes Western businessmen. That TAGOil is currently being represented by Robert Coulthard inevitably makes him interesting. And for a man with ambitions to branch out and trade under his own steam, Markowski might yet prove a valuable ally to the Scot, albeit that it would always be that Markowski would set any rules.

Something makes Robert Coulthard look up and he catches sight of a pair of eyes watching through the cracked pane of glass on the roof. Now the gowk is moving him out. Coulthard's ankle strappings are cut. Hands grab him and the thugs are running him into the blue night. Hard paving gives way to rough ground. Prodded into jogging then Coulthard is being half-lifted between two men over a pile of rocks. He hears someone call out. A second yell, a barked order. And again. The heavies pause, though it's the middle of the night, it's bright enough for Coulthard to make out a car parked several feet away. The Plough winks conspiratorially then vanishes. The apocalypse has begun.

A hail of falling stars. No, not stars. Brilliant lights. A hail of silver bullets. An exquisite whine of discharged shells. Coulthard's legs tremble as he wills them to run. Around, crumpled and broken, lie three corpses de ballet.

Coulthard is in the back of Zhdanov's car, travelling fast. Gliding through a dark landscape of blurred shapes soaring and shrinking with the lights from oncoming traffic.

'How did you find me?' asks a relieved Robert Coulthard as he rubs his raw red wrists.

151

'We follow them. Wanted to know what they were up to. No idea you were there. Lucky you, huh? Lucky we didn't shoot you, too.'

Sergei Dolgoruky sits up close, his long slender thumb tracing the star emblem on his Makarov PM semi-automatic pistol. Coulthard is being observed through the driver's mirror. An ashen-faced, coal-eyed stranger, as near a snowman as damn it or a ghost. Yes, a ghost, he supposes. Marley from Dickens' *A Christmas Carol*. But he knows he's looking at his own reflection. Same face he'd seen on the journey there, only in a different car. Desperate. Desperate for a drink. Whatever they have in mind for him, a drink would help. He lowers his eyes. Leans over. Head over knees to get the blood flowing back to his brain. Trying to sort out his thoughts. Feeling bad. Fearing he's losing it, again. Right there in front of these Leningrad Johns. Is he still working with them? No doubt time will tell. For comrades and rescuers, Dolgoruky and Zhdanov are being surprisingly uncharitable.

'We save your life, Englishman, you bloody shit. You should be grateful.' The lips part, emitting a jackal howl across the din of the car's engine.

Yuri Zhdanov swings around from the driver's seat grinning broadly and nodding in agreement. Then he reaches over and chucks a bottle into the back.

'Be gentle with our guest, Sergei. Robert, this is for you. You look like you need it. Keep it away from Sergei or he will have it drunk before you know where you are.'

Dolgoruky picks up the bottle and passes it across to Coulthard. 'Take it, it is your funeral, Mr Coulthard,' smirks the clown.

Coulthard pays no attention. He feels fine again. The mirror ghost gives a half smile. Coulthard cranks off the golden top and lets the liquid wash the inside of his mouth. The sweetest sensation soaking into every crevice, every single cell around his mouth, throat, down into his stomach, cell by cell by cell. Sweet sensuous sensation. Never has a mouthful of booze tasted so bittersweet. A second swig washes over his gums, around his tongue. Then another. Then the rush as the alcohol hits his brain, radiates along his arms and down into his legs. Christ! This feels good. Like his old self. Good old Stoly. He wants to leap to his feet and holler, 'I am Stoly Man and I'm raring to go!' But doesn't.

'Okay, what's the story? What d'you know about those Johns? Where're we headed for?' His tongue slurs the words. 'What's the plan?'

Nothing is said immediately, then Zhdanov pipes up.

'Robert,' Zhdanov whistles to him from the driver's seat, 'have you heard this one, Robert? Three prisoners in gulag are asking each other why they are put there. Say first, "I am here because I am always five minutes late for work and they charged me with sabotage". Second prisoner say, "I am here because I was always five minutes early for work and they charged me with spying". Third prisoner say, "I am here because I was always on time for work, and they charged me with owning a Western watch".' Zhdanov puts on a mock glum expression. 'Patience, my friend. You are back with us so that is good. We could not leave you with Markowski's hooligans now could we? Markowski's people leave trail as big as herd of reindeer in snow, yes? They should go back to Odessa. Oh, no, they cannot. I forgot. They are dead. Well, not all of them. That little bastard disappeared but we'll sort him one day.' He shrugs.

Coulthard suspects the big talk is for his benefit. Markowski is the real deal. Greater than Dolgoruky and Zhdanov. But he can't fault their ambition. Not until their luck runs out at any rate. Coulthard wonders how much of this will work its way back to Dinger and Tart. He imagines the pursed lips and highly-polished, handmade shoes from Paddington Street padding silently down London's carpeted corridors with requests for, *a quick five minutes in your office*. Not out of concern for his safety. Not part of Tart's make-up. Tart might reluctantly acknowledge how she depends upon men such as Coulthard – active at the margins; smash and grab artists of the highest calibre but Tart's anxiety would be reserved for any wreckage left by Coulthard which could be traced back to London.

The road winds around high banks of dense green fir trees reaching like gigantic fork tines into the blue and grey-streaked sky. Pallid moonlight kindles Dolgoruky's frightful face, illuminating his beak and wire brush hair. As though roused from slumber, the savage head rises, beak sniffing the air. Coulthard helps himself to another slug of vodka. He could down the lot but the beak is pecking at the bottle.

'You mixing your narcotics, comrade?' Zhdanov is watching again in his mirror. 'Remember we work.'

Sergei Dolgoruky stares at his own reflection in the window, raises the bottle to his lips and swallows hard before resting it against his thigh – the Makarov pistol on the other. An exhausted Coulthard closes his eyes just long enough to catch Hugh Bell's quizzical expression the day greed finally caught up with him.

A tip-off from the Soviet Embassy in London alerted Tart that something was afoot when its mole there realised Hugh Bell was not going to show up for their rendezvous at a grubby Knightsbridge hotel. Bell was pulled in by Tart and gently interrogated but played the innocent card throughout. Not that any of that washed with intelligence. There was a strong sense among the privileged and select body who crewed SS Tart that one of their own had let the side down and, while nothing could be definitively proven against Bell, once his friends had deserted his cause, Hugh's days were numbered. TAGOil was bugged. Bell's telephone at his mansion in Aberdeen's west end underwent "repairs" by a very quick and efficient telephone engineer following its sudden failure one pleasant spring evening. Around the same time, Hugh's brother had been called back to London from NI to be advised that loyalty to the crown came before family and he should prepare to undertake a change of duties.

The Brigadier's submission that a different resolution be found, one which did not involve harming Hugh, was politely heard by Tart's disarmingly charming intelligence officers over a stodgy club dinner. The atmosphere reminded the Brigadier why he preferred being out mixing with his men: the tiresome toadying wine waiter hovering like a great black crow out of sight but watching all the same to ensure the distinguished claret flowed smoothly for men who could stomach nothing less. The Chief had to take him to one side. *The good colleagues that they were. That they had always been. Not colleagues. More than colleagues. Regrettable. Always a price to be paid. Here, some more claret, Roderick. Good friends. Best of friends. Trusted associates. No alternative. Sorry.*

A man in his sixties could easily slip on icy rocks, tumble backwards, strike his head, lie stunned and confused and exposed on the ice and snow lapped by the silver- tongued waters of Loch Muick. No-one around to hear his cries for help; if he were able to call that is. Snow on the ground. Brilliant white snow that falls on the Cairngorms. Dazzling walkers. Blindingly bright in the eye of a stunned man. Blood rushes to the brain; sparkling, guttering flashes followed by their partial eclipse and deepening shadows merging into dimming confusion, disorientation and shivering. Big effort to crawl. Try to stand up. Mire … mire on boulders lapped by those silver tongues. Ice and mire underfoot. Slipping. Down on his knees. Cold. Raw. Rippling, glistening, light sparking. Pretty sensation. Huge effort. U-u-u-p onto feet. Must walk clear of the licking silver tongues. Up and stumbling, corkscrewing and down. Face gently licked by the lapping waters. It might have been.

The harder he tries to rub out the memory of that day, the more fixed it becomes in Coulthard's head. Difficult to understand why given the number of men he has dispatched in his time. Well, people to be exact. Mostly men. One of the things they taught you when you joined Dinger's cell was how to control your mind and not allow negativity to come between you and your own survival. Coulthard had been warned at the outset it wouldn't be easy: years of socialisation make you who you are – average with a conscience – then along comes someone whose specialism is mind-meddling and all the learned stuff goes out the window, for an average man is not what intelligence wants. Not for NI. Not for lots of areas. What use is one more average guy there? What's needed is someone unfettered by conscience to carry out deeds that would sicken your average civvy. Not the likes of Basher's lot, of course, they imbibed bigotry with their mother's milk. Their butcher's mentality reinforced through every action and relationship in their unquestioning existence. There were differences between Dinger's unit and Basher's boys although some might argue that came down to semantics. Prying journalists like Ian Ross for one.

Robert Coulthard has become adept at suppressing his emotions, as his women will testify. After years of adopting various personas; service names, cover names, travel names, operation names, names, names, how could his real self have survived? He is an actor … agit-prop. And sometimes he gets sick of being someone else. His head is full of different people. Hugh Bell. That bastard just will not leave him alone.

Hugh Bell, Scottish businessman on the conference circuit, expert in his field, sometime agent for Tart, amateur in his field. Successful arms shipper, crony of Russian gangsters and a British security risk. Hugh, his real name. In his other line of work, Hughs were informants and that tickled him. Hughs could materialise after arrest and be persuaded to spy in their own back yard. It could be a risky business being a Hugh. No-one trusted a Hugh. Once someone sniffed them out, Hughs would be fed false information which would hand back the advantage to the home side and then everyone was on the Hugh's back. In the world of Hughs it was vital to avoid exposure. TAGOil's Hugh Bell wanted everything: personal fortune as well as fronting Tart's relationship with Oktneft. He might have got away with it if he hadn't been quite so high profile. There were advantages to being a nobody, mused Coulthard, Meet Mr Nobody.

What was that? Robert Coulthard clears a roundel on the misted up window. An ambulance with its siren wailing speeds past. Solitary workers heading for the early morning shift shuffle down the avenue of tower blocks. Zhdanov slows up. They've arrived at the rear of Alexei Grigoryev's studio apartment. Walking fast through the scruffy entrance hall, they arrive at the medieval, leather-clad door. Homely sounds and the smell of cooking meet them. Coulthard expects to see Grigoryev in an apron emerge from the kitchen but he doesn't. Sergei Dolgoruky gestures towards the livingroom. Coulthard obliges and parks himself in the armchair. Dolgoruky takes up lookout by the window.

'You expecting a visit from Markowski?' Coulthard asks matter-of-factly.

It would have been clear to the gangster by now that three of his boys weren't coming back. Dolgoruky ignores Coulthard which makes him curious about his apparent fall from grace. Zhdanov appears with mugs of tea and a plate of omelette which looks like it might have been sitting there for some time. His face is drawn and puffy.

'We don't have much time.' Zhdanov passes Dolgoruky his tea. 'We think it best you leave soon.'

'What's going on? Is it Markowski?' Coulthard takes the mug and eggs offered by Zhdanov. 'Why all the drama?'

'When we found you there and realised you were in danger we had to act fast.' Zhdanov takes a drink of his tea.

'I can take care of myself. Thanks for the care and all that but next time…' Coulthard adds facetiously.

'It does not look like it. So eat and remember you owe us your life.'

Coulthard is not so sure. He thinks it strange they just happened to turn up when they did and he still hasn't worked out what they have on Alexei Grigoryev that has him tied to them. Zhdanov is still talking.

'First there are things we must arrange. We know that criminal Jew Markowski is trying to get you to work with him. This makes us think we should not trust you. But, we already have deal with you. This is certain. You see our problem?'

'I've not gone over to Markowski or anyone else. I'm where I was when I first came here. You've had me checked out so let's not start playing silly buggers now.'

'Why should we trust you, a foreigner?' Zhdanov's tone is not exactly menacing but heading in that direction.

Coulthard keeps things calm. 'There's no problem as far as I'm concerned.'

'Except we find you with Markowski's thugs,' barks Dolgoruky.

'They didn't give me any choice.' Coulthard laughs.

'What is it he wants with you, Robert Coulthard? Do you come from Odessa? No, so why does Markowski send his men to talk with you? He kills people like you. You should be careful who you are friendly with.'

Coulthard takes the warning on-board and lets him go on.

'We are not afraid of Markowski. No, we can handle this guy. Markowski talk big but he has many enemies. It is said he has lost the few friends he had in politburo. When our government falls, and this will be soon, Markowski will vanish like snow on stove. This Jew is greedy and wants everything for himself.'

★ ★ ★

157

TAGOil's inroads into the Soviet energy sector received a setback with its interference into a scam operated by Soviet oil tankers which involved altering their IDs to avoid export fuel tax. It was a clumsy move which alarmed Oktneft's management sufficiently to require kid glove treatment. Warnings came out of London that any system built on corruption was never going to be transformed into one of openness. Of course, this was a very partial view. Neither could it be reasonably argued that Tart and TAGOil were acting above board either. Still, TAGOil learnt to bite its collective tongue when confronted with rigid industrial practices – after all, the game was long-term.

★ ★ ★

Sergei Dolgoruky is muttering under his breath and making hand gestures. Something through the window has caught his attention. Zhdanov cocks his head, his face a picture of concentration. Dolgoruky and Coulthard stare at him, listening. Then they hear it. Scarcely a sound. A breath.

They're onto it in a flash. A thin hose has been squeezed under the apartment door. It must have been there for a while for the lobby smells strongly of gas. Zhdanov makes a grab for the tube but it won't budge. On his knees he tries desperately to get more purchase but down close he's taking the full effect of the gas. He keels over unconscious. Dolgoruky draws back the door's bolts and turns the key. The door won't budge. Coulthard pushes Dolgoruky out of the way and tries to press down on the tube with his foot to shut off the gas but there's too little of it projecting to succeed. Dolgoruky is back with a wet towel wrapped around his nose and mouth and tries to cut off the supply with his hands until Coulthard wrenches the towel off the clown and stuffs it around the bottom of the door, finally stemming the flow. Both men pull on the door but it doesn't give an inch. Their eyes are stinging. Coulthard shrieks for gaffer tape. Dolgoruky finds some in a cupboard and scrambling back along the passage, his foot glances off Grigoryev's son's football. He falls, hitting his head against the wall and topples over Zhdanov. Coulthard pulls away the towel and succeeds in taping the end of the tube but he can do nothing with the door. He goes back into the sitting room and uses a small table to smash through the window. A gunman down on the street aims an automatic up at him. Another gunman runs up and fires at the window. A woman is calling from the landing. Someone is banging on the door. Coulthard rushes through the lobby. The door is open a crack and Mance Stresemann is pushing it against the weight of the two unconscious men on the inside. Coulthard can see a gas cylinder behind her 'I've turned it off ... and jammed the door downstairs,' Mance Stresemann gasps.

Coulthard bundles Dolgoruky aside. He pulls on Zhdanov's arm, which appears to stretch so that Coulthard can only drag him a little way. His eyes are pricking, red-hot needles. Zhdanov groans and rolls over, choking and spluttering. Dolgoruky is coming to and attempts to stand up. Robert Coulthard takes Mance's outstretched hand and joins her on the landing.

'Where did you spring from?'

'Never mind. My God! What have they done to you, Robert? Your face is a mess.'

Coulthard shakes his head and looks over the banister. He can hear a commotion of kicking and shouting from below.

'Don't think it'll hold them for long. Up here.' Mance is manhandling the gas container into the flat and locking the door.

'What're you doing?'

'To be safe, I will lock them in,' she replies.

They take the stairs to the next floor. Gunshots ring out. Peering over the stairwell, Coulthard can see three men dodge and weave their way up the stairway from the ground floor, faces turned up in his direction. He doesn't need introductions to know they are more of Markowski's minders. Coulthard and Mance try door after apartment door.

'Here,' Coulthard hisses. 'There is a God.' They step inside and let the door swing shut behind them. No-one appears. Mance draws the bolt.

'God! This stinks, sorry.' She screws up her face. Coulthard has noticed the smell too and is breathing through his mouth.

'Robert ...' Mance begins. She touches Coulthard's bruised eye but he's still annoyed with her and draws away. Mance follows him into the first room off the passage, where Coulthard is pulling open the window's inner casement. He turns when she squeals. A decaying mass of fur and flesh is draped over a chair.

'Oh, Robert, a dog, how awful.' Mance stares in disbelief and horror at the putrid remains then picks up a heavy brass ornament and smashes the filthy window. A blast of air freshens the rank atmosphere in the room. Mance pulls out loose jagged shards of glass held in the putty around the frame and clambers out onto the sill.

'No, wait, don't jump, drop.'

'What?'

Coulthard edges past, and lowers himself down onto the roof of an adjacent utility block.

'Hurry, Mance! Keep relaxed. Don't tense up.' He gestures at her to follow.

Mance is gripping onto the window ledge and looks as if she's frozen to the spot.

'For God's sake, Mance, let go!' Coulthard hisses through his teeth.

Then she's pushing off and down. Coulthard steadies her.

'Just like the movies.' She flashes him a beautiful broad grin.

They jump the final ten feet to the ground and start running. They run on until they hit Prospect Serebrjakova. Outside the metro, there's the usual line-up of worn out old women selling gaudy long-stemmed gladioli.

At the ticket barrier Coulthard groans at no-one in particular and hurries back to a ticket kiosk. Its queue looks semi-permanent. Coulthard searches his pockets in front of a ticket dispenser. 'Have you change?' Mance pulls out a handful of tiny rouble notes and shakes her head. A whistle rings out followed by a yell from their right. The two look at each other for a fraction of a second before sprinting away to the left.

Aberdeen

Stanley Shaw watches the police officers' car roof glide past the bank of yellow potentillas which line TAGOil's drive and sucks in air between his teeth, sounding like a deflating balloon. He punches in a number on the phone on his desk and is about to speak when Sue Cromarty bursts in following the briefest of knocks. She's brandishing a fistful of papers.

'Just one moment,' he speaks softly into the receiver at the same time as he dismisses Miss Cromarty with a turn of his wrist. She closes the door and Shaw resumes his call. A trace of perspiration is wiped from his brow by his free hand. In his nasal London accent he reassures the person down the line that all is well. 'It's all fine. Stop worrying. Only, remember what we said, it's not a good idea to contact me here. The weekend. As we arranged. You still on for that? Great. See you then. And you.' He folds a tissue and runs it over his neck and under his collar then leans a cooling hand against the window, very much as he did the day he watched Donald MacMillan leave TAG for the last time.

Moscow

In the thick of the shrubberies at the Botanic Gardens the pair eventually draw up. Winded and bending over to catch his breath, Coulthard is further reminded how far his condition has declined in his time out of the field.

'You okay?' Mance places a hand on Coulthard's back.

'Fine, just give me a minute,' is Coulthard's panted reply.

Mance leads him deeper into the bushes, which Coulthard recognises from Dinger's Aberdeen garden as laurels. Laurel for wreaths.

Mance is looking back, listening for signs of their pursuers.

'How d'you keep so fit?' Coulthard asks now that his breathing has returned to normal.

'You know us Germans – sport and survival … also I am younger than you.' The angelic smile flashes mischievously. 'You Scots rely too much on porridge, it makes the blood sluggish.'

Coulthard stands his hands on his hips and returns her smile. Mance leans over and they kiss away the Dolgoruky incident.

'It does no such thing, it's very good for you.' Coulthard straightens up.

'So I see.' Mance Stresemann laughs at him.

'It's just that these daft Ruskies they insist on cooking it with sugar.'

Mance looks happy. 'Are you feeling better?' she asks him. 'And your eye? It still looks painful.'

'Aye. A.O.K.' Hands back on hips, he stretches his back.

'Come on then, I think we should get a move on.'

Coulthard longs to linger there to kiss that beautiful mouth again but Mance is already making her way into the open. A couple of stocky women, heads draped with enormous Gunnera leaves in place of sunhats, happen to be waddling by and are startled by Coulthard and Stresemann but exchange knowing glances.

Mance brings up last night's incident, explaining how Dolgoruky had been elated following the meat lorry incident. He had wakened her by fanning banknotes in front of her nose and she had humoured him. Asked if he was going to share the money with her. 'Some of it,' he'd replied, if you are good to me. Very good. Then he'd kissed her. 'We shall hit town tomorrow night!' He was so upbeat she had used the moment to reveal that she had arranged to meet Coulthard the following evening. 'Screw Coulthard.' He'd screamed. 'Stand him up. Phone him. What do I care? Tomorrow we will be together.' Mance painted it so vividly that Coulthard couldn't help getting the picture: Dolgoruky's mouth, set in its terrible rictus grin as he brought her face up to his, screaming, 'Screw you, bitch!' before throwing her out.

Coulthard listens but says nothing so Stresemann slips her arm under his and together they stroll through the park to the VDNKh, the Soviet Union's tribute to its vast empire's life and work. Coulthard half expects to meet Mickey Mouse strutting between the extravagant ice-cream cornet pavilions: symbols of Soviet accomplishments in engineering, agriculture, space exploration, education, atomic energy, culture, radio-electronics – a manifestation of bizarreness, sham confections in bricks and mortar while ageing vendors in whitish laboratory coats served up the real McCoy.

Coulthard and Stresemann are surrounded by sun worshippers

stretched out on benches as they lick their ices from wee wooden spatulas. With the sun high overhead, Coulthard thinks about Dinger and his Greek wreaths while sunlight javelins rain down from golden statuettes circling the extravagant fountain and he sees broken faces from the gowk's photographs. Real world, political duplicity.

Coulthard squeezes Mance's hand and draws her close to him, noticing how warm and damp she is from their flight. Muzak wafts across the park from loudspeakers on poles, waves of sound rippling in and around the exotic shrines to the great socialist revolution. Mance leads the way to the far side of the park and a long barn packed with wooden pens where a solitary knock-kneed lamb bleats plaintively. And deeper within the vast shed resonates the rich cry of a ewe and another and another until a virtual sheep chorus fills the rank air, but for those who choose to hear there remains a lament between lamb and its ma, still audible above the din. For Coulthard it is a Tommy MacHardy moment. Tommy the soft touch. Coulthard hardboiled. He seeks out the silence of the caged rabbits. But is it a sign of contentment? he wonders.

'Oh, look here, Robert.' Mance is pointing at a pen packed with pink roly-poly piglets which has become the focus of attention for a group of children pressing against the wooden struts and prodding grub-like fingers towards the animals.

'Come on, Mance Let's go.'

Between animals and families it's getting very crowded and hard to watch who's coming and going. He and Mance have fallen into behaving like a regular couple of tourists instead of that morning's prey. They follow two men and a child along a path at the rear of the park which leads into a small plantation of trees behind a quiet stretch of road. The child, a boy, breaks away, running up to a ramshackle hut, crying, 'medvedye! medvedye!'

'A bear,' mutters Coulthard.

'Oh, can we see?' Mance is on tip-toes, her nose pressed against the shack's single grimy window. Out from the gloom rises a fleshy snout. It bobs up, bobs down, bobs up again.

'The only trampolining bear in Moscow,' jokes Coulthard.

'It is a pity,' Mance laughs, 'do you think he will come out?'

'The door's padlocked. Probably just as well. Might be a monster if let loose. Better to leave the Russian bear in its isolation. Safer for the rest of us.'

'Mmm. Maybe.' Mance squints at Coulthard. 'Are you thinking about our friends?'

'Do you mean Zhdanov and your friend or the other lot?'

'Those two will be alright, I believe. I meant the men who tried to kill you.'

'Can't think of much else. Y'know I had the feeling I'd come across the one pointing his gun at me from the street before.' He's talking more to himself than to her.

'Are you going to tell me?' enquires Mance.

'Yeah,' he replies thoughtfully, 'a meeting I went to with Alexei, Tovarischchestvo Russkikh Khudozhnikov.'

'Your Russian is good. I'm impressed. Russian artists' group? Are you sure?' Mance's eyes sparkle.

'Pretty sure, aye.'

'And what was a Scotsman doing at their meeting?'

'Being sociable. Getting the feel of the country – we're a very curious race. A nation of inventors and explorers. And extraordinarily cultured. Anyhow, Alexei's into all that arty stuff. Persuaded me to go along with him.'

'I've seen your culture – in Pitlochry.' The right eyebrow arcs above one sparkling eye.

'Ah, well, you'll know then.' Coulthard has remembered where he's seen those Johns but it wasn't with the artists. No, these two had been guarding the door at his meeting with the colonels and airmen. So, now they were tailing him, he muses. And loaded. It isn't apparent to Coulthard why they might be keeping tabs on him, after all, the arms negotiations had gone well. Everyone left apparently satisfied. He put it down to Russian angst.

'Are you ready to move on? We'll get a bus to Babu?kinskaya metro.' Coulthard feels the light pressure of Mance's hand on his arm and he looks down at the long pretty fingers.

'Aye, let's go.' Then the hand is gone and, not for the first time, he's struck by a physical sensation of emptiness.

'Run!' Mance is screaming.

He runs to keep up with her. They're gaining on a white and red bus.

'Before it gets to the stop.' Her words come broken up between breaths.

They fling themselves onboard, the driver and Mance shouting at each other. She pushes Coulthard past passengers packed into the aisle, away from the driver's view. When the bus draws up at the next stop, the line of those waiting explodes into anarchy. A model in total equality: men, women and children pushing and shoving to get on board but it's packed full and most are left out in the cold.

★ ★ ★

A phone is ringing in a darkened room. Robert Coulthard quickly picks up the receiver so as not to disturb the sleeping Mance. Jeff Bull comes straight to the point. As he swings his legs out of the bed, Mance grabs hold of Coulthard and gently holds him back. He turns around and leans over and kisses her long and softly on the mouth and allows himself to relax back into the warm sheets, content that at last things are working out for him.

16. PIE TOMORROW AND BORSCHT TODAY

Moscow: Thursday 8 August 1991

Robert Coulthard curses himself for not stopping to buy a wristwatch from the pedlar on the Borodinsky Bridge. Whatever else he might say about Moscow, an excess of public clocks is not the first thing that springs to mind. As he nips down the steps leading to the boulevard, Coulthard glimpses, out of the corner of his eye, a woman struggling with a large pram. He turns around and approaches her. She's flustered, agitated. The steps are filling up with people emerging from every direction, like a scene from one of those foreign films he's seen in the Cowdray Hall. Uncomfortable place. Tubular chairs with canvas seats and the sound all to hell. Subtitled, he remembers. Set in Russia and a woman manoeuvring a pram down some steps during a gangster shoot-out.

They're at the foot of the stairs. No sign of hoodlums in spats. They turn up. Late. But they turn up. Shadowing him like he expected they would. He's stopped for a street beer and looming over his shoulder, as he picks up the aluminium cup from the kvass vending machine, are two figures built to an entirely different blueprint from himself. In English just good enough, they explain they've come from Mr Markowski.

As well as being of interest to Tart, hence Dinger, Markowski had also attracted the attention of the CIA since the time his name popped up over a two billion dollars launder through one of New York's oldest and most respected banks. It was Tart's view that the CIA's willingness to share its intelligence on Markowski, amongst others, came down to the alarming rate that Soviet crime syndicates were infiltrating American financial circles and the fear that major fiscal frauds could bring down Wall Street. Tart shared their concern. In a twist of fortune,

Tart's eagerness to reach into Oktneft owed its success to precisely this drive of Soviet interests. TAGOil joined company with those businesses quick to grab the initiative while others held back out of caution and timidity, unconvinced it would prove a case of pie tomorrow and borscht today.

Tart regarded Markowski as a determined bastard who would continue to scratch away at the UK's energy industry in Aberdeen, with its university academics and oil company executives every bit as materialistic as the big wheel himself. TAGOil's Hugh Bell had been one of Markowski's easier conquests and when their cosy trysts at Markowski's dacha, nestled discreetly among the long grass up on the Finnish border, came to light Tart sat up and started to pay closer attention to their TAG operation. Enter Dinger.

Markowski was still smarting from losing Hugh Bell, having cultivated the fiscally promiscuous CE of TAGOil, and was seeking revenge for Bell's death. For just that purpose he unleashed a couple of hounds recruited in Aberdeen to sniff out the rodents responsible – thought to be a business translator and an engineer for an offshore service company in Dyce with links to Moscow. Tart had got wind of his activities and alerted Dinger. Dinger then primed Coulthard. Despite appearances, Markowski's men in Moscow were no simple brainless hulks. Their boss wanted a friendly word with Coulthard about a mutual acquaintance and there was talk about Russia's consumer-starved masses and their buying potential for everything Western. Everywhere, everyone daring to speculate about what might be. The land of the free: gas, electricity and water but excluding the press, challenging opinions and liberty of movement. Rock bottom wages economy justified by there being very little to spend money on but mouthfuls of gold teeth and black-market Western tat. Such is life for the ordinary consumer cum non-consumer at least, for Party apparatchiks were already channelling their not inconsiderable wealth into overseas banks and financial ventures of questionable legality.

'You will be safer with us,' murmurs one of the shadows. 'Mr Markowski apologises for the mistakes earlier. There was misunderstanding with some of our boys. Mr Markowski is very upset about what has happened.'

All things considered, Coulthard believes this might be the truth or part of it. Markowski could have been demonstrating what could happen if he didn't play straight with him. Despite Gorbachev's dalliance with Western governments, the Soviet Union was still a place where foreigners stood out like sore thumbs and the natural disposition of Russians was suspicion, not just of foreigners but foreigners most definitely. If its indigenous people had their movements restricted and monitored, where did that leave a north easter from old Caledonia?

Out from the shadow of a pewter granite wall glows a line of tombstone teeth. 'You've heard of Anatoly Savelyev, Mr Coulthard?' They have been joined by a third fellow, shorter than the other two, his English syntax polished by charm and application. 'Savelyev is the man to know round here. He is someone to do business with. I quote your Mrs Thatcher, who said this of Chairman Gorbachev.' He ends by spitting out a great gob of saliva.

Robert Coulthard guesses it's directed at Gorbachev not Thatcher.

'Savelyev knows people who matter and I have him here.' The short man pats a pocket. Instead of the near ubiquitous black or caramel leather worn by Soviet men with cash in hand, the short man sports a well-cut designer jacket in beige linen.

Coulthard examines Marat Markowski: lean, dark haired and almond-shaped grey eyes flecked with brown magnified behind heavily framed spectacles. The little man is round shouldered so his designer jacket takes on a certain tea cosy appearance. Marat Markowski is a big shot in many ways but, so far, the energy industries have eluded his Midas touch.

'A Party man?' Coulthard enquires.

'Indeed he is.'

Coulthard realises how times have changed. Markowski senior would not have entertained Savelyev, even if he did come with a pass key into the Kremlin. But the Party isn't what it was and Markowski junior is an empiricist at heart.

'Have you ever seen anything so impressive?'

The cityscape stretches for miles below them, Moscow University at their backs. With both hands on the balustrade, Markowski leans forward, a self-satisfied Napoleon looking over his realm. 'A magnificent city. So many prospects. Its time is yet to come. Believe me my friend, you can share in the future. We are at the start of something. Soviet oil flows now through Eastern Europe and we can push further into the West and across Black Sea to Turkey. This is a very rich country, Robert Coulthard, but the wrong people are in government. They hold everyone back. I think you know this. They do not know how to use our resources to make us wealthy like you Westerners.' Behind the spectacles, his eyes blaze with emotion.

'And you want to make your people rich?' There's impertinence in Coulthard's repost.

Markowski tugs at Coulthard's sleeve and the strong face lights up into a smile. 'My people do not live in this country. One day I will take my family to the promised land of our people and live out my days there quietly as old men should. Until that time I will get as much out of this unholy place as I can. It is foolish to think everyone can become rich but that is no reason for some of us to miss out.' He snorts.

'From what I hear, this is already what goes on in Russia.'

Markowski takes a step back. The almost feminine nose wrinkles up at some unpleasant thought. 'Yes, this has been the way that things work here. Our government is corrupt and runs the system in their interests so it is our national duty to correct this wrong-doing. We must do what we can for the most unfortunate among the people.' Again, he closes in on Coulthard, touching his sleeve. 'Not your duty. You are not a Soviet citizen. I speak of us,' and he draws an arc with his arm, encompassing his stooges.

'And Savelyev, where does he come in?'

'He is a friend. He is one of us. Savelyev the citizen. No! Savelyev the patriot. We are standing on the brink of a great and prosperous future. I intend to make many friends at Oktneft and you have friends who would like to do more business with these people. I am a man with many, many friends and I can help you and your country. You understand what it is I am offering?'

Coulthard pulls a face. 'I don't know who you think I am, Mr Markowski, or what I might be able to do ... '

Markowski cuts across Coulthard's response, 'No. No. I know

who you are and what you are doing here.' He draws Robert Coulthard to him. 'I'm an important man in this country and it will be of great advantage to your people if you work with me. We will take care of you. We like your TAGOil. It will be in our interest to look after you.'

'Like you looked after Hugh Bell?'

'That was unfortunate. We have lost Mr Bell but we have learned from this. He was grateful for our assistance at one time. Mr Coulthard, I run a strong business. Mr Bell understood that. So much bureaucracy in this country, you will agree.' He turns his dark head slowly from side to side. 'The time is not yet right for foreign businesses to make inroads here but one day soon it will be. It is impossible without people on the inside who can grease wheels for Western companies. It is co-operation that is required. Co-operation, Mr Coulthard. I may call you Robert?' Markowski purrs on, 'Mr Hugh Bell was helpful in developing bonds between our energy industries. In this competitive world, Robert, we must seek out valuable associates who can help smooth our way. Hugh Bell understood this. Simple business enterprise. Hugh Bell set up second company, like TAGOil, you do not need its name for now.' He wags a finger. 'You will have it if you work in Scotland for me. For now, the name is not important. This is a small company but, like TAGOil, it imports and exports – oil products and services. This second company is more wide-ranging. We transfer, say, a few million sterling – if we are lucky maybe it is billion sterling. You understand that sometimes business is good and sometimes not so good. Of course it cannot come direct from here. Your British government is suspicious of the Soviet Union. And this is good. Soviet Union is full of bad people, communists. I am a good Jew. One day I will leave this place and take my business, all my business, to Israel. Someday soon.' He tugs at Coulthard's sleeve again. 'Money takes the tourist route to Scotland: first to the Caribbean and then it is transferred to a bank in Cyprus and then to Scotland. Too many nosy parkers there. You know this term, nosy parkers? Mr Hugh Bell would say this, "Marat, conceal the cash, let it see the world, confuse nosy parkers." Good man, Mr Hugh Bell. He did not want to waste time with the black marketeers you hang about with, this Dolgoruky and Zhdanov. They are criminal elements from Leningrad. They should not be here in Moscow. One day we shoot them dead. Never mind.' Marat Markowski gestures dismissively with his hand. 'Look, it was good we had Hugh Bell when he was working from TAGOil and we repaid our gratitude by introducing Mr Bell to business people who can open doors that are normally closed to Westerners. We are powerful people, Robert.'

The diminutive villain shifts his attention to the cityscape below. Markowski, in common with several Soviet godfathers, operates overseas through trusted or fearful associates, expanding criminal networks via fictitious companies to launder cash before transferring the funds into friendly foreign banks naturally delighted to service such large investors.

Coulthard has few doubts over the kind of power Markowski could wield and he feels the squeeze but when he looks deep into Markowski's eyes he sees himself. It had been an instruction from Dinger that he behave in a consolatory manner towards Markowski, if approached by him, to string him along in a sense, but he also cautioned Coulthard against being inadvertently drawn into Markowski's web of corruption. Hugh Bell's name had come up, "And we all know what happened to him" Dinger had added, which, given the circumstances, sounded curious to Coulthard. Coulthard had seen the way Dinger had looked at him that afternoon. Reading his man. The raw recruit he had shaken up and moulded into the highly disciplined officer he had become. Days well in the past. Both of them knew it. Had Dinger expected Coulthard to use the job to launch himself on his very own enterprise trail?

Robert Coulthard faces Markowski. 'Okay, you could look after me here in the Soviet Union but what about when I go abroad, go home?'

Markowski lifts a hand. 'Mr Coulthard, there is no place on earth our people do not touch. But do not go away with idea you are being recruited into my organisation. Mr Coulthard, you are a fine fellow, indeed, but you are not from my people. Only my people work close to me. You will simply provide a way into industry and banking in your country for us. We are the important ones, Mr Coulthard, Robert, not you, with respect.' He dips his head to the side. 'Those who join us take an oath of loyalty and silence and in return they are richly rewarded, but if the seal is broken then there is a price to be paid. Life is safer that way, I'm sure you will agree?'

Put that way, Coulthard admits that Markowski has explained it beautifully.

The Russian goes on, 'There are risks, sure thing, but not significant. I have people in the police, prosecution services, in the courts. Everywhere we are covered. In the Party. Of course in the Party. Right to the top. Anatoly Savelyev takes good care of any tricky problems within government but mostly he helps seal agreements.' Again he pats the breast pocket of his tea cosy. 'Money silences even the greatest chatterboxes. Here, take this watch. I notice you do not have one. Here.' With that he pulls a flashy gold bracelet from his wrist and thrusts it at Coulthard, who feels it would be churlish to decline.

The Soviet mafia has been mounting pressure on its government to dismantle trading restrictions outside the USSR and racketeering families have been jostling for position ahead of the pack for when the signal comes. Hugh Bells' death had been a blow to Markowski, given that he was one of the Western contacts he had built a good relationship with, and an even greater blow for the over-ambitious Hugh Bell. A touch too greedy. Much too sloppy. Bell had been trying to cut it all ways. He had taken TAGOil's expertise and equipment into the Soviet oilfields when perestroika lifted the latch off the gate under a General Secretary who understood that industrial growth required his government to rethink its attitude towards the rapacious West. Not that expertise was a one-way stream. The oil running from under the North Sea into Scotland coursed through pipelines manufactured from methods developed by the Russian Boris Paton.

Hugh Bell had sealed a deal which allowed his company to buy into the distribution of oil which was not strictly legal, not the way he played it but potentially very lucrative. Nobody lost. Well, nobody who mattered. Bell was in there like a shot. Inevitably, Tart found out and tried to reel him in but Hugh Bell had become too entangled. Tart's intention had been to use Hugh as a lever to persuade business managers in the SU's key industries to instigate conflict with the government, create a kind of corporate vanguard for a capitalist revolution. But Hugh Bell's contacts turned the tables on him, being less ideological than entrepreneurial in their ambition, seeking Western attachments for personal enrichment and he had liked the notion of TAGOil figuring in Oktneft's future in the event of it being sold off in a post-Party Russia. Hugh Bell's problem was that he began believing whatever the Sovs promised. In the end there was no saving him. Tart fretted she was compromised and at the same time there was growing resentment within British intelligence that Hugh Bell had been allowed to become a maverick.

Shadowy minders lurch over Coulthard. A glint of white enamel. 'Call it a down payment on your acceptance of my offer.' Markowski presses the watch into Coulthard's hand.

'And if I don't accept?'

Markowski gives an exaggerated shrug of the tea cosy shoulders. 'What is there to refuse? It is just a trifle.'

Coulthard slips on the watch. The hands point at ten to ten.

Coulthard has come across Russian generosity before. This is not it.

Markowski's line has been cast into a whirlpool and Coulthard is nibbling on the bait. He looks over to where Markowski is being devoured by the thugs of darkness as they fall into step alongside him. One opens the door of a white Volvo. Half in half out, Markowski calls out, 'We know where to find you. We will be in touch. Soon. Everything will be fine, Robert. I am not a monster. I am going to have lunch with my daughter. She studies fine art. In Russia there are many beautiful paintings. They deserve to be appreciated by people in your country and in America. I love art. I am not only a man of enterprise. Perhaps soon I will combine my current interests with art. There is too much art for us here. We should share it with the world. One day, with the help of my daughter, perhaps we will. Oh, and one last thing. Stay away from those Leningrad hoodlums if you know what is good for you. They are two fucking idiots who think they can swagger in here and snatch away my business. That incident with the meat truck – they will pay for that. But do not worry, we will get them.' A flash of the divine smile and he is gone.

Coulthard is aware he has been joined by a courting couple apparently more besotted with each other than the view. They leave him to his musings.

173

He had become bored in Aberdeen after fleeing NI, then South Africa. And broke. Dinger's offer of one final chance to get back on his feet is already throwing up a wealth of possibilities. So, here he is – in this country of half-defeated, half-outlawed people. Secretive. Trusting no-one. Isn't that the advice he is forever getting? Exotic.

Moscow: evening

The militia officer is in a filthy temper when he turns up with a van full of men to deal with an unauthorised public meeting, as Alexei Grigoryev can testify. Being the only person in attendance, Grigoryev receives the full blast of the official's interrogation and it is apparent that none of his answers satisfy the policeman in charge. The hall is locked and in darkness, until the militia let themselves in. Has he made a mistake? Alexei Grigoryev is consulting the note he has taken from an entry in Dolgoruky's diary and assumes the meeting has been postponed or cancelled. Not so extraordinary. But the militia officer is not easily placated. His men planned to watch a football match on television and are as mad as hell with him. More importantly, the officer's superiors will be furious for the overtime payments due to his crew for the abortive call-out. He demands to know from an apologetic Grigoryev why he has wasted their time.

There is no apology forthcoming, however, for Robert Coulthard, who also made his way to the hall and is observing from the cover of a shop doorway as the wagon full of armed men pull up and proceed to batter down the locked door. This commotion alerted the hall's caretaker who proceeded to berate the militia for their actions while denying any meeting had been booked for that evening. Further, he remonstrated with the chief officer that he never allowed any illegal gatherings to take place there.

Also observing the scene, and Coulthard, is a tall, athletic-looking man with bristly hair, who melts away as the police wagon drives off.

Grigoryev phones Coulthard after being released from police custody, although he makes no mention of the incident during his call.

174

Grigoryev wants to show Coulthard his recently finished city landscape which he hopes will be accepted for the artists' group's forthcoming exhibition. The Tovarischchestvo likes urban subjects, he explains to the Scot as they make their way to his Arbat apartment.

'You don't mind Zhdanov and Dolgoruky staying with you?' Coulthard asks Grigoryev bluntly. He doesn't mention Mance Stresemann.

Grigoryev makes a face. 'No. Not really. They stay at the studio.'

Coulthard looks surprised. 'Zhdanov and Luda were very much at home here a couple of nights ago.'

Grigoryev is holding the door open, at the same time as calling to Irina that he is bringing in a guest. Irina Grigoryeva peeks out from behind the kitchen door to say hello then disappears again. Grigoryev takes Coulthard's jacket and goes to have a word with his wife. She then reappears with a bottle of red Moldovan wine and moments later Sasha, the Grigoryev's young son, sidles round the door pitching a football from hand to hand. The child's English is very good and he chatters away happily to Robert Coulthard about school and football. Sasha tells Coulthard he supports Dynamo Moscow but what amuses Coulthard is that he can name several players in the Scottish First Division. Grigoryev brings in the painting which everyone admires. He says he'll take it back to his studio tomorrow to frame it but he intends it for Irina whether or not it is accepted for the exhibition. Then Grigoryev notices Sasha playing with the ball and orders the boy to put it away.

They eat a dinner of wild mushroom soup, fried carp with oily fried potatoes and tomatoes followed by a cake made from cream cheese served with a sweet liqueur. The boy finishes everything on his plate then helps his mother clear away the dishes. He skips back into the room to say goodnight to his father and Coulthard before Irina whisks him off to bed.

Grigoryev waits for them to be alone then mentions Mance Stresemann. His tone is friendly but sombre as he tells Coulthard, 'There is more to that young woman than you might imagine. Fräulein Stresemann is not a stranger to Russia. She is an enthusiastic ambassador for her cause.' His brow is creased as he speaks.

'Her cause being?' Coulthard asks almost incidentally.

'Oh, I think you know. Fräulein Stresemann believes that Europe's salvation rests with a new holy alliance which would reverse the avariciousness of the 20th century.' Leaning close, Grigoryev ensures he has Coulthard's full attention before he continues. 'Here, the government is losing its control and authority which means very soon the USSR will become a magnet for anyone anywhere in the world to exploit it for their own political or economic ends.'

Robert Coulthard sips his drink. 'D'you mean, like TAGOil?'

'TAGOil is a very small fish but might stand to make a lot of money but no-one knows what might happen here if a political vacuum is created.' He refills Coulthard's glass.

'Your English is very good, Alexei.' Coulthard raises his glass in salute.

Grigoryev takes the compliment and considers the Scotsman. His spectacles magnifying his eyes into round chestnuts.

'How did you come to get in with Zhdanov and Dolgoruky?' asks Coulthard.

Grigoryev takes a drink of wine before replying. 'I came across them in Leningrad. We fell into conversation. They were full of talk about making a big impression in Moscow. As Leningraders it was a challenge to take on their rivals.' He laughs. 'They are nothing if not ambitious. All big talk. I think they saw me as a person who might be helpful to them, you know, because I work in the Institute of Precise Mechanics and Computer Technology, although they also had their eyes on making money from exporting our antiques abroad. They don't know about art. So I am useful in that way. Yes, they see me as a tool for their ambitions.'

'And what's in the arrangement for you?' Coulthard asks but Grigoryev appears not to have heard him. Robert Coulthard's suspicion is that Grigoryev has some connection to British or American intelligence. His job with government computers would give him access to state files and this alone would mark him out for the attention of Western intelligence. Coulthard is tempted to ask Grigoryev how aware he is of the illegal trade in Western computer programmes whose software has been doctored for export to the

USSR with the aim of sabotaging the Soviet's computer systems. But he says nothing, for if he is wrong about Grigoryev then he risks jeopardising an active operation. And, it occurs to him, that the Soviets already suspect tampering is happening, but there is little they can do about it given their dependency on Western information technology. Coulthard's guess is that Alexei Grigoryev is an active conduit for information between Moscow and London. His intelligence, urbanity, fluency in the language fit the bill nicely. But his relationship with Zhdanov and Dolgoruky continues to puzzle him.

Grigoryev is talking. 'We can wait until Gorbachev is toppled, or we can prepare now to make the new regime better.'

'Isn't that dangerous speculation?' Coulthard suggests.

Grigoryev pauses and regards the Scot ... 'I believe I'm with a friend?'

Coulthard reassures him with a half-smile. 'So, is it when or if?'

'Definitely when.'

'And then TAGOil will make a move to buy a share of Oktneft?'

'More likely a contract for specific services. Perhaps an interest. Even so, the risks will be enormous – enormous for any Western company – but the money to be made, is immense. You can see why companies and individuals are hanging about in the wings waiting for something to happen here. The USSR's vast land area alone is rich in resources which is why nationalist movements have been so active in recent times. They can see what it would mean if they were to break away from Russia. Whatever lies ahead, everything will be up for grabs and what a scramble there's going to be.' Grigoryev narrows his eyes, contemplating his own words.

'You have to speculate to accumulate.' Robert Coulthard wants to keep him talking, to discover more about Grigoryev. 'Isn't that what those intrepid dealers in the city of London and New York have carved into their hearts?'

Grigoryev tilts his head to the side. 'Well, there are calculated risks and there are wild gambles.'

'And if you're right about the way Russia's going, I think you'll find Westerners will steer shy of getting in too quick, wait to see which way the wind blows, y'know?'

'But not you, Robert? You are keen to do business in the heart of communism.'

The wine is exceptionally fine and pours like rain on the west coast of Scotland from the hand of Alexei Grigoryev. The two fall silent.

Robert Coulthard is first to blink. He is drinking too fast and an angel has plucked a sensitive string which renders him emotionally volatile. He sees Hugh Bell in Grigoryev's eyes and in his mouth. Coulthard presses his tired eyes. He's thinking about Markowski and the little that Dinger has said about him: how Hugh hadn't listened, that he had become a liability. Last resort called for …. Summon Coulthard. Hero with dirty hands – metaphorically speaking. No, literally. Everyone said literally. Coulthard would have put money on Alexei Grigoryev getting it right. The man in question has withdrawn into the comforting hug of his armchair, watching Robert Coulthard, who has broken one of the golden rules: he is very drunk and has started rambling about TAG and Hugh Bell.

'Man, I just wish we hadn't chosen that spot to do the drop. It used to be one of my favourites. For walking. Kind of spoiled it after that. Am I being sentimental?' He turns on a bleary grin. 'Funny how some things take you. Y'know it's often the little things, isn't it? I was chuffed when he asked me to do it. Hadn't been doing too well, myself. Got this good pal, Tommy. Got over it, like. Pretty much. Done that kind of stuff a hundred times before. Exaggeration'. He smiles groggily.

Grigoryev is watching Coulthard the whole time. He pours him another drink, which Coulthard swallows down without even noticing. He scarcely knows who he's talking to. He's just talking. 'Don't know why Muick was chosen. Random, suppose. Maybe no. He never did random. But it was just that place that bothered me. Later, not then.'

'Not the man?' asks Grigoryev.

'The man. Hell, no! Just another jumped up snob. Why should I care about him? Did he care about me? I'm paid for what I do. Point is, he went over the score … ' Coulthard is fascinated by the ruby highlights in his glass, 'And got caught. Never, never get caught.' He is oblivious to Alexei Grigoryev, who is studying him with deep interest.

Coulthard's alcohol infused chatter rapidly descends into morbidity. He has become the epitome of a miserable drunk, spiralling into factor X in the face of the Soviet's greatest weapons of mass destruction: vodka and red wine. Coulthard squints from behind his fringe and notices, Grigoryev's habitual, benign expression has gone. What can he read behind those spectacles? Who's he kidding? He can't read anything. Grigoryev has the patience of a saint.

'Russian architecture.' Robert Coulthard sways gently before a line of bookshelves, narrows his eyes and removes a single slim volume.

'Something you're interested in?' Grigoryev's voice is flat.

Robert Coulthard hesitates and, without looking round at Grigoryev, slurs, 'I know someone who is. You collect books in English?'

'I speak various European languages and have books in several of them.'

'No wonder your English is so good.'

'Thank you,' replies Grigoryev inaudibly.

17. EVIL BRINGS MEN TOGETHER

ARISTOTLE

Moscow region: Friday 9 August 1991

The peak on the bald colonel's oversized cap forms a perfect screen from the afternoon sun and, as added insurance, he reaches in for a pair of expensive-looking sunglasses from his car's glove compartment. He checks out his reflection in the driver's mirror and appears happy with what he sees. Robert Coulthard is more interested in the familiar contours of a 9-milly pistol he spotted alongside the glasses in the glove box.

He had been contacted by the bald colonel after the arms for Ulster meeting he'd attended with Grigoryev. The invitation had been for him only.

'Follow me,' directs the colonel while turning his key in the car door. They have walked only a short distance, and are about to cross a stream via a broad plank, when the colonel holds up his hand. 'I have forgotten something. Wait here.'

Coulthard can imagine what he's forgotten and longs for the reassurance of his Llama.

Moments later the colonel is back by Coulthard's side and the two men walk on for around 500 yards, skirting a settlement of houses, and close to a steep-pitched timber church with extensive keyhole patterning around its eves. The colonel explains how the church was removed from another village twenty-five or thirty years earlier.

'It is museum piece. No nails, see? Even then things were not easy. You like?'

Robert Coulthard nods his appreciation.

The colonel slaps his hand against the heavy timbered wall. 'There are many churches here – too many.'

Coulthard is impatient. 'I haven't come here to discuss religion and Russian architecture,' he snaps.

The colonel pushes his cap back on his head. 'Be patient, comrade. It is something you learn in Soviet Union. Patience. It is virtue, yes? In this country we go slowly. Life goes too fast.'

As if choreographed, a skinny young woman with an old woman's face hurries by, her flimsy dress hanging loosely from a lean shoulder. She makes no eye contact with the men but draws her two young children a little closer to her. Ahead a market is just visible beyond a stand of trees. Coulthard watches them go. Pure Kathe Kollwitz. His mind wanders back to Dinger again. Thinking about what kind of person he might have turned out as if Dinger hadn't picked him out.

Dinger was Coulthard's *developmental*: responsible for socialising his intelligence recruit in the ways of the world, according to Tart. Some might say mental was appropriate but developed? Coulthard's slender artistic hands had suggested that lurking within the morose ill-educated youth was a mind capable of appreciating creative culture so Dinger whisked him off to an exhibition of Kollwitz's work in Berlin. "A socialist, you can see it in her art but look beyond the bloody obvious, lad," was how Dinger had put it. And Coulthard had been surprised how her drawings had brought his mentor close to tears. "The ache of life at the margins, son." Yes, Dinger could be a sentimental old bugger, reflects Coulthard.

One of the kids sees something in the grass and pulls away from his mother's grasp, running towards the thing. Coulthard lets out a scream. The shocked child recoils, scampering back to the woman, who is staring open-mouthed at the foreigner.

Bending down, the colonel picks up a shiny torch and throws it towards the boy, who retrieves it, eyes locked on Coulthard the whole time.

'I thought it might have been a bomb.'

The colonel grins. 'You spend too much time with bad people. You must learn to relax. You are in Soviet Union now. There is nothing to worry about. We have no bombers here.'

A self-conscious Coulthard walks ahead of the colonel so he can't see the embarrassed flush on his cheeks or read the panic building within him. The incident has re-awakened his self-doubt. But only for a moment. Coulthard is playing mind games with himself. He doesn't want to live any other way. He could never settle down. He misses the excitement of NI: and is terrified of the monotony of mainstream. Maybe the murky depths of arms and drug dealing will be the making of him. If not he'll die trying. He practises the breathing techniques he'd been taught. His own mind a minefield – a mess of self-doubt, fear, ambition, his father, NI. He has to persuade himself he is a changed man. In lucid moments, Coulthard accepts how his mind has become scrambled more than Dinger will ever know. Sometimes then he thinks he is himself. But he doesn't like himself. He likes being other people. This isn't Coulthard talking but one of the other blokes, whoever the hell they are. His real self wants to get clear away from Moscow and the Soviet Union.

His fingers tighten as though around the cap of a bottle. Just imagining it makes him feel better.

'There it is, see?'

Coulthard follows the colonel's finger to a trim wooden pavilion with a slight list to the left and forest trees growing right up to its walls. He steels himself. "Mental attitude is as important as physical endurance," Dinger had drummed into him often enough, and through all the years he worked with the unit and Tart he'd succeeded in keeping himself in great shape, mental as well as physical. Considering. Escaping the nightmare in Ulster had brought his world tumbling in on itself. Living the nightmare had been bearable and only when risk of his exposure got too great and he was pulled out did the impact of those years begin to eat away at his sanity. Yet he still believes in himself and his dreams.

'It is best we do not spend too long here. He is waiting.' The colonel and Coulthard reached the house, which is not much more than a hut. It shows no signs of life. Coulthard lets his fingers run inside his jacket. Habit. He remembers the Llama is someone else's pet now.

The colonel taps his sunglasses against a window shutter. They hear the creak of a floorboard and the door is flung open. In the doorway stands a man in profile; very tall and willowy. A hand shoots out a welcome. Eighteen inches above it is a grin so wide you could park a bus in it. Above it a high brow topped with silver white hair in an Ivy League cut.

'It's good to meet you, at last, Mr. Bull. An unusual spot, this godforsaken forest.'

Bull takes Coulthard's hand and draws him in. 'There's an airstrip not far away,' he says, as if that's the answer.

Jeff Bull is wearing a dark navy suit with a white shirt and navy tie that has a single diagonal red strip going from left to right. When his jacket falls open his tie is fixed by a gold pin with a delicate chain that ends in an oval moonstone inlaid in gold and a gold bar that secures it through his shirt buttonhole. Bull pours out three drinks and detects the faintest tremble of Coulthard's hand as he reaches for the glass.

'I hear you have nerves of steel?' Bull faces Coulthard, getting the lie of the land. Sees the bruised eye.

The cabin's interior is more shabby chic than rustic. They sit on cheap red plastic chairs. Fifties retro in the West; nineties contemporary in the SU. Bull can't take his eyes off Robert Coulthard, sizing him up.

At last he gives a kind of shrug as if casting out whatever doubts he's been harbouring. 'I've got fairly good relations with our Soviet cousins. As Mrs Thatcher observed of their esteemed President, he's a guy I can work with. And where there's one, there's lots of others trying to emulate him. And it's Jeff.' He raises his glass.

Coulthard allows a mouthful of vodka to drain down his throat. 'I was surprised to hear from you. That you were here, I mean. Suppose I'd assumed you were Stateside. Letting others do the legwork. People like me.'

'Well, indeed like yourself, Robert. You don't mind Robert? Robbie? Or have you moved on from Robert?' The lips are set but the eyes are quick, omnipotent.

'Robert's fine.' Coulthard's response is all but lost for Bull is still talking, talking fast without waiting for an answer.

'I like to dip my feet in the water periodically. Never ask others to do what you wouldn't do yourself. You agree?'

Yes, Coulthard does. Not the guff about rolling up your sleeves and becoming one of the boys. Men like Bull are intrinsically paranoid. They think everyone down the line is ripping them off. Which, of course, they are. He is there to do a spot of checking up.

The colonel finishes his drink, whispers into Bull's ear and leaves the room.

'Glad to see you're back in the frame, Bud. You slipped out of things for a while. Everything okay?'

Coulthard makes reassuring noises, mumbles his speculate to accumulate turn of phrase, happy to let Bull lay down chapter and verse on the latest deal he has going in Mozambique. The American is animated: his deep, gritty drawl excitedly describes the extent of the next fortune he stands to earn across Africa.

'It's a well-worn trail between the West and Africa.' Bull coughs and blows his nose, checking his handkerchief then returning it to his pocket before explaining that if he doesn't follow the money then someone else will so what's the point in becoming over-righteous. A new scramble for Africa. That's what he calls it. Bull takes Coulthard's empty glass and refills it straight off. No questions asked. Coulthard knocks it back. Instant relaxation therapy in a tumbler.

Jeff Bull makes for easy company. His effortless banter gives the impression he's being free and open about what he does but Coulthard knows he is only getting the abridged version. Bull tells him he is about to fly to Burundi. The way he sees things, the split between Tutsi and Hutu is a heaven-sent market opportunity promising big, big profits from prospective weapons deals.

'Just watch this space,' he tells Coulthard. 'Get yourself down there and grab a piece of the action. Gather up all the Akies you can get your hands on; Kalashnikovs – they can't get enough. Even the kids. They're so simple even a child of ten could fire them and frequently does.' He chuckles. 'You got family?' He doesn't wait for a response from Coulthard. 'Sometimes it's easier without. Western squeamishness. Not everyone, though. You'd be amazed how many family men pay their kids' school and college fees from this business. But, what was I saying? …. yeah …. did you know Mozambique has the Kalashnikov on its national flag? Don't hang about Robert, get in and make your bundle then go get one of those coats of arms for yourself with a brace of Akies over the gate to your pile in the old British Isles. I might even see if I can arrange one for myself. Can you still buy peerages in your country?'

'Don't really know. I expect so,' replies Coulthard.

Bull is amused by the thought.

'These guys are not particular where they're from. I mean just about everyone's making them nowadays. The Chinese, Iraqis, Egyptians. The point is they come cheap and sell effortlessly. The perfect supply and demand. No messy customs probes. Just purchase and payment on delivery.'

Bull continues in this vein for some time. He's the sort that once he's got into full flow, wouldn't notice if you sneaked out raided a bank and went for a sit-down meal of kung po prawn at the nearest Chinese before slipping back into the room. The perfect alibi. Or maybe Bull is pure ego with a mouth. What he was saying was interesting but most of it Coulthard already knew and when he thought back on it, Bull hadn't really said a great deal other than *Hey guys, look at me, I'm the rich big shot in these parts.* As for Coulthard, he needs no persuading that there is a bright future to be had from servicing the needs of East Africa and every other part of Africa come to that. An old pal from military intelligence who'd got in with a British company specialising in exclusive shipments to bankable war zones described Africa as *a peach of a continent* – a continuum of small arms opportunities. If Coulthard had read Dinger correctly, and he realises his record in this department isn't as good as it used to be, then his handler had also cocked an eye to the trade. Before cancer slowed him up that is. Bull is keen that Coulthard has the full picture.

'Air traffic control system for a central East African state.' He takes a pull of vodka. 'For the sake of argument, let's call it Tanzania. Now, Tanzania's dirt poor. Dependent on food exports. But, y'know, Bud, here's a place built out of gold, gas and diamonds. Incredible! But it costs to extract them and needs experts in the game. You're not going to find these guys locally but that's the beauty of it. They need investors, guys happy to sink their bucks into mining. Tanzania, if we stick with it as a case in point, Buddy, gets £100 million of its debt to your country wiped out – oh, just listen to your little Englanders screaming about the government writing off more Third World debt – but what your government gives with one hand it takes with another, gets Tanzania straight back in hock to them to the tune of £30 million. Strike up the bleeding hearts orchestra ranting on about dumping an air traffic control system on Tanzania that'll do nothing to feed its hungry or being picky that the price of the system's been hiked way over its true value but y'know, Bud, these guys are not taking into account the jobs it'll create for the UK. Tanzania gets a loan from a British bank – charging big interest rates – and there's the 250 jobs for the British engineering company that'll build the system.'

Bull draws his hands apart in an imaginary underline, always studying the short, eager-faced man before him, then carries on.

'It's a great set-up. Tried and tested format and simple. Always go for simple solutions. Supplier wins, UK wins and there are Tanzanians, too, who'll be grateful for their cut. Always make sure you pay for favours, Bud. Greasing of palms; if that's what it takes, that's what it takes. It's prudent to have friends anywhere there's gold, gas and diamonds, wouldn't you say, Bud?

You heard of Sir Basil Zaharoff? There was a guy who could stoke up war on a Sunday school picnic. One goal in his life to make money. Said to have fired up the arms race before World War I by spreading rumours through his own newspaper. I'm not there yet but I know some media guys who don't disagree with my line of work. Wasn't fussy who he supplied, Sir Basil. Can't afford to be in this business, Bud. What he called "doing the needful". Ambition above patriotism, you'd have to say. You hit the nail on the head, what you said about having to speculate to accumulate. Slap, bang, centre. Sir Basil paid out to the tune of millions in bribes and to some of the most important men in the world. No use slipping the envelope to a no-one, is there? You Brits liked him enough to give him his title but it would have been the fortune he made supplying the First War through his Vickers company that tickled him most. Just goes to show there's no shame in this business.'

Bull pauses and nods in the direction of the absent colonel. 'You see the crap they call aircraft? More tread on my old man's slippers than those tyres. They patch them with duct tape. You believe that?

God, is this place falling to bits. Still, Buddy, if any of it drops in our direction, well, there's bound to be some profit attached to its tail. Their pilots are good, or should I say obliging? They'll agree to most things for the Yankee dollar.' Bull is rubbing his thumb and fingers together. 'Get yourself one of the flying bedsteads lined up at Tomsk and a co-operative pilot – y'know, the guy missing the action down in Afghanistan and boy, you're most the way there. You'd need to register it – somewhere discreet, y'know, Liberia maybe. Pack it up to the gunwales both ways. Never fly empty. That's the credo. There's a market for everything. Just have to know where to go. Weapon parts into anywhere, Central Africa, load up with blood diamonds, rare minerals, pretty rugs, whatever they come up with. Well not anything. We're not doing barter here, Buddy. You know what I'm getting at? Negotiate hard. They need you for shipments in and out. Let' em know it. Had a load of frozen chickens one time. If there's a space, fill it. Empty space is an empty pocket.'

Cultivating life-long friendships is never high on the agenda of the small arms dealer but he does rely on his network of contacts, kept at a Smith & Wesson length. Today, Bull's bonhomie is full on. He flatters. Comes up with a couple of names from Tart in London just to signal to Coulthard he's in with some of its operatives.

'Not that I'm boasting. Know what I'm getting at? They ask a favour. They're in my debt. Get to know them a bit, over a drink perhaps. Sometimes a name slips out. I don't talk, Bud.'

The truth is Bull's interests are so vast that he is always scouting for runners who can trail blaze. He believes Coulthard is clean. Clean in the narcotics sense. Only a bit wide off the mark. He had never been your squeaky-clean, bloke next door but that was never the type Bull was interested in recruiting. The main proviso he set was his operators couldn't be junkies. That was his particular idiosyncrasy. He wasn't bashful when it came to supplying the means for killing people individually or en masse, civilian or otherwise, innocent victims caught up in a technicality called war, yet Bull recoiled at the sight of a junkie. Wealthy businessmen are no strangers to irrationality but seldom allow prejudice to interfere with their blood-soaked profits.

Jeff Bull comes to the point. He knows Coulthard was part of

Dinger 's team in NI. Had him checked out. Nothing emerged which alarmed him, which is reassuring for Coulthard. Bull is familiar enough with Mire to recognise that anyone who played a part in it is likely to fit into his set-up. If he has any misgivings, having seen the tremble in Coulthard's hand, Bull is giving the impression he's let them go. He talks virtually nonstop. Reminds Coulthard of Tommy when he was under pressure. Not that he'd describe Bull that way. He's back onto Africa. Completely besotted by the place.

'Where would we be without the great, dark continent, Robert? Africa needs us and we, sure as hell, need it. Its hunger for weapons is insatiable, Bud. It's a business that just keeps on growing. I don't have to tell you this. War is a way of life. Whatever else has to be sacrificed in their countries it sure as hell ain't gonna be the gun. Yeah, war, it's a way of life there, Buddy. They live to fight and they fight to live. Good for people like us. It's kids and candy, Bud. Low effort and big returns. I know this business like the back of my hand, Robert, believe me.'

Coulthard does.

'We'd make a good partnership, Buddy. You agree?' The pale blue eyes are twinkling and the broad grin can't get much wider as Jeff Bull replenishes Coulthard's empty glass. His aim perfection. 'I just know you're eager to get some of the action, Robert, and I've been thinking, y'know if TAGOil were to get in with us some way it would be just great for tapping government aid missions. Think of it like this – we get a chance to push an aid project, say, to develop the petrochemical industry in one of these godforsaken areas. Your government'll smooth over whatever issues might crop up from the IMF, y'know, outstanding debt, that kind of thing. Wipe them out. Happens all the time, like I was saying. Then TAGOil tenders for the aid project knowing it's going to get the thumbs up. We could be talking $70 million dollars here, Rob. The bulk, the government would pay up front to TAG in lieu of payment by the buyers. That is a helluva good deal. Everyone gets something from it, specially us, eh, Buddy? Y'know the guys I work with out in West Africa would jump at the chance to sign off something like this. Who says Africa's the white man's burden? No more it ain't, Bud. Only a fool would turn up his nose at such sure-thing speculation, if that's not a contradiction? Way I see it, if it isn't me or you then it'll be that other guy driving down the highway in a bigger, shinier automobile. You gotta believe it.'

The mention of TAG sets off a niggle in Coulthard's mind. Everyone wants to know him because of his tie-in with TAG. He'd have to find a way of working something out with Dinger. After all, Dinger owes him in a way. Not that he'd ever say that to his face. Just not what you did to Dinger. And MacHardy's having his tuppence-worth. Never far away. Coulthard takes a mouthful of Stoly. It catches the back of his throat and he suppresses a cough. The two of them controlling his thoughts. Tommy MacHardy forever complaining about his 'misguided loyalty' to Dinger. Dinger's loyalty to Tart. He'd be straight on to Tart once this gets out. Or is he being naive – does Tart already know who he's been seeing, what he's been saying? His paranoia again? British intelligence sneaking around in the Soviet Union spreading the word according to Westminster. Is he missing something? Why has Bull not gone to Dinger? Perhaps he has. Dinger would never let on to him. And MacHardy harping on *why you, mate? You're nothing.* Well, MacHardy, I'll show you who's nothing. You're the one who ended up in the loony bin. Dinger wasn't wrong when he said, "The only people who matter are those who can and those who're willing. The British government's defence policy – same line – if we don't provide the goods, France or Germany or whoever will." Same line as Bull. Winners' talk. Dinger's friends. London establishment.

Going to make him military attaché to China, Dinger recently told him. Coulthard is sure he said China, certainly somewhere in the east. Until Hugh Bell's demise. Predictable career move for someone with Dinger's military background. *Nice thank you for the support in NI. Couldn't do it without you. Set the standard. A bit of time out, Bell.* Nice sinecure. You believe it. Coulthard looks into his empty glass. *The reliable types deserve our gratitude. And we need just your sort of chap to represent British interests in the East. A lot going on in China.* Dinger's world. The pals' network. Used to confide in him during those early days in Germany. Nothing incriminating. Just talk about how things happened. Arms industry personnel seconded to the Ministry of Defence putting the insider squeeze on the government to free up restrictions on arms exports by pressing the unemployment button. No government liked to be held responsible for job losses. The arms industry was, after all, vital to the country. Ding dong Bell would throw that look, a caution against his men believing what they heard; always check sources. Dinger openly discussed how the arms producers had won a victory in public relations over a credulous population. No-one bothered to check the facts. But when did government and industry let the facts get in the way of effective propaganda?

Bull drags his seat in toward Coulthard. 'You sure you're okay?' Bull cocks his head to the side, his shrewd, handsome face up close with the Scotsman's. 'You want to share anything with me?'

'I'm fine,' Coulthard brushes aside the American's concern.

Bull smiles and nods. 'Look, we've been around for long enough, Robert. Long enough to know the score, eh, Bud? Me more than most. Hell, I was a young pup in the CIA in the days we toppled what's his name? Old Mossadegh's government in Iran. Course that was before your time. You're a fresh faced upstart compared to me.' Bull reaches behind him, and as if by magic, conjures up a second bottle of Stolichnaya. 'Sure you're okay with this?' Not hanging around for an answer, he continues, 'About the best thing that comes out of this place, right?' He twists off the cap and runs the clear spirit up to the rim of Coulthard's glass. 'Where was I? Ah, yes. Well you don't want to listen to an old man reminiscing. Thing about age is you go off the point. Like I was saying, I was acting as a consultant with some company, advising on softening up the target client, you know, enticements, something that'll be attractive to a government minister with tastes beyond his income, you know the type. So we smooth the way for him and this company – that company, whatever.' Bull closes his eyes, savouring the slug of spirit. 'You can always get agreement but you have to know the client.' He holds Coulthard's eye, reading him like a book he's read a hundred times before. 'I know you can do it. It's not such a bad life. Believe me, you get used to shifting the morality goalposts if that's what's worrying you.'

Robert Coulthard thinks it likely Bull has been trying to convince himself he's approached the right man. But as far as he is concerned he's ready to walk through temptation's door. Something he's good at. Coulthard clears his throat. Slight irritation there. It might be MacHardy. Usually is. Coulthard gets impatient with MacHardy and his vulnerability. That just isn't the way Coulthard lives his life. Tommy is a good John and it's the burden of all good Johns to struggle through this world. Coulthard regards himself as tough, a graduate of the old escape and evasion and resisting interrogation training. A chance to go in with the bluff American. Aces dealt. Make a hand from them or be stuck with the pair? A chance of a trio in the flop. Exotic, in Russian parlance. Bull is still reading Coulthard. Patient. Coulthard shows his deuce brace. Bull studies the Scotsman then deals him a third card.

'Well, Bud, me and the colonel back there are willing to take you down to meet with some colleagues of ours. If you're happy with that, and you and them get on okay, then we'll give you a try out. Up for that? There's something we've got brewing which I won't tell you about just yet except to say it'll relieve the colonel's comrades-in-arms of a quantity of their baksheesh arms stocks. You've met them. As keen as mustard, boy, I think you'll agree. More of that later. Let me repeat, we're talking cleeeaaar profitsss.' He stretches the words to emphasise that the good times are just around the corner. 'Can't find faster turn-around for your money than shifting weapons around the globe. Even food's not in such demand. You name it – parts, pipes, pedalos, there are clients out there. Look, Bud, I don't really need you; no offence, Robert, but I've a great thing going here. But, y'know, there's too much for me right now and I reckon you could be the extra pair of hands I've been looking for, and in your part of the world. How about it, Bud? You up for it?'

Robert Coulthard is sitting on three of a kind, maybe even a full house. They're being driven by the colonel some ten kilometres down the road to a stretch of track doubling up as an airstrip where an Ilyushin 62 is waiting. Jeff Bull explains that an Ilyushin 76 will be at Moscow's Vnukova airport on Saturday.

'Before I go down to Burundi, there's a bunch of stuff going out to Somalia but we'll take it to Kenya first.' He gives a crystal clear account to his potential business associate. 'It'll be straightforward stuff, Czech-made AK47s, Wolf brass jacketed 7.62 x 39mm high velocity cartridges, a batch of 30-round magazines from the Tula plant south of Moscow – they're good, can fire 600 rounds a minute and lethal to a hundred yards. There's also ammo pouches, green-khaki hessian. Sealed into foil crates. Give us a return of $450,000.' He looks at Coulthard for a reaction and reckons he's impressed. 'We secured it through a relation of Comrade Siad, ex-President Mohamed Siad Barre. Y'know? He's currently holed up in Nigeria.' He goes on to explain that this is one of several consignments being channelled through the Soviet Union, he's signed off with the colonel and his Siberian comrades.

Robert Coulthard is on a high, there's no question about that. He's beginning to believe the bleak lean times are behind him. In fact, he's had the kind of boost that is just likely to send him rocketing skyward with Gagarin. Coulthard is consciously suppressing a few stray negative thoughts. Now is hardly the time to get the jitters or is that a conscience? Perhaps in a previous life. He's fallen too deep into the vortex to settle for humdrum now. When was his life ever so? Always rent to pay. He isn't going to be choosy. But … but in with the high there's the niggling doubt. The dichotomy. It occurs to him that, good as Bull is, there are Johns out there who are better. Market forces always shifting and Bull looks stuck in his groove. Narcotics are quick and clean. Grigoryev mentioned how regular deliveries were arriving in the SU from North Korea courtesy of itinerant lumbermen on government contracts but which can't keep up with the demand. Grigoryev hadn't been setting out any kind of offer, it was only something that came up in conversation.

And yet, and yet, Bull knows the arms trade inside out. For him, arms dealing is a piece of piss. He knows everyone – all the powerful suits who strike poses in corridors of power and hitch rides on every available gravy train. Types who will say one thing in public and something entirely different privately, scurrying around whispering promises into open ears, generating loopholes as big as nooses to enable their lucrative deals to slip through. The kind of public figures who mop up spilled-over public outrage with platitudes and exploit every bloody civil or cross-border war that might boost their already obscene fortunes. Just the kind of men to talk up scare stories about the impact of job cuts in the defence sector, aka arms manufacturing, whenever discussion about their tawdry technologies comes under scrutiny. Wars fought with British hardware which bring slaughter to the hopeless, the jobless, the diseased and the starving in lands far enough away so they are never going to impinge on the conscience of any Westerner with a mortgage on his house. Tommy MacHardy, Robert Coulthard's alter ego, likes the certainties of life, so he says. Coulthard cannot fully understand what MacHardy stands for. Tommy is his soul mate but he is soft. Tommy expects good wherever he is. Coulthard knows different. He understands that life has made him who he is. Nearly twenty years of self-discipline and he's proud of his record. He thanks the regiment for being in loco parentis to a lost youth in desperate need of stability. For providing him with a raison d'être for going on living. He has come to believe that the military is essential to society as its defender and an authority model and he seldom tires of telling MacHardy so. 'The great thing about the army is you know where you are and what's expected of you. The country needs people who're prepared to do the things others won't to keep everything flowing smoothly. You know, a price worth paying kind of principle … if you want to keep the United Kingdom united.' It was a source of regret to Coulthard that he'd been born too late to play his part in defending the British Empire. He could see himself as a staunch defender of the pink.

Robert Coulthard was grateful to Dinger and the Ruperts, as he called them, who'd picked him out from other young corporals in West Germany to groom him for special duties. His first faltering steps into intelligence work in Germany during the 1960s and the move into Dinger 's unit in Ulster during the 1970s when he was required to penetrate deep within the enemy. New boy, new job, new identity. Still that was then. He's finished with the unit. Holed up in Aberdeen after his spectacular expulsion from NI.

Aberdeen

'Where did this come from?'

'What?' Detective Sergeant Dave Millar is miles away, tapping the keyboard on his computer, not really listening to his DI.

'Is this yours? Christ! How long has this been here? For Christ's sake, Dave!' DI Young squawks as she extracts a damp package from the bottom drawer of the filing cabinet. 'Were you planning a barbecue later?'

Dave Millar looks up to see what all the fuss is about. 'What's the matter? Looks like it was a chop. Evidence or dinner?'

'For God's sake, Dave, this place has been honkin' for days. I didn't like to say anything but I was pretty sure it was you. What're you playing at?' Young drops the piece of meat into the carrier bag lining the bin and ties a knot in it.

'Not mine.' D S Millar turns back to his screen, whistling softly between his teeth. 'See this. That scallywag Ross. His bio keeps flashing up when I key in the names of terrorist groups.'

'Ross? Ian Ross. He's no terrorist. Just a lefty.'

'Oh, no? Think so … just take a look at this lot – demos, groups, contacts, his job. Got sacked from a paper for his comments on the PM's visit to Dundee. He's into everything. And he's here.' Millar jabs aggressively at the monitor with a finger. 'This punter's got something to hide. Been in Ulster on and off for years. Pally with the Fenians. Was mixed up in that car bomb scare. Mind?'

Bonnie is listening.

'Must be a marked man. UUF or one of that crowd. They must be keeping tabs on him.' DS Millar leans back into his chair.

'Or maybe he's onto something,' his DI suggests.

Millar looks surprised. 'Like what?'

Young shrugs. 'Like army connection with the UUF.' She sounds unsure, not having thought through what she is saying. 'Could be. It's been in the papers. Complicity between the army and loyalists –hmm, and RUC.'

'Don't believe all that rubbish, d'you? Renegades in the army working with unionists?' DS Millar's tone is disparaging. He can see which direction Young is coming from.

The DI's face flushes but she sounds confident. 'Maybe more than that. Maybe it's unofficial government policy, the hidden agenda, using the likes of the UUF to tackle their insurmountable problems. Makes sense.' Young drums her thumb on her desk, waiting for Millar to say something.

'That's just imagination. Where's your evidence for that?' her DS scoffs.

'In the same place as your evidence for Ross being our man.' Young comes back at him.

Dave Millar is disgusted by her position. 'You know the government's trying to develop a policy for peace in Northern Ireland. They're not taking sides. One's as bad as the other. What would be the point?'

Bonnie Young cannot disguise her irritation. 'The point would be … . would be to rid the North of some of its most recalcitrant political figures so the peace would not be compromised when – if – it comes.'

Millar is slow to shift his attention away from her and Bonnie Young feels intimidated by her Detective Sergeant but sticks to her guns.

'It's naive to think there's no link between the loyalists and the government or MI5, Dave.'

'Phew. Too deep for me, quine. But it doesn't mean Ross is not our man. I'd put money on him.'

DI Young stands up and peers over Millar's shoulder, reading his computer screen. 'Something's been nagging away in my head. Something about that guy Shaw. He's been in the papers. Can't put my finger on it. Oh, well,' she points to the screen, 'not exactly watertight evidence that he's blackmailing the Rear Admiral, Ross I mean, but we could tail him for a bit – to make sure.'

'Aye.' Millar looks up at her. 'Supper Tuesday?'

'Well …' Bonnie hesitates. 'Where?'

Millar points his mouse at the computer screen. 'The meat was for my supper last Tuesday. Forgot I'd put it in the drawer. Keeping it cool, out of the sun. Is it cooked?'

Bonnie Young's face relaxes and she kicks the bin with Millar's supper towards her colleague. 'I hope you choke on it.'

'Oh! Touchy!'

Siberia: evening

The Ilyushin 62 glides gracefully through a navy-blue sky stuck with ginger to a perfect landing at Irkutsk in Siberia. The private plane has been borrowed from every rascal's favourite comrade in the Politburo, Deputy Savelyev, on the promise that Bull will take great care of the minister's perk and cut him in on the deal. On the short drive in from the airfield to the town they pass a Russian cowboy riding the Siberian plateau astride a handsome bay stallion. The colonel draws his eyes away from the rider and places an elbow over the back of the passenger seat he's claimed for himself. He's in mufti and very relaxed.

'You know they say this is one of first anti-Bolshevik jokes. It is 1917 and old woman visit Moscow Zoo, where she sees camel for first time. "Bah!" she splutter. "Just look what the Bolsheviks have done to that horse!" Jeff Bull and Robert Coulthard both indulge him with easy smiles.

They've crossed the bridge over the raging Angara River where some labourers are making heavy weather of sweeping the walkway with twig besoms. Bull catches Coulthard's eye.

'It's a system to cultivate comradeship not efficiency, wouldn't you say?' A line of three men come into view; they're also rigged out in workers' attire but show none of the deficiency of purpose of the quartet. An old timber building with blue shutters, and surrounded by a picket fence, is their destination. They're joined by the trio and the door is unlocked. The interior is pitch black. Someone flicks a switch and a comfortably furnished room materialises. The shutters must have been closed for some time for it's distinctly chilly and there's a whiff of damp about the place. A very large blue and white tiled stove takes up most of one corner with a stack of logs and kindling alongside. One of the men packs the stove and in no time the room is alive with its crackling and hissing while the colonel, Bull and the other two comrades indulge in a short burst of noisy greetings.

'Welcome to Irkutsk, Mr Coulthard.'

Robert Coulthard guesses overalls are not the usual mode of dress for the man welcoming him with an open hand.

'We understand you are here to make us all rich,' says one of the other men. They laugh. Clearly it is Coulthard who is the only new boy here and the butt of their humour. He takes it in good part.

Bull and the Colonel had primed Coulthard on the meeting

during the flight. They had completed several successful deals with the men previously which is what led to the current plan to ship out a consignment of arms to Somalia on the 17th and from this deal others will follow for larger pieces of military equipment and the odd batch of gold and diamonds.

Bull wants to see how Coulthard and the men from Irkutsk gel. He needs someone who can speak good Russian to work this end when he's preoccupied elsewhere.

'Well, I'll do my best,' Coulthard quips. 'I'm impressed with what's going on over here.' Bull is leaning against the stove in conversation with the colonel.

The same local man speaks again. 'When Mr Bull put it to us that we should speak to you down here, we agreed to see you. You speak Russian, we understand?'

Coulthard feels the mist from his words. He's up real close. He obliges him by conversing in Russian until Bull breaks in.

'Whoa! Boys. Not in my company, if you don't mind.'

This is the moment of no return for Coulthard. He knows that once he's drawn in to Bull's activities, everything will change. Even on the plane ride down, the idea still seemed fairly academic, but here the pressure is on. Again, it's Bull doing the talking.

'We're looking to establish a small business in West African Guinea y'know, nothing more than a front really. From this company we create a stash of fake end-user certificates. Y'know the geography of the place? West of Lake Victoria – Rwanda, Burundi, through Zaire as far as Angola – plenty of places to build landing strips away from prying eyes. We've got an address book full of small airlines lining up to work as sub-contractors who'll ship-out locally-mined minerals – y'know, coltan, cassiterite, that kind of thing. For free traders like ourselves, gentlemen, it's reassuring that export licences fly out from the Great Lakes region like ticker-tape on the 4th of July. I'm a Washington DC man and this trade's in my veins.'

★ ★ ★

Robert Coulthard is back in Berlin. He's about 22 years old and he and

Dinger have arrived at the Wannsee. Dinger is on great form, reminiscing about his time as a fresh-faced officer in 1960 when a serious young African was elected to lead the Republic of Congo's Nationalist Party in government.

"Thirty-four, bloody young for a Prime Minister, don't you think, son? Too bloody smart by half," is Dinger's verdict. The "too bloody smart one" is called Patrice Lumumba. Coulthard remembers because he thinks it sounds like a girls' name. Dinger is whispering, "All a mistake. Usual faction disputes, too bloody young! Course the Yanks were up in arms, bloody commies and the like taking over. Belgians as well. Used to be their neck of the woods. Suppose y'know all about that, don't you, son? Land of copper and diamonds, the Congo. Couldn't have that going to the commies, now could we?"

'We?' Coulthard asks him, 'You said Americans and Belgians?'

Dinger winks, "For a start. Some British boys thought Washington was going too far, dirty business. But the President demanded they get him so Lumumba was kidnapped. Gagged him, drove him somewhere, tied him to a tree and shot the poor bugger. Created some hullabaloo among the usual suspects. Bloody great outcry for the body, then. What did they do? Panicked – dug him up, carved him up and dissolved the bits in a pit of sulphuric acid. Protests of course, in Trafalgar Square. Wouldn't you just know it? Eisenhower took some criticism that they'd overstepped the mark but as the late Herr Hitler observed, one of the essentials for achieving your aims is the use of constant and regular violence. The world's no place for dreamers, son."

Coulthard recalls the excitement he felt back then listening to Dinger and what he had to say about violence and success. He knows, has always known, he's no dreamer. If anything, his world touches on nightmares. Back then he was being moulded. Fiercely loyal to Dinger and the country. Acquiesced with Dinger over what was morally justified to preserve the Union: Dinger's own moral map which he shared with his men. Had outsiders known about it they might have condemned it as the law of the jungle. But he and his comrades from the Joint Force for Research were in agreement that patriotism is best served through discretion and secrecy. It was how things were, until

1987. Always the certainty that he was acting in the interests of, and at the behest of, the British government. But, nothing is permanent, Coulthard muses: times and people change. Now he is much more in tune with Sir Basil.

Coulthard is full of anticipation. If he had religion he might be praying that the dark days of the last year are well and truly behind him. Of course, he knows that Tommy MacHardy'll say he's heading for more trouble. MacHardy the loser. Given to outrage over the expediencies of politics: members of the UN's Security Council's domination of the international arms trade. Coulthard is pragmatic. If it's alright for them then why should he feel guilt? Defence is an industry like any other. Where would Britain's GNP be without the billions taken in from weapons' deals? Why else would the British government hand out tax relief on the generous sweeteners the industry has to pay out to prospective buyers? Back scratching as high art. No-one is hurt through it. Metaphorically speaking.

For almost a century the Soviet Union has maintained peace of sorts within its vast empire but the voices of dissent are gaining confidence. Azerbaijan, Georgia and Ukraine are among Mother Russia's ungrateful children, kicking out at an overbearing guardian. This is the message from the Irkutsk three. Huge weapon silos already in place to defend their republics.

Bull drags a tanned hand down his dark navy suit jacket as he discusses the movement of heavy-duty Antonovs out of Tomsk: the school buses, or air freighters, now imported from Mielec in Poland. The An-2 or the 24, with its high mounted engine, built to take-off and land on the tiniest rough strips, and the great workhorse of the sky, Ilyushin, up and away, fully laden from a take-off no greater than 6000 feet.

★ ★ ★

Immediately after fleeing Northern Ireland, Coulthard found himself in South Africa. He had been whiling away an evening in a bar when he noticed the same pretty girl who had smiled at him the previous night. This time when she patted the empty stool next to her, Coulthard had been happy to accept her invitation. It was then that the boyfriend turned up and, as fate would have it, it turned out he was a one-time colleague of Coulthard's. Took the Scot a minute or two matching the face to the voice but, yes, it was him, the Special Air Services Rupert who'd taught him the art of bypassing alarm systems, tapping phones, picking locks and associated techniques during his initial immersion with Dinger after joining the Gordons.

The girl introduced the guy as Mark but the name didn't ring any bells with Coulthard, but then neither would Coulthard's with the Rupert. In their business, identities changed with their socks. If the Rupert had clocked Coulthard then he never let on. The handshake was firm and confident and he gave him a look that could say whatever he wanted it to.

The three drank lager with Glenlivet chasers while discussing Oliver North's suspended sentence for his part in the Iran-Contra affair. Mark's view was that the operation had been justified and misconstrued by lefty Western journalists. Coulthard and the girl agreed with him that the deal between the US and Israel to ship weapons to Iran for the release of the six Americans held by Lebanese Hezbollah Shias was both justifiable and reasonable; its execution was its only flaw. They were still assessing the merits of the operation when they were approached by a large balding man of North African appearance. From behind his dark bushy moustache the North African talked to Mark, his words largely inaudible, at the same time as the girl kept up her rapid fire chatter about this and that. Coulthard did his best to screen out her prattle and he was able to pick out references to a contract the company had with the SADF, South African Defence Force, and that Mark was, or had been at one time, an officer with the SADF.

Coulthard wondered, then, if Mark had been involved in '85, when a contingent of Ulster loyalists flew in to Johannesburg with £325,000 of stolen cash from the Northern Bank in Portadown to purchase AK47s, grenades, pistols and rocket launchers for Northern Ireland. Dinger's intelligence cell and MI5 had reassured the paramilitaries that once they got the nod, Her Majesty's Customs and Excise Office would be otherwise engaged, leaving the County Down coast clear for landings.

The deal had been going well and they got as far as being signed off in Paris when the French police stepped in and arrested the Irishmen along with a South African SADF officer and an American called Bull. The Ulstermen had been fined and the cases against the South African and the American dropped. A couple of members of the South African embassy in Britain and France were sent packing for appearances sake but this did not detract from the embassies' crusade against the African National Congress with professional support from a number of former British army personnel.

The three met frequently, usually in the same bar for beer and malt whisky. Once or twice, the North African businessman turned up and would pick up the tab for any previous unpaid sessions. 'Loaded,' remarked Mark one time in way of explanation. Then one evening, late on, Coulthard was asked if he would deposit some money for the businessman in a bank account in Switzerland – all expenses paid, naturally.

Coulthard had been edgy. He'd only recently been sprung from NI. It was a risk getting involved with these companions but living on his military pension had proved impossible. He needed the cash. The way Dinger saw it, Coulthard craved the adrenalin rush, the risks. Whatever his motivation, Coulthard became the ferryman, carrying money from South Africa to Switzerland, usually. Not that Dinger knew about what was going on. Not as far as Coulthard was aware, at least. After a few weeks of this he was trusted not only to deposit funds but to sign for their withdrawal as well. The North African businessman then disappeared from the scene altogether leaving the two former soldiers operating the bank account; Coulthard acting on Mark's instructions.

In due course, Coulthard set-up an investment holding company in Switzerland at Mark's instigation. Several smaller offshoot trading outlets followed, more nominal than actual, commercial enterprises for the express purpose of enabling the deposit of cash and bearer bonds, stolen as it happened, into the Swiss banking system. During this period, Coulthard had been sent to the UK for a meeting in London with three financiers including a certain Mohammed Ali Khan, whose interests ran to exporting weapons through an office in Mayfair in

London courtesy of an £80,000 bank loan underwritten by the UK government's Department of Employment. They were in Britain to discuss a $60 million deal with South Africa for NBC suits – military clothing capable of protecting against nuclear, biological and chemical attack. Mohammed Ali Khan had asked that a performance bond for some $3 million be issued by the company selling the suits: one of the subsidiaries set up by the North African businessman. This had been agreed by Mark and, subsequently, the money was transferred as a bond into an offshoot of the holding company's account. In return, Khan was asked for a letter of credit for the deal. But Mark, or perhaps the North African, had not been satisfied with the letter issued by Mohammed Ali Khan and had put a hold on the bond. Khan cried foul and demanded $1.5 million against his loss. Eventually, something less was agreed and Coulthard later dispatched to Paris with a cheque and a demand for a second letter of credit from Mohammed Ali Khan. This was refused outright at which point Coulthard then refused to hand over the cheque. In a phone call to Mark he explained that he had called off the deal but Mark began screaming down the line, obviously suspecting Coulthard of fixing up his own agreement with Khan. That was when Robert Coulthard decided to return to Scotland.

Rumours followed Coulthard home that he'd been involved in false documentation practices and he was interviewed by MI6. It was shortly after this that he had his first experience of being in a mental hospital. Dinger had a quiet word with some friends and Coulthard's denial of any criminal activity or involvement with ghost companies was eventually accepted. Besides a testimonial from his handler, Coulthard's service record in NI persuaded the British authorities he had no case to answer. As for Mark and the North African businessman, they moved to other shifting sands companies to attract other Mohammed Ali Khans with their disposable millions. Fast deals. Fast profits. Deal, play and move on.

★ ★ ★

The spokesman for the Irkutsk three knocks the ash off the tip of his cigarette into a cup and studies Coulthard through eyes half shut against the smoke. His American buddy is a big hit with these Russians and he can understand why. Bull's curriculum vitae reads like a *Just Go And Do It guide*: a signed-up member of the American-based International Freedom Foundation which promotes liberty, independence, choice, self-determination; everything from free thought to the free market – except for communists, anti-apartheid supporters, left-wingers, liberals, environmentalists, socialists and freely elected governments disapproved of by the USA.

Throughout the 1980s, aided and abetted by the CIA, Jeff Bull had supplied the Mujahedin with firepower for their jihad against the Soviets. When the Soviets withdrew from Afghanistan, Bull switched to providing arms to the USSR's increasingly alienated republics. If Coulthard was looking for a role model he needed to look no further than this person who had successfully combined official government work with his own private enterprises.

Bit by bit Coulthard is picking up the basics of his future trade. Buying captured weapons from one party, clearing them out fast by plane, transferring them into sealed freight containers, removing the steel seals, switching the contents and redirecting the consignment to new destinations. Essentially sending shipments on a world tour, zig-zagging continents from America to Europe to Africa; in and out to the US, to Germany, to Israel, to Afghanistan, to the moon if the money was right. Shipments travelling through more entry and exit ports than a season of Japanese tourists. Within the hour, the five are outside filling their lungs with fresh Siberian air and in the vicinity of the bridge the same four men are still engaged in the serious business of retrieving wilful scraps of litter.

18. PURE RUSSIAN

Moscow-Leningrad Express: Saturday 10 August 1991

There is a lively game of Black Maria being played on the Moscow-Leningrad express, which means none of the seven tourists, nor their Russian guide, is paying the slightest attention to the uncommunicative passenger dozing by the door. Tommy MacHardy even retains his anonymity when it emerges that the middle-aged couple and their teenage son come from Aberdeen. The rest of the group consists of three men, two from Glasgow and a German from the Black Forest, and two English women, along with their Intourist guide, Larissa. Larissa doggedly refuses to take winning seriously – all competitiveness having apparently been bred out of her – making the whole exercise of Black Maria pointless. Jane, one of the English women, who is a producer at the BBC and knows Paddy Ashdown, is discussing street violence with the couple from Aberdeen, who mention an assault at the city beach some months earlier when a taxi driver they know discovered the male victim lying by the roadside. He'd been set upon while walking back from his work at the Bridge of Don. The card game and discussion are interrupted by a commotion in the adjoining compartment. Someone has lit a stove and smoke is filtering along the carriage creating panic among the train's travellers. The coach attendant is called, a friendly twenty-something sporting a blond ponytail and utterly unconcerned by the neighbours' domestic arrangements. She informs everyone that the samovar at the end of the corridor has built up its head of steam and is ready for anyone who wishes to have tea. A voice calls out in English, demanding she confiscate the stove, but either she does not understand or has decided that would go beyond the call of duty. In any event, she ignores it and returns to her samovar. Pure Russian.

19. SILVER MOONLIGHT EELS

Leningrad: Sunday 11 August 1991

Flanked by Zhdanov and Dolgoruky, Mance Stresemann descends the few steps leading to the meeting hall. While she checks her notes, her companions mingle with some of the thirty or so people already assembled. Among them a huddle of some eight or nine black-clad individuals; contemporary equivalents of Ivan the Terrible's evil Oprichniki.

Zhdanov steers Mance Stresemann through the throng of excited men and women to a trio of middle-aged men.

'I want you to meet Vasilav Mikhailov, Dmitri Dichev and Nikolai Vasiliev. They have been with us for several years.' He lays a hand on Mance's arm. 'And this is our guest Mance Stresemann.'

'We are honoured that you come.' Dmitri Dichev takes Mance's hand. The other two follow, include bear hugs. The five then move onto the stage with its backdrop of twin oversized Romanov flags suspended from the ceiling. As Vasiliev climbs the wooden steps, he whispers something into the ear of Dolgoruky and both men turn to look at the main door into the hall.

★ ★ ★

An infestation of silver moonlight eels dart along mile upon mile of Leningrad's coiling waterways which wind under bridges, in and out of its majestic architecture. Pedestrians slow up, savouring the strains of the musical recital percolating out from the Yusupov Palace.

Tommy MacHardy watches the navigating river traffic, his mind straying back to his home town. Not an exact comparison. Aberdeen is no Leningrad. Twenty years of oil and gas and the second largest number of millionaires in the UK living in the area but Aberdeen wears its wealth lightly. Just another Scottish town lacking corporate pride and afflicted by lack of ambition, imagination and foresight. Thinks modernisation means discarding heritage. 'Auld fashioned.' Decades of myopia. What Aberdeen needs is a bloody good revolution, thinks MacHardy. Its architects and masons migrated east, creating municipal splendour on a grand scale to prove what might have been achieved if only Scottish Presbyterianism had cast off some of its prim sparseness for the passion and sybaritic attributes embraced by Russian Orthodoxy.

'You like our city?'

Tommy is surprised by a tanned elderly man who has joined him. 'Oh. Eh, yes. How d'ye know I'm British. I mean.... '

His companion rolls his head from side to side.

'You are British, so? I think this. British people – they look, well, British. I am Armenian. I look Armenian. No?'

Tommy takes a step back and gives the man the once-over. 'Well. I don't really know what an Armenian might look like.'

'Don't worry,' beams the Armenian, 'they all look like me.' He inclines his head towards the palace, listening. 'Such music. So beautiful.' He looks at Tommy. 'Do you like to listen to music?'

'Don't go out of my way for it.'

'That is Vivaldi, my friend,' the older man lets his eyelids close. 'He was great composer of exquisite music. Did you not come out of this recital?'

Tommy MacHardy doesn't take his eyes off the boats working the river. Nor does he give the man an answer. The Armenian's eyes stay closed.

'Not like Russian. Vivaldi was Italian so his music does not have drama of Soviet works but it flows like Neva,' he sighs.

★ ★ ★

Mance Stresemann's is the only non-Russian presentation to the meeting of Znamya, or The Banner, an organisation set up in Leningrad in 1979 by a group dedicated to halting what it regarded as the moral and political decline brought about by seventy years of communism. Recently Znamya had been approached by Mance Stresemann's ultra-right Erinnerung organisation from East Germany, which was now making inroads across the west of the country.

Stresemann became involved as a teenager in her home town of Solingen, the city of blades. The ideologies behind the two movements were remarkably similar, both promoting chimeras of the past and holding up authoritarianism as the only way forward for the citizens of their respective countries.

With echoes of the Black Hundreds from earlier in the century, Vasilav Mikhailov's thin, reedy voice strikes a resonance with his audience.

'I stand before you, as my grandfather did in 1905, urging us all to join in opposing socialism. Communism has failed to lead our people from poverty and is responsible for bleeding life from our land, leaving decay and misery. For more than seventy years, agents in the Kremlin suppressed the real expression of Russia's people and now these same agents are leading us into a pact with capitalism. Citizens' minds have been contaminated so they no longer know their history; they have strayed from the path of morality. They are feeding their hopelessness with alcohol so that they can no longer think for themselves. Only one thing in their heads is how to get their next fix. Our country cries out for a powerful leader. Our movement must provide this man. He must be someone who will not bend with the wind but will stand firm. This is the mark of any great leader but do you see such a man in government? The answer is no. Liberals and moderates are moving us deeper into moral and political bankruptcy.'

At this point, Mikhailov throws a quick look in the direction of Zhdanov and Dolgoruky, whether out of comradely recognition or examples of moral bankruptcy is not clear. Mikhailov goes on to sum up to rapturous applause. Stooping down to the microphone, he roars the Znamya slogan, 'Stand united for leadership, church and motherland!'

★ ★ ★

The Vivaldi quartet plays on.

'I thought I might see somethin' of the work of a Scottish man who came here for work. Called Adam Menelaws,' says MacHardy.

His companion has a twinkle in his eye. 'After our President makes policies of perestroika, many come here from your country.'

'But the guy I was tellin' ye aboot was here two hundred year ago. A builder. Sort of.'

'And he helped build this city?' enquires the old man. He sees the foreigner steady a tremble in his leg against the railings.

'So it would seem.'

'International co-operation. We are all same under skin.' A warm smile wrinkles the brown face.

★ ★ ★

Outwardly, Mance Stresemann is calm when it is her turn to speak but imprints of sweating palms on the table reveal her nervousness. Her audience listens attentively as she addresses them in English. They applaud her call for closer links between her German faction and Znamya, which will bring about an international right-wing movement based on radical Christianity.

'We will unite all classes in our cause to defeat the scourge of Zionism. We must expose the extent of its worldwide conspiracy, of its ambition to control every aspect of our existence. The dangers to Aryan people have intensified greatly over the past fifty or so years since our shared ideals were smashed by the tyranny of the Zionists and their abetters. Let us take our fight to the people so they can be left in no doubt that there are universal truths which must one day be realised. But we cannot hope this will happen without a struggle. The agents of the left have constructed a great bulwark of lies which the media drip-feeds to the masses, who have little perception of what is really happening in the world. But, friends, we are strong and we have support in many countries. We must continue to grow and for that we must keep up the momentum. Keep the movement strong. We must be active at all times, countering arguments of the left with the truth. We must stop liberal, leftist scum from subverting – .' Stresemann glances up from her papers. Some fifteen or so young men are rushing into the hall, their shouts and screams aimed at both the speakers on the stage and their supporters.

'Young communists!' snarls Dichev.

Sergei Dolgoruky pushes Mance aside. 'Wait here,' he barks as he jumps down from the stage and sets about a seventeen-year-old stick insect with fists and feet. The boy is no match for the agility and power of Dolgoruky, who grabs his long hair and pins him to the floor while beating the wind from his belly and the good looks off his face. The teenager goes limp, blood oozing from a nasty cut to his mouth, his nose spread like messy dinner over his face. Dolgoruky sticks the boot in for good measure.

All the young comrades are finding the evening difficult. One by one, each is ejected, painfully, into the Leningrad night. As the last youth is dumped onto the street, Zhdanov reassures Mance. 'No longer a problem. You okay?'

'Of course. We have this kind of thing at home, you know. The same scum.' All the same, she looks shaken.

'But we showed them, yes?' Zhdanov can't contain his glee as he stretches bruised and raw knuckles.

Vasiliev is calling for the audience to settle down. 'We have just been reminded that our fight will always be difficult, friends. We must beat back the forces of darkness whenever and wherever they crawl from their evil nests. We here are all true patriotic Russians and know,' he addresses Mance Stresemann, 'with our allies abroad,' he continues, 'we know that vigilance will always be necessary. Know this, our enemies are everywhere and will not always be as clumsy and easy to recognise.' His words are drowned with exhilarated shouts and Vasiliev waits for the clamour to subdue before continuing. 'We must rise against the anti-Christ. Russia is at the crossroads. Which way will our beloved country take? There are some who would take us into cosmopolitanism, to democracy and other Western traps which will spell destruction for Russia. People in our country are being corrupted and infected by Satanists who promote new progressive life styles. There are organisations everywhere, we cannot know how many, that will not be content until they wrest away the last vestiges of our great Russian inheritance established by our forefathers over centuries. We look to other nations. Share their visions for future. We may speak different languages but we are together, have same objective. We believe in God and in our nation and together we can forge a future that will belong to us. We will trample society's trash beneath our boots. We will restore our culture; destroy those lies responsible for diluting our traditions. We will restore belief in strength and in obedience. Our road will be dangerous and we must remain vigilant. Eighty years ago, forces of evil destroyed our noble leader and his family. They were murdered by Zionists. And that evil act sent our people on the wrong path, away from way of truth, thrust our children out naked to a wolverine world bereft of faith. Always we must remember our dead and pay tribute to our warriors who fought our fight, in Russia and Germany. And we remember those lying and scheming Zionists who tricked our people to die for the cause of corrupt government. But there are many in Russia who never betrayed our Orthodox faith and who are ready to come together to tear down the chains of communism and tyranny of Zionism. For Aryan unity and solidarity!'

Vasiliev finishes by thumping the table with his fist. Chairs scrape then topple over onto the parquet floor as the enthusiastic audience rises in rapturous applause. Nikolai Vasiliev gazes over the heads of his wildly appreciative audience. One or two people press forward to shake his hand but they are pushed back by self-appointed bouncers from the front row. Vasiliev resumes his seat beside Yuri Zhdanov, a small smile of satisfaction playing on his fleshy lips.

The remainder of the meeting is a variation on his theme; speaker after speaker reiterating Vasiliev's sentiments and each hailed with similar approbation. When the meeting is finally wound up, members of the top table gather in a post-meeting post-mortem while the rank and file dutifully stack their seats and leave.

★ ★ ★

The older man falls into step with MacHardy. A working barge steams by, all but drowning out the Scot's words.

' … that man to man the warld o'er, shall brothers be for a that.'

'Ah! Robert Burns.' The Armenian has his ear close to MacHardy.

'I'm impressed. You've heard o' Burns here in Leningrad?' MacHardy is genuinely surprised.

'Of course we know Robert Burns. He is not just Scottish poet but great poet who speak for all people. Here in Soviet Union every year we celebrate his birthday. Yes, of course, we know of your poet. His 'Tree of Liberty' is about poor peasants throwing off chains of tyrant.'

The Armenian's bowed shoulders straighten as he closes his eyes and carefully recites:

'Fair freedom, standing by the tree,
Her sons did loudly ca', man,
She sang a song o' liberty
Which pleased them ane and a', man'

Tommy MacHardy nods his approval. 'That's the first time I've heard it recited in a Russian accent.'

'Armenian,' mutters the older man scarcely audibly, as he shakes his head at a white Volvo accelerating past. 'There was so much that was good about our country, so much. Now our young people have no sense of past. When history is forgotten, what will become of us? History is future. Our enemies were once outside our great state. Now they are everywhere. Our young people look to West. They are ignorant and greedy. They want everything and give nothing. They do not know what they do but one day they will learn.'

'People just want to get on.' Tommy's glib observation doesn't appease his companion.

'Now we have criminals. Like Al Capone. If you want car like that,' he points in the direction of the vanishing Volvo, 'Chechens will get it for you, at price. If you do a favour for them, they will return favour. We no longer have leaders. They have lost our respect. In Soviet Union there is only suspicion and poverty.'

'You don't think Gorbachev has the answers then?' Tommy asks.

'Not in Soviet Union. Maybe in your country. Maybe in West. He is not good leader for us. His power slips away each day. Just you see. Perestroika! Glasnost! All nonsense. We are not Europeans like you. What is good for your government is not good here.'

211

MacHardy is in no mood for political discussion. 'Well, I don't know about any of that but this seems like a great town.'

'It is great city. Great city.'

'At least there's no-one like Stalin anymore.' MacHardy is scarcely interested, his mind preoccupied. He keeps on looking around him, as if uncomfortable in the man's company.

His companion narrows his eyes then as if taking Tommy into his confidence, says quietly, 'Stalin was great man. Great leader for Soviet Union. We had food on our tables under Stalin. I stand in line to buy fish yesterday. I was number one hundred. This was Leningrad's main fish shop. Where else would you go for fish, I ask you? When I get to counter I am told all I can buy is frozen seaweed or grey fish. This is fish I used to feed to my cat. You cannot eat this fish. Even cat will not eat this fish. It stink.'

A woman strolls by, her jacket the shade of unfurled lilac leaves and her knee length skirt as red as Stalin himself. She is pulling on a recalcitrant pooch that yelps and bites on its lead. The Armenian tracks the woman's clicking heels with his gaze.

'We must be careful when we speak.' He pauses, waiting for the woman to move further away. She lingers while her dog cocks its leg against the railing. The old Armenian embarks on a short circular walk, muttering under his breath as he does.

'Even people you know. I tell you, in Soviet Union, most people, they spy. In this city, thousands spy on neighbours, on family. Thousands. In work, in metro, in shops, in hospitals, in hotels, here on street. So it is crazy to speak openly. Do you agree?'

'You seem open enough talkin' to me,' remarks Tommy as he hurries to keep up with the older man.

'You are Scottish. I take my chance with countryman of Robert Burns.'

'Well, maybe it's a cultural thing, but back home we trust everyone until they show they're unworthy of our trust. We speak openly. Even leave oor keys wi the next door neighbours if the gas man's callin'. In some places folks don't even lock their door at night.'

The wrinkled tanned face cracks open in a golden grin. 'Exotic.'

Tommy returns the smile and flicks a finger towards his

companion. 'Russians go in for gold teeth. You have a few yourself.'

'Well, I am not Russian but we do. There is nothing to spend money on here so we turn our roubles into gold and jewellery.' He brandishes ring-adorned fingers. 'Now, I go. Enjoy your time here and always listen out for music.'

★ ★ ★

A stiff breeze blows up off the Moika River. Buffeted white-winged gulls wheel and shriek above the esplanade where Mance Stresemann and Zhdanov are talking.

'I like Vivaldi,' Stresemann remarks on the strains of the composer drifting their way. 'Many Germans believe he is not grand enough. That he lacks, um, gravitas. Do you know this word?'

'I think so. Yes, for sure.' Zhdanov twists around so his back is to the railings. He looks over towards the Yusupov Palace.

Mance Stresemann breathes in. 'But I love those rhythms. When I was young, my mother used to hum his music to get us to sleep. I find listening to it now is comforting. So sentimental.' She grins at Zhdanov.

'So sentimental,' he echoes and places his hand on her head at the moment Sergei Dolgoruky walks up. Mance shakes the hand away.

Zhdanov looks his compatriot up and down.

'Mance spoke well. They liked her in there.' He thumbs in the direction of the meeting hall. Dolgoruky is silent. His dour face a picture of self-pity.

Mance fills what looks to become an awkward silence. 'We all went down well, I think. Except for our unexpected guests.' She and Zhdanov laugh, recalling the rather one-sided fight. Dolgoruky shifts uncomfortably.

Zhdanov punches his arm playfully. 'We did pretty good, eh, Sergei, for old men.'

Dolgoruky steps back, his mouth a perfect horse-shoe, 'You can keep her. The ungrateful bitch.' Then, turning on his heels, takes off into the night.

Zhdanov turns to Mance. 'Look, I am sorry. He does not mean

that. You know where he has been – shooting up. He's a mess nowadays. He will cool down and all will be well.'

Mance leans over the railing and speaks to the river. 'I don't want to come between you both. I'm leaving here. He and I are nothing. We use each other but I cannot cope with his addiction. It is not good for our organisations. We must be always conscious of everything that is happening and Sergei is losing it. He will become a liability.' She looks up at Zhdanov. 'Look, there is no need for you to worry about me. I am not afraid of him. I can handle myself. It is the movement which is important. When I leave here, I will go to Britain and to Ireland.'

Zhdanov nods. 'I envy you in some ways. Free to travel as you do. One day I will go to Britain. They are not like us Russians. I think they have no passion or commitment.'

Mance breaks in, 'Oh, I wouldn't say passion was lacking in Ireland. It seems there is a great deal of that on both sides … '

'Okay,' Zhdanov agrees, ' but they do not wage war against whole state. In Britain many people have sympathy for Irish loyalists but we, in Russia, have been victims of persecution by government since 1917. Here, state kills millions and still we are not defeated. Struggle only makes us stronger.'

Stresemann shivers. 'Mmm. You know, Yuri, I thought the worst when Markowski's lot turned up at Grigoryev's place. Couldn't believe we all got out of there alive. If I'd come round the front, I'd have run straight into them. Thought the worst but all you had was a good sleep.' She giggles.

'Yes, thank you for putting in the gas cylinder and locking them out or we might still have been sleeping.' Zhdanov squeezes her hand.

Mance Stresemann grins back at him. 'Coulthard was so convinced they were after him. He is up to something. I would say there is more to him than appears on the surface. But, Yuri, I was scared. I didn't know if they might get in. What they might do to you.' She frowns at Zhdanov, who scratches his head and pulls a face.

'They only wanted to scare us off,' he says. 'You most of all. You are an even greater enemy of Markowski than Sergei and me. So he succeeds, for now. And if Coulthard is confused about where he stands with Markowski then all the better.'

214

Mance Stresemann becomes serious. 'I think he might be able to help us, Coulthard, I mean. I will see him again and put more pressure on him. He could be an important link in the chain between us and Ireland so I would not write him off. It is essential that we forge further international alliances. Sometimes I wonder how strong we are, if we really will win some day.'

Zhdanov moves in so close Mance can feel his warm breath on her neck.

'Why is it you want to talk this way? Meeting was good. Everyone knows what we must do. Now you relax. You are with handsome guy who thinks you very intelligent and very pretty. We should not waste evening. Our comrades have gone to drink beer. Would you like a drink?'

Inside the bar, a mere stone's throw from the monument to Russia's author of fables, Ivan Krylov, Zhdanov and Stresemann mingle with their fellow travellers in an atmosphere of sour vinegar and spilled beer. Two men, set apart from Znamya supporters by their identical haircuts and absence of conversation, attract the attention of one or two of the campaigners who suggest they all adjourn to another bar. During the boisterous relocation it is observed that the haircuts are accompanying them on the opposite side of the road and, shortly after, are joined by three others, happy to keep in step with the outspill from the meeting. Secret service, police, Markowski's goons? An hour of noisy drinking takes place in the next bar and when a smaller group of Znamyas, including Zhdanov and Mance, set out for a third public house, the five again follow. There appears to be no connection between the original two haircuts and the three others and the conclusion among the old guard of right-wingers is, whoever they represent, there are two different organisations involved. In all, five of Leningrad's drinking dens are visited by all three parties and, at the end of the night, no-one is quite sure who anyone else really is.

★ ★ ★

The elderly man drifts off along Gorokhovaya ulista, leaving MacHardy to his own thoughts. As it happens, the Scot is not entirely

215

comfortable with them. In fact, he's quickly withdrawing into the sort of mindset which can make him retreat under the bedclothes for days or weeks at a time.

Tommy's hand goes into his pocket. His insecurity is the worst he's felt since arriving in the Soviet Union. Nearby in the Yusupov Palace the string quartet plays on. MacHardy's head hurts enough to make him want to scream. He presses out some pills from the foil in his pocket and swallows them easily out of practice. Why did he come to Leningrad? Moment of madness. He walks away from the Yusupov and past the hall where he saw a group of young protestors being violently ejected earlier.

20. THE GOWK

Moscow: Monday 12 August 1991

Robert Coulthard wonders if he will ever shrug off his sense of isolation. Although isolation isn't the right word watched over, as he is by the city's omnipotent eye: in every building, every park, every railway station, every street, wherever he is, whoever he meets. Good luck to them. Maybe once they work out who he is they could let him know. He is paranoid. He knows he is paranoid. His psychiatrist told him so it must be true. It doesn't matter. None of it matters. And reminding himself of that helps. So he allows himself to go a bit manic. That business with Bull. Everything happening at once. "Biting off too much of the proverbial, old chap," Dinger might have cautioned. Coulthard bites his lip. He should have explained. To Dinger. Of course, he couldn't have. "Never show weakness. Never let the enemy see you have doubts. Fight them. Don't let them surface. If you have real doubts, you shouldn't be in the game. You'll only become a liability to the others. I need all my men fighting fit. Strong minds. Strong. Hear me? Doubting Thomases are no use here. The unit can't carry anyone like that. You depend on your mates and your mates depend on you. A team. Remember we're a team."

Coulthard stares into the bathroom mirror. He can't get Mance Stresemann out of his mind: her fumbling attempts to draw him out over Northern Ireland. He can tell she wasn't comfortable with it. Her turning up like that at Grigoryev's studio when he needed saving. Robert Coulthard's shoulder shakes as he gives in to an overwhelming sense of loss and he holds the bath towel tight against his face. Nothing is making a lot of sense. He had been contemplating passing on her name to Dinger. But that would have been betrayal. He drops the towel and composes himself. Betraying her, Coulthard? That's a funny term to use. Betraying. Someone had to be doing something they didn't want revealed to be betrayed. Can he say that about Mance? Can he? Has done. Before. Not Mance Stresemann. A different Mance with a different name. Look what happened to her. And Dinger's questions would begin. Calm and methodical, getting to the crux of the matter in the end. Does he want that? It is clear she is into some kind of far-right activities, trying to forge links with extremists in Ulster. That she'd been tweezing him to get at what he knew. Traced him. Lucky speculation on her part? The whole world knew about the British army in NI. Why had he come out and admitted being in the army? Still, too late for that now. Might be he likes what she stands for. The only kind of political principles he's ever really considered are the regimental sort. Had to believe in that. Wouldn't have joined up otherwise. Had his own opinions, to be sure, fairly mainstream. Went with what the army told him. Pretty well everyone did. Taught what to think. Told everything they needed to know. Dissent not encouraged. Give them the facts. No, tell them the facts. Fact: a concept whose truth can be proved. Facts based on information supplied. *Supplied by whom*? Tommy MacHardy had asked him, *Proven to whose satisfaction*? He was an irritation. Always thinking around what was perfectly clear and sound. Army didn't encourage debate. Facts. Hard facts. Army source facts. No room for prevarication. Side with violent nationalists? At least the loyalists were on the side of the British state and the state was grateful for that. And gratitude takes many forms.

Aberdeen

Ian Ross steps out of his room at the Tighnamara Guest House and into the arms of DI Bonnie Young. Close on her heels waddles his landlady, Mrs Milne, a large, ungainly woman with a short nose that is remarkably snout-like.

'Ah! Mr Ross, I wis jist comin t'tell ye, y've visitors. The police. I'd appreciate ye getting packed up and oot richt awa,' sniffs the redoubtable sow.

'Mr Ross? Ian Ross?' Bonnie Young offers a slim hand

accompanied by a tentative smile. 'I'm Detective Inspector Young and this is Detective Sergeant Millar.'

Ian Ross shakes hands but to DI Young's eye he has the knowing look of the wary and to DS Millar's, defensive.

'We'd like to ask you some questions relating to a serious matter. Might be better if we go inside.'

The inflection in her voice leaves Ross in no doubt over his options. Besides, Mrs Milne shows no intention of leaving them on the landing so Ross leads them into what the sow had euphemistically described as *a fine, cosy room* furnished in a hit or miss style. Ross reaches for a packet of cigarettes lying open on the bedside cabinet. He lights up with a black and silver lighter and inhales deeply. 'Want one?' Ross offers belatedly. Neither detective responds so he drops the packet and lighter onto the bed. 'So what's this about?'

The detectives notice his refined voice, its local burr smoothed off by years of exile in the south.

DI Bonnie Young begins. 'We'll come to that, but could you tell us why you're in Aberdeen?'

Ross slowly smiles. 'Why shouldn't I be? I can go anywhere I like, can't I?'

The DI gives him a quizzical look.

'I used to live here. Catching up with old friends. Y'know the kind of thing,' the journalist adds.

DS Millar pitches in. 'I believe you've just come from Northern Ireland where you've been working on a newspaper story about Ulster loyalists and their contacts abroad. Is your being here anything to do with this article?'

Ross draws on his cigarette and blows smoke off to the side. 'Pretty well informed. Look, I'm often dropping in here between assignments. Roots are a great thing, wouldn't you say?' And then, 'As I said, taking a breather.' He's not happy to have the local law scrutinising his movements and assumes he's been the subject of a phone call to his editor. 'Ulster's a claustrophobic place when you don't belong there. You have to get out to get things back into perspective.'

'You're not answering my question … ' presses Millar.

'I am. Just not what you're looking for.' The journalist takes on

Millar, eyeball to eyeball. 'Look, I really don't understand why you're interrogating me. Phone the newspaper if you don't believe me,' he adds, knowing they will already have done that.

'We're not interrogating you, Mr Ross,' Young says, helping herself to a chair, 'only asking a few questions. You invited us in. We've an investigation going on that may have a connection with Northern Ireland and we understand you've just flown in from … '

Ross cuts in, 'How d'you know?'

'I'm sorry, Mr Ross, we can't divulge our sources. Can you confirm you're working while you're here? If you could tell us who you've talked to since arriving. Only you seem very political. Well versed in these groups – and their contacts with ultra right groups … ' The question melts in Young's mouth.

'You've been reading the Sundays. I'm impressed.' Now Ross sounds smug.

'Only your Special Branch file,' Young counters his jibe, 'which suggests you're deeply into politics.'

'My Special Branch file? You don't hide these things any longer then?' Ross draws on his fag.

'No point, Ross,' smirks DS Millar, 'you know you're on file. Have been for years. Interesting reading.'

Ian shrugs dismissively. 'At least one of us is interesting.' Then, pulling in his horns, he adds, 'Goes with the territory.'

'Indeed it does. And you're an activist.' Dave Millar's hostility is obvious. He has no time for political stirrers and he has Ross placed firmly into that category.

'Is that some kind of accusation? An activist?' Ian Ross has heard it all before. 'What the hell d'you mean by activist? You mean I've opinions? I'm not some mindless stooge of the state?'

Millar bristles. 'Watch it, pal.'

'Would you mind if we take a look around?' DI Young tries to inject a note of calm into the conversation.

'Bloody right, I would mind.' Ross stubs out his cigarette then follows the detective's gaze to a hypodermic syringe on the bedside table. 'I'm diabetic. Want to make something of it?'

'I think we'd be more comfortable down at Queen Street. You have any objections?' DI Young makes for the door.

Ross bites on his lip. 'Am I being charged?'

'No,' replies the DI, 'but the sooner we talk this through, the sooner you can get on with catching up with your friends. You don't have to agree to come with us but … ' She hasn't finished before Ian Ross' arms are raised in surrender.

Millar and Young watch as he gathers together a few items.

'By the way,' the DS whispers in an aside to his boss, 'you were trying to remember something about Shaw? It was in the papers that he got some sort of medal for bravery – in France. Saved some kids in a house fire.'

'What was he doing in France?' Young asks absent-mindedly.

'Business. Oil. Y'know, pick the best places.'

'Mmm. When?'

'Couple of years ago, got it in the office, from the *P & J*.'

'Oh well. Goes to show you can never tell.'

Ian Ross is ready. He and Young move into the hall, Millar follows behind then steps back into the room. 'Here, you might need these,' he says and stretches over to retrieve Ross' cigarettes and lighter from the bed and an empty, scrunched up packet abandoned on the bedside cabinet which has a couple of numbers scribbled on it and a sketch of a face that looks familiar.

Moscow

'Alexei Grigoryev! You look like you are in a rush? We have been looking for you.'

Alexei Grigoryev has not been giving much attention to the evening commuters as he made his way from his studio to the metro and back home. A solitary woman sits on the pavement on a scrap of blue blanket. As he approaches her she holds up a pink plastic necklace. The sight of the sunburned hand with its cheap offering touches him and he stops to look. Now he is committed. He can't walk away without embarrassing himself but he doesn't want the tatty necklace. It would never do for Irina. He looks down at the other shabby items lying on the blanket: a couple of toy cars with most of their paint missing, a wooden bird with half a beak, a rickety green plastic photograph frame and a cellophane fish. Grigoryev picks up the red fish by its tail and lays it on the palm of his hand. It's head and tail immediately coil up. He smiles and drops a few kopeks into the woman's tin cup. Sasha will love the fish. Grigoryev slips it into his jacket pocket and adjusts the small watercolour he's carrying under his arm, a study of a bridge over the Moskva River picked out in shades of blue through white. It is a delicate work, sombre and figurative with details of masonry and patches of snow on the pavement and bridge parapets, really quite sweet and not at all representative of Grigoryev's usual output of flamboyant oils but it pretty well sums up his mood of late.

For two decades Grigoryev has created a life for himself in the Soviet Union but it feels that instead of becoming easier, his existence here is becoming ever more fraught with difficulties. A life so carefully assembled might be reaching the point when it will have to be deconstructed; relationships and networks meticulously choreographed to be torn asunder regardless of consequences.

Grigoryev tightens his grip on the little picture he hopes will be accepted by his peers. Irrespective of everything else going on in his world, his art is a constant.

Zhdanov and Dolgoruky catch up with their artist friend. 'This your picture?' Zhdanov draws a finger over the canvas. 'Maybe you will sell it?'

Grigoryev shakes his head. 'Present for my wife.'

'Ah, nice.' Zhdanov looks at Sergei Dolgoruky while nodding, comet-like, towards the picture. 'It would be nice to see her face. Can you see her face, Sergei? Pink and happy. You are a very lucky man, Alexei, to have such a beautiful wife and child. Oh, wait! What was it we came to tell you, Alexei Grigoryev? Remind me, Sergei.'

Sergei Dolgoruky snarls something inaudible as Grigoryev turns in front of both men, preventing them from continuing along the pavement.

'What is it? Has something happened to them? What's going on?' demands Alexei Grigoryev.

'You talk too much, Grigoryev.' Zhdanov cranes his neck, zooming in on Grigoryev's face.

Grigoryev feels sick. His association with the two racketeers has been an alliance made from necessity. Just moments ago it had been one of the relationships he was looking forward to putting behind him and now the initiative is with the two gangsters. Something's wrong and Grigoryev feels a shiver run along his spine. Dolgoruky and Zhdanov present a nonchalant demeanour in contrast to Grigoryev's obvious anxiety, and they refuse to be drawn on what has happened for this change in attitude towards him.

Arriving in the Arbat, Alexei Grigoryev is relieved to discover Irina and an excited Sasha coming up the stairs behind him. He unlocks the apartment door and steps aside to let Irina and his son go through. Irina immediately lets out a gasp and drops the blue cotton shopping bag she's been carrying.

The place is in chaos. She rushes from room to room calling on Alexei to phone the police but Grigoryev suspects those responsible are probably standing behind him. He looks at Dolgoruky and Zhdanov. Neither show surprise at the state of the place. Grigoryev puts his painting down on the dining room table and tells his son to go to play with his friend Stefan. Sasha begins to protest. He wants to see what's happened to his bedroom but Grigoryev is angry and begins shouting at the boy to go so they can clear up the mess without him getting in the way. Irina comes into the room, her eyes red. Quietly, she persuades Sasha to do as his father tells him and that he should come back for supper in an hour or so. Dolgoruky steps up as though he is going to prevent the boy leaving but Zhdanov holds him back. Grigoryev waits until he hears Sasha close the apartment door and only then does he really take in the full extent of the damage. Books pulled off shelves are strewn across the floor, drawers and cupboards emptied, precious plates and cups smashed, food jars opened with their contents strewn over fine damask chair covers, soaking into upholstery and cushions, and paintings taken from their hooks on the walls have disappeared altogether. Tiny down feathers from ripped cushions fly on currents of air from the balcony's open door. And there, as Grigoryev knew it would be, the flower pot where they had been growing fragrant red tomatoes, shattered and exposed, the once plastic-bagged radio transmitter exposed.

Irina Grigoryeva sinks down into a torn and stained chair, her eyes transfixed by the radio.

'You too, Grigoryev, sit down.' Zhdanov walks up to Grigoryev and stands squarely within his personal space, spraying him with his warm, garlic breath. 'I have the militia breaking down the door to my apartment in Leningrad. My family are all terrified. Terrorised. I am being accused of smuggling heroin into the UK. Say they know for sure it is me, and him.' Zhdanov gives a flick of the head to where Sergei Dolgoruky looks ready to pounce on Grigoryev the moment his comrade steps aside. Zhdanov raises his right index finger towards Grigoryev's face, brandishing it as if a finger could damage him. 'How they know about this? They tell me they have an informer. Who can this be? Him?' He wags now at Dolgoruky. 'I know it is not him. But *you*, Alexei Grigoryev. *You* are maybe that man. Sure, you are an informer. With your books and music and painting. You are not like him and me.'

The stench of garlic fills Grigoryev's nostrils and diffuses into his lungs. He tries to edge backwards but Zhdanov places one of his great hands on the wall behind and moves in even closer. Grigoryev sinks his hands defensively into his jacket pockets. There is the cellulose fish. He has forgotten to give it to Sasha. A garlic mist from Zhdanov's breath settles in cool droplets on Grigoryev's mouth and eyes. He gives a shake of his head, and begins to speak. 'I did not do anything. I haven't talked to the militia …. '

'You lie. We watch you. We know you think you are a clever bastard. But you are a bastard. Traitor! We listen to you. We take you into our organisation. You make money. This is what you give back to us. How do you think we should treat a traitor, Alexei Grigoryev? What would you do to such a traitor?'

It is clear that Zhdanov has already decided the answer to that. He is fired up and not yet finished with Grigoryev.

'What you think? You are more honourable than me, than him?

You were against us dealing drugs. What is it to you if people want to kill themselves with narcotics? What business is it of yours?' They choose this life. *We* live hard life here. We find a way of making a difference, to make life better for *our* families and you want to stop this, Mr Moral Man who gives the police our names and scare *our families* in early morning raids.'

Grigoryev stiffens. 'I did no such thing.' His entreaty of innocence falls on deaf ears.

Zhdanov snarls. 'So how do you explain that police know about us meeting Taliban drug lords in May?'

Grigoryev continues with his denials so Zhdanov spells it out for him.

'At the markets in Tajikistan. On the border with Afghanistan.' And as if explaining it to a child, 'Where we exchanged guns for their heroin. They know we did not use money, only barter. Thirty Aks for one kilo of heroin.' He pauses with a look of self-satisfaction on his face as if allowing himself to appreciate the neat and profitable deal they'd pulled off. But Zhdanov's conceit is short-lived. 'So we know it is *you*, Alexei Grigoryev, who must be informing on our businesses selling these drugs to the West where people are happy to pay us a lot of money for them.'

Dolgoruky is bored of being left out and berates Grigoryev with his own accusations. 'Yes we know you are not with us, you piece of bloody shit. Then we find *that*,' he kicks out a booted foot in the direction of the radio receiver on the tiny balcony. 'What is *that*? Something big is going on with you. Maybe the police would be interested to know about *your* secret life, comrade Grigoryev, but we are first.' He picks up the picture Grigoryev has painted for Irina and smashes it against his knee. Irina stands up and begins to say something then swallows her words, her face a portrait of despair. The frame is split and the canvas hangs loose. Dolgoruky tosses it down to the floor and works his boot over it as if stubbing out a cigarette.

'The militia accuse us of arming the Taliban, of giving them Soviet machine guns, rifles, whatever – that kills our own people. So they want to hurt us. But maybe they have some scheme and want us out of way to get a bigger cut of the action for themselves. Maybe you are part of their plan. Is this why you tell on us, Mr Artist? You are just greedy, Mr Artist? You want more Helmand heroin for yourself and your new colleagues?'

The tension in the room is unbearable.

'This is between you and me,' Grigoryev says, attempting to calm things down. 'Let's go to the studio to talk about it.'

But it's clear neither Zhdanov nor Dolgoruky are listening to him.

'We settle this here,' snarls Zhdanov.

A shaken Grigoryev asks, rather hopelessly, 'What are you going to do?'

Zhdanov takes a step back, turns his shoulder and shoots Irina Grigoryeva clean through the face.

Grigoryev's legs buckle and he gives a low moan as Zhdanov informs him matter-of-factly, 'This.'

Alexei Grigoryev crawls to where his wife's body lies in the pretty white and pink cotton dress he likes to see her wear, with its pearl buttons running down the front. He notices she has on her white open-toed sandals with straps around her ankles. Grigoryev strokes those thin ankles and presses his head against the soft feet, feeling the cutting edge of the leather strap rough against his face. The buckle catches his wire, John Lennon spectacles and they fall from his eyes. Grigoryev clasps them in his hand and stands up but cannot bear to look at his wife's head.

'You have betrayed our organisation!' Dolgoruky is screaming. 'So you pay. You all will pay. You bloody shits.'

Grigoryev is still taking in what he has said, *Betrayed our organisation*, and realises that the only reason they've killed his beautiful wife is because he had been careless enough to get found out informing on their filthy, right-wing group and they will kill him and almost certainly his boy for that. Only for that. They know nothing about the bigger stuff. There will be no government statement denouncing him as a traitor to the USSR; no British denial that he is "one of ours"; no international outcry against continuing Cold War espionage which furthered the separation of people into friends and enemies. But he will now simply vanish.

Tart in the UK will arrange for someone else to replace him; there

226

will be no shortage of candidates. His brother Roddy will be the last of the Bells. He tries to think of everything that doesn't matter, to stop his mind contemplating what might be in store for the boy. If he is lucky, they will kill him cleanly and quick. Should he plead for the boy's life? He decides no. Both Dolgoruky and Zhdanov are psychopaths and that might only spur them on to making young Sasha's death long and difficult.

Aberdeen

Ian Ross had telephoned his editor, who in turn had phoned Aberdeen's police Chief Superintendent, who had then informed Young and Millar that they had better know what they were getting into or their private lives would end up over a two-page spread in the Sundays. This may go part way to explaining Young's and Millar's inability to make any headway with Ian Ross. He was sticking to his story that any associations in Ulster were strictly professional and once he had completed his work there he would be glad to leave it behind. Young was inclined to believe him. She had never shared Millar's speculation that Ian Ross' political views meant he was a dangerous blackmailer. Millar stuck to his guns, he was certain Ross was hiding something that might be relevant to the TAG case.

'You don't like big business, do you, Mr Ross?' Millar cannot contain his dislike for the newspaper man.

Ian Ross knows Millar is just being coy. He wants to accuse him of being a lefty, agitator, commie.

'Agent provocateur,' Millar throws into the mix.

Ross wonders what is coming next. Too much contact with authority makes him uneasy. He hopes his editor is doing all he can to get the police off his back.

DS Millar takes a notebook from his pocket. 'What d'you know about a Colin Riddle? Ulster. Come across him?' He's watching Ross closely and thinks he sees a faint smile on his lips but the reporter presses those same lips together and shakes his head.

'This is going nowhere.' Bonnie Young looks at her watch

impatiently. She's feeling as frustrated as Millar by Ross' unco-operative behaviour but knows they'll get nowhere with him.

'We'll have to let him go.' DI Young replaces the phone receiver. 'The Chief wants to know why we're still holding him.' Dave Millar scratches his head and stares hard at his boss but Young returns the defiant look. 'C'mon, we've nothing on him. You've not turned up anything to tie him into Brigadier Bell's little problem other than he's been in Northern Ireland recently and, if that's all we have on him, there must be an awful lot of suspects out there. We have to let him go.'

Millar groans and starts fiddling with a biro. 'Riddle…. I know there's something fishy there.' There's an audible sigh from Young. 'And just where does Ross come into the picture? All I'm hearing is Riddle and precious little about anything he's done that links him with any of this.'

'Well, I think there might be something in it, y'know?'

'If you have something then let me have it. Don't keep stuff from me, Dave. I need to know what you know.'

Dave Millar is uncomfortable. Young picks up on it.

'Well? Is there anything else? Come on.'

'And what about this punter Hugh Bell, the brother of the Brigadier?' DS Millar throws back his head. 'I'm sure there's a tie in with MacMillan's death.'

Bonnie Young knows Dave Millar has been after every promotion going without success. She imagines it could have something to do with the way he flies every kite he stumbles across. Young claps her hands. 'We'll have to drop this for now, Dave. Wouldn't life be nice and simple if all our enquiries led to one conclusion? Unless you've something concrete to connect these guys, which you haven't.'

'There's this.' Millar rummages around his desk.

'What?'

Millar hands Young a number scrawled on a piece of paper.

'And?' Young shrugs, not comprehending. 'Whose number is it?'

'None other than our blackmailed Brigadier's.'

'You're keeping me in suspense again, Dave. Where did it come from?'

'Spotted it on a fag packet in Ross' room, that's all. Picked it up when we fingered him.'

'And you're only telling me now? Okay, let's ask him.'

'He's not going to say anything, is he?'

'Perhaps not but we have to ask, anyway.'

'Maybe we should root around a bit more first. Then hit him with whatever we find.'

The Chief Superintendent's head appears round the door. 'A word, Bonnie, please.'

'So that's it. Ross is free to go. And that's not all. The Chief says to cool it with Shaw down at TAG,' Young says to Millar when he comes back with their coffees.

'Yeah?' Millar whistles softly through his teeth. 'He's obviously the sensitive type. Was it something we said?'

'Mmm. Makes you think, I admit,' DI Young seems distant.

Dave Millar leans over his desk. 'The Chief's turning out to have more strings than Pinocchio.' He blows on the hot coffee.

Bonnie Young puts on a face, 'Just don't ask me. It's curious, though.'

'Curiouser and curiouser. So what are we going to do about Ross? Up he pops, puts in an appearance at TAG HQ and then MacMillan decides to take a short cut across the railway line.'

The DI, however, is having none of it. 'As I said, Dave, we've nothing on him. Look, he's just a reporter who knows a lot about what's going on in Ulster. He's come back here on holiday, like he says. Coincidences. They happen you know. For a guilty man, he's behaving boringly normal. My bet is he'll take off south soon and it won't make a bit of difference to the case.'

'I still think we're missing something. Okay, so I can't prove it but I'd put money on Ross being mixed up in some way.'

'Come on, Dave, let it go.'

A frustrated Detective Sergeant Millar holds his tongue. She's right, he grudgingly admits to himself. Since coming north, Millar has struggled to fit in with its culture of quiet plod, which he assumed had gone out with Sergeant Dixon. Oil capital it might be but to him it is just another small town hanging off the edge. Millar has convinced himself of a link between Ross and Brigadier Bell. Why else would Ross be carrying the Brigadier's telephone number? Unless it wasn't the Brigadier he was in touch with but Margaret Bell? he muses. Now that he might understand. He considers mentioning this to the DI but decides to keep it under his hat for the present. She'd not listen. That is also the reason he hasn't told her about the phone call to his former colleague when he found out Brigadier Bell's file was security blocked. His contact had whispered that the Brigadier was tied in with military strategy in Northern Ireland. She couldn't elaborate. Told him he'd get no further. Warren of dead ends.

DI Young knows Millar keeps records of his work in personal notebooks. She'd asked him about it once but Millar had shrugged it off.

'Just something I've done since I was a kid. Got into the habit.' The routine of keeping his diary has become second nature to him. He became a prodigious writer-downer but the irregular hours mean he finds it difficult to keep his notes up-to-date so he has taken to carrying a notebook with him and jotting down observations whenever he can grab a minute. Colleagues and family pull his leg that one day he will write them up into a book and sometimes Millar likes the sound of that but it isn't his motivation. They have simply become an obsession.

Back in the office, Millar looks back on his impressions of Ian Ross and decides he is a man with powerful friends; the proverbial Teflon-coated hack. Millar digs his elbows into his desk. It makes him sick that Young has submitted so easily to pressure from the Chief Superintendent. It isn't that he dislikes Young, in fact, when he first arrived he quite took to her. Everyone does. She is one of the lads. Not like some of the skirts who wear political correctness like badges of honour so that he has to be constantly guarded in what he says. The point being driven home the time someone reported him for a comment made over lunch in the canteen. That was why he was assigned to Young. Being under a woman DI was seen as the best learning curve for him.

Moscow

Robert Coulthard draws the curtains and fetches a leather holdall from a shelf in the wardrobe. He's in two minds. Part of him is all for upping and leaving. Just getting out. His other self is cautioning against rash decisions. "Never run away from your responsibilities, men, they'll catch up with you eventually." Coulthard tosses the bag to the floor. Closes his eyes. Was it Dinger's way of manipulating him? All that talk about his men. His team. "All in this together, boys." He didn't see many of the others when he was up to his neck in it with the UUF. Where was Dinger then? Sitting pretty back in HQ. If he'd gone down, they, Tart, Dinger's real boys, would have sent a wreath. Laurel. Discrete. Nothing showy. Aunty Madge won't forget you. A lone piper might play 'Flowers o' the Forest'. He'd never know.

Aberdeen: evening

The Chief Superintendent chats amicably with Margaret Bell, who looks every bit the radiant hostess, at TAGOil's reception for senior staff and their peers from the business world: oil and gas executives, representatives from fishing and farming, plus a sprinkling of local MPs, councillors and local authority bureaucrats.

Brigadier Roderick Bell is full of admiration for the way his brother's widow works the floor. She is utterly enchanting, as his wealthy associates never tire of telling him, hinting with knowing looks that he could do worse than consider making her Mrs Bell twice around. That Margaret Bell might be otherwise inclined never occurs to these smug, alcohol-sodden bores who measure achievement in profit margins and attendance at such social events. They enjoy rubbing shoulders with the charmingly amiable Brigadier Bell, deaf to his own caustic views of them as shallow tentative creatures who will leave no lasting legacy despite their wealth and positions.

All three of the young Bells had left the family home with the well-rehearsed words of their father ringing in their ears that any society was only as good as the contribution of its individuals and that each man should be prepared to sacrifice himself for the greater good. A credo adopted by two of his three sons.

When the drawing-room door swings open, Brigadier Bell spots Stanley Shaw sneaking into the kitchen. TAG's Financial Director is something of an unknown quantity to the Brigadier. Frequently away on business trips and a bit of a loner, in the Brigadier's view. He's made a point of reminding Shaw he is welcome to bring along a guest but as usual he has turned up on his own. Brigadier Bell once asked Donald MacMillan if he thought Shaw might be "one of those." A suggestion dismissed by MacMillan. Bell was not persuaded but abandoned his attempts at matchmaking after unsuccessfully encouraging Shaw and Margaret to attend a formal dinner together in the Beach Ballroom.

'Margaret, can you talk?'

Margaret Bell is in the kitchen where she's checking that the caterers are keeping up with demand for refreshments in the drawing room.

'Not now, Stanley, can't you see I'm busy? The long dark hair falls forward as Margaret Bell rearranges savoury bites into regimental rows.

'I'm away for the next few days. I need to speak to you.'

'Okay, but not now. I've starving guests to see to.'

21. BASHER AND BROTHERS

Aberdeen: Tuesday 13 August 1991

Following his hasty departure from Mrs Milne's guest house, Ian Ross moved his possessions a few hundred yards along Crown Street, nearer the Union Street end. This time he didn't bother unpacking, he had no intention of spending more time in Aberdeen than he had to. He was making connections alright but not of his choice. But there was the outstanding matter of Brigadier Bell still to be resolved.

A woman answers his telephone call and Ross waits while she goes to fetch the Brigadier. She comes back onto the line to ask his name.

'Tell him it's Ian Ross. We share a mutual acquaintance.'

'Ian? Is that you?'

'Who is this?' Ross is thrown by her familiarity.

'Ellen. Ellen MacHardy that was.'

'Ellen! Hi, Ellen! Sorry, didn't recognise the voice. But … what're you doing there? I was given this as Brigadier Roderick Bell's number,' begins a surprised Ian Ross.

'Yeah, yeah,' her voice is soothing, 'I'm his nurse. He's no … ' she stops herself saying more.

Ross cuts in, 'I heard. Look, great to hear you, Ellen, but I need to speak to him. Is he there?'

'Ian, look, I hope yer nae bringing him trouble.' There is concern in her tone.

'Ellen? Don't know what you mean. I just need to talk t'him, that's all. C'mon, Ellen.'

'You're always mixing it, Ian. That's what you do. Which is good. But he's nae weel. Just dinna get me involved. How are ye, by the way?'

'Doing pretty well. And yourself? Been ages since we met up.'

'Well, I've been here. It's a while since you've been home, maybe?'

Ross agrees. It has been. The hotel's pay phone is guzzling cash coins and Ian is frantically searching his pockets for loose change, he hears a muffled conversation in his earpiece followed by a refined male voice taking over the call. The manner is abrupt. Asks Ross what he wants. Feeding the call box with the last of his money, the reporter answers, 'I'm determined to speak with you, Bell. I won't just disappear.'

'What is it you want?' the Brigadier repeats.

'I want us to meet and have a talk.'

'I've already said I have no intention of speaking to the newspapers. You've a nerve .... '

'I'll write what I have in that case, without your perspective.'

'You won't get it published. I've already had a word with Alistair. He's most concerned you're now the focus of the police's attention.'

Alastair McNaughton is Ross' newspaper editor. A rich, conceited, overbearing type, not averse to suppressing articles which might embarrass his pals.

'I'll go freelance,' rejoins Ross.

'Not to be recommended, sunshine. A recipe for a brief career move, I'd say.'

Ross imagines the supercilious smirk behind the remark. It is clear that Brigadier Bell considers himself untouchable and with good reason.

Brigadier Bell's circle comprises a self-sustaining network of self-serving, powerful and rapacious individuals and families who determine boundaries for British society. The Bells had served in the three most powerful of Britain's services – military, intelligence and diplomatic – and are used to dealing with irritants like him. Try as he might to uncover the tangled web of deceit and collusion between the army and RUC Ulster, Ross' allegations are met with flat denials or obfuscation. It's a shock, to Ross however, that his editor has allowed himself to be intimidated. And if the Brigadier has scared off McNaughton then life is going to get a whole lot harder.

'I'm willing to take that risk,' Ross rasps back down the line. His throat is dry; the start of a cold or apprehension? Best not to think about it. 'But as the cops are still sniffing around, we'd better make it well out of town unless you want them circling you as well. I'll meet you at Stonehaven harbour front in an hour.'

'Out of the question. I can't get away at the moment. I have a diary full of appointments.'

'Or I'll turn up at your door, or TAGOil, wherever you happen to be.'

Moscow

The wind roaring along Prospekt Marx feels as if it has blown straight in from the arctic, not that Robert Coulthard is concerned with the temperature. He is on the lookout for faces, familiar or suspicious. He nips into a bar, mainly to use the lavatory, and is startled at his reflection staring out from the filthy cracked mirror. What, he wonders, do people see when they look at me? Eyes, the mirror of the soul.

Dodging in and out of shops, taking off down side streets, crossing roads, retracing his steps, loitering to see who goes by again. It takes him longer than it would most to get back to his hotel. Not that the hotel is secure. Staffed round the clock by double-timers, regular shift personnel picking up second salaries for informing on guests and their movements. Feeding government or crime syndicates; indispensable eyes and ears of the great machinery of state, from burly concierge to diminutive elderly needlewomen darning the sheets.

The last time Robert Coulthard felt this insecure was five years ago on Belfast's Falls Road. The point he knew he had to get out of Mire and out of Ulster. Only a matter of time before he'd be exposed as a plant within the UUF. There had to be quick footwork from the Joint Force for Research to circulate credible false information to the loyalists to buy him time, which is how Tony Pagliari became another statistic of the Troubles.

Alarm bells began ringing the moment the UUF discovered two of its members were, in fact, Mire walk-ins. That's how the JFR gets most of its intelligence – plants and walk-ins. Turned out the girlfriend of one of them, a guy named Robert Keenan, discovered their secret so she had to disappear. But, by then, she'd already let the cat out of the bag. No surprise then when the pair were picked off the street and held in a UUF cold store in east Belfast. Coulthard didn't know how long they'd been held there but when he saw them they looked in a poor way. They'd been stripped and were trembling. From the cold, clearly, but mostly from the sheer terror of what lay ahead. Coulthard had had to do his bit. Taunting and burning. Cigarettes mainly but someone had taken in a poker. This was never what he signed up for. But he knew when he agreed to become Cassidy's man inside the UUF that life wasn't going to be a birthday party.

To be honest, a small part of him didn't mind the violence too much. Take those two in the cold store: they'd killed a young woman so had to take the consequences. But he couldn't prevent the nagging doubts at the back of his mind that his handler Cassidy's reassuring justifications could never excuse his behaviour completely.

For the RUC they were just another couple of mutilated corpses dumped by the side of the road. The post-mortem report showed that death was caused by two shots to the head. There was no mention in the report of how long and hard the men had begged their brothers in the UUF for their lives or perhaps their deaths. Struck Coulthard as odd that a man could be undergoing horrible torture and plead to be allowed to live, prolonging his suffering. All the time he was there in the stinking torture chamber he was thinking about his own precarious situation. Made up his mind then to make a bolt for it. A fresh start somewhere new. Once again. Or he could go back to being himself, he toyed with the notion. If he could remember who the hell he was.

The memory of those days never stayed away for long. Little wonder. They was something. Almost immediately after they'd dumped the youths' bodies, speculation had been rife about a British agent embedded within a republican group and then the possibility that the loyalists too had been infiltrated. This all coincided with an old photograph of the Queen inspecting British forces in Berlin turning up in a *Look back at Yesterday* feature in the *Belfast Times*. Clear for everyone to see in the line up of troops on parade none other than himself. He'd contacted his handler at Castlereagh Barracks and it was decided there and then that he had no future in the province.

In the Berlin days, Captain Cassidy, as Dinger was then known, had misread the wild streak in his young squaddie as nothing more than a youthful search for excitement. He felt pity for the boy, for the traumas he'd been through – his father convicted of murder. It didn't occur to Dinger that there might have been mental instability there. Besides that, fear and self-pity were never part of Dinger's character and he didn't probe too deeply into the boy's make-up. Yet he recognised something fragile in it. Fragility could be an advantage in the kind of men he was looking for. Not really men yet but they would become them one day. Dinger learned how to sustain his young charges. Provide the support each desperately sought though they might not know it. He saw something vulnerable in the raw recruit: his mood swings, a reckless disregard for his own safety which threatened to impinge on others if not directed.

Aberdeen area

Ian Ross had taken the coastal train the fifteen or so miles south from Aberdeen and walked the short distance downhill from the little railway station to the harbour. He's sitting on a bench outside one of the hotels, staring out over the water and up to the Bervie Braes, when a silver Mercedes purrs around the corner, drawing up alongside him. Ross slips into the passenger seat. Brigadier Bell reverses and they drive past the courthouse and up to the cliff top ruin of Dunottar Castle without a word being exchanged. The Brigadier parks and leads the journalist down the grassy slope towards the cliffs.

Ross breaks the impasse. 'So we meet again, Brigadier.'

Brigadier Bell is concentrating on placing his feet on the slippery path.

'I wasn't aware we had met … '

'Not met in a formal sense, I attended one of your briefings – in a scruffy community hall in Derry.'

'I don't think … ' begins the Brigadier.

'It's all very different now by the looks of things. Businessman and all.'

Ross watches the Brigadier but doesn't detect much change in his demeanour. He's convinced the Brigadier would have seen his piece on TAGOil in which he referred to his new role as its Chief Executive, and that Brigadier Bell wouldn't have been too happy about the publicity.

The frail figure before him has retained the bearing of a serving officer: the stance, straight back, head tilted back, self-assurance which doesn't invite understanding, which is just as well as Ross has none to give him. With Dunottar stretching verdant and rocky to the right, the two adversaries stand side by side, awkward in each other's company.

'I know your association with Wright,' begins Ross, watching the other for a reaction.

Brigadier Bell goes on the offensive. 'Not a word until I'm sure you're clean.' The strong voice belying the thin, sick body.

Ian Ross holds up his hands. 'I'm not wired.'

Brigadier Bell attempts to reach into Ross' jacket pocket but the younger man steps back.

'I check or nothing,' insists the Brigadier and expertly frisks Ross.

Ross can't understand why he's jittery and hopes it doesn't come over in his voice. By contrast, the Brigadier exudes all the confidence in the world.

'I served in Northern Ireland, of course I know the man. He's a key figure there.'

'Indeed he is, Bell.' Ian Ross stresses the name and pursues his quarry. 'He's right up there, the government's man in the north; protected and empowered to wreak the kind of havoc helpful to the Union.'

'You're getting carried away with your own rhetoric, man,' the Brigadier cuts in.

'Am I? So why has the British state been acting like his nanny? Why did your own unit cosy up to one of Ulster's most notorious terrorists? Don't you think that makes your hands as bloody as his? There's no way he could have survived this long without having the backing of the British government. And your own intelligence unit colluded all the way with him and his mob. All very cosy and very repellent.'

238

'I might agree with you if it were true, but it's a complete fabrication, of course. My advice to you, Mr Ross, is to go back to where you came from, taking your absurd allegations with you. If there was anything worth printing about me it would be in the papers by now but you've nothing, nothing at all because there's nothing to tell. You're only trying to make a name for yourself at the expense of my reputation. Now if that's all you have to say … '

But Ian Ross is not to be put off quite so summarily. 'It's all going to come out. Some day people will know exactly what the government was doing in Northern Ireland, and Gibraltar of course … '

'Come, come, Mr Ross. I wasn't even there. C'mon, we both know you're not going anywhere with this. I wouldn't have thought you naive but I'm afraid that's precisely how you appear. You barge into my life making all manner of accusations about some underhand goings on … without a shred of evidence. Where wars are fought, nasty things happen. That's just how it is. Brave people have to put their lives on the line to carry out actions that most wouldn't consider … but they may be necessary. I've never commanded anything remotely illegal. Look, from time to time a man might see things he doesn't like and perhaps someone's squealed to you. I don't know. But what kind of man is prepared to place his own country in danger because his conscience has been pricked? As I say, a lot of bad things happen in war. No-one knows everything that goes on. No-one.'

'Not even you?' Ross presses him to say more.

'Not me. Now you may think you have the moral high ground here but war is a dirty business and we had to play the enemy at their own game. It ill becomes you and your lefty comrades, cowering behind our splendid boys who daily face up to death, to complain about what's done to preserve Britain's security.'

'So it is a war, then? There's some who'd deny that.'

Brigadier Bell examines a cloudless blue sky. Men like Ross are thorns in the flesh which must be endured. In the world of journalism he might enjoy the reputation of being a principled hack but to Brigadier Bell, Ross is simply a despicable individual hell-bent on trying to destroy him. He has faced tougher enemies in his time and Brigadier Bell reckons he has little to fear from Ross' pen. Lowering his sights from the sky, the Brigadier fixes his shrewd eyes on Ross and thinks he might have found his blackmailer. Looking more closely at the pasty pinched face, Brigadier Bell reads disquiet and wonders just what Ian Ross' concerns are. But the thought is quickly shrugged off. It could be that Ross might soon be making his own headlines? There is no question, he will have to mention this to Tart.

On the way back to the car, Brigadier Bell underlines his position. 'My role in the province is all in the past. I'm out of the army. Been so for years … '

Ross shakes his head. 'You don't just retire from something like this. You're responsible not only for the deaths of suspected IRA people but for innocent civilians too.'

'Steady on, man. This has gone too far. Anything I did then was strictly official and in accordance with my duties. I had … '

Ross cuts across him, 'Precisely! The government's Northern Ireland policy was built on collusion with a bunch of thugs and criminals. And then there's Colin Riddle. I was speaking to a source down south who gave this guy a name check and then, what d'you know, it's the same name came up from a pal of mine. Coincidence or what? Now I can't find my pal, but you're here. What I've gathered is that this Riddle is tied in with you. That he's a useful man to have in a crisis is Mr Riddle. Your flexible friend: agent, courier, dealer, fixer, stringer – I believe he's been the lot. I've found out that your unit, Green Mire, passed on dossiers to loyalist paramilitaries that led to them shooting Tony Pagliari to protect this Riddle. Riddle jumps to your tune.'

Brigadier Bell looks as if he is suffering from premature rigor mortis. 'Look, I've given you enough of my time … '

★ ★ ★

Detective Sergeant Millar had been going through material on the Bell case, determined to discover what, if anything, Ian Ross had to do with Donald MacMillan's unexplained death and the TAG blackmail.

He's hunched over his computer, tapping on his grey mouse, and watching the menu screen appear. Clicking on an item, he scrolls down the page, cursing the time it's taking. The technical guys should have been in to repair it last week. He steadies the cursor over an entry marked *Strictly Classified* and notes down its ID reference and the few biographical details that appear: date of birth – 19 February 1936; place of birth – Germany; school – Robert Gordon's College, Aberdeen; career – army cadets, commission based in England and the USA, retired from the army into commercial industry in Scotland, TAGOil. Bare-bones.

DS Millar smiles wryly. Concealment of information being the modus operandi for the body of state whose function, on the surface at least, is exposure. His brief secondment to Special Branch had opened Millar's eyes to the extent of accumulated intelligence gathered, collated and archived on people living in Britain. Remarkable, given the conceit of the system, that it is somehow more open and accountable than everywhere else in the world.

The designated ID at the top right of the page confirms the file is available for authorised viewing only. Millar follows a cross-reference from Roderick Bell to two other Bells. Hugh Bell's education and business career are listed along with his move into oil and the establishment of TAGOil, and his disappearance and grim discovery by a party of school children walking by Loch Muick.

Millar lifts the phone. Someone still owes him one and he is calling in the debt.

★ ★ ★

'It's no longer a secret, Brigadier.' There's irritation in Ross' tone of voice. 'So it's only a matter of time before the whole story comes out. Naturally, I want to have a hand in it when it does. Talk to me and we'll see what can be done to play down your role in this circus macabre.'

Brigadier Bell snorts. 'Just who the hell do you think you are? You think you can come here and undo me? You think you have any influence with anybody? Well, I know something about you, Ross. You're not the only one who keeps tabs. Not the squeaky clean protector of the public interest you like to paint yourself to be.

Remember, we had intelligence on every reporter covering the Troubles in the seventies and eighties and to say many were rotten to the core would be no exaggeration. Frequently came across your name.' Brigadier Bell shakes his head, the pretence of his being unfamiliar with Ross has been laid aside. 'We set you up more than once. Didn't know about that then, did you?'

Ian Ross squints at a reinvigorated Brigadier.

'As I recall, you had your own special relationships with some dubious characters, one being a certain James McKerny. He fed you titbits about IRA movements and in return you'd pass on what you'd picked up on the grapevine. What you didn't realise was the grapevine was being cultivated by our boys so, whatever you discovered, we wanted you to know. Like the faithful lapdog you were of the IRA, off you'd scuttle to McKerny. Sad to say, you delivered one message too many for Mr McKerny's good. Perhaps you remember the day word got out that loyalists were going to attack the home of Councillor Joe Nicholas? An easy rumour to circulate. Nicholas lived with his mother in that old, rundown farm of theirs and, well, he'd made lots of unionist enemies in his time. Get into bother in that neck of the woods and there was little use in crying for help. Only the old lady to hear. We made sure you got to know and, of course, what you knew was whispered into the ear of McKerny who, true to form, assembled a bevy of IRA beauties dutifully dispatched to ambush the UUF. Sadly, there were no UUFs there at all, only our boys who stumbled on a car full of paddy gangsters armed to the armpits and obviously intent on no good. When cautioned, they tried to escape, tried to run one of our boys off the road, so what alternative was there but to open fire? Zig-zagged all over the road did their little car, zig-zagged until it came to a halt halfway up a tree. A spectacular success. Everyone said so. Couldn't take the credit, of course. We gave that to the regulars but we're all brothers under the uniform. So, there you go. You contributed to clearing out some of Ulster's seedier characters and didn't even know it. Some were good friends of yours, I believe.'

Ian Ross feels pole axed. He can neither talk nor think straight. He frantically tries to remember. He remembers. Couldn't forget. He was speaking of McKerny. McKerny had supplied him with a lot of background for his articles. Supplied him material for several of the pieces he'd sent off to London. He'd grown to like the man, spent time with him and his family. A great big family of daughters, girls of all ages between two and fifteen. Thought the world of those girls did Jimmy. Ross remembers their kitchen always warm and smelling of pancakes and scones. Always buzzing with life. One of the children begging her dad to play, to throw her up into the air and catch her safely in his arms. Wee girls screaming with excitement at the thrill, breathless with giggles, imploring their daddy to *Do it again*. Deirdre was the oldest and the serious one. She had lost the happy-go-lucky recklessness of her siblings. More mature than many at her age. They'd got Jimmy as well. Ross pictures those same girls, distraught, gasping with anxiety when he called in to pay his respects after it happened. No more swings around the family kitchen. Deirdre comforted her young sisters, dry-eyed in shock, her darkest nightmares about her daddy in the Derry badlands had been realised.

Ross can't look at the Brigadier. Had he let himself be duped? Blindly falling into British intelligence's well-formulated scheme. He'd underestimated them.

Beyond the tumbling parapets of Dunottar a black and white inshore fishing boat is clinging to the coast as it makes its way northwards.

Atoms of recall are spinning out of control in Ross' mind. *A word, Ian. Look out for Riddle but he goes by different names. From your neck of the woods. One of Mire's lot. Go for Bell, and you've got him.*

Two men cleaning the deck. He is sick to the pit of his stomach. Let Jimmy down. Couldn't let anyone more down than getting them shot. When he looks up it's into the composed features of Brigadier Bell. No show of malicious pleasure. Ian Ross is determined not to let him off the hook. 'You've another man deep under cover with the IRA, haven't you?'

Bell looks skyward. 'Absolute nonsense. These things just don't happen in this country. It's people like you who put our servicemen's lives on the line. Quite disgraceful. Quite disgraceful.'

MI5 did not advertise Bell's role in Ulster, in fact, it had gone to considerable lengths to keep his name from the press and Ian Ross had been one of the most determined hacks, ferreting away to lay open the murky closed world of civil and military intelligence to public scrutiny. The atoms are gyrating furiously in his sceptic's brain. Riddle. Why hadn't he twigged when Tommy mentioned the man? Only later, when he heard it again, when he'd called down south. Then he'd punted it back to Tommy or had Tommy punted it back to him? He can't get it clear. In Ma Cameron's, and Tommy MacHardy mentioned something about Riddle's reaction to his exposé in *The Irish Times* about allegations of shady alliances between Mire and the Royal Ulster Constabulary. Tommy said Riddle had dismissed it as 'A fucking load of old shite,' and, that he'd said 'the poncy press in London know bugger all about Ireland.'

Tommy laughed it off as the drink talking. Told Ross Riddle was obsessed with Ireland, had given him the lowdown about its history: at the time of the First World War when the Tories had vowed to ignite civil war if the British government didn't pull back from creating an independent Irish state and how a former British colonel had revived the Ulster Volunteer Force to resist republicanism and defend Ulster. Then when Ross had asked Tommy's own opinion, Tommy MacHardy hadn't seemed very interested. 'Know nothing aboot it, mate, but Colin was right worked up, like.'

★ ★ ★

It is usual for Dave Millar's shoulders to slump in relaxation once he closes his front door on the world but today his shoulders are saying something different to him. The key turns in the door no differently. Millar's left hand pushes open the door no differently. He steps inside no differently but the shoulders remain tense. Dave Millar stops, tilts his head and listens but and hears nothing. In the sitting room a couple of jackets are slung from chairs where they have been for days. A handful of loose change is scattered on the telephone table. Nothing out of the ordinary.

His life. He goes into the bathroom. Usual mess. Tap still dripping into the wash basin from his rush to get out. The bedroom is deserted as he hoped it would be. Unkempt bed, its covers pulled hastily across, pillow still dented from his sleeping head. In the kitchen he discovers he'd forgotten to empty the bin for the morning's refuse collection. Its black plastic liner bulges out over the top. Dirty coffee cup and side plate with sticky knife just where they'd been abandoned at breakfast. The lobby cupboard door lies ajar. Millar prods it with his outstretched hand. The door swings back, crashing against the wall creating a nervous ripple through his body.

The Detective Sergeant's senses are on red alert despite being surrounded by the normality of his domestic life. His head speaks to his shoulders. Tells them to relax. But the shoulders have a mind of their own.

Back into the bedroom. Millar pulls at the wardrobe doors. Nothing. He drops to his knees and checks under the bed although there are scarcely eight inches between it and the floor. Systematically he re-visits each room. Cupboards. Behind curtains. The shoulders must have got it wrong. Something, his nose is telling him. A faint odour? Perfume perhaps. Not his. Someone has been in. He is sure now. Trouble is, his place always looks as if it has had a good going over but the scent ... careless of whoever has been in.

Millar pours himself a mug of coffee, feeling the steam, hot and moist, against his face. Nothing, as far as he can tell, has been taken. So it isn't robbery. Reluctantly he concludes it must be connected to his awakening a slumbering giant.

The visitors were obviously highly professional so why wear perfume that would linger? The more Dave Millar thinks about it, the more he realises the scent has not been an oversight on their part. Quite the contrary, it is a visitor card, a subtle Post-it, to make sure he gets the message. Now that he's tuned into their frequency, Millar begins to see their tracks like footprints in the snow: a coffee jar at the tea side of the cupboard; the morning's post he had riffled through at breakfast and left by the toaster is neatly stacked against the bread bin; the soap dish at the wrong end of the bath; cushions on his chair and sofa switched over. Tiny clues to someone else's presence. Tiny clues but deliberately obvious so he would know he is under surveillance.

★ ★ ★

'You were promoted to Brigadier during your stint in NI. Must have pleased someone.' The question draws no response. Wasn't a question. Ian tries again.

'In '66 the UVF firebombed a girls' school in Ardoyne.'

'Where did that come from?' Brigadier Bell laughs. 'I assure you that was well before my time in Ulster.'

'And then they went on to kill an old lady, a protestant.'

'And you think this had something to do with me, do you? You're out of your mind.'

'I've never killed an old lady,' retorts Ross.

'And, I assure you, neither have I. Satisfied? War is no Sunday school picnic.'

'Like the UVF killing twenty-eight people, mostly women and children, on 17th May 1974.'

'The IRA were at it too.'

'We remember IRA bombs but strangely forget UVF's. And that day the killings were meant to put a stop to the plans for power sharing in Ulster, were they not?'

Roderick Bell adjusts a cuff. The black and white boat is rounding the headland. Both men watch it sail out of view.

'And what can you tell me about Cassidy?' Ian Ross throws the name into the mix.

Roderick Bell buttons up his jacket. Composed but perhaps a chink in the armour; Ross has noticed. Had he not been up close, he might have missed it. A slight flicker across the gaunt cheeks.

Cassidy went way back to the time he was freelancing in Berlin, covering stories about East Berliners attempting to escape over the Wall. Best stuff came from squaddies oiled by the booze. Used to go on pub crawls with them. One began blabbing about a fellow Gordon Highlander, an officer called Cassidy. This Cassidy had grown his own team of agents and ran them throughout West Germany and, according to the squaddie, the East as well. Cassidy, he hinted, was the cover name to protect the fluent German-speaking officer engaged in anti-communist activities. 'Infiltrated the Easty Beasties,' he'd blurted out just as his mates joined them. They weren't half as drunk as him and not so press friendly.

Ross recalled an incident when a colleague among Berlin's press pack passed a remark about a rising star in the British army who'd been promoted to colonel and transferred to Ulster. The same Cassidy, he presumed, who turned up there in charge of a unit operating virtually outside of the law; rumoured it had carte blanche over its operations. No accountability. That's power. Then Cassidy slipped under the radar until a whisper linking him with Bell.

'You're lucky you've made it this far, Brigadier. Imagined it would be easy to vanish into this backwater? Except you haven't really. Vanished, I mean. I've known others run and reinvent themselves this side of the Irish Sea but they don't usually hog the limelight. Is it an ego problem you have or is it the Goebbels' dictum to tell a lie as big as you can so they'll swallow it? We're onto you, man.' Ross doesn't get the feeling he's shaking Bell's confidence for the man he's confronting continues to ooze complete self-control.

It would surprise Ross to know that Bell's demeanour defies his true emotions. It's frustrating for the Brigadier that his health is so diminished and fragile in the face of Ross' onslaught. The indignant, oh-so-righteous Ian Ross; haranguer of the establishment, Conservative government and all-things military. Who is he, anyway? Self-styled liberal conscience for the middle classes who makes a good living writing about the very things he professes to despise. He can condemn army practice as vociferously as he likes but without it Ross would be a no-one going nowhere. Brigadier Roderick Bell can scarcely contain his loathing for the journalist.

'Look here, Ross! Where do you mean to go with this?' The Brigadier's tone is indignant. Ross shifts uncomfortably and before he can say anything Bell goes on the attack. 'Your everyday bloke on the street isn't interested in what happens in Ulster. He sees it as nothing but trouble. Happy to leave us to get on with it. You think you can just trample over someone's life making outrageous accusations which are bound to attract the attention of republican fanatics. Utterly irresponsible.' Bell's sick pallor flushes pinky-yellow and he pauses to clear his throat.

'I can cut and paste it so you don't come out too badly, but I need you to confirm what I have to convince my editor there's a story here,' Ross interrupts.

'You really expect me to co-operate with you?' Bell's voice is shrill. 'A pretty good offer considering what could be written. Readers will find it incredible you didn't have any qualms about working against the interests of the British army or the police in your twisted conception of patriotism.'

'That is an outrageous accusation!' The Brigadier is back on the offensive. 'Do you really think the British public gives a hoot about the claptrap you make up? Anything you think you've found is past history. You're talking about lies propagated by commies and IRA terrorists. Of course I've heard them and I can assure you there's no foundation to any of them. Look, nobody gives a monkey's about people like that, apart from a few fey liberals that is, and they can prattle on as much as they like, in the end it's people like me who make the difference, not the bleeding hearts.'

'But your game continues, Brigadier. You're still acting a role. Maybe it's time you got some recognition for your performances. Royal Variety show?' It's a rash, indulgent comment which Ross immediately regrets. He knows that if it wanted, Whitehall could easily slap an injunction on him.

Bell strides back to his car, turns over the engine, selects first gear and holds the clutch on bite while Ross hurries to take his place on the passenger seat.

'It doesn't really make any sense for me to speak to you, does it?' The Brigadier's anger is plain.

'Of course it does.' Ian Ross forces home the seatbelt buckle into its port.

The car picks up speed and Bell half turns to Ross. 'You're innocent in the ways of the world. You spin the line that you're exposing some dangerous element in UK security but you're missing the point, Ross. Whatever activities we carried out were always at the heart of Britain's national security.'

If he had been anyone else, Ross would feel sorry for the man next to him. Bell is sick. Looks it. Worn out. But it makes no difference to Ian Ross. Everything coming his way, Bell has brought on himself. He chose to play a lawless game behind a banner of loyalty to the state.

Brigadier Roderick Bell has already made up his mind to get Tart's help to deal with Ross in the light of his own state of health and the absence of Riddle. They owe him that at least. It's as much in Tart's interest as his own to keep the lid on the Ulster pot for a long time to come and it is imperative that Ross be prevented from jeopardising national security through his misguided principles. Ross would never understand the investment his men put into defending this country. The simplistic analysis he applied to his news stories, describing the casualties of the struggle for peace in Ulster as victims of mindless violence when in fact they were often the result of precise operations. Heroes dressed to kill in mechanic's overalls smashing through flimsy doors, heavy boots pounding up narrow stairs, kicking down bedroom door after bedroom door, confused, half-asleep, hysterical naked targets. Never people. "Don't personalise them, boys. No point in making things more difficult for yourself. Heroes don't have time to wipe away tears. Heroes' maxim: all is fair in love and war. Heroes' number one weapon is fear. You can't argue with a bullet in the night."

They have almost completed the short car run back to Stonehaven when Ross asks, 'Brigadier, how long do you think it'll take for the whole story about your agent in NI to come out? This Riddle, for example. It's not as if I'm the only one uncovering this stuff and if I've been able to work out what's been happening, so can others.'

Bell is concentrating on the narrow curving road, with its steep descent into the town, and ignores his passenger.

'How many men and women have been killed to protect this one man at the top of the IRA? Is this what Riddle's been doing? How many others have been suspected of compromising IRA actions and been subjected to torture? Do you ever stop to think what it must have been like for these people?' Ross continues to hurl a barrage of questions at Bell.

They've arrived at the railway station before the Brigadier finds his voice.

'Don't waste any pity on them. IRA – people! Since when did they show pity for any of their victims, tell me that?'

'So are you judging your actions by the IRA's set of values? Is that what you're saying, Brigadier?'

The Brigadier looks for a place to pull in.

'Burned by cigarettes, hair set alight, shocks from cattle prods, heads submerged under water before the relief of a bullet through the brain. Could you tell which ones died because of you?' Ross fights the impulse to shut up. As Bell took delight in telling him, he's now implicated in one death at least and Jimmy McKerny's been praying on his mind ever since. Not knowing he was compromising Jimmy doesn't make him feel any better? His face colours. Ross can smell the decay from Bell's body swathed in a coat that has outgrown it. 'Did you actually save any lives as a result? One life? Or is it that no-one is quite sure who the bad guys and the good guys are anymore? It's clear your man took part in torture and murder. Did Riddle take part in torturing people? In murder? Was that how he was able to maintain his cover? It had to be like that. You couldn't risk drawing your man out into the open if too many bombings or robberies were compromised. No, the only way to avoid pointing fingers would be for him to get down and dirty like everyone else. None of the people interrogated would have gone easily, would they? A cigarette lighter under the nostrils, stamping or cutting or singeing for hour after terrifying hour before that final trip into the countryside where they'd be found dead in a ditch. A hard death, you might say, Brigadier, by the IRA's Nutting Squad. Any of them yours? Certainly they were. Government or military spooks dying by the hand of someone else undercover. And another peculiar thing: your unit didn't like sharing its intelligence with Special Branch or MI5. Why was that? Something to do with sacrificing another agency's agents? Who was innocent and who was guilty? Any idea how many we're talking here? Thirty? Forty? Fifty? Could you have saved any of them? Policemen and women, soldiers and ordinary Johns around Ulster. Thomas Nicholas in County Louth was one, wasn't he? Shot after passing on information on the IRA to the Guarda. Did you ever stop to count the number of lives you wrecked?'

Ross has succeeded only in silencing Bell, whose mouth under his trim moustache is a resolute line in the otherwise flaccid face. He knows he's only talking so much to stop seeing the faces of Jimmy's young daughters.

Ian Ross walks the short distance to the platform to wait for the next train back to Aberdeen. He's disappointed and he's desperate to get away from the place. Instead of finding the information he was after, he's become the centre of attention with the local constabulary and his editor's ready to put the knife in.

He books himself onto the early afternoon flight to Belfast and rings a friend at the *Sunday Herald* from the airport. They exchange some idle chit-chat. A colleague has suffered a fatal heart attack. The news shakes Ian. The three of them covered each other's backs in many a battle hotspot around the world. Ian Ross remembers something about his dead colleague when he realises Jim is saying something he hasn't quite caught. 'Say that again, Jim,'

'Best way to go. At least he didn't have to suffer a drawn-out death, unlike that wee shite Wright.'

'What d'you mean,' Ian's hand tightens on the receiver as he presses it hard against his ear. 'Wright's dead?'

'Yeah. I assumed you'd have heard. News not get all the way up there? Farm accident. Nothing suspicious. Son was driving. Tractor. Some bad injuries, took a while to finish him off but finish him off they did. Happened a day or two back. Didn't make much of a splash in the papers here. Bets on a spot of pressure from upstairs to smother it. But no loss, eh?'

'Look, James, good to hear you again. Meet up soon.'

Wright is dead. The tannoy is announcing immediate boarding of the Belfast flight. An accident, Jim said. Opportune for some, Ross is thinking. He hurries through security and into the departure lounge. It's further than he remembers. There's a final call for the flight. A member of the ground crew tears his boarding pass. 'You'll have to hurry, sir'.

As he picks up his bag, he's overtaken by a businessman; immaculate in a dark blue suit. Ross hopes he won't be sitting beside him. The bloke reeks of sweat.

Stanley Shaw settles back into seat 3A. He relaxes and flicks through the in-flight magazine. It was a piece of good fortune that Bell changed his mind about sending him to the conference in Ulster. The past couple of times he's been over he's had to pay his own fares.

'If you could hurry and take your seat, sir.' The air stewardess ushers Ian Ross down the aisle. He breathes a sigh of relief after row three. He doesn't have to sit beside the guy after all.

Shaw fastens his seatbelt. The flight will give him time to think. Is he wise trusting Margaret? She'd been behaving oddly. What if she says something to the police and the RUC are waiting when he disembarks? But that wouldn't make sense. He pulls a handkerchief from his pocket. If he had been under suspicion, the police would have arrested him before he boarded. And they would have found the letter on him. What game is Margaret playing? He's been the one taking all the risks. She could turn round and deny everything. Court will take her word against his; after all, she did get part of Hugh Bell's estate. Not as much as she'd wanted but something. He didn't even get a promotion. Why had he let her persuade him that getting the police in to investigate would be a good idea – to cover her – knowing she'd be the last one suspected? Had she outwitted him? Stanley Shaw looks down on the diminutive houses and pocket-sized fields and feels hot and bothered.

★ ★ ★

Millar starts up his computer. His files are still there. He can't think how to discover if anyone has been in looking at them but he is convinced they have. Double clicking on the recycle bin, Millar's saliva runs dry. It is empty. Evidently the garbage man has called and cleaned up. There is only one thing for him to do: start worrying. He's already there.

Millar knows he has to get back into work without drawing attention to himself. Already he's dispensed with the idea of waiting until the following day. For him it seems that time is an asset in short supply.

The handful of detectives at work hardly acknowledge his arrival as Dave makes straight for his desk. There is no sign that anyone has been in the drawer. It is locked, but he knows they have been in it. Why would they turn over his flat and not his desk? Still, he hopes they haven't taken what he hopes to find. They have. Fortunately he'd already taken away much of the documentation he had been gathering but what had been left in the desk has vanished. The Ross folder is there and a couple of documents but everything else has gone. Millar looks around. He thinks of trying Bonnie Young's desk. Of course it will be locked. He makes sure. It is. Millar speculates about her involvement. He assumes she knows more than she's letting on to him but that she won't have been in on the search of his flat.

One of the guys down the room is watching. 'Something the matter, Dave?'

Dave Millar lifts his hand dismissively. 'Got it mate.' He takes his wallet from his inside pocket with a flourish. 'Thought I'd dropped it in the street.'

'Someone would've handed it in. When have you ever heard of a dishonest Aberdonian?'

'It's after it was handed in I'd be worried.' He locks the drawer, remembers, tugs it back open. Ignoring the contents, he switches the folder around until he sees the number, practically indecipherable, pencilled on the flap. The second number from Ross' cigarette pack.

On the way back home, Dave Millar drops into the Glentanar Bar for a beer, runs into a couple of his neighbours and hangs around for a couple more. By the time he gets back to his flat it is around eleven. Millar is tired, but he finds the phone directory and checks the lists of dialling codes until he finds a match for the one on Ross' cigarette packet. Phoning from his own flat might not be such a sensible move and neither would using his phone at Queen Street so at quarter to midnight he's back out on Holburn Street making for the phone boxes at Alford Place.

With each ring Millar can feel his heart rate increase. The surprise comes when, instead of the Irish accent he had expected, a pukka English voice reports that he is through to 12 Company HQ. DS Millar blanks for a second when asked the nature of his call.

'Oh, I was dialling a Lisburn number,' Millar stumbles over his words.

The detached voice confirms he is indeed through to Lisburn and again asks who it is he wishes to speak to. Millar does his best to retrieve the situation.

'Who am I talking to?'

'You should know we don't divulge names, sir. Perhaps you have inadvertently dialled a wrong number.'

'No, no, this is the right number. I'm sorry, I'm not making much sense.'

'No problem, sir. It is late. You're through to the support HQ for British army personnel in Northern Ireland. If you leave your name and number, someone will contact you in due course, sir.'

'Thank you,' is all Millar can muster as he replaces the receiver.

Despite having promised not to implicate her any more, Millar can only think of one person to turn to.

22. GUARDIAN OF THE MORAL MAP

Leningrad: Wednesday 14 August 1991

Mance Stresemann did not return to Moscow. Since chancing on Markowski's crew playing with gas outside Grigoryev's studio, she has been determined to keep well out of their way. As it is, she has finished what she came to do in the Soviet Union, to reinforce the relationship between her own Erinnerung organisation and the Russian Znamya, and her presentation to the Pamyat meeting in Leningrad had gone down well with the audience there.

'Will you go back to Cologne straight away?' asks Zhdanov.

'Not straight away. I have one or two other places I must go to first. And I don't want to make life too easy for Markowski.'

'Will you be alright?'

Mance Stresemann holds Yuri Zhdanov's face between her long tapered fingers and kisses his forehead. 'I will be fine. I may go back home to Solingen to see my family when things settle down and I am finished in Ireland. But I worry for you, Yuri. You too must take great care.'

'The Angel is not so determined to get us as he is you, Mance.'

'I think maybe now he is.' Her chocolate drop eyes are full of concern.

The influx of Soviet Jews who used Germany's open door policy and financial incentives in the 1980s to migrate to the country which had tried to exterminate their forebears did not meet with universal approval. Among the tens of thousands who applied for entry and succeeded was one Polina Zanevskaya, who moved into the town of Solingen with her husband, a blade manufacturer formerly employed at the Leninets Leningrad factory, and their children. It had been a fairly obvious choice for the family given Polina's husband's

255

occupation but unfortunately Solingen, apart from being the source of over 90% of Germany's domestic blades, was also home to a small but active right-wing extremist group and within months of her arrival Polina Zanevskaya was dead. No-one was convicted of her murder, which took place in daylight in a public park where she had been stabbed and her throat slashed. Rumours spread of a domestic incident but among the several people questioned by the police were members of the local Erinnerung cell. When it became known through the press that Polina Zaneskaya was a sister of the head of a criminal organisation in the Soviet Union, sympathy for her and interest in her case waned. Waned, that is, with most people, though not with her brother, Marat Markowski.

Zhdanov and Mance Stresemann ate dinner in the Literary Cafe on Nevsky where Pushkin enjoyed a meal before his fatal duel. It is an extravagant farewell but neither knew when they would see each other again. Zhdanov told Sergei Dolgoruky of their plans but he did not turn up.

Later in the evening, Mance Stresemann caught a flight from the city's Pulkovo airport to Berlin and from there to Brussels.

Aberdeen

MacMillan's funeral has put Bell into a reflective frame of mind. He used to envy MacMillan's ordinariness. Then again, it was probably that ordinariness that had made him incapable of coping when the heat was turned up. It struck Bell, not for the first time lately, that his cancer was not only destroying his body but his self-assurance as well.

Then there was Tart; his malicious mistress's cooling relationship with him over concerns about Coulthard. And Ross. Others too, no doubt. Psychotic bastards not content with trying to destroy a man but enjoying seeing him squirm. Bell prided himself in never having taken pleasure in anyone's suffering. It was his privilege to have produced professionals who only took a life out of necessity. Masters of a broad range of skills: efficient assassination; doctoring bullets to explode in the gun barrel, killing the gunman; arranging for targets to "win" holidays so their homes could be fitted with surveillance bugs inside their televisions – whenever they were tuned into *Coronation Street*, every pick of the nose, every intimate tête-à-tête, every unguarded exchange between comrades would be televised into the blue van. Reality TV. His men were highly trained, vigilant sleuths; tappers of conversation; readers of faces; adaptable; skilled; cool; silent killers. His men. Loyal British heroes. Patriotic men. A very precise policy of expediency. Necessarily ruthless, recognising that the protection of the state takes priority over the individual.

★ ★ ★

Detective Sergeant Dave Millar does not usually approve of taking work home but today proves an exception. Viewing classified files is not an activity to be done in public, even when that is Police HQ in Queen Street. As well as the restricted records, he'd accessed copies of newspaper reports from visits to the Central Library. A cursory glance at the files tells Dave Millar he is onto something. There are police copies of material that could only come from Ross' own archives.

Millar reads down Ross' list of contacts, some with telephone numbers or parts of numbers, presumably without area dialling codes. No addresses but Dave Millar recognises several of the names; these men could be found in a Who's Who of Irish political life.

Millar spreads the documents over his living room floor. The press cuttings mainly carry the same by-line: Ian Ross. What becomes apparent to the DS is that Ross' consuming interest in Northern Irish politics has earned him unprecedented access to significant individuals and organisations on both sides of the divide, but most interesting of all to Millar are the references to Roderick Bell and to Colonel Gordon Cassidy, commanding officer of the Joint Force for Research aka military intelligence aka Mire, active in Northern Ireland during the late 1970s and 1980s. Dave Millar discovers several documents with references to this Cassidy. *Colonel Cassidy/Roderick Bell – promoted to Brigadier at the end of his stint in Ulster.* A picture is emerging of Bell as Cassidy in West Germany, Cyprus and Ulster. Millar finds a quote from Colonel Cassidy he'd attributed to the Bible, to Luke chapter 11 verse 23, "He who is not with me is against me" and a pencilled aside, presumably from Ross: *Catch-22/ Korn to Yossarian/ You're either for us or against your country. It's as simple as that.*

This is the sort of smart Alec attitude DS Millar objects to from the likes of Ross. In one of his articles he remarks that some of Cassidy's team regarded their commander as a surrogate father; one what had hand-picked recruits with personalities which would be most responsive to his strong leadership. Flawed youngsters who'd become dependent on him. Manipulation of the individual: cultivate, coach, convert, condition, care, charge, channel, command, conduct, captain, compel, campaign, crusade and control.

According to Ross' view, Cassidy's was a world of black and white in which recruits were willing to believe whatever they told them. Straightforward, easy to remember certainties essential to every good soldier but especially his sort of man. Bare bones lessons in politics: communism – bad; every other form of regime – good or tolerable. Irish republicanism must never succeed – responds only to the firm hand. Mediator Bell, aka Cassidy, appeared to attract enemies like fleas to a dog. Ross wrote that Cassidy's wars would never end. Enemies could come and go, names and nationalities could change but one of life's certainties was that the future would always throw up fresh targets. Flexibility in foreign affairs. Flag and Crown. In the greater scheme of things it wasn't your past adversary you had to be concerned with but those yet to be identified. Friends or foes only words beginning with " f ". Simple philosophy happily accommodated by the British establishment through its networks of interests, its clandestine activities, its surveillance systems and, most effective of all, its confidence in a docile and indifferent population.

Gordon Cassidy was a temporary prop in the life of a recidivist chameleon. Employee of state. Protector of interests. Guardian of the moral map. Executer of strategy. Whatever was required of him. Selfless. Anyone he was asked to become. Identities taken from real people so backgrounds checked out. Protected by legend, by Tart, by the system, by agreement.

There is so much to take in that Dave Millar wonders if he should throw in the towel. He tries to arrange the documents in piles: relevant and not relevant. Into the not relevant pile he puts a tiny cutting, no more than a single paragraph about a Russian criminal called Markowski, alleged to have been implicated in a plot to frame a British soldier over an alleged relationship with an East German prostitute working for Soviet intelligence. The soldier had been fast-tracked out of West Germany once news of the scandal broke.

Millar starts a third pile: stories relating directly to Ross himself. A handwritten item about his being gagged by the British courts for trying to publish an article on an undercover British army intelligence officer who'd switched identities to evade charges of serious misconduct. He reads it again and drops it into the not relevant pile.

It is only when he glances over several more documents that Millar really begins to appreciate what he's stumbled on. A stack of evidence pointing to British military involvement in sectarian murders where army issue weapons had been picked up at the scenes of crime. Ross described incidents with unmarked vehicles said to have belonged to army intelligence: Q cars equipped with concealed radios and eavesdropping equipment for surveillance sweeps around Ulster streets where their personnel were active or simply out to spy on the enemy.

Millar finds he's scribbling notes: *the Quick Reaction Force, or QRF, and the RUC were geared up for fast response whenever a call came through of trouble brewing.* He puts down his pen. He's uncomfortable reading Ross' material. He resents having to question some of his certainties about the British government's policy in NI.

Despite becoming absorbed by the information, his sympathies still lie with the men and women risking their lives in covert activities – firmly on the side of the army and RUC. Ross was out and out hostile, contesting Margaret Thatcher's pronouncement that there was no war in Ulster when she denied paramilitary prisoners POW status. But if Ross' information is accurate then this same QRF was more proactive than defensive.

In a separate paper Ross recounted an episode in which three IRA men died. The way he reported it, army intelligence had got wind that the Provos were planning to attack a loyalist bar so they set up an operation post close to an arms cache they knew was near the target area. They'd guessed right. Under cover of darkness, three masked men were spotted making their way towards the dump. From the OP, Mire combatants successfully took the men down with a volley of shots from their German HK53 assault rifles. The final fatal shots, however, came from army issue Browning 9mm automatic pistols, which miraculously pierced the men's skulls without penetrating their black balaclavas. Ross highlighted the inference drawn by lawyers for the men's families that an attachment of special forces had incapacitated the republicans with the HKs, peeled back the injured men's balaclavas to confirm their identities, fired at them point blank with their Brownings then pulled back down the balaclavas. The case never made it to court but as the RUC had destroyed the dead men's clothing and any evidence of powder burns, it would have been impossible to prove what had taken place – despite evidence that the victims' weapons still had their safety catches on. The newspaper had headlined the piece *Better Safe than Sorry*, a reference to the 117 rounds of fire pumped into the three. Ross' report ended with an observation that a fourth IRA man had been arrested, uninjured at the scene, and this man was later released without charge. His body turned up a few days later, the apparent victim of summary justice from within the IRA for being a tout or informer.

Everywhere Dave Millar looks there are fresh disclosures, more speculation. The most recent document is a badly typed note from May 1991 with "1970s" scrawled across it. Millar assumes it had been typed up fast and amended by hand before Ross forgot a conversation. It takes him a little while to make sense of the typos and Ross' comments on the poor copy which, of course, is a copy of a copy and badly faded, as if one or both Xerox machines had been short of toner. Millar screws up his eyes, straining to decipher it.

Clandestine team of serving soldiers setup under Scottish commander from Gordon Highlanders' Regiment/ Colonel Gordon Cassidy. Media-shy Cassidy hand-picked men able to tackle Ulster's violent paramilitaries and beat them at their own game. Source said (NB serving but not from elite unit but shares barracks) unit is known to members as Mire, as in bog, and set up with primary aim of infiltrating loyalist and republican groups to undermine them. Source

260

unclear how far Mire involved in paramilitary activities – sectarian murders, torture, car-bombings to maintain cover. Scribbled alongside the margin of the typed note is the figure *1* and *in UUF*. Millar understands this to mean that a member of Mire had become embedded within the loyalist UUF but there are no details and nothing to identify the person.

In a different document, Millar comes upon an addendum to a copied published article: *Europa Hotel – photo Mire informant/ UUF.* And he wonders if Ross had ever attended that meeting.

There is further evidence in the cuttings of a highly sophisticated web involving the army, the police and paramilitaries: catholics randomly abducted and subjected to systematic and vicious beatings; lurid descriptions of shocked and terrified victims, their skin flayed as they swung from carcass hooks in an Ulster slaughterhouse, of others butchered by hammer-wielding, hate-ridden crazies shattering limbs, using pliers to twist and crush, cleavers and knives to slice and nick, often to the bone; the victim's tongue extracted lest the dead should rise up and offer evidence against their executioners.

A subdued Dave Millar fills the kettle. He wishes he'd never become so involved but he's hooked and while waiting for his coffee to cool he unfolds a note made on a sheet of hotel writing paper.

'86 Derry car bombing … first on the scene – an army patrol?? … cordoned off – no press access for several hours … the few human remains recovered passed to families for burial but no formal identification possible. Brian Anderson, Tom Dooley and Terry Nicholls. Check "Riddle" – 2 dead? 1 spirited away? Why? Deep cover? … Bombing a convenience? Embedded soldier/ moved to safety/given a new identity??

More conjecture on Ross' part, concludes Dave Millar. He is dog-tired. It's late but he's reluctant to stop reading. Something else catches his eye: a reference to TAGOil and some thoughts on Aberdeen's oil boom.

TAGOil Aberdeen set up by Hugh Bell in 1974. The early, heady days spelled boom time for North Sea companies. Time served turners were making small fortunes in Scotland's neo-rig system: run-rig to oil rig. They may not have been 20thC 49ers but many a train limped into Aberdeen Joint Station loaded-down with drunken Geordie's keen to grab a share of the bounty spilling out from the North Sea. The government kept up the mantra it wouldn't last. People cautioned over the excitement of Scotland's Klondike. The moment the drills hit the ocean floor up popped the gloom and doomers. They said it in the seventies, they said it again in the eighties, they'll be saying it through the nineties and into the new millennium. In a sense the gloom-mongers are correct. Wealth will never find its way into every pocket. The majority of us have to be content with crumbs which fall from the masters' table and each year those crumbs will diminish. The two weeks on two weeks off passport to riches will become a struggle for workers' rights and basic safety measures. Eventually the naysayers will have it and north east industries will turn inland from the coast, having stripped the North Sea of more of its resources – first fish then oil and gas. Until then the sceptics will have to put up with the level of success that has come to the myriad of energy sector businesses such as TAGOil Aberdeen, a world leader in the field of well completions and intervention solutions, whose employees take their skills around the globe as trouble shooters in the difficult and dangerous world of oil and gas extraction.

Millar checks the clock over the fireplace: 2.40am. He rubs his tired eyes and begins to tidy away the mess of paper when he chances on what appears to be an original document which has attached itself to the reverse of a page of type, a faded scrap torn from a newspaper with its date intact: 16 April 1970. He reads the brief account of an accident at the Catterick army base in the north of England in which an officer had been accidentally killed by live ammunition. The officer is named as a Captain Sandy Bell, whose two brothers were serving officers in the army. No picture, no more details but tantalising for the sleepy Dave Millar. He leafs through his notebook and finds the note he'd made when speaking to his source in records. Three Bell brothers.

She'd hesitated – 'Not certain, Dave, think there are three.'

Dave Millar tosses his notebook aside and closes his eyes. Three. Three little pigs. Eek. Eek. So who is this third eek? Restricted access record. One he knows about. Dead and buried but where? Makes up his mind to check the local paper for details of Hugh Bell's funeral, or he could just ask Margaret Bell. Yes, that is what he'll do. No point in making extra work for himself.

23. BELL AND BROTHERS

Moscow: Thursday 15 August 1991

Markowski's people at Moscow airport had alerted him to the imminent return of Zhdanov from Leningrad which is why the gowk finds himself back in the apartment where he'd been humiliated head-down in the lavatory pan. This time he is alone, except for a faceless corpse in the dining room.

The gowk walks slowly around the body, revolver in hand, just in case – trying to figure out if it's Mance Stresemann. Too tall, he thinks, and hair a shade darker, but it's difficult to be sure. The last he had heard, the boss's boys were onto her, the Jew-hating bitch. He looks again and thinks it could be her.

The gowk has come from Grigoryev's studio to check out the Arbat apartment and satisfies himself there is no-one else there, well no-one alive. Evidently, Zhdanov and Dolgoruky are elsewhere on business or have decided to hightail it back to Leningrad. It is all too great a temptation for the gowk to ignore – the place is in such disarray. He packs a few keepsakes into a blue bag he's found in the hall, including a very nice painting of a sailing ship at sea which he found under a bed.

One of the Grigoryev's neighbours had alerted the police to what sounded like gunshots from the apartment. She didn't trust foreigners and explained how she'd been keeping an eye on the comings and goings of various strangers, including two giant Leningrad hoodlums who turned up at all hours of the day and night. So when she saw armed officers bundle a diminutive man with a blue shopping bag into their black police van, she reflected in the warm glow of knowing that she had done her duty as a good citizen of the USSR.

While searching Grigoryev's apartment, Moscow police officers discovered that their little prisoner had not only tried to make away with some priceless antiques, including a seascape later appropriated by the officer in charge, but that he'd murdered the female occupant of the flat and would face charges of first degree homicide as well as burglary. They were also curious about why the occupants of the apartment kept a radio transmitter among the plants on their veranda.

★ ★ ★

Alexei Grigoryev was fortunate to survive into the summer of 1991 given that his cover had been compromised at Moscow's International Trade Centre on 31 March 1987. British Prime Minister Margaret Thatcher was among the guests at the official inauguration of the British-Soviet Chamber of Commerce established to reflect the UK's welcome for Gorbachev's open door approach to Western commerce: nearly 600 UK companies considering tie-ins of some kind. On the Soviet side, a mere sixty trade organisations attended but it was a start.

That evening there was much talk about joint ventures, a logical stride forward following some delicate negotiations among delegates from Central Europe, the US and the UK over the development of the 4,500 kilometre pipeline between Urengoi and Uzhgorod to carry Soviet gas to the West.

The majority of guests were from the worlds of government and commerce, well-connected Soviet business managers and their Western counterparts eagerly calculating the lucrative profits soon to be theirs from forthcoming joint ventures.

When Mikhail Gorbachev made his declaration from the sumptuous grandeur of London's Savoy Hotel that his government intended a vast expansion in trade links between the SU and Britain he thrilled a listening Thatcher. Glasnost had one supporter, well two, at least; three if you counted Alexei Grigoryev.

It had been a deeply buried cherished desire of Grigoryev's that once day he would be able to board an aeroplane with his wife and son on a trip to Scotland where he would take the decision to return or to stay, so when he turned up appropriately rigged out as a guest for the launch of the Russo-British Chamber of Commerce at the World Trade Centre in Moscow, it is likely that this thought dangled like a mobile somewhere near the front of his mind. Precisely what he was doing there was never fully understood by Luda Semenova, who was herself a guest of an Oktneft representative. Following her initial surprise, Luda concluded that Grigoryev's job with the Department of Computing must be more important than she imagined.

The man who was running Luda Semenova was a commercial secretary at the British Embassy and would no more have been disposed to discuss Grigoryev with her than Alexei's handler would be to reveal Semenova's role, had he known about it. There were others in the room with links to British intelligence and at least two who ran between the UK and Soviet agencies. It was natural in a climate of glasnost that there was some blurring of identities but it did very little for trust in relationships.

Alexei Grigoryev had given twenty years of his life to the cause and there was part of him that longed for the CPSU's collapse, clearing the way for his return to the West in the knowledge that his mission had succeeded. What that might have meant for his family in the Soviet Union was quite another matter.

Aberdeen

DS Millar rings into work to tell them he has a doctor's appointment first thing, then dials the Rubislaw Den number he found on Ross' fag packet.

'Ah. Mrs Bell. I suppose Brigadier Bell has already left for the office? Fine. Fine. No. No, it doesn't matter. Really. Actually, I'd quite like a quick word with you, if that's possible. This morning? It'll only take a few minutes. No, just you is fine. We've already spoken to the Brigadier. Fine. Around twenty minutes. See you then.'

Dave Millar waits to be served in his local corner shop. He glances at a paragraph at the foot of the front page of the Aberdeen's *Press & Journal* about how a former north east man was taken ill on a flight between Aberdeen Dyce Airport and Belfast. A spokesman for the airline had told the paper that the man had been transferred to a hospital by private ambulance on arrival at Belfast. The man's companion had mentioned that his friend was diabetic. Initial reports that the man had died during the flight were denied by the airline. No name would be issued until relatives had been informed.

Millar pays for the newspaper and a tube of Polo mints.

Stepping into Margaret Bell's drawing room, Dave Millar occupies the space by the window he'd got to know so intimately on earlier visits with Young.

'Beautiful garden,' he remarks, raising a slat on the Venetian blind.

'Thank you,' is the rather prim response.

DS Millar runs his eyes over the display of photographs which had fascinated him previously. His searches through old copies of local newspapers in the Central Library during his lunch break the previous day had turned up Hugh Bell's death notice. When he'd followed this up with a call to the council, Millar was given Bell's layer number and area of Allenvale Cemetery where he'd been buried and in the evening he walked along the River Dee to check out the gravestone.

In loving memory of

Alistair Graham Bell

Died 11 February 1953 aged 66

In Bonn, Germany

Jane Isabel Grigor

Wife of above

Died 10 April 1978 aged 72

Their oldest son

Hugh Alistair Bell

Drowned Loch Muick 8 March 1987 aged 60

Hugh Bell. Oldest son. Not elder. More than two. And two he knows are dead. Two dead, one dying. So three in all? "Grigor" he notes it down. The Scots' way. A wife retains her maiden name although she might take on her husband's, as a courtesy to him. *Jane Isabel Grigor, wife of the above.* Into his notebook.

Dave Millar recognises Hugh Bell in many of the photographs: Bell lying on a beach; Bell stepping into a gondola on a Venetian canal; a number of Bell socialising with men in suits. And an older picture, in a particularly striking art nouveau frame, of two young men and a younger teenage boy rigged out in striped rugby shirts, all tall, lean, fair-haired. One of them has a nose with a leftward list.

'Your late husband?' Millar points to one of the boys. Margaret Bell, graceful and poised, virtually glides across to the table and cradles the picture in her hands.

'Yes, that's Hugh,' she delicately traces the slight, youthful figure with a manicured crimson fingernail.

'His death must have come as a great shock?' The DS wonders if this tiny, shy woman enjoys sharing the house with the bluff Brigadier. Margaret Bell replaces the picture on the table, smoothing away a smear left by her hand cream from the frame.

'They telephoned to tell me he was missing. The police, the Chief Superintendent, actually. I was away at our house in Nice at the time. Hugh was going to join me there but … '

DS Millar feels self-conscious but he has a job to do. 'His brothers?' he asks, pointing to the two other youths in the photo.

Margaret Bell brushes aside a stray lock of hair from her face. She wears her hair loose over her shoulders. It is jet black and shimmers where it catches the light. Millar thinks he would like to smell it, and it occurs to him that this exotic flower of a woman is so utterly out of place in the reserved and faded gentility of her granite mansion.

'The Brigadier and another brother?'

Hugh's widow goes to sit down, 'Please take a seat. Can I offer you tea or coffee?'

'No, I'm fine. Thanks. What was the other brother's name?'

'I didn't say it was a brother.' Mrs Bell's dark eyes sparkle and she smiles mischievously.

'Oh, I assumed,' begins Millar.

'Yes, I'm only playing with you. Roderick you know and the other was Alexander, Sandy. He died many years ago. Before I met Hugh. A tragic accident.'

Dave Millar looks over the table crammed with family pictures.

'Your husband enjoyed being in front of the camera. Not everyone's that comfortable.'

'Yes, he loved the attention. I took some of those. Not the earlier ones, of course.'

Hugh Bell had looked considerably older than his wife. Millar thinks she could be Philippino. Had Hugh Bell discovered her on a trip abroad or had they met through a dating agency? DS Millar is curious to know but declines to ask.

'This one looks like he's been in the wars.' He points to the broken nose.

'Ah, the result of a rugby tackle, I believe.'

Millar loves hearing Margaret's soft lyrical voice. 'That's the other brother, because the Brigadier doesn't have a broken nose, does he? Who's the old lady?'

'The old lady, as you put it, was my husband's grandmother. She virtually brought up the boys when their parents were abroad. Had a place in Aberdeenshire. She died soon after that photograph was taken. So Hugh told me. He was very fond of his grandmother. She lived a remarkable life, you know. As a young woman she was involved with the Pankhursts, campaigning for women's rights. I believe she remained a strong character to her dying day.'

Millar smiles weakly. He sometimes regrets how far women's rights have affected men like him. 'Why were the parents abroad?'

'You're a very inquisitive young man. Look, if this has to do with those dreadful Irish blackmail … '

'Irish?'

'Yes.' Again, there is caution in her tone. 'Sent from Ireland, wasn't it'

'What makes you say that?'

'The postmark, of course. Londonderry.'

'You saw the postmark?'

'Yes.'

'On the envelope?'

'Of course on the envelope. Where else would they be?'

'And the Brigadier showed the demand to you?'

'Look, what is going on? Perhaps I've said too much. This really is not my concern.'

DS Millar is keen to placate her. 'I'd forgotten, that's all. But I thought the Brigadier had told us he didn't have an envelope.'

'Well presumably he's misplaced … ' her reply fizzles out.

Millar considers what this means. Sue Cromarty had suggested a London suburb. But it hadn't been a suburb. The London might have been Londonderry.

Margaret Bell makes a show of consulting her wristwatch. 'Look, Detective Sergeant, I don't wish to appear impolite but … '

Dave Millar has more he wants to ask. 'We need to build a broader picture of the target in cases like this. Sometimes the people themselves are too close to events. It can help getting some background.' He blushes as Margaret Bell scrutinises his face.

'I think it best you come back when Roderick is here.'

On the spur of the moment, Millar blurts out, 'Why do you think he didn't report the blackmail to us sooner?'

'If I may say so, that is an odd question, Detective.' It's Margaret Bell's turn to appear flustered. 'Roderick was not at all pleased I'd discovered the … the … he was trying to protect me, of course, but I insisted he call in the police. You've met Roderick, he believed he could handle it all himself but he's not a well man, so I insisted.'

'You did the right thing, Mrs Bell. Any blackmail has to be investigated. You're very protective of your brother-in-law.' Millar notices a flash of irritation in the woman's dark eyes but he presses on. 'What d'you think the blackmailer was getting at by threatening to disclose embarrassing information about the Brigadier?'

'I've really no idea. I'm sure everyone has something to hide. Only very dull people have lives so bland that they have no dirty linen.' The friendly tone has gone from her voice.

Millar smiles at her. 'Oh, surely not you, Mrs Bell.'

'I do not appreciate being patronised, Detective Sergeant. If there's nothing else.'

Dave Millar is buying time. 'I apologise. I didn't mean … eh, how long have you known Brigadier Bell?'

Margaret Bell thinks before she replies. 'Back to that again. Well, I feel I've known him most of my adult life. He's my late husband's brother, after all. Although it was only after Hugh died that Roderick and I actually met. Rather strange, don't you think? I'd been part of the family but we hadn't physically met. Lots of letters and cards and that sort of thing. Phone calls too, of course. So although I feel I've known him forever, it is only a little over two years.'

'There weren't family holidays? Get-togethers?' Millar asks.

'Hugh and Roderick would go on golfing holidays together. Mostly Portugal. I can't stand that sort of thing. Intensely boring, don't you think? They kept up.'

'It must be very comforting for you, having someone so like your husband …'

'Roderick's not in the least like Hugh. Whatever gave you that idea?'

Again the eyes flash. DS Millar notices that Margaret Bell wears red on her lips.

'Now, if you don't mind, Detective Sergeant, I must get on with my life, dull as it might appear to you, no doubt.'

'Thank you, Mrs Bell. You've been a great help.'

'I can't imagine why.'

From his car Dave Millar waves back to the slight figure framed by the unrelenting hardness of granite.

★ ★ ★

The lovely Margaret Bell lifts the telephone receiver as soon as DS Millar has gone.

'Ah, there you are! Where have you been? I've had the police here asking questions. No, you listen! This Detective Sergeant was really fishing. No, I'm not being melodramatic.'

★ ★ ★

Stanley Shaw walks his fingers along TAG's reception desk where Sue Cromarty is dropping off outgoing mail.

'Got to pop out. Any phone calls just explain I'll be back about three. No later. Maybe two-thirty. Three to be on the safe side.'

Sue Cromarty makes a face as he leaves the building. 'Make it never, Mr Shaw, please make my day.'

270

TAGOil's glass plated door had been wedged open to air the new carpet in reception. Sue Cromarty holds her breath until she reaches her office.

'That smell's not getting any better. They should evacuate the building. God knows what deadly cocktail of chemicals we could be breathing in. Greg? Hello, is there anyone there? Have the nasty fumes eaten your brain?'

Greg signals for her to be quiet. Sue crosses the room and peers over his shoulder. Greg's holding up an envelope. 'It's got Bell written across it but inside it's addressed to someone called Gordon. Who do you suppose that is?' Greg turns his head to face Sue Cromarty, who's biting on her lip.

'Is it another of them?'

Greg puffs out his cheeks and blows air out slowly. 'Will I?' He's flapping the envelope back and fore.

Sue Cromarty takes it from him. 'No me. Let's see.'

Greg reads aloud as Sue flattens the page. 'Credit Suisse, Zürich. Payment through Swiss Interbank clearing from your bank to – there's a bunch of numbers. Suppose that's the account … good grief! It's the blackmailer alright but why Gordon? Look, it finishes by saying balance must be left … the west chapel … a tapestry footstool.'

Sue Cromarty shakes her head then carefully folds the note and returns it to its envelope. 'I'm going to leave it with the rest of the mail. See if he picks it up.'

'Who?' Greg knows he sounds silly.

'Old man Bell, of course. Could be the scumbag doing this has got things mixed up, could be there's something more to this than we know. Let's just see if he takes it away or queries it with one of us.'

★ ★ ★

Brigadier Roderick Bell stares at the envelope. He closes the door of his office and re-reads the instruction. £3 million to Switzerland and £100,000 in cash. Details for making the bank payment. A warning that failure to follow the instructions would lead to information being leaked which would undermine his reputation. If it had indeed been

Ross responsible then Bell knew he could afford to feel relaxed, but it isn't clear that it has come from him. This isn't turning out to be a great day. He weighed himself on the bathroom scales before his shower. Looked like he had lost more weight. For a split second Bell considers making a copy for MacMillan and leaving it at reception but somehow it doesn't seem quite decent. He smiles at how much he's changed over the past two years. Should he take it to the police? He has little choice, after all, Sue Cromarty has seen it. He will have to phone Tart for advice.

★ ★ ★

'Brigadier Bell? Detective Inspector Young here. We've got some news.'

Bonnie Young has just hung up the receiver when Dave Millar appears with her coffee. 'He sounded pretty happy. On his way back from TAG. We're seeing him at 3 o'clock at home. No sugar, I hope.'

'It's all stored up in here,' Millar taps his temple, 'no sugar in coffee but sugar in tea; no milk in tea but a good skoosh in coffee; no cheese and onion crisps because the punters object; never prawn cocktail because you have a shellfish allergy although no prawns have ever been harmed in the making of crisps. I know you better than you know yourself, methinks.'

Moscow

When Alexander Bell abandoned his identity and life as an enthusiastic communist undergraduate in Moscow in 1970, that part of his life went into abeyance, waiting for the day British intelligence deemed it suitable for him to resume his former persona. There was some consternation about whether or not he should be brought out at the time of his brother Hugh's death. A certain queasiness in intelligence that the Soviet government was questioning the extent of TAGOil's intrusion into Oktneft. It would never have been possible to extract Sandy Bell and have him pop up as CE of the Scottish company without raising acres of shaggy Kremlin eyebrows and creating a furious international reaction. It was therefore decided that the third brother, well known to Tart, should be pensioned out of the military and into civilian life as himself, Roderick Bell, brother of Hugh. Bell was then awarded a titular promotion to Brigadier to help compensate him for his disappointment at having to forego a pencilled-in move to China as military attaché. His command of Mire had been exemplary. His men were renowned for their loyalty and efficiency but arranging his return to Scotland was regarded as the best outcome, given the circumstances.

There was a second person Grigoryev recognised that evening at the Moscow Trade Centre reception, outside of his contact in the embassy that is, an Andrei Karpol. Karpol was a very talented portrait artist, long-time participant in Tovarischchestvo Russkikh Khudozhnikov and outspoken opponent of the Kremlin. TRK had been originally set up from Western funding although this was known only to a very select few. In the days when hard currency was virtually impossible to get hold of in the USSR, Tovarischchestvo Russkikh Khudozhnikov provided an ideal platform for Western inspired criticism of the state's apparatchiks within the USSR. What Alexei Grigoryev did not know was that the Kremlin had been alerted to what was going on from the start; two members ensured most of the hard currency received by the brotherhood from the West was transferred directly into the state's coffers. Neither did Grigoryev realise the degree to which membership of the TRK had been subjected to scrutiny by the KGB.

Alexei Grigoryev had a guardian angel within the walls of the Kremlin, one who was materially rather than spiritually inspired, and who had been motivated by the expectation that one day Grigoryev might realise his weight in hard currency. As loud as some comrades might roar against the system, there was never any question of prohibiting TRK for it contributed substantial sums to the Soviet Union's Cold War chest.

Grigoryev squeezes the hand of the young son he has been reunited with in the unlit cellar. The room smells of damp, fungus and stored potatoes, earthy and musty. Any fight he had within him at the outset is being slowly extinguished by the thought that their captors are about to murder his wonderful, bright, funny, talented boy. As if sensing his father's distress, the child reassuringly nudges Grigoryev's leg with his knee as he plays with the red fortune fish, flattening it against his small palm and then pressing it against his father's cheek. It is so dark Grigoryev can't even make out his child's face. They have sat like this, side by side, hour upon hour.

At the sound of feet on the stone steps they turn to each other and then to the door. A key turns in the lock and a strip of smoky light reveals the figure of a man. Alexei Grigoryev strains to see through the murk and recognises the shadow. He gets to his feet to greet a comrade from the artist's group.

The light from the corridor reveals the shadow's expression. There is to be no miracle rescue for there's something in the other's face he's never noticed before, something familiar.

'We meet again, Grigoryev. Different circumstances. Come.' Andrei Karpol steers Grigoryev closer into the glare of the fluorescent light. 'No, not the boy.' The child has followed his father and is clinging to him. 'I'll return for him,' Karpol says quietly.

'No! He comes with me.' Alexei Grigoryev feels a ripple of terror convulse through his son's slender frame and holds him fast. 'Why are you doing this, Karpol? I am of no consequence.'

'You undervalue yourself, comrade,' is Karpol's sneering retort.

'Here, come. I will take good care of your boy. I am a father. I know how you must feel but come.'

Karpol is not alone. A brick shithouse emerges into the grey light. 'You know my cousin, Andrei Karpol!' quips Yuri Zhdanov impishly as he pushes past Grigoryev and pulls Sasha from his father's desperate clasp. Karpol holds the struggling Grigoryev in a fast arm lock and marches him away from the cell.

Aberdeen

Contrary to what Bonnie Young believes, Brigadier Roderick Bell is anything but happy but always capable of rising to the occasion, even when his heart isn't in it. He can't help feeling tense where this blackmail business is concerned and, settles on the very edge of his sofa, feet wide apart, the top half of his body tilted forward over his knees, he holds a whisky tumbler with one hand while the other explores the silver salver on the occasional table by his elbow. Uncorking the Laphroaig, he liberates the genie. The act of swallowing soothes a searing pain shooting across his back. As he puts down the bottle, Roderick Bell catches sight of his rippled reflection in the salver; it is pale and drawn. 'Wee, sleekit, cow'rin', tim'rous beastie, O what a panic's in thy breastie!' He croons to the silvery spectre.

The impressive door, with its heavy brass letterbox and lion knocker, closes behind the two police officers. Roderick Bell detects unease in the female detective as she makes her way into the drawing room. He notices that the hem of her skirt hangs down below her coat on one side. This pleases him. Carelessness. There are situations when that is reassuring in others. The young man sends out a different message. More confident than at their last meeting. A nonchalant slouch of a man with an air of cockiness about him. Bell pulls at his toothbrush moustache.

The Brigadier helps Bonnie Young off with her coat. As the DI sits down, the dropped hem catches her eye. Nimbly, she tucks the skirt behind her legs, casting a fleeting glance around to see if the men have noticed. DS Millar is preoccupied with the photographs by the bay window but Bell, she realises, is watching. DI Young gives him a silly, embarrassed smile and lowers her eyes. A gold and black lipstick nestles by the bulbous wooden foot of her chair and, absent-mindedly, Young picks it up, sees it is called Orange Ice and places it on the side table beside the whisky bottle.

The horizontal window blinds create a room starkly striped into light and shade. From where Dave Millar sits, blades of sunlight slice into the Brigadier. Pure Hammer Gothic.

Brigadier Bell listens politely as DI Bonnie Young reveals that colleagues in the south have passed them information which suggests responsibility for the blackmail lies with an insignificant left-wing group whose numbers can be counted on two hands and who are scattered around the British Isles. A Special Branch report on their background has thrown up a history of direct action against prominent companies, especially multinationals. At this very moment, known members of the group are being rounded up and are to face questions, although, as in many of these cases, it is not always easy to find sufficient evidence to prosecute successfully. DI Young goes on to reassure the Brigadier that permission has been received from the Home Office for the Special Branch to tap group members' phone calls, intercept their mail at Post Offices – the usual means used to monitor leftist organisations in the United Kingdom. As if to emphasise just how little the obviously sick man across from her should be concerned, DI Young explains how the group involved is idealistic but mainly preoccupied with circuitous political discussions and in-fighting and with the odd public swipe at corporations. Precautionary questioning and continued monitoring should ensure that threats to blackmail him will go no further.

Brigadier Roderick Bell relaxes into his cushions. Tart has obviously acted swiftly to stifle further police enquiries but DS Millar appears reluctant to let matters drop entirely.

'Remind me, Brigadier, where did you say the blackmail had come from?'

Bell arches his eyebrows like furry, trampolining caterpillars and mumbles something Millar can't quite make out and then, 'I don't recall a postmark. The Brigadier looks directly at him and sucks on his moustache.

Young is looking as pleased as Punch. 'They'll be interviewed and we think our colleagues will put the fear of death into them.' She's talking as if Bell needs more reassurance. 'We deal with these types all the time. They're pure hot air.' Now she's rubbing her hands together and Bell takes the cue and fetches Young's coat from the hall and is holding it open for her when Dave Millar pipes up.

'Do you have another brother?'

The question hits the floor with the finesse of a falling skydiver in tackety boots. Young's coat slips from her shoulders. Millar's back is to the window, his face in deep shadow but it amuses him to observe the discomfort on the faces of the Brigadier and Young.

276

DI Bonnie Young flashes him a warning dart. She already made it clear to Dave Millar that they would not be carrying on with the case; that she had been instructed to let it drop and that whatever he imagined might be going on, it was no concern of theirs. The case was closed, she had told him firmly.

'Sergeant!' Young frowns as she rearranges her coat over her arm and follows his eyes to the lipstick on the occasional table.

'What the hell did you think you were doing in there?' Young is furious.

Millar sighs exaggeratedly.

'I had to say it. You know there's more to this. That old punter's making a couple of turkeys out of us. We can't just let it drop. I think I'm onto something … '

Bonnie Young leans over the roof of the car. 'I don't give a shit what you think you know or don't know. In this organisation we follow orders. I've been instructed to drop it and you'll follow suit. We're not a couple of private investigators, Detective Sergeant. We can't make up our own rules. Don't you see? You're making a fool of yourself, which is fair enough but don't drag me into this. Look, just forget it. It's gone.'

'I thought you were different?' Is all Millar can think to say.

'Different! Different from what? Of course I'm not bloody different. I'm a systems person. I work within the system because I believe in it. I don't know what you know or more likely what you think you know and I don't bloody care. We're the guppies in this ocean of shit and we don't stand a chance against them so we swim away. Okay? We swim away.'

'Organisation! You make it sound like the KGB or something.'

Detective Inspector Young shakes her head. 'I never took you for a naive boy, Dave. You haven't a clue what you're getting into. Take my advice and stop this now.'

'And if I don't?'

'You'll be treading on some very influential toes, sunshine, and they're not going to like it. Not like it at all.'

It comes as a consolation to Dave Millar that they wouldn't like it.

It upsets him how many of his generation of cops have won the promotion which eluded him. In a moment of introspection, he develops the theory that if he is ever going to make an impact on the force's gold braids, he will have to do something which makes them sit up and take notice of him. Risky, he knows. But so too is not taking that risk. The evidence is all around at the station. Men all out of ambition. Disillusioned. Dried up. Depressed. Riding out their time. Hanging around for the early pension and winters spent on the Costa Brava.

Moscow

Tethered to the chair, Alexei Grigoryev looks a shrunken version of his former self. Someone has removed the wire-framed glasses and his hazel eyes are having difficulty focussing on Zhdanov and Dolgoruky and another man he doesn't recognise. In the way that he'd been drilled, his denials are mechanical. His computer voice in denial mode.

He has known since they killed Irina that they know nothing about his activities as a spy for the UK and that his fate will be sealed solely on passing on information to the authorities about their right-wing organisation. He's been careless – has underestimated their ties to the police and militia and Kremlin, he supposes. Dolgoruky, meanwhile, had been content to let Zhdanov do the talking until his patience runs out, which is around ten minutes into the one-sided conversation. Language not being Dolgoruky's strong point.

Without warning, Dolgoruky strides up to Grigoryev's chair, raises his left leg and kicks Grigoryev hard on the chest. Chair and man go down. Hands bound behind his back, Grigoryev is unable to right himself and gasps for breath at the same time as trying to make himself as small a target as possible, but Dolgoruky does not come back at him. Instead, Zhdanov picks up the chair and helps Grigoryev back into it. Instinctively, Grigoryev thanks him, as if he's forgotten Zhdanov has shot his wife dead.

For a further half hour the three men try to extract an admission from Grigoryev: that he has passed on information about food scams they have only just set up in Moscow and district to Markowski, undermining the whole venture; that he's revealed where they were living; that he's alerted Markowski to their would-be partnership with Coulthard. Alexei Grigoryev can't believe that his wife is lying dead, his son, God knows where, and all that these maniacs are interested in is some misinformation that he's betrayed them to a rival crook. It is all too obvious to him they have no idea the extent of his activities for Britain since arriving in the Soviet Union. It occurs to Alexei Grigoryev that these neo-fascists might even approve of what he has done. Not that he will say anything. Who knows how many lives will be at risk were he to talk. It could make no difference to Irina and will make no difference to Sasha and, as for himself, he doesn't care anymore.

Grigoryev closes his eyes against the world that has contracted to a room no bigger than four metres square. He concentrates on feeling each application of pain on his skin, through his skin, into nerve endings on his hands and head and face and body. He wants to feel the depth of the torture but it is unfathomable. Only by keeping his head full of pain can he atone for whatever has happened or will happen to Sasha. He cannot plead for Sasha's life, will not plead for Sasha's life, since he knows that will only motivate his assailants to greater cruelty on the child. His head fills with noise. Through his ears. Flooding into his brain. There is little Sasha and victims of the traders in death. Victims of war and terror. Girls and women subdued and controlled by rape. Old and young, male and female casualties of sexual violence. Fighting robots of death with children's faces. Terrified abductees, enslavened and ransomed. The violated. The looted. The persecuted thrashed from their homes and livelihoods by sadistic bullies screaming hate dressed up as religion. A cord of hopelessness tethered around half the world; victims of collective suffering.

Alexei Grigoryev thinks he hears someone calling to him. He can't make out if it's a man or a woman. He doesn't think it's Irina. Someone told him Irina had died. He thinks it might be Veronika. But it's been such a long time since he heard Veronika's voice so he can't be certain. He tries to call back but he can't hear his own voice at all. It's strange that he can hear someone else but not himself. He hears the voice again. Yes, he's sure it is Veronika, his first wife. He can see her now, her hair tucked under a green cotton bandanna. She is holding his hand, like she did in the dark of the dormitory when she told him about her father.

As the daughter of a man convicted of subversive activities, Veronika Titova had been lucky to get a place at Moscow University, where she and Alexei met. He sees that dormitory, as clear as day, where he's comforting her as she explains that her father had been sent hundreds of miles away from his family to Camp 17A: the gulag where hope is extinguished; where he regarded his political status with pride; where he abhorred the criminals he encountered in the camp – the suki, as his fellow politicos disparagingly labelled them, the colluders and informers.

Prisons polarised between dissident and criminal factions, both being victims and perpetrators of savage cruelties. The suki conspired in argot, their secret language. They lived with their own rules in the camps, operating through their own chains of command: suki laws and courts which tried fellow-suki who stepped out of line.

Alexei Grigoryev had had a lot to learn about life in the Soviet Union. He knew nothing of the Vorvovkoy Mir, the Thieves' World, until Veronika explained about it.

The Vorvovkoy Mir is feared by camp inmates because they have so much power. My father was a strong man to stay clear of them. He despised them; how they had privileges that other prisoners did not get. And they hated intellectuals like my father. They were scared of the politicos and would beat them. My mother was always expecting to hear that my father had been murdered by them.

And Grigoryev had said nothing but drawn Veronika's head close against his own and wondered about his own future.

Released Thieves' World brothers went out into every nook and cranny of Soviet society. They assisted each other with introductions, money, information, ladders, whatever was required to get to the next level. What else were brothers for? And fellow brothers recognised, not by their Masonic-style handshakes, but by their fingers, hands, arms, faces, necks, torsos, legs, feet – picture language, pictorial legends of life in the gulag recorded through tattoo.

Once married, Alexei and Veronika would travel with Veronika's mother to Bratsk in the Chita region of Siberia, near its border with Mongolia, where Ivan Titov spent his remaining years in exile. After the long journey it was always a relief to arrive at their wood-panelled room at the Taiga Hotel, which appeared to have been built from a blueprint for a shoe box. There, on top of bright red counterpaned beds, still in their travelling clothes, they would curl up, exhausted. And later they would sleepily gaze out from behind the stiff, shiny, moss-green curtains to a broad boulevard of prairie-wide proportions sprinkled with trees and shrubs and precious little traffic.

This was a hydro-electric town where workers lived in regimented ranks of blue and white apartment blocks, five or ten stories tall. However, despite the hydro nature of the place, the rectangular pond beneath a larger-than life poster of Vladimir Ilyich Ulyanov, aka Lenin, was invariably dry.

Grigoryev recalls it as if it were yesterday. Bratsk Dam, where they strolled until it was time to visit the camp. Bratsk Dam beach, just the place to walk off anxiety amid bright polygonums and dandelions that flourished in the scrub above the sands. On warm summer days, Bratsk presented its best face; flurries of blossom snow, drifting from pavement trees.

He thinks about the occasion they'd arrived with time to spare and explored a reconstructed pioneer settlement set deep inside the mosquito-ridden taiga. Stories of early settlers; battling tough terrain and dense forests and fording fast tumbling rivers to subdue the land and create ideal prison camps. And, in an effort to forget their sadness, the family would finger the hanging cribs, spinning wheels, samovars and decorated pediments in the ethnographic museum and remember that their hardship had a long pedigree.

Ivan Titov never strolled the banks of Bratsk Dam. But neither did he succumb to ill health while in exile. For that he was grateful. So, too, was he grateful for never having had his eyes gouged out; that he had not had his hands crushed by iron weights; that he had not been hanged under the gaze of indifferent camp personnel; and that he had not been sent to the mines in the Donetsk region.

'My father is really a very lucky man,' Veronika had confided to Alexei after their daughter was born.

As for Alexei Grigoryev, when not with his in-laws, he would tell anyone who asked that he was from the Caucasus, from the pretty village of Privolnoye, which could easily be mistaken for Smallsville, Wyoming. But in truth he was not; his wife, Veronika, was. Her family home, a simple timber house with a thatched roof, later upgraded to red corrugated iron, and with sweet blue and white shutters surrounding the windows. Like many other houses in Privolnoye, the Titov house had its own fruit and vegetable garden, surrounded by a white picket fence. In the evenings, the family would sit out on the porch under grapevines threaded around the arbour, reading and talking and listening to music while ducks and hens scratched contentedly on the dirt track out front.

Villagers in Privolnoye had rarely been touched by hunger until the year Stalin's men appeared and took away all the grain from the harvest. Privolnoye's farms were collectivised and anyone with the audacity to resist the directive risked arrest and banishment from the area. Some paid with their lives; their bloated bodies floating down river like upturned canoes. Veronika's grandfather became one such canoe. His son, Ivan of Camp 17, never forgave Stalin and never tired of condemning him. Growing up during the violent days of collectivisation, he dared to speak out wherever he saw injustice, which is why he came to reside for a time in that camp.

His son-in-law was not from the state of Stavropol. He was not from anywhere in the Soviet Union.

Grigoryev feels something pressing on the tail of his spine. He starts laughing. *Only three minutes to go. Hold in there, Sandy.* Scramble of legs and arms and heads. Bang. *Oh, I felt that* … jarring my neck … someone's got me again on the back … Grammar School always bastards in the scrum … *two minutes and we'll have taken the match. They're turning the scrummage … is that mother?* … picks her moments … always gets worked up when her boys are on the rugger field, specially me, being the youngest – *You've a nose for trouble.*

Alexei Grigoryev had been born in Germany, in 1948, to Scottish parents. Christened Alexander and known as Sandy, he was the third son of British diplomat Alistair and his wife Jane Bell. All Bell brothers had gone to schools in Scotland and all seemed destined for military careers until, in 1966, Sandy appeared on the roll of Berlin University as a language undergraduate. It didn't take him long to get embroiled in student politics, in particular with the SDS, the Social German Student Association, when it eventually surfaced in Berlin after gathering support in the student campuses of Heidelberg, Cologne and Saarbrücken. It was therefore no surprise that, given the SDS's links to East Germany's Socialist Unity Party, Sandy should head to Moscow to pursue his studies there. So after a brief appearance in Scotland in 1970, he began a course in Russian Studies at Moscow University. It was there that he began to use his full name, Alexander, dropped his father's name for his mother's to become Alexander Grigor, which was Russianised to Grigoryev, and obtained a new passport and documents through a Soviet government official and friend of Bell senior in exchange for a case of malt whisky, a box of Cuban cigars and a stuffed brown envelope.

'It is you Veronika! It is you. I've missed you.'

Veronika stood out from Sandy's average students at Moscow. Tall, very blond and with vivid violet eyes. Grigoryev was envied by all fourteen other students in the dorm in Stromynka's vast utilitarian barracks ... so crowded the only place for books and clothing was a suitcase under the bed.

Veronika Titova was in turn attracted to the cultured youth whose experience of the outside world marked him above the usual run of undergraduates. Veronika had inherited her father's integrity, his intolerance of discrimination and stupidity and soon she and Alexei became active in student politics.

Grigoryev steels himself for the next onslaught of pain. It is his punishment for what he's done to the people who loved him. His tears are for the child, the daughter he had with Veronika.

When their marriage broke down, Grigoryev resigned his position as a teacher of languages and moved back to Moscow to study computer science during the day and painting at night. He never saw Veronika or their child again. Then, in 1981, he married Irina Priminova and within a year Alexander, known affectionately as Sasha, was born. The child turned out to be a very proficient footballer and his parents encouraged him to believe that one day he might play for Moscow Dynamo.

Alexander Bell, the talented linguist and cheerleader for the Soviet Union was, in fact, always a fifth-columnist; Grigoryev the sleeper. Deep sleeper, as it turned out. It was a decision of youth never regretted by the man whose duty it was to be patient. When the time came, he would be told. Meanwhile, the destabilisation of the Union of Socialist Soviet Republics that had welcomed him in 1970 – the year US troops invaded Cambodia, four anti-war students were shot dead by the American National Guard at Ohio's Kent State University, the Soviets landed Luna 16 on the Moon, Aberdeen FC defeated Celtic to win the Scottish Cup by three goals to one and CSKA Moscow defeated Dynamo Moscow to take the Russian League title was moving along nicely. Grigoryev got on with living a fairly normal life in the USSR. He joined the Tovarischchestvo Russkikh Khudozhnikov, in pursuit of social and political change. He secured a job with the Institute of Computing ,which gave him access to all kinds of useful data. Anything of particular significance was slipped into a football and taken to Sacha's soccer coaching sessions in the park. A keen observer might have noticed how a mother's regular outings to the same park included ball games with her three children and how invariably the ball ended up in the shrubbery at almost the same time another boys' football landed among the same bushes. It would have taken a very keen eye to detect a swap. This energetic mother was the wife of the visa official at the British Embassy in Moscow, and it was her role to retrieve documents from Sasha's football and pass them onto Grigoryev's employer.

24. THE INCIDENT IS CLOSED
POEM BY MAYAKOVSKI

Aberdeen: Friday 16 August 1991

Roderick Bell picks up his pink appointment card, dog-eared from constant use, and slips it into his inside jacket pocket. He doesn't mind attending the oncology clinic; it reminds him how fortunate he has been to have lived an eventful and relatively long life before his cancer struck. Clinic D with its waiting area full of toys and children's books as well as the usual out-of-date magazines meant to occupy anxious patients, patiently waiting as patients generally do, hoping for the best and dreading the worst.

The City Taxi cab arrives in good time. Bell always uses the same firm so he takes no offence when Wattie, his driver, questions having time to stop off at the Mither Kirk en route to the hospital. As for Wattie, as soon as the words are out he could kick himself. Who wouldn't stop off for a prayer or two? Well, Wattie for one, he reflects. He's never found a good reason yet for attending the kirk but rebukes himself, nevertheless, and keeps the car engine running in case one of the dreaded "yellow peril" brigade shows up on Schoolhill to slap a parking ticket onto his windscreen.

About the last thing on Roderick Bell's mind this afternoon is prayer. Striding confidently up to the south door of the Kirk of St Nicholas, he enters Drum's Aisle and goes into the West Kirk, listening. Then when he's content that he's quite alone he slips into the fourth pew inside the tiny side chapel and tucks a package full of cash under the red tapestry footstool he finds there.

Stepping back into daylight the largest carillon of bells in Britain peals out high over his head. Wattie gives him the thumbs up as Bell returns to the cab.

285

'Was that you who started that row, then?'

The Brigadier chortles with relief even though he has just parted with £100,000 of TAGOil's money.

★ ★ ★

Paranoia is a term DS Millar has often pitched at recidivists incensed at being pulled in again on suspicion; *You're out to get me,* their cries of proclaimed innocence. Now, however, there are signs of psychosis developing within his own head. He's notices an unusual level of dedication to the job shown by his fellow officers, not to mention a definite lack of eye contact between them. And while those impressions are gelling in Millar's mind, DI Young bursts into the office drenched in smiles and affected bonhomie.

'Well, Dave. Someone's been listening to you. That bit of fishing. We've to see Brigadier Bell about developments in the case.'

'So it's back on? This is like a bloody yoyo.' Millar can't suppress his surprise.

'Watch it. Not completely shut at any rate,' comes her qualified reply as she searches through the Bell dossier. Bonnie Young looks at him, her smile intact. 'Well?'

'Good. That's good,' he manages limply.

'Only good. What's got your goat? I thought you were desperate to carry on with this?' A note of irritation has crept into her voice and the smile freezes.

'Oh, just tired. Haven't been sleeping too great. Knackered that's all.' Millar stretches his arms above his head as if to emphasise the point.

'Well get yourself a coffee then we'll get off to speak to the Brigadier again. Won't that be nice?'

'So what about the lefties who were supposed to be behind the blackmail?'

'Lefties?'

'Yeah, you know. An open and shut case, Brigadier. Bunch of lefties on a counter-capitalism trip.'

'Couldn't get evidence to stick.'

'You mean they weren't guilty?'

Young shrugs. 'Bell has come back with something, it seems.' She returns the dossier to the desk drawer. 'You getting coffee, or what?'

'No, I'm good. Oh, here.' Millar hands Young a cutting from the *Press & Journal*.

'What's this?'

'Bit on Shaw getting that medal. Same time that Hugh Bell disappeared.'

'Medal for what, again?'

'Medal! You told me about it, remember? Bravery. A place called Grasse, beside Châteauneuf-du-Pape.'

'That's the place with the wine, isn't it? What was he doing there?'

Dave Millar knows everyone around is listening in, following every twitch of his neck muscle, his taut jaw.

On the drive out to the Bridge of Don, DS Millar asks Young who authorised the reopening of the case but she brushes the question aside.

'You know what they're like upstairs. Moods shift with the wind.' Her DS is looking at her. 'What? All I know, Dave, is the Brigadier's been talking to the Chief. Been poking around. Found out something. Chief's asked that we listen to what the Brigadier has to say. Tie up loose ends, y'know. Possibly nothing to it.'

DS Millar turns away, puzzled. 'So it's not that the case is being reopened. You don't believe there's anything in this. Whatever it is.'

'Dave, if that's what you want to believe. Look, I was going to go and see the great man myself but then I thought you might want to string along.'

Dave Millar clenches his teeth to stop him saying something he might regret. Now he's a piece of string.

DI Young is still talking. 'Actually, the Chief was insistent I take you along. Somebody loves ya baby.'

Millar resents Bonnie Young's flippancy. Further confirmation she's covering up something. The nerves in his neck ripple in nervous spasms. 'You don't sound too convinced Bell has the answers.'

'Sorry?'

'You said it looks like he's been poking around. You think he's making it up?' Millar watches his boss' expression alter.

'What are you talking about? We're going to see him because he has information for us. Information that might help finally allow us to drop this bloody case. What's your problem? God, I should have done this on my own.'

Dave Millar holds his tongue for a good thirty seconds then says, 'If it's an open and shut case like you say, why don't you sound convinced?'

DI Young stops at traffic lights. 'Let's just drop this, okay? We're nearly there. Let me handle this. Remember it's me the Chief's been speaking to … there's going to be no spilled blood.'

'But,' Millar turns ninety degrees in the passenger seat to confront Bonnie Young, 'earlier you hinted the case was being reopened because of something I'd done.'

'No I didn't'.

'Yes you did. Fishing you said. Remember?'

'I said the Brigadier had been fishing.'

'You said I'd been fishing.'

DI laughs at him. 'There's a helluva lot of fishing going on. No wonder fish stocks are low. Look, it's just a figure of speech, Dave.'

'Meaning what exactly?'

'Meaning you weren't happy this was a simple case of blackmail. I mentioned that in my report to the Chief …. and … well, I don't know. He called me in … asked me to say more about where you were coming from … I think he'd got onto the Brigadier and … I really don't know much more.'

'But you do know some more?' Dave Millar knows his DI is holding out on him.

'Not really. Look, this is not the place. Let's just have a word with Bell and then we'll see where we are.'

As they draw up in front of TAG's flashy entrance, DI Young adds, 'I expect that Margaret Bell has been ear-wagging the Chief again, to move his arse into gear.'

Brigadier Roderick Bell looks washed out but his mood is light as he welcomes the two detectives into his spacious office.

'Thank you for coming. It appears we've good news at last.' He holds a chair for DI Bonnie Young and indicates with the tilt of his head that DS Millar should also take a seat then places himself, straight as a poker, in front of the window. Silhouetted laird of the North Sea. From the blacked-out face comes a buzz of words apparently directed at DS Dave Millar.

'One of my colleagues was in Belfast on business when he was approached in his hotel by men claiming his life was in danger. Something about a plot to lure him from his hotel and ... well ... linked to this ... blackmail.'

Millar half laughs, half coughs.

'TAGOil is a thriving business,' continues Bell, 'and this individual imagined he could take advantage of our success. ' He pulls on his moustache.

'So you think the blackmailers belong to this group, whoever they are, and they planned to kidnap your colleague?' DI Young is business-like.

'That's correct but he's safe.' Brigadier Roderick Bell crosses to a small cabinet behind his desk containing a selection of spirits and glasses. He pours a drink for himself and brandishes the bottle. 'Care for one?' he says to neither detective in particular.

'No, we won't but you go ahead.' DI Bonnie Young motions to him. She's aware Bell is possibly using whisky for its palliative qualities, although it appears to be doing nothing to improve his skin's pallor and increasingly cadaveric appearance. 'In your opinion, the threats will now go away?'

Bell allows himself time to swallow a mouthful of spirit. 'Certainly. Police over there are onto them. Won't be long before they're behind bars.'

Millar watches the Brigadier sip from his glass, covering his moustache with his lower lip to draw off the spirit.

'You spent some time in Ireland, with the army, Brigadier?'

The Brigadier swirls the amber liquid around the bowl of his tumbler. 'Northern Ireland, yes I did. It's one of those arenas most of us chaps have to do a stint in at one time or another.'

'So could this blackmail be connected with that?' Millar enquires.

'No, Sergeant.' Bell sinks another slug of malt.

'Ah, well, it looks as if you might be right about this, Brigadier Bell. Certainly the Chief Superintendent thinks so. He thought we should have a word with you just to make sure you're completely happy with where things are.'

DS Millar glowers at the DI. Why, he wonders, is she rambling on?

'I still think,' Millar begins and is instantly cut up off by Young.

'Likes to keep me right.' Her expression darkens.

Dave Millar is on the back foot and obviously ill at ease but attempts to carry on. 'But the case is still wide open, isn't it? D'you mind if I ask something?'

The Brigadier indulges the junior officer. 'Anything you wish. I'll help if I can.'

'You didn't say who this colleague was.' Millar leans forward as if he wants to be sure of hearing Bell's reply.

'Oh, didn't I? It was Shaw, Stanley Shaw. I believe you met him. Our Financial Director.'

Millar squints at Young but she's concentrating on the wall in front of her, which Dave Millar takes to mean she's already in on what Bell's saying. This briefing has been laid on for his benefit. Rather half-heartedly, Millar perseveres. 'Did he receive any blackmail demand?'

'No, he didn't.'

'So … why would he be targeted in Belfast? In Ireland?' There's tension in Dave Millar's voice.

At this point, DI Young is about to say something when Bell raises his hand.

'A legitimate question. We don't know where the blackmailer comes from but this was a major event. Well publicised. Shaw was representing TAG. Anyone interested would have known he'd be there. They're not fussy, these people. Probably seemed a good opportunity.'

'And the blackmails came from Northern Ireland?' Millar can't stop himself asking questions.

Bell coughs. 'I didn't imply that.'

DI Young's eyes narrow.

'One last question.' Millar reads impatience in Bonnie Young's face. 'D'you know Ian Ross? He's a reporter.'

Brigadier Roderick Bell puts down his empty whisky glass but his attention lingers on it as if he hoping it might refill itself. 'It's odd you should ask that. A man was murdered in Belfast last night. His name was Ian Ross. Possibly same one. Of course, I don't know that. Reporter. Heard it on the news.'

It was lucky for Millar he wasn't at sea. The Brigadier's revelation took the wind clean out of his sails. No sooner had he come to see Ross in a more sympathetic light than he'd been eliminated.

'And the Chief's opinion is this Ross is our blackmailer,' announces Bonnie Young. 'He was fascinated by republican politics. Wrote about it all the time. Newspaper articles. And it's no secret he was friendly with many unscrupulous types in Ulster. The blackmails may have been postmarked Londonderry not London, after all. He is, was,' she corrects herself, 'always going back and fore between here and there. All a bit too obvious. Likely Ross went on the run when he realised we were taking an interest. Getting too close.'

If Millar's scepticism has not already been as plain as the nose on his face, he leaves Bell and Young in little doubt about his view. 'There's no evidence Ross had anything to do with any of this. Why should he? He'd nothing to gain.'

DI Young is quick to reassure her colleague. 'Naturally we've been onto intelligence. Ross been under surveillance for ages. MI5 were very interested in what he's been up to … '

'And what? They let someone carry on blackmailing a British company?' Millar's tone is scathing.

'I suppose they didn't want to reveal themselves. But they have passed on what they know to us. Look, it's not that easy. Somebody could have been hurt if they acted impulsively.'

'Somebody did get hurt. More than one person. There's MacMillan and now Ross. So much for intelligence.'

'Not the place to discuss this, DS Millar,' Bonnie Young reprimands the Detective Sergeant.

Millar is dejected. He has listened to Bell talking nonsense and now his DI is at it, but they won't have him. He clears his throat and asks, 'How did Ross die? Who's investigating?'

'Sergeant!' Young's voice trembles with fury. She moves towards the door. 'This is now going to be investigated by the RUC.'

Legs akimbo, cool as a cucumber, Bell considers the blunt policeman in front of him. 'It wouldn't surprise me if they never find the men who did it. I wouldn't blame the RUC. Don't envy them their jobs. Where would they begin? The whole place is awash with evil … and it might surprise you to know the networks set up to protect these people are very intricate. No, this might be a blessing in disguise. If the Chief Superintendent has seen the evidence to link Ross with my blackmail, then I'm more than happy to concur with his proposition. That would be a resolution of sorts. I don't advocate this type of thing, of course … but I'll sleep easier in my bed tonight knowing the menace has been removed.'

Dave Millar has very little to say on the journey back to Queen Street. Sure, he had suspected Ross of being in on the blackmail, but that was before finding background on Bell and discovering Ross was battling the odds to expose the activities of the intelligence services in Northern Ireland. Ross hadn't been the one behind the demand, Millar was convinced of that. And what of Bell? He'd been much too eager to paint Ross as the culprit. Bell was altogether too smarmy and self-assured. Too excited by Ross' death. What if Ian Ross had uncovered something the Brigadier would prefer to be under wraps? And who were the guys ready to stick their necks out for him? Millar's ruminations are interrupted by Bonnie Young offering to recount the full grizzly details of Ian Ross' demise. Millar watches her profile as she races the lights at West North Street. It is evident the little goodwill and trust they have enjoyed in their relationship has gone. What else does Young know about the case? She's staring steadfastly in front, as if aware that Dave Millar's eyes are boring straight into her.

'Do you want to know or what?'

'You're going to tell me anyway.'

'Only if you want to know,' she adds unnecessarily, 'I know how much you like to be kept abreast of events.'

'Go on then.'

'It appears Ross was taken ill on the plane as it was landing at Belfast and he was transferred by private ambulance to hospital. Except he never got to a hospital. Not then at least. Someone knew Ross was on the flight. If he really was ill or something happened, we don't know. Could just have been coincidence. Anyway, whoever was after him got their man. Word from the RUC is that he was taken to a slaughterhouse and … well, slaughtered. You want more?'

Millar doesn't react. He's searching out of the window for something he doesn't find. They're at the junction of King Street and Union Street: no cars, no buses, no shops, no tenements, no people.

'You've probably read about the sort of thing they did. Y'know,' says Young, ' sectarian assassinations … and before you ask, there's no proof Ross was connected to any particular group. Not yet. Maybe it was someone, more than one, getting their thrills from digging, as they put it. Whatever. There was evidence of bruising from kicks and punches on his corpse, although how they could tell they'd hung him from a meat hook? … why would people do that? Just the provisional report from the RUC so far. Post-mortem proper later. Only had four teeth left in his mouth. Someone had carried out basic dentistry on him with a pair of pliers.' Bonnie Young's voice falters but she doesn't stop. Is she punishing Dave Millar or herself? 'RUC suspect someone in the protestant community, a butcher or a slaughterhouse employee – you know, for real, with animals. They've got their suspicions but no arrests so far. So there you have it. You wouldn't wish it on your worst enemy, would you, Dave?' She finishes with a nervous cough.

Dave Millar's thoughts are miles away, on Ross' meticulously researched newspaper articles.

Back at the office, DI Young complains her head is splitting and goes off in search of aspirin.

Millar waits for her to leave then goes over to her desk and opens the drawer with the blue dossier. He isn't sure what he is looking for exactly but comes on a list of items found on MacMillan when his body was recovered. Then he sees a printed text in a transparent poly pocket and a sticky label marked D on the front. Densely typed, the manuscript has nothing to indicate the author but Millar recognises the style as Ross'. A draft article maybe. It contains names of people and towns: Belfast, Dublin, Londonderry, Lisburn. Too much to read here and now. Millar weighs up his options. He reckons he has two. Option one: he could be completely open with Bonnie and ask her outright about it. Why wouldn't he be curious about a possibly vital piece of evidence? The fact that she hadn't shown him it might have been just an oversight. Option two: make a copy.

He's stuffing the papers back into the file when he notices a long brown envelope. In it is a folded newspaper cutting. Millar smoothes it out. It's an article on TAGOil and its CE, complete with a photograph of Brigadier Bell.

Millar checks the corridor that houses the photocopier. 'Hope you're no in a hurry. I've a mass of stuff to do.' One of the girls from admin is surrounded by stacks of paper. 'You're okay,' he says but Millar is frustrated then he remembers there's another copier in a corridor one floor up. When he gets there he finds it's available but then a scrum of officers spill out into the corridor at the end of their shift. He waits, nervously, until the coast is clear. He's starting back down when he hears the clackety-clack of DI Young's ankle boots on the stairs below.

'Where've you been?' DI Young is leaning against a filing cabinet, glass of water in one hand, two white tablets in the other. She squeezes the pills between her lips and throws back a mouthful of water.

'Bog.'

'Sorry I asked. You okay?'

'You're the one popping pills. Are you?' He can't remember if he put the folder back into the drawer when he went off to the copier. There's no sign of it on top of Young's desk.

'No, my head's throbbing. What I need's six months away from this place.'

Dave Millar sinks into a chair. 'I thought you liked your job. What's brought this on?'

His DI shrugs and shakes her head. 'Sometimes you're asked to do things you don't agree with,' she says behind her hand, as if trying to prevent the words escaping.

It doesn't take a genius to work out she's talking about the Bell case. The working relationship between Millar and Young has always been open to misrepresentation. What some might construe as synchronicity in their partnership is in reality a game of shadow boxing. Prevarication. Despite the irritation he feels when he's with her, Millar knows Young is nobody's fool. He imagines she's already detected the close typed sheet clinging to the skin under his pants.

'What does that mean?'

'Oh, nothing. I think it's time I settled down and started a family.'

'You don't mean that?'

'No. I don't. Let's change the subject.'

For the best part of forty minutes the two detectives play dodge ball on the subject of Bell, MacMillan, TAGOil and Ross. On at least three occasions Young even consults the blue dossier, apparently failing to notice any missing items. She repeats that, as far as she's concerned, Bell and MacMillan had been targeted by Ross so he could raise cash for the IRA. TAG was more or less selected at random. Big business. Big coffers. But, unfortunately for Ross, his scheme fell apart and he paid with his life.

DS Millar recognises bullshit when it flies through the air. Whatever the reason for Ross flying to Ireland, it wasn't for the purpose of collecting on blackmail. And, however much Bell and Young had appeared satisfied of Ian Ross' guilt, DS David Millar is certain it is a cover. He's more sure than ever that Ross' sole interest in NI was as a bona fide journalist trying to unearth evidence of underhand British tactics there and the part played by the arrogant Brigadier. Had Ross been naive imagining the biggest threat to him was the censor's blue pencil?

Bonnie Young is sticking to the official line that Ian Ross had been nothing other than a corrupt hack on the take. 'So, Dave, you were right to suspect him from the start. I should listen to you more often.' She drags her hand across her forehead as if still in pain.

Millar puffs out his cheeks. 'So, it really is case closed this time?'

'Take it as read.' To emphasise the point, Young reaches into the document drawer in her desk and hands him the dossier. 'This can go to central filing. Will you take it along, Dave?'

DS Dave Millar nurses the blue folder. A test? Is he being watched to see what he does with it?

The door to central records is wedged open and two filing clerks are chatting away to each other as they sort through boxes of documents. Millar loiters outside the door and pulls arse-shaped sheets of paper out from inside his pants. Balancing on one knee, he returns them to the file and neatly folds the Xeroxed copies he'd made into his jacket pocket.

He lowers his feet from Bonnie Young's chair when she returns to the office. Young brushes the seat with her hand.

'D'you mind, DS Millar!'

'Sorry,' he mutters, nose stuck in a magazine.

'On your break?' Young reaches for her phone and begins dialling.

'Keeping up with the latest in mind control methods. D'you know the Russians are experimenting with microwaves to induce nervous breakdowns and heart attacks? Implanting thoughts into someone's brain without them knowing it.'

'What else would you expect from them?' his boss asks vaguely, not really interested.

'Not just them,' Millar continues in the vein of the *Readers' Digest*, 'the Yanks have been developing a machine that can read minds.'

'More useful with some people than others. Haven't you any work to do,' she asks.

'In a minute.' Dave Millar has a point to make. 'US military is right into this stuff – plugging into a person's brain, psychotronics.'

'Wish I could do that. In my day we called it brainwashing.' DI Young wonders what her sergeant is up to.

'Still happening.'

'Only if you have a brain to wash.'

'High frequency radio waves and hypnosis can transform anyone into, well, anything you want.' Millar stretches his tight jaw.

'A working policeman? Any chance of that?' Young gives up on her phone call and turns the pages of an atlas. 'Checked on Grasse, that French place, it's only thirty-five kilometres from Nice. D'you think Shaw enjoyed tanning himself on the beach while he attended conferences?'

Nice. Millar takes it onboard, and doesn't Margaret Bell have a house there? 'Activated by passwords and numbers.' Dave Millar carries on reading. 'Russian mafia use this stuff. According to this report.'

Moscow

From Brussels Mance Stresemann phoned Zhdanov but got Sergei Dolgoruky. There was no mention of their quarrel. Dolgoruky told her that he and Yuri had been packing up items from Grigoryev's Arbat apartment when they were confronted by a woman in the shop threatening to call the police, so cutting their losses they took what they had bagged up, and were driving away when they spotted one of Markowski's hoods heading into the building. Next they knew the guy had been banged up, accused of murder and attempted robbery.

Dolgoruky asked Mance Stresemann if she was alright. Told her he missed her. They arranged to meet in Egypt in September. Holiday permits to Egypt were never any problem and once they had sold Grigoryev's antiques they'd be rich.

Aberdeen

Margaret Bell is surprised there is so much to pay on her excess baggage, although she shouldn't be. It is more than six months since her last visit back to her family. This time she's taking more with her than usual. It's a relief for her to escape the oppressive atmosphere of Aberdeen. There was a momentary pang of conscience about deserting Roderick but she knows his favourite health visitor, Ellen, won't give up on him. This is not her principal concern, however, as she waits for the Amsterdam flight to be called. The blazing row she'd had with her brother-in-law persuaded her to leave. Nothing more than accommodating was how their relationship could ever have been described and her way of coping with the frequent tensions had been to disappear abroad to one of her other homes. But she had always come back. She doesn't think she will this time. She hadn't meant to shout and scream at him but when he brought up Stanley Shaw something had snapped. She had accused Roderick Bell of taking advantage of her dead husband: living in his house; forcing her out; taking over at TAG and leaving its more experienced men to carry him along. Infuriated by his unresponsiveness, she'd suggested he was in some way to blame for Hugh's death. It was at that point that she had stopped, gathered her wits together, gone up to her room and telephoned Shaw.

Stanley Shaw had initially demanded reassurances from Margaret that she hadn't revealed to Bell what they'd discovered about him while searching his desk. In truth, Margaret couldn't quite recall everything she'd said and those doubts reinforced her decision to leave.

Death had claimed Hugh Bell before he'd made adequate provision for his young, beautiful and indubitably elegant widow. What expectations she might have harboured about becoming an active partner at TAGOil were summarily dismissed when Roderick Bell arrived. Everything that had been her husband's had become his, herself excluded; she'd made that plain enough to him. Her disappointment at how events had turned out was shared by other Board members who'd expected promotion on the death of their Chief Executive. Finance Director, Stanley Shaw, felt the disappointment more than most. Not only had he not benefitted from a move up the Board on merit, but his dream of marriage to Margaret, with all likelihood of becoming CE at TAG, were shattered when Roderick Bell came on the scene. Out of a sense of entitlement, he and Margaret Bell had devised a plan to extract from TAGOil something in recompense.

★ ★ ★

A shroud of silence hangs over the house in Rubislaw Den as Brigadier Roderick Bell enters the hall after his radiotherapy session. He stares into the empty drawing room. Margaret has left. MacMillan gone. It hits him how few people he knows in the city. He has grown accustomed to regarding Margaret's and MacMillan's sets of acquaintances as his own and now there would be no-one. Perhaps not quite no-one. The one person left who is anything like a true friend is Ellen, and he can't call her at home in case her husband answers. Brigadier Roderick Bell looks at the silver salver on the occasional table and resists taking a dram. Instead, he goes out to the kitchen to make himself a pot of tea.

It is one of life's certainties that unless a Tart Johnny is guilty of gross criminality, he can always be confident he will find assistance from behind its grimy, net-draped windows.

Roderick Bell opens his front door to the charming woman who dropped her lipstick on her last visit. A pretty and unusual shade of tangerine, he'd mentioned when she phoned. As they sip tea together he listens when she explains that Stanley Shaw has been picked up, cash in hand, from the Kirk of St. Nicholas. A report will be going out to Grampian Police from Tart with instructions to search Shaw's home and, to save the Force time and manpower, will include a statement for the press that a considerable quantity of pornographic material had been obtained during the search, indicating that Shaw is a danger to women and, possibly, children.

'As for her,' Bell's guest wipes traces of lipstick from the rim of the teacup, 'we've had to move fast on this but very soon it'll be shown that the lady concerned has been found to have a criminal record as long as your arm. Don't know how we never spotted it before.'

Bell catches her meaning perfectly. Routine clean up. He lets her continue.

'We've already blocked her access to her bank accounts and investments. Got lots, all over the place.' The tone is disapproving. 'Quite a smart young woman, your sister-in-law. It's unlikely she'll ever to get back into this country and she'll find it damned hard to enter anywhere that's a friend. She'll just have to go back to waiting on tables or whatever she did before gold digging her passage here. Shame. A pretty little thing. At least she's still alive.'

Roderick Bell carries their tea things back into the kitchen when the woman has left. He feels well enough for a slug of Laphroaig. It's a weight off his shoulders that the blackmail mess has been cleared up and to get Tart's reassurance that nothing relating to him would be made public.

Bell is dozing in his armchair, surrounded by the oppressive silence that he imagines will mark his future, when the insistent chirping of the phone by his elbow jolts him awake. On the end of the line comes a familiar voice, from an office overlooking the Thames that he knows well, with its grubby net drapes and odour of decay. Brigadier Bell's colleague, whom he hasn't seen in years, expressing concern that nothing has been coming in from Russia lately. Bell feels a surge of annoyance although he had been expecting something of the sort, so takes the Tart tongue lashing over his employment of Coulthard, 'In his present state of health. Presenting, as it does considerable danger to Tart.' Bell mutters something akin to regret that any such interpretation could be placed on his actions. Then London fires the bombshell. 'A body was recovered from an apartment followed by the discovery of a second at Moscow municipal dump. We won't go into details, if you don't mind. But we've had positive identification that the latter was Longview. Condolences and all that. Bad outcome after so long in the field. If there's anything we can do … '

Brigadier Roderick Bell stares down at his rippled reflection in the silver salver. He raises his whisky glass to his dry lips but his taste for it has left him. He lets the silence in.

How long he sits for, Bell has no idea. Hugh and Sandy. Roderick Bell is exhausted: the cancer, radiotherapy, Coulthard, blackmail, Hugh, even Margaret; now Sandy. Sitting alone in that empty mausoleum, staring into a cold marble hearth, Brigadier Roderick Bell experiences something quite uncharacteristic – tears moisten his parchment thin cheeks.

He and Hugh have returned to their alma mater for a charity game of rugby. It's a chance to see Sandy again, the baby of the family, still at school. Their mother got them rounded up to take their photograph before the match. Her wise council was for them always to be themselves and have lots of children who would love them and give them the same pleasure she had from her own three boys. The same mother who uttered, 'My brave, brave boy,' when her youngest child went off to Russia. She knew then she would never again talk with him or hold him. And, while she never said so much, Roderick Bell believed she never quite forgave Sandy for placing himself in danger for, what she regarded was, misplaced patriotism which separated not only the two of them but a grandmother from the children Sandy might have. She never reconciled herself to being denied the pleasure of holding his children's fingers; kissing them and receiving their smiles. And it did not escape Bell that he, whose entire working life had been played out in dangerous and violent arenas, would be the one to die a slow, most ordinary death.

★ ★ ★

'I see ye've got yersel' a girlfriend at lang last.' It's Mrs Walker, Dave Millar's downstairs neighbour as she sweeps the second floor landing. She eyes up the bulky manila envelope he's holding. 'Trouble with you police lads is yer aye marriet t'the job.' She gives him a look as if to say he's a lost cause.

Since he moved into her tenement on Howburn Place, Mrs Walker has taken Dave Millar under her wing, reminding him of his day for hanging out his washing (not that he ever does, the launderette, five minutes down the road); how far down the tenement stairs he should sweep and polish (not that he ever does, leaving it to the dust fairy); when the bins should be put out for collection (he does that but often forgets to bring it back in between times). He used to apologise to her for his shortcomings, using long working hours as his excuse. Mrs Walker would just give him one of her looks. She doesn't really expect a man to do the washing or the stairs. That is why she is keen for him to find a girlfriend. Dave Millar likes Mrs Walker. As well as being a friendly old soul, she is his only source of information on what neighbour is doing what, to whom and when – nothing happens in the tenement without her being wise to it.

'Someone looking for me?' Millar has not been expecting visitors.

'A bit auld fur ye, loon. A fine, turned oot lad like yersel' could come up wi somethin a bit mair exciting than her, I think.' Plainly Mrs Walker is enjoying teasing him.

'What d'you mean?'

'Ah well a' body his a right te their opinion but, loonie, she's a bitty o' the soor plooms aboot her, has she nae? Ken fit I mean?'

'Mrs Walker, you've lost me.' Millar laughs but he feels his oxters growing damp.

Mrs Walker pulls herself up to her full five feet and stretches her aching back. 'Talk o' mutton dressed up as lamb! Dyed hair, nithin o't, no right on a wifie her age, and that horrible lipstick – orange! I was thinkin' the womin must hiv put herself the gether in the pitch dark.'

Then, reaching out a hand to Dave Millar, she adds, 'But tak nae notice o' me, laddie. If she's the ane for ye, then ging for it.'

Dave Millar's mouth is as dry as a sand quarry. In a voice that isn't his he blurts out, 'She's no my girlfriend, Mrs Walker. When was she here?'

'Oh, nae lang since. I heard someone ring a bell doonstair. Kept on, ken? Couldna tell fa's it was exactly. My hearin's no fit it used te be, laddie. Someone must have rung the buzzer te let her in, no me. I went oot te the landin, here. Seen her come past. Never spoke. Seen her go up te yer flat. She catched me watchin' but that never bothered me 'cause, well, I bide here. She rings yer bell. I ken the sound o' it so I shouts up, he's no in. Whilie later she comes doon. Then she spiks.'

'What did she say?' Dave Millar tries to clear his throat but the sands have slipped down there too.

'Gie's time, laddie, I'm just tellin ye. Says the lady in a toffee-nosed voice, "I'm looking for Detective Sergeant Millar. Do you know when he's expected home?" Mrs Walker pronounces the words slowly and with care in the way people do with a foreign language. 'Of course I kent then she wasna really yer girlfriend. Fit lassie wid ca her man, Detective Sergeant?'

'So did you say anything else? Did she say anything … ?' Millar wipes a sweaty palm down the side of his trousers.

Mrs Walker brushes aside his question. She'll take her time. 'Dinna tak me wrong. I've nithin' against the English, but some are that snooty kind. Ken fit I mean? Oh, says I, David works a' oors. He could be here ony minute then again maybe he winna. Then says I, was he expectin' ye, like? But she just ignored that. An' she smiled. No a real smile, ken. Ane o' them turn on turn aff jobs. I've te be honest, David, I didna tak t'her.'

'Thanks, Mrs Walker. If she comes back, let me know.' Dave Millar pats the old lady's arm.

'A' right, son. Hey! Maybe ye could get me a job in that police station o' yours?' Her smoky, rasping cackle from a lifetime of tobacco follows Dave Millar as he mounts the stairs to his flat on the top floor.

Two grainy photographs taken through long camera lenses provide a challenge for Millar. The first picture shows British troops in West Germany. The other had been taken a few years later and shows a youngish man stepping out of a car. In the accompanying article, Ian Ross recounted the dishonourable discharge of one of the soldiers in the first shot. He is identified by a white circle around his head and an exclamation mark, possibly made by Ross. Ross went on to claim that the same man then turned up in Ulster a couple of years later, apparently with the SAS. Known as Brian Macdonald in Germany, this former squaddie was also known to use the cover name Gary Hannah, who worked for about eighteen months on undercover duties for a branch of British intelligence known as Tart. Ross had discovered that Hannah had been involved in at least one surveillance operation on the border between Ulster and the Irish Republic when a republican under surveillance ended up dead.

Neither photograph is well-focussed; cap visors down level with the nose but the stature of the soldier in question is plain – the short, well-built man in the Berlin photo could be the individual getting out of a car in Ireland. According to Ross, this man was a covert operator for the British government who had been involved in planting an explosive device later attributed to the IRA. In another case, Ross claimed that Hannah was the operating name of a plant within a loyalist group thought to be connected with the killing of a family man at a house in County Down in which the gunmen escaped in a stolen blue Orion. There had been continuing speculation that this had been a botched operation in a case of mistaken identity and that the intended target was an alleged IRA member who lived at number 123 in the same street as the victim at number 132. He cited an unnamed source, a civilian working with the RUC. One of the weapons used had been of a type issued to undercover personnel in the province. Similar weapons had been used in the deaths of other suspected terrorists.

Millar unbuttons his shirt at the collar. He's not sure what to make of Ross' claims. How much of the information is accurate? He has no way of telling. It doesn't prevent him reading on.

SAS operators sabotaging IRA detonators so they blow up the bomber before

303

the charge can be laid – impossible tell if interference/ failure of fuse/ occasionally used/ protect agent plant within IRA/ mil. intel

Millar reads Ross' scrawled jottings. Tongue-in-cheek references to a particular agent's b.o. problem, suggesting that was the reason he'd been deployed deep within the IRA.

DS Dave Millar sits on a desert island surrounded by a sea of documents. He's dipped his feet into the water and now is worried he might be getting out of his depth. There's still a way out. I can burn this stuff, he tells himself. Not say another word. He knows that's not going to happen. Dave Millar has turned the key in Pandora's box and now the evil is encircling him. The phone rings. Marooned on his island, Millar stares out to the horizon. Beyond the armchair. Even beyond the coffee table.

It's approaching 7.30pm when Dave Millar returns from Mrs Walker's flat. He drains a pan of tagliatelle and is reaching into the grill for the warming dinner plate when the downstairs doorbell rings. Millar turns off the cooker and hesitates. Should he answer it? He's not expecting anyone. He might just leave it. He doesn't make a move. He just waits. There's a second ring, this time at his apartment door. Someone must have left the outside door open again.

Not exactly orange is Dave Millar's take on the shade of lipstick. Still, he can see what Mrs Walker meant. Definitely more Dundee United than the Dons. The lipsticked mouth is set hard.

'Detective Sergeant David Millar?'

'That's me.' The Dave Millar agrees with his elderly neighbour. No way would he fancy this woman if she were the last …

'I think you might find it more acceptable if I come in.'

The powdered nose wrinkles, reacting to the aroma of boiled pasta, but there's no apology for interrupting his dinner. She comes straight to the point.

'We know, Mr Millar, that you're involved in some extra-curricular investigations and that these include accessing classified material. I should not have to remind you as a police officer that you have placed yourself and your … your accomplice open to very serious charges. This illegal use of your powers directly undermines the security of this country.' She searches Dave Millar's face for clues about the kind of man she is dealing with.

Millar tries to stay relaxed while being confronted by the painted lady from hell. His accomplice. How much does she know about who supplied him with the classified stuff? He won't allow himself to think what might happen to his source but can't help feeling bad that he's got her mixed up in this.

'I have to impress upon you, Detective Sergeant, that you must desist from taking this any further.' She pauses as if expecting something from him. 'Look, it should be possible for us to settle this amicably; after all, we're both on the same side. Concerned with the security of England … '

Millar gives her what he intends to be a supercilious stare.

'You should know as well as anyone, Dave – may I call you Dave? You should know better than most how essential it is for all of us concerned with state security to work as a team.' Miss Ice Cool is beginning to sound a fraction exasperated. 'This silence only highlights the bankruptcy of your position.'

So Millar speaks. 'My position? What's my position? I'm a cop and I've been trained to investigate when I smell a rat. And fuck me, if there aren't rats scurrying around all over the place just now. Now, I've no idea what you have to do with it all since you haven't even said who you are, but if you've been sent here to put the squeeze on me there must be some helluva pile of rat shit you're trying to hide.'

'Your language is very colourful and, if you don't mind me saying, a touch naive. I don't think this is the place for formal introductions. I think we know what's happening here.'

'You've got a nerve, coming here and accusing me of, I dunno, plotting against the state or something. The reason I went into uniform was because I wanted to make things good and safe, okay, so you might think that funny but it's not me at fault here. There's bad guys out there, so why's MI5, if that's who you are, going after me instead of them?'

The woman takes a long deep breath.

'Look, these bad guys, as you put it, place their lives on the line for all of us in the United Kingdom, Detective Sergeant. They are the men and women who safeguard the freedom we all enjoy in England.'

'Aye, well we're no in England here.' Millar jabs a finger into her face.

'I'm sorry?'

'And this is all about Ireland, as far as I can work out.'

'Not entirely. Let's not get bogged down in silly semantics and parochialism … '

'No, let's not.'

The stiff lips degenerate into a twisted smile. 'Very well, the last thing I want is to become embroiled in a tedious discussion about PC terminology. You're already in serious trouble and may be facing a long term of imprisonment for procuring classified material. It's been agreed we should have a talk with you … '

Millar has heard enough. 'Whoever *we* are and whoever *you* are there's only one of us in this room who's contravening the laws of this country.'

'Look, you know that's simply untrue. I have to warn you, Detective Sergeant, that you're being extremely imprudent and I cannot guarantee your personal safety … '

Once more Millar interrupt. 'Is that a threat?'

'We don't threaten, Mr Millar. Look, you don't know the people involved here and what they're capable of. Be sensible and drop this whole affair now.' The orange mouth closes. From a large black shoulder bag the woman draws forth an assortment of papers. 'Look, there's a way out of this … '

'Aye, the way you came in. Out,' growls Millar, colour blotching his face. He strides to the door and holds it open.

The woman tightens the grip on her bag and fixes on Dave Millar's stare for a fraction more than is comfortable for him before taking her leave.

Mrs Walker's television can be heard through the floor. Millar looks out of the window. The street is busy. He supposes it is for he's not really focussing. Never changes from one evening to the next. People and cars. People in cars. Meeting other people. Dave Millar sits down and listens, second-hand entertainment courtesy of Mrs Walker. He should feel angry. Outraged. But he doesn't. It's a different sensation. He thinks it's fear. He tears back the ring on his lager can and phones his mother's number. It's not something he does very often but tonight it seems appropriate. He checks his watch. 8.20pm. His mother rarely goes out in the evenings; too many stories on television about Scotland's high streets. Once her realm. No longer safe at night. The police not doing their jobs. Excluding her son from her criticism. *You don't know what it's like, son. If only you were here to look after me.* The son assumes he's inadvertently punched in the wrong number and is about to try again when it rings.

'Mother?' He steadies the beer can at his feet.

'I bet you say that to all the women.' Bonnie Young's voice on the other end of the line startles him.

'Sorry, thought you were somebody else.'

'Yes, evidently – your mother. How is she? She fine?'

'Don't know, was trying to phone her.'

'Look, Dave, I'm just phoning to warn you off. It's been noticed … your behaviour around the nick. You can't carry on like this. You're not some one-man private eye agency.'

'You've said.'

'Well, I'm saying it again.' Millar detects a shrillness in Young's tone. 'You have to keep me in the picture. At all times,' she continues. Dave Millar realises he's travelling the wrong way down a one-way street. 'If you want to get on in the force, you have to toe the line, Dave. Simple enough. I thought you knew that. Anything you came across on the Bell case should have been passed onto me and then taken to the Chief. That's how it works. No secrets here, Dave. We operate as a team and if someone's not playing ball, they have to accept the consequences. A team. God bless.'

Dave Millar replaces the receiver, gulps back a couple of mouthfuls of lager then tries his mother's number again. This time there's no dialling tone. Mother can wait. He'll get it fixed in the morning. Leaning back in his chair, he kicks off his shoes, drinks his beer and reflects on his visitor. What with the events of the day, the lack of food, the alcohol … Millar closes his eyes.

He's going to have to go down to Mrs Walker. Music full blast. He starts up off his chair. The red light on his hi-fi is glowing. Sound turned up loud. Dave reaches out to turn it down.

'What the fuck!' Millar is thrown back into chair. He attempts to get up. An intruder with a considerable weight advantage pins him to the seat.

'You are Daveed Meelar?' The accent is distinctly East European. 'Do not talk. Nod your head if you are Meelar.' The intruder takes Millar's lack of co-operation as an affirmative.

Dave Millar struggles. Trying to get on his feet. The hand at the end of the camel sleeve depresses the carotid artery on both sides of his neck. Millar feels pressure building in his ears. He pushes with all his strength. Grasps on the thick wrists. Tries drawing them down. To get breath. His mouth gasping for air. Fighting off his attacker. He can't see him anymore. He thinks he's going to be sick. He's not sure but he thinks he can feel the prick of a needle on his forearm. He can breathe again. A craggy, weather-beaten face and crazy paving neck is so close … bearing down on him. Millar's butter-pat hands and shoelace arms lash out.

25. WELTSCHMERZ

Moscow: Saturday 17 August 1991

Robert Coulthard had taken some sleepers. He comes around under the capstan at the Banana Pier.

★ ★ ★

The store had not been designed for browsing, the system laborious and chaotic; constantly the orderly queue fragments and tired shoppers elbow into spaces opening up at the counter. MacHardy looks along the shelves until he spots the spirit he's after, waits to pay the cashier, joins a different queue which is more a scramble than a queue, attracts the attention of a woman on the other side of the counter, hands over his receipt from the cashier, points to the shelf of Stolichnaya, takes them from the assistant and realises he's forgotten to bring a bag with him so self-consciously retraces his steps to his hotel, a bottle in each hand.

MacHardy phones home. He has descended into a dark place and Ellen is emphatic that he has to get himself back to Scotland. She tells him he's in deep trouble. MacHardy knows she's been told to relay this message, that he should have returned to Aberdeen days ago. That they want to know *what the bloody hell he thinks he's doing. There would be no more help. He's overstepped the mark this time.*

The receiver is still in his hand long after his sister has put down the phone at her end. He presses it hard against his ear but still the sound of the rain pouring out of a blocked drainpipe echoes through his head. He needs to prove himself to so many people but most of all to himself.

He buries his head in his arms. Maybe he should go back to

Aberdeen. Just for a while. Even if he needs to go back into hospital; he will be out again, eventually. Better than before. Different medication.

He stands up and closes the curtains. The darkened interior gives him respite from the battle for his mind. Lying back on the bed, he submits to an irresistible force, something between sleep and contemplation.

1958 and just another Saturday evening. Most Saturdays his Granny MacHardy had him over to stay with her. Never Ellen. She was older and preferred going out with friends. Tommy MacHardy was only little. He loved the Saturday routine: dropped off by his mother sometime after dinner, usually around two in the afternoon, then he and his gran would go down to the river to feed the swans or sometimes cross the suspension bridge to Duthie Park. Supper was something quick and fried then they would settle down together listening to the radio or playing cards until his father rolled by, after a long session in the bar, at some time between seven and eight.

The day had been sunny and warm and he was tired from his walk back from the park, too tired to eat supper so Granny MacHardy told him he could sit and wait for his father. His Dad would invariably turn up with fish suppers, sometimes a red or white pudding and a couple of pickled eggs from the chipper on Menzies Road. Part of the ritual.

But that Saturday was different. When his Dad still hadn't turned up at the back of ten, the wee boy was shooed off to bed despite his pleading. So he lay under the covers, silent and angry, frustration boiling up in him, listening for the familiar sound of the key in the door.

MacHardy forces his eyes open and grips the sides of the hotel bed. This is the point at which he always opens his eyes. He gets up and digs an aluminium strip of pills from his jeans pocket, presses one out with his thumb, goes back to the bed, gets up again and takes out a second tablet then lies down again.

The turn of the key in the lock at last. Streaks of daylight leaching through the thin curtains. His Dad whistling. Living room door opening. Surprise in his voice.

'Ma, Tommy, having a lie in?'

MacHardy tries to get up, to look out the window. The second pill prevents him from moving. Day stealing into the night. Day stealing into the nightmare. Whistling.

'Dad!'

Figure at the bedroom door sensing something wrong. He's stopped whistling. 'What's happened?' Even in the dim light, Tommy can see the colour draining away from his Dad's face as he approaches the bed.

'It wasn't me, Dad. Wasn't me.' Tommy returns his father's gaze, defiant.

'Son! Son! Fit've ye done?'

Tommy watches as his Dad picks up the razor-sharp fish-gutting knife from the bed and squeezes his own tiny child's hand. He takes the knife into the living room. Tommy hears water gushing into the sink, knows it will be splashing over the blade, rinsing it clean, over its handle, rinsing it clean. From under the covers on the bed in the other room, Tommy puts his hands to his ears to stop the rush of water.

His Dad is back in the bedroom, running the knife blade down his sleeve. Now he's kneeling by the side of the bed, hugging him and crying uncontrollably. He feels his Dad's hand cold through his thin pyjama jacket. Sees his Dad gripping the knife handle and placing it by the side of the body.

'C'mon son, let's get this sorted and you hame. Let's get your jacket on.'

Tommy feels his Dad's hands trembling as he zips up the jerkin over his pyjamas and takes him by the hand for the short walk along the road to the red phone box to call the police. 'You've done nothin' wrang, son. It's nae your fault. I'll take care o' this. Never spik te anyone aboot it. Niver. Y'hear? Oor secret. Dinna cry, loon. Ye'll be fine.'

The police shook their heads over young Tommy. Cut and dried case was what was reported to his mother. An argument, the gutting knife was produced, the old lady had defended herself by grabbing the blade, severely cutting her hand, and died from a heart attack.

Tommy MacHardy's mother never had a good word to say about her man from that day on. Couldn't face her neighbours and friends. What kind of man would do that to his own mother because she criticised him for going off with a fancy woman? In front o' his ain bairn, an' a. And folk thought his few years for the manslaughter of his mother was too lenient a sentence. Came out of jail eventually. Went to live in Lochinver. Straight back to sea. Drank himself to an early grave.

311

'Good riddance to bad rubbish,' MacHardy's mother never tired of saying. Ellen went over to the west coast to attend his funeral. Brought MacHardy back their father's gold watch, awarded to him for his bravery in saving the life of a fellow seaman just after the war. Presented at the Seamen's Mission in Aberdeen, it was inscribed on the back. MacHardy had to be persuaded by Ellen to accept it. He felt awkward, not having been to the funeral. He'd been working undercover at the time but could have got back if he'd chosen to. Chose not to. Something he had to live with. His father's legacy to him: guilt. The guilt that moved a father to protect his wee son from the sleekit look; the whispers behind hands; the charge he *wasn't right*.

He resented his mother changing their last name to her maiden name, banishing all associations with his father, but eventually he retrieved it from the scrap heap of his family's discards. He again became Tommy MacHardy, who would retrace his footsteps along the Bay of Nigg road to the Banana Pier. Salty seawater spraying the grass. Slippery under his feet. Licking salty tears from his lips. Eyes fixed on the grey horizon to where his father's trawler would emerge steaming towards Aberdeen harbour. He was the same person, who as a boy, stared, dry-eyed out of the railway carriage of the train carrying him away from Ferryhill, Duthie Park, Tullos and Cove to unfamiliar country on the long journey to Ireland. Returning for school holidays, never once spent with his father who was hundreds of miles away in Sutherland. Banana Pier; father in absentia.

Different fishing boat at the harbour mouth low down in the water after a successful trip. Another son's father on deck waving to a speck at the end of the pier.

MacHardy covered his head with the bed covers and suppressed his memories.

26. EYEBALL TO EYEBALL

Aberdeen: Sunday 18 August 1991

DI Bonnie Young is deep in thought as she walks back from the newsagents. Sunday mornings are the highlight of her week and unless there is something pressing to be done at Queen Street, she has the whole day to do whatever she wants, which is usually nothing very much. It is unusual for her to be up quite this early but since the Chief Superintendent telephoned late the previous evening she has been distracted and on edge. Precisely why he had phoned she isn't certain. He hadn't said much to her except thanking her again for co-operating over the Bell blackmail. She looks at the piled up newspapers on the shop floor. Usual nationals: London with a smattering of football from the north of England. She picks up the *Sunday Herald*.

Waiting for the kettle to boil, Bonnie Young flicks through political tittle-tattle, celebrity gossip and ads for conservatories in search of something to read. She finds something: a page four report about a break-in at the RUC's Special Branch offices at Castlereagh Barracks in Belfast. Documents had been taken said to relate to an undercover agent working within the loyalist UUF. Young tells herself to get a life and turns to the book reviews. The kettle clicks off. She makes herself coffee and settles down in the sitting room where she reopens the paper again at page four and reads how two years earlier the *Irish Sunday Tribune* had been due to run a piece about an agent referred to as B but then took the decision to hold back the story. The updated article in the *Herald* picks up some of the issues covered in the original feature by the author of both, the Northern Ireland specialist journalist Ian Ross, well known for having connections inside Ulster's paramilitary organisations and military intelligence. Ross maintained his source had supplied him with details about the British government's dirty war in Ulster including *Its practice of using a special unit within military intelligence to run a series of agents in the north who provided the British state with vital information while feeding back to the loyalists the names of republicans the UK would like to see eliminated.*

Young skips down the page. *Ross believed Agent B's cover was compromised and he was smuggled out of the country but that desperate for cash and determined to sell his story he was about to meet up with him. However, when this came to the attention of the authorities the matter was raised at Cabinet level and a statement was issued from the Northern Ireland Office that it supported the measures being carried out in Ulster but denied any illegal activities were ever sanctioned or carried out by its armed forces who put their lives on the line everyday to uphold the safety of the United Kingdom.*

Ross described a meticulously planned break-in at the Castlereagh barracks, which housed the military intelligence records for Ulster.

Every trace of Agent B and the mysterious plant within the UUF disappeared. The break-in at the barracks was a professional job. Entry had been swift, involving official passes. The people responsible knew exactly where to go and made their way to the room where agents' files were kept. They knocked down the Special Branch security man, hooded him and threatened him with a syringe if he tried to get up. Locks were expertly picked and all incriminating material seized. Two of the intruders carried the SB guard outside while a third disabled the fire alarm and telephone system before setting fire to the office. There were also questions being asked at top level over reports that a member of army intelligence was whisked out of Northern Ireland under cover of being blown up in a car bomb. The government and the Northern Ireland Office deny any such incident occurred.

When the Super phoned Bonnie Young again she knew something serious was amiss. She went straight over to Dave Millar's flat and called in on Mrs Walker.

'You'll maybe ken fit te dee wi these, lassie.' Mrs Walker holds out two large packages stuffed full of documents. 'Dave asked me te hold onte them for him. He must have bin expectin' something like this, would ye say? Must have given them te me just before it happened. Terrible, just terrible.'

DI Young recognises missing papers from Ross' folder along with

items Millar had taken from the Bell file. She has no idea what she'll do with them, if anything. There's no doubt in her mind Dave Millar's death is connected with the Bell case. Young shudders. Was it out of fear or shame that she'd been so easily bought off? Bonnie Young herself doesn't dwell on the thought.

When she leaves Howburn Place, she goes straight to the office, where she drops the flotsam and jetsam from Dave Millar's desk into a black plastic bag. There's very little of value – a few pens, half-filled notebooks, assorted paper clips, an old copy of the *Radio Times* salted away in his bottom drawer. She shakes it to dislodge anything slipped between its pages; there is nothing. None of Dave Millar's own notebooks are where he had normally kept them in the desk.

Moscow

MacHardy stands out on the street. Moscow is different from Leningrad. More noisy somehow. More urban. He imagines Adam Menelaws sharing a comic aside in his soft Scottish burr with a companion as they watch a procession of carriages and riders, happed-up against Russian frost, and recalling the Royal Mile in Edinburgh and the sensation underfoot of the deck of the *Betsy and Brothers,* rolling over the waves before stepping onto land, at last, and an uncertain future in exotic Russia.

The taxi has been taking its time. An anxious MacHardy paces up and down, watching out for its arrival. Two mousy-headed, skinny street boys, fists full of lapel badges: adept traders sizing up a stranger. One grubby hand proffers the golden features of Lenin, scarlet flag flying on the winds of change; synthesis of enamelled ideology. His friend plumps for a symbol of Soviet CND: an elongated globe pierced through by a nuclear missile and HET emblazoned across it.

'Just say, nyet,' MacHardy mutters, 'How much?'

The boys refuse kopeks in preference for a couple of Biros apiece. At the same time, MacHardy slips them a US five dollar bill.

Pinched faces light up in a duet of squint-tooth grins. Pins of all description are turned out of pockets and pressed into the hand of the generous stranger, leaving him in a quandary as to what to do with a palm full of propaganda costume jewellery.

Dmitri Fedotov's cab slows to a halt and MacHardy climbs in. 'Had to wait in line for three hours for petrol. Still, I am here now. Nice seeing you again, Tommy, but you don't look so good, huh? Been talking to too many of our beautiful girls, is it? Next time you come back you will stay with me then you will see how to have good time and not suffer for it.'

At Sheremetyevo airport, when Dmitri reaches out to shake MacHardy's hand, the Scot turns it over. 'What does this mean? This tiger?'

Dmitri Fedotov looks into the face of the blue tiger on the back of his hand, hesitates, then his face softens.

'I told you – my father. I searched for person who sent him to psychiatric hospital. It took long time but …. ' He shakes his wrist, making the tiger jump. 'Tiger is sign of avenger. I avenge my father.'

'You avenged him?' MacHardy's eyes narrow.

'I am not ashamed. Any son would do this for his father. There is always a link between a father and son. I feel that.' He raises his right hand to his heart and MacHardy notices Dmitri's chest rise and fall with emotion.

MacHardy turns away and makes to get out of the car.

Dmitri is still talking, misinterpreting the gesture as disapproval. 'Four years they held me. Tommy!' His voice is raised.

MacHardy waits.

Dmitri is looking at his tattoo of a four-pointed star. 'Four years – one, two, three, four – each year, one point of star. Now people see that I am man who takes no shit.' And, lowering his tone, he confides, 'In camp we used wire to draw tattoo. Wire and shoe rubber, soot and piss. My prison log.'

'So, what did you do to get four years?' MacHardy has got himself together and is again listening to his friend.

'Robbery. I am no robber but I did it to get into camp. Then I avenge my father.'

'You mean you hurt someone?' asks MacHardy.

'This I do not say. You do not know these places, they are wild and dangerous. Things happen in them that should never happen but they do.'

MacHardy's brow wrinkles. 'You didn't get caught, then?'

Dmitri Fedotov places both his hands on the steering wheel and stares straight in front. 'You learn to handle it or become its victim. Guards, they know to keep away or I kill them.' Then he grins and his eyes glance sideways towards MacHardy, half-in, half-out of the car. Fedotov lists left and draws something out of his pocket. 'Keep this with you. Believe in its healing power. It will also make sure you come back here. I like you, Tommy. Call me next time. You keep my number.'

At the airport check-in MacHardy turns the iridescent blue gemstone over in his hand feeling it smooth against his skin. He's waiting in line with the other quitters behind a group of American students and their teachers negotiating passport control. A head nods from within the eyrie and he moves forward with his passport. A bespectacled, serpentine eagle examines it against something out of sight of MacHardy. Two stalls down, the last of the Americans joins his party retrieving their luggage before moving onto the next security hurdle. That's when MacHardy feels a hand on his shoulder.

'Is there a problem here, Jim?' MacHardy emphasises his Aberdeen accent.

'This way, Mr MacMillan.'

'MacMillan? You've made a mistake. My name's MacHardy. Thomas MacHardy.'

The Americans move aside to let the lofty Russian official through with his detainee. The familiar clamour of an airport concourse disappears behind a set of heavy double doors. They're in a small room with a couple of office chairs, a table and a mattress on the floor. Two strip lights extending the length of the room make up for the absence of a window.

'You come in to the country in one name and leave in another. Is this normal where you come from?' asks the official sitting across from him.

MacHardy shakes his head. 'This is my passport.'

'But not the one you entered with.'

317

MacHardy opens his mouth as if to speak but pulls it into a grin instead. 'It looks odd. I admit. It's just – look, I ken the man you think I am but he's deid. I used his passport because … visas, the whole lot were set up for him and the work needed someone in quick. Thought … just this once, it would be okay … someone in the office … I believed … '

'Sit here, Mr MacMillan, and save your breath. You travelled here as Donald MacMillan, who is under suspicion by police in Moscow. He is with company called TAGOil. Authorities are watching TAGOil. You are this MacMillan. We have orders to hold you so we can ask questions. Make yourself comfortable, Mr MacMillan.'

'You're making a big mistake, I am not MacMillan.' MacHardy's mouth hardens into a rigid, determined line. He gets to his feet.

'You say you are different person, not person in other passport. This is not good. Not good. Now, please, sit.'

The institutional orange plastic chair is offered. MacHardy sits. He is the urban terrorist in the orange seat in the bus shelter at the Springhill terminus.

'Mr MacMillan, I must call you something.'

'My name is MacHardy. It's here in my passport.'

The antagonist peers at him.

'I'm … '

A raised hand suppresses MacHardy's protestation. 'Mr MacMillan or MacHardy, it does not matter, you have been observed during your time here. Sometimes you are like tourist. Sightseeing here. Going there. But not all of time. You are fascinating subject for us. TAGOil,' the Russian articulates it slowly, 'in Scotland. There was deal. Yes? We know all this. Oktneft has many people working there and some of them are eager to be rich. They do not always have best interests of country at heart. Still, I go on. What is your business with Oktneft?'

MacHardy answers calmly. 'We provide technology and expertise to oil and gas companies across the world.'

'Good sales talk. Expertise, I like this word. You are seen going here, there. You are busy in Moscow. Very busy. You keep our people busy. Then you appear in Leningrad. These are both beautiful cities.

Specially Moscow. I am from Moscow. You agree, Mr MacMillan, sorry, Mr MacHardy, that Moscow is more beautiful than Leningrad? It is not necessary for you to agree. But, if you do not, I know you lie.' The man considers the figure on the plastic chair. MacHardy stares back and his inquisitor breaks into a sideways smile. 'I joke. This is just my sense of humour. But, make no mistake, Moscow is prettier. We leave that. Would you like to empty your pockets?'

MacHardy pulls out his handkerchief, a few kopeks, a long handled comb, a receipt for drink, a pen, a small diary, a foil strip of tablets and a number of enamel badges.

His interrogator turns the pages of the diary, looks up at MacHardy then picks up the pills and asks, 'Headache?'

'Something like that,' replies MacHardy. He pushes down on his left leg to calm its trembling.

Picking up the CND badge, the official tosses it into the air and as he catches it, comments thoughtfully, 'Peace is good but, unfortunately, we Soviets cannot trust West. We wait for you to remove your weapons. Then we talk. Now I think we shall wait until you are ready to be open with me. Of course, I do not have flight to catch. Then again, Mr. Mystery Man, I do not believe you will be going home today … do you?'

'Hey, man. You go on about my name. I don't know yours. You got a name? Look, you can call my work. They'll tell you the man Macmillan died. I'm nae him. I just took his place on the plane. I had some papers to deliver but I'm here on holiday. That's it.'

'This is legal in your country to travel under different name?'

MacHardy concentrates on the grey snaking indentations on the ceiling tiles.

'A simple mix up. Nae offence meant. One phone call. That's a'. I'll do it, if ye like.'

Reaction. MacHardy's interrogator crosses his arms and tilts his gaze upwards, beyond the white asbestos tiles upwards, upwards, heavenward, lower, lower, lower and captures it right there in the room.

Divine tranquillity. Nothing stirring but the consciousness of minds. Utter peace. A dead silence. Deathly hush. Silent as the grave.

Stillness. Patience. A'body haudin' their weesht. Deafening silence. A swishing in ears. Wind-rustling bamboo. Two hunted men running into a grove of tall, swaying bamboo – hushed exchanges, muted panic showing in their eyes and one captive forced to the ground, feeling the tickle of young bamboo shoots under his naked body, securely pegged into place by rope and long stakes. Left there. Natural justice. Fast growing bamboo. Up to three feet. Each day. Strong shoots, sharp, pierce through human flesh like any growing medium. And soft tissue. Human organs. Between bones. Towards the light. Phototropic. Negative geotropic. Earth to earth. A film. Only a film. In Belfast a long time ago.

Back in European central time it is clear to Tommy MacHardy that this pseudo interrogation is nothing more than a time wasting exercise. Leading to what he doesn't yet know. A few half-hearted accusations about broken deals and trading energy secrets that appear to have been Hugh Bell's legacy to his second in line at TAGOil. Allegations which drip off the officer's tongue and are followed by his mantra that MacHardy isn't who he says he is.

'You say you are not MacMillan, you are MacHardy. You travel on different documents. Maybe you have other documents? You are other people too? You are one day one man then other day somebody else. So, today, you are Mr MacHardy? Are you sure you know who you are?' MacHardy's interrogator tilts his head and smiles as MacHardy shifts uncomfortably in his seat. 'Do you know the criminal Markowski?'

MacHardy does not react.

'His sewer rats run all over my city. You meet this man Markowski, Mr MacMillan, MacHardy?'

MacHardy closes his eyes. He isn't feeling that great. Bloody awful in fact. And his head, drilling, drilling, drilling into his head. He pinches his nose and forces air into his ears. Sometimes it helps. Now it doesn't. His eyes spring open. He puts a hand into his inside jacket pocket. The man opposite bristles. Dmitri's lapis lazuli drops from his fingers. MacHardy picks up his little black diary and points to a number scribbled in blue ink. 'My work's phone number. You can phone in and ask anyone there. They'll confirm fit I'm saying. I don't know anything about MacMillan's deals with anyone. That was him. This is me, MacHardy.'

The Russian is back in no time but doesn't come closer than the doorway. 'There is no reply. Only answer machine. You're friends, they do not pick up.'

MacHardy groans. 'Of course, it's Sunday afternoon, they'll be shut until Monday. It's the weekend.'

'No pick up. No reply. No confirmation of what you say.'

'Can I get a drink, Jim?'

The man looks back at MacHardy from the open door. 'There is Russian proverb: only free cheese is in mousetrap.' And he leaves MacHardy to contemplate its meaning.

The official hasn't returned his tablets. Not that Tommy MacHardy has been scrupulous about medicating himself recently. Still, not having them at all doesn't help his mental stability. He drops his head into his hands.

For how long he sits like that is anyone's guess. He squints towards the door. Thinks he hears someone speaking to him. It's still closed. There – he hears her again. Going on and on and on. Like she did when she said as far as she was concerned his good-for-nothing father was dead. Her hard-set face telling him, not explaining, that they would have to leave the city. Everyone was talking about them. She couldn't stand it. It was for the best. MacHardy had hung his head. Let her go on and on.

He's no good for us, son. No good for anyone. Killed his own mother! Killed his own mother! Tommy listen t'me. We have t'go. Ellen, she'll stay. She's all grown up. Started a job. We'll be fine, son. My family'll take care of us. Don't you worry, son. You're father never cared for any of us. Let him go. Tommy! Where are you off to? Come back …

Tommy MacHardy feels the cold stone of Banana Pier. He rubs his hand across the pier's roughcast concrete until it becomes so numb he can't feel anything. He does the same with his other hand and would do it with his whole body had it not been paralysed with fear. The look of horror on his Granny MacHardy's face and the shadow of his father. And a flash of something terrifying in his father's dark eyes as he speaks quietly to the pathetic, trembling child, transfixed by the sight of the knife. That memory isn't his. That horror is someone else's to deal with. The spell dissipates into the salty spume of the sea and wind thrashing his small child's face, discharging the explosive tension building in his head.

Clear thinking. Discover what he's up against. His pulse is racing. The least thing and his mind takes off in every direction. Calm down. Calm down. He'll demand access to the British Embassy. A single phone call. Christ! His mind. Racing again. He tries shouting. Demanding they give him back his medication.

When eventually the door to the room opens it's to offer MacHardy a glass of tea and some food. Behind the uniformed youth with the tray hovers his inquisitor.

'Please, eat.' The voice is soft, almost feminine in pitch.

MacHardy examines the plate of potatoes and cabbage coated in gray gravy.

'Please, eat,' echoes the youth as he places the tray on the table.

'Would it be possible for me to phone the British ambassador?' MacHardy hears himself ask politely in a staccato of broken biscuits words.

'We are not in business of telling every Tom, Dick and Harry ambassador what goes on here. They are nosy bastards. Think they have right to ask all sorts of questions of us. This will be sorted out without assistance from any such gentleman.'

MacHardy coughs to clear the stickiness from his throat. 'But there's been some terrible mistake.' It sounds unconvincing even to himself, but he perseveres. 'Look, I'm really not the man you think I am.'

'This is of no consequence now.'

He is about to be locked in again. MacHardy stands up. Makes a move towards the door. 'What d'you mean, of nae consequence? You grabbed me because you thought I was MacMillan. So how can me nae bein' him be of nae consequence? You canna just keep me because I'm here!' He has hold of the younger man's arm when the inquisitor hits him hard across the jaw, sending him reeling back into the room.

'Do not tell us our business. If your story is right, you are of little importance, so it is not in your interest to start pushing your weight

322

around. We do not stand for this sort of thing. Learn fast, comrade. Run fast or learn fast. That's what gets us through life. Now, eat your food while we decide what we will do next.'

MacHardy retreats into a kind of void. He's angry. Angry at his captors but mainly angry with himself. He'll have to calm himself down to get out of this mess.

MacHardy had come to believe in the maxim *What doesn't crush you makes you bold*. He was the disturbed child thrust into an alien culture by his bitter run-away mother – running from her husband's shame, her shame, his father, stripped of his father's name, his name, given her name, maiden name – two lost souls lost in the heartland of unionist Belfast, his mother's heartland, never his, his mother's *Good little boy, not at all like your bastard of a father*. For her, the perfect end to a distressing episode but for him the start of his confusion.

The young child scarred by insecurity found release in reading adventure stories of clean-cut heroes overcoming swarthy, unscrupulous foreign types with strange names and disgusting eating habits; disappearing into a dark corner of his local picture house to escape into the make-believe world of *filims* – *Carry on Sergeant, The Vikings* and *Spartacus* with his favourite actor Kirk Douglas whose Scottish sounding name was Hollywood's cover for his real self, the Russian Issur Danielovitch.

In 1960 Tommy was still only fifteen but a girl he knew at the ticket kiosk let him go in to watch the X-rated *Psycho*. He sat surrounded by courting couples who were oblivious to the tension Hitchcock had created on the screen. With eyes wide he soaked up the lessons of dramatic creation. Impressed teachers with his ability to draw and to act, his visual memory, eye for detail and character. Yet he grew into the troubled and anxious youth who swapped *filims* and plays for shooting neighbours' cats and dogs with an air rifle and who liked to watch rabbits somersault from the impact of his uncle Robert's Weihrauch 50V.

Eleven years in Belfast from the age of six was bound to have had some impact on the personality of a child, especially one as vulnerable as young Tommy. And if that was not enough, there was the episode in which his cousin, just four years older than him, was found murdered on Belfast's lower Antrim Road. Why he'd been there remained a mystery. Protestants knew better than to venture near that quarter so rumour had it that he had been seized on the street after seeing his girlfriend home, driven to the Antrim, shot and dumped. The shock of the youth's death hit the family hard. He was the youngest and most talented of three children and the only son, a happy-go-lucky lad who stayed clear of sectarianism and who planned to go to London to study music.

His death illustrated the random cruelty that befell many innocent souls in Ulster. The murdered youth's father, MacHardy's uncle Robert, an officer with the UFF as well as a convicted petty thief and failed bank robber, vowed to avenge the boy's death by taking out as many catholics as he could for as long as he lived.

So, in that land of myths and bigots, a young man emerged bearing scars of both it and tragedy in north east Scotland. Reminiscent of his mother eleven years earlier, the boy, whichever one he was, Scot or Irish, walked out of the family home and into an army recruitment office.

If his mother had stood on the quayside to wave off the Larne to Stranraer ferry with a prayer that on the mainland her son might be able to shake off the morbidity that had blighted his teen years then her son would never know. He had gone straight down to the buffet. What interest was it to him what his mother did? She'd dragged him away and poisoned his mind against his father, or tried to. If she waited, hopeful that he would join the rest of the passengers leaning over the port rail to call out their fond farewells to family and friends, then she did so in vain. Had she resolutely waited on the quay, as the distance between the boat carrying her son and her grew greater, then it was only to increase her own suffering. Her lost child was equally resolute and would not indulge her by going up on deck to look back at the speck that was her. She would never see him again, although he did return to arrange her funeral. By then he was a different son in some ways, her family, his family, said. A confident, grown up kind of son. Perhaps the army had been the making of him, they had said. When they told him he was doing well on it he'd turned away reluctant to agree. Reluctant to leave them … his mother cold and alone in the cemetery. He did, of course, go back. Would have been for the high-jump if he'd absconded. Yet, in no time, eyebrows were raised when he emerged once again out of the bowels of the ferry. Wanted to be home, he'd told them. Desire to return into the bosom of his mother's family.

Uncle Robert helped find him somewhere to stay and stay he did, hanging out with old pals, laughing about girls, cadging drink off older men in bars, sometimes buying a bottle of cheap wine when his unemployment benefit came through. Got back into reading adventure stories; spending whole afternoons and evenings at the pictures, sometimes with a few of his pals, mostly by himself. Watched re-runs of *Robbery* every day for a week when it came out, liked to imagine himself as tough guy Stanley Baker; and *Cool Hand Luke* with Paul Newman. An aunt once told him he was a dead spit for the American hunk. Not that he believed her. Sometimes he just wanted to watch horror. *Dracula: Prince of Darkness* or *Rasputin the Mad Monk*.

When he wasn't sitting in front of the big screen, the young man might be turning his hand to a spot of rewiring and repairing radios, that kind of thing. Always short of cash but, unlike some of his pals, he never resorted to doing anything which might meet with the community's disapproval to raise it.

Uncle Robert became something of a surrogate father to the youth. Apart from a bit of time spent back in Aberdeen, MacHardy could be found on Uncle Robert's farm with his cousins, helping to dispose of rats and rabbits or loch fishing for perch and bream. His uncle had often been exasperated trying to interest the youth in home-grown politics. *Yer too much yer father's child, Tommy, I'm thinking. It's time ye remembered it was yer Mammy that brought ye up in her homeland. Yer no a Scotty now. We were here for ye, Tommy. Sometimes in life ye have te pay folk back.*

But Uncle Robert had failed to appreciate that when the young Tommy escaped NI he had left its petty sectarian hatreds behind – to a large extent at least. When he returned, it was as a soldier to a war zone.

Berlin was the birthplace of the chameleon. Eighteen months of intensive classified training before being posted to Ulster. Patience in abundance. Picking up the old life. Blending in again. Same old crack.

Excited by the challenge. Dangerous. Could it get more dangerous? "Deserve a medal for what you're about to do. Wait … wait … wait. Patience."

One day Uncle Robert took him aside. *Young man like yerself should be givin' somethin' back t'is people. Look at yer cousin. What the bastards did t'im. Think on it, boy.*

The training he'd got in electrics did not go to waste. Always somebody or other at the door looking for a repair on the cheap. It couldn't be said either that he skimped on his work for he was adept at fitting surveillance cameras into light switches and televisions. His skill as a sparky was probably one of the reasons used by Uncle Robert to get him into the UFF. Knowing his way around circuit boards meant the organisation was keen to enlist him. And they gave as much as they took, developing his skills in interrogation techniques, torture and elimination.

It was a highly dangerous existence being back in the bosom of his family. He did have the reassurance of a slick back-up team with a fleet of vehicles permanently on alert should he need them. But it was impressed on the young agent that his survival was probably best guaranteed by relying on his own wits.

It was a difficult area for military intelligence. Although Mire's activities had been sanctioned from the very top of government, there were plenty of grey areas that might be seen as running counter to the principles of open democracy so it was essential that no awkward questions were raised in parliament. Simpler all round for bald denials to be issued whenever there were queries over the legitimacy of the government's military tactics in the province.

When, more recently, the part played by military intelligence in infiltrating illegal organisations within the province was aired, the Northern Ireland Office prevaricated then implied that any action which saved lives and prevented further sectarian atrocities was justified. By this time, one of the key figures involved had already left the UFF, had left Northern Ireland and believed he'd left the nightmare of living a double life in the city where murder and bombing was pretty much the norm. But then, life is never so straightforward, and the human mind is complex.

Robert Coulthard conjures up an image of his handler, malt whisky in hand, calling him every bastard name under the sun. But uppermost in Coulthard's mind is Alexei Grigoryev.

Grigoryev puzzles him. Every inch the educated anglicised Russian. Not so unusual in the cities. Obvious reason why he'd been drawn to him in the first place: the low key personality.

Then, as quickly as thoughts of Grigoryev flit into his mind, they evaporate and a tidal wave of exhaustion sweeps over Coulthard, compromising his ability to reason. One minute he's slavering with anticipation at the cornucopia of opportunities promised by the collapse of the Soviet empire and the next he's free-falling into wretched depression; as if his mind is possessed by Tommy MacHardy. He is determined to keep the sad MacHardy as far away from him as possible. For an hour or so he remains in this agitated state before surrendering to his dark demons: haunted by the face of the man slumped on the helicopter floor.

Coulthard's mind is playing tricks on him. It is as if his head is in a constant battle with itself. Better to forget. Concentrate on other things. Not MacHardy. So he allows Hugh Bell back in. A large man but easily overpowered by the two of them. Over-confidence had been Hugh's downfall. Thought he could set himself up as a sole trader on the back of Tart. Like eating an elephant, the Soviet Union is best tackled one bite at a time and Bell's downfall was due to his pecuniary gluttony.

It had been a simple life in Tartland: rules drawn up with the expectation that everyone would be complicit. Unequivocal. Crisp. Certainly the theory. So why is he now contemplating following in the footsteps of Hugh Bell? Because, Coulthard tells himself, he will succeed where Bell failed. His will be a subtle game. He will avoid treading on significant toes. Dinger had reassured him of Tart's appreciation so why would Tart care if he takes on a sideline or two if they didn't compromise the organisation?

★ ★ ★

327

A brief knock and the door handle turns. A different official comes into the room and behind him a figure with a mouth full of piano keys glances in then passes a package to the other man who invites MacHardy to follow him. Beyond the double doors, the paymaster melts into the crowds jammed into the airport's main concourse. Crowds are good, MacHardy cheers himself. The officer pats the fat bundle deep inside the pocket of his uniform. He accompanies MacHardy through security and hands him his passport and boarding pass.

'Your flight. Look,' he points ahead, ' it is from that gate.'

Tommy MacHardy slips the boarding pass between the pages of his passport. When he looks up, he's alone. His interrogator has evaporated into the fog of fellow travellers. Fog has its own distinct smell which suffuses confusion. Bamboozles rationality.

It was particularly foggy during the early hours of the 10th June 1972 at the Rudolphstein – Hirschberg border crossing which controlled the main highway between Berlin and Munich. The West German guards on duty shared a few jokes with a group of British soldiers who happened to be at the post. Visibility was poor with the floodlights from the control points scarcely able to penetrate the murk and the few vehicles passing through were forced to slow right down as they travelled from the East into the West. A meat truck had just come in from the East when its driver pulled up metres from the border post. The cab door opened and the driver jumped down to the road. He was carrying what looked like a bunch of papers. What happened next is disputed. It was said that he hesitated for a few moments then he began walking back towards the GDR sector and was quickly swallowed up by the swirling fog. Muted gunshots were heard and muffled shouts, and an amorphous shadow seen moving away. The driver lay dead. The Brits evacuated the scene *sehr schnell,* leaving the West Germans shitting themselves. The press had a field day. It was revealed that the meat truck driver was an Italian working in Germany – "Some kind of commie sympathiser" – Dinger told Coulthard and the rest of the men. "Not as if he had been trying to reach freedom in the West." It further transpired that the little Italian had been carrying a key ring with the hammer and sickle on it. No-one admitted to killing him. The Easties rejecting accusations they were responsible or that they had started the shooting. And the Westies were cleared of firing their weapons. Italian opinion raged against the GDR until eventually an official expression of regret for the driver's tragic death was issued.

East German claims of unexplained activities along the Western part of the crossing – of an armed man running under cover of fog into the unauthorised zone from the West, of not responding to shouted warnings and ignoring instructions to halt – were never resolved. Neither was there resolution over accusations that a Western soldier had used the weather conditions to move in on the GDR border point. Among the strong denials made by the East German authority of its involvement in the death of the Italian, was the notion that the Italian had been ordered, by them, to return to their checkpoint after clearing security. It insisted an armed soldier from the West border station had ordered him to return to the GDR barrier with his papers after noticing the hammer and sickle on his key ring.

MacHardy walks up to read the screen showing the gate for the departing Glasgow flight then continues to the men's lavatories, with its long mirror running the length of the stand of washbasins, and comes eyeball to eyeball with his old mucker, Robert Coulthard. He checks out the beige chinos, blue open-neck shirt, black cotton jacket and polished black leather shoes, touches the bruise by the side of his eye, and goes into the empty cubicle. He slips the end of his comb up behind the cistern and draws out a package. He peels off the plastic wrapper and lays two passports on the floor. Removes his right shoe, extracts a third passport from under the inner sole and places it in his jacket pocket. Replaces it with Riddle's passports from the floor then rewraps MacMillan's adapted passport with MacHardy's and pushes them up behind the cistern.

A small truck is parked at the exit on the far side of international departures. Robert Coulthard checks the time on his gold wristwatch and jumps aboard for the short transfer to the waiting Ilyushin cargo plane. Bull is already on board. Coulthard sucks in his cheeks, the beak sniffs the air. He pats his chinos pocket and reassures himself he has sufficient Doxepin to last him until he can find a doctor to write him another prescription. He's as agitated as a fly in a bottle but game for *doing the needful.*

Moscow: Monday 19 August 1991

Gorbachev's overthrow begins.